THE
WINTER
DUKE

THE
WINTER
DUKE

CLAIRE ELIZA BARTLETT

Little, Brown and Company
New York Boston

Copyright © 2020 by Claire Eliza Bartlett

Cover art copyright © 2020 by Billelis. Cover design by Karina Granda. Cover copyright © 2020 by Hachette Book Group, Inc.

Hachette Book Group supports the right to free expression and the value of copyright. The purpose of copyright is to encourage writers and artists to produce the creative works that enrich our culture.

The scanning, uploading, and distribution of this book without permission is a theft of the author's intellectual property. If you would like permission to use material from the book (other than for review purposes), please contact permissions@hbgusa.com. Thank you for your support of the author's rights.

Little, Brown and Company
Hachette Book Group
1290 Avenue of the Americas, New York, NY 10104
Visit us at LBYR.com

First Edition: March 2020

Little, Brown and Company is a division of Hachette Book Group, Inc. The Little, Brown name and logo are trademarks of Hachette Book Group, Inc.

The publisher is not responsible for websites (or their content) that are not owned by the publisher.

Library of Congress Cataloging-in-Publication Data
Names: Bartlett, Claire Eliza, author.
Title: The winter duke / Claire Eliza Bartlett.
Description: First edition. | New York : Little, Brown and Company, 2020. |
Audience: Ages 14+. | Summary: When all of her family succumbs to a magical illness, Ekata Avenko reluctantly assumes the throne, seeking a cure and fending off unwanted suitors while seeking the culprit.
Identifiers: LCCN 2019028073 | ISBN 9780316417341 (hardcover) |
ISBN 9780316417334 (paperback) | ISBN 9780316417303 (ebook) |
ISBN 9780316417310 (ebook)
Subjects: CYAC: Nobility—Fiction. | Courts and courtiers—Fiction. |
Blessing and cursing—Fiction. | Magic—Fiction. | Fantasy.
Classification: LCC PZ7.1.B37287 Win 2020 | DDC [Fic]—dc23
LC record available at https://lccn.loc.gov/2019028073

ISBNs: 978-0-316-41734-1 (hardcover), 978-0-316-54043-8 (international edition), 978-0-316-41730-3 (ebook)

Printed in the United States of America

LSC-C

10 9 8 7 6 5 4 3 2 1

*To my parents, who, unlike the parents
in this book, were unconditionally loving,
encouraging, and supportive of a little girl
who wanted to go far away and live strange
lives. I love you.*

CHAPTER ONE

The night could be worse, considering. The likelihood of a public death was low.

All the same, I kept my opulent coat buttoned up, despite how my neck itched in it. The more layers I had between me and my sister Velosha, the better. Last week she'd nicked our brother Kevro's arm with a poisoned stiletto at Wintertide mass, and I wasn't about to let her try her tricks on me. "Ekata," she whispered. I pretended not to hear.

My favorite tutor said that other people's siblings were noisy, argumentative telltales. *My* siblings tried to murder one another.

But not this night. Tonight we had a strict no-murder policy. Tonight we had a brideshow, and the world was watching us. And nothing said *get out of here* like an unstable, bloodthirsty family. I should know. I'd been begging my father for the chance to leave from the moment I was old enough to take a place at a university. He'd promised that when the brideshow was finally over, I'd be free to do it. Provided I lived so long.

The brideshow candidates stood on the long, narrow balcony that ran around the Great Hall—fifteen people who thought that marrying into our family was a good idea. Some of them giggled with one another. Some observed the floor, pointing out their delegates to the candidates next to them. More than one looked tired of waiting. A pretty girl with a dark ponytail and an emerald-and-gold riding suit covered a yawn with her hand, earning a laugh from the girl next to her. Her arms were bare, tan from the kiss of a foreign sun. A bold choice for a palace made of ice. But something about her *seemed* bold. When she caught me watching her, she raised an eyebrow. I rolled my eyes at the absurdity of it all. Her mouth twitched into a lazy smile.

My stomach lurched. I flushed, looking away before I could cause a scene. I had no desire to create an international incident, and she was here for my brother, not me.

Mother had sent written invitations to twenty empires, duchies, and kingdoms. Fifteen of the invitations had been answered with delegations, who now stood on the floor of the Great Hall and waited for the festivities to finally begin. Most eligible royals would be interested in a deal with Kylma Above and access to trade with the prosperous duchy Below. Kylma Below was the only source of distillable magic in the world, which meant that our cold, tiny country on a frozen lake commanded policy alongside kingdoms a hundred times our size.

Even so, it surprised me that fifteen people could be interested in Lyosha. That, more than anything, was a clear indication they'd never met him.

The restlessness was infectious. We'd been waiting for my father, mother, and brother for half an hour, and up on the royal dais, we didn't talk. I glanced at my maid, Aino; she lifted her chin, and I did the same. Aino had never steered me wrong at a social function.

A door on the side of the Great Hall opened, but it was only Prime Minister Eirhan. He'd been prime minister longer than I'd been alive, and his oily demeanor left me with a sour taste every time I had to speak with him. That was happily rare; I preferred the study of bones and trees and the denizens Below to the study of politics.

Eirhan spoke to a guard next to the door. The guard, dressed in ceremonial silver and blue, struck his iron-tipped halberd on the ground. The guards lining the hall took up the movement, creating the iron tempo that announced my father.

The hall went dark, and whispering began. A dark hall heralded magic, for magic did not work well with fire. The candles burned low in their sconces, reflected like diamonds by the ice walls.

Light descended from above, instead, in round pearls that fell like feathers. They glittered as they drifted, shimmering blue one moment, orange the next, clumping together like the thick pollen that blew in from the mountains during what passed for summer in Kylma Above. There was a great intake of breath from the hall, and I tilted my face up to catch some of the pearls as they fell. My father was the only man in the world Above who could refine magic and control how it manifested, and it never failed to mesmerize. It was his declaration of wealth, his declaration of power, and it reminded the rest of us what magic could do, if we only had the imagination for it.

The pearls turned into flower petals, filling the air with a sweet scent. *Rosaeus brumalis*, I thought, breathing in the faint smell of winter roses, the only kind that grew here. Before they kissed our faces, they burst apart again, showering us with needled points. I covered my face with my sleeves. A few of the delegates shouted. A crack shook the palace walls, and dark wings snapped above us. An enormous eagle winged around the top of the domed ceiling, golden eyes flashing in the dark. Its cry made my ears throb, and its wingbeat nearly blew me into Velosha.

The eagle pulled its wings in and hurtled to the ground. Delegates stumbled out of its way, and even I, who'd seen my father's displays at least twice a year, flinched. With a screech, the eagle raked its talons across the floor, leaving deep gouges that would stay long after the bird had disappeared. The power of magic: It was temporary, but the effects were permanent. And only my father had the secret to it.

I hated him for that more than I hated him for other things.

The eagle launched back into the air, knocking over the nearest delegates, and sped toward the ceiling. I was certain it would slow down or disappear—but instead, it crashed through the dome. Ice shattered and plummeted toward us. We ducked again, but the ice slowed and spun, turning into snowflakes that dusted our shoulders like sugar. Wind howled through the cracked dome, but winter roses grew over the cracks, smoothing the wall; ice climbed toward the starred sky. The hole became smaller and smaller until the last of the roses knit together, leaving us with our ice dome and sealing us off from the elements once more.

Light flared. The room became golden and warm. The show was over, and the grand duke stood before us. Everyone knelt.

That was Father's grand trick for our guests. Show them the power of magic—its constructive, destructive, and trans-formative glory. Because magic was our most exported resource, Father wanted the wealthy delegates to imagine what they could do with it. They could impress kings. They could bring down city walls. With the correctly refined pearl, they could change the world.

My father's very presence demanded silence. I'd feared him for almost as long as I could remember. Where he walked, the air seemed thin and sparse, as if his broad shoulders and fur coat pushed it out of a room. As if it tangled in his snow-and-stone beard or got bitten off by his sharp teeth when he smiled. As if his brown eyes could pin it down.

Mother stood next to him in a dress of white doeskin. She and I shared the same pale hair and skin, the same gray eyes, the same pointed chin and nose. I hadn't managed to inherit her elegance, but I made up for it by being less abhorrent. And on Father's other side stood Lyosha—eldest brother, heir-elect, and groom for the brideshow—who had Father's height and dark hair and pale skin, but still looked like a weasel in a coat. Unlike the rest of us, he wore the brown-and-white wool that was spun from the shaggy goats we kept at the base of the mountains, eschewing the bright colors and fine-spun cottons that could be purchased from abroad. Lyosha liked to consider himself a man of the people—provided the people wanted nothing from him.

My father motioned for the hall to rise. I straightened reflexively. As Father began his welcome speech, I kept my hands clasped in front of me; I knew if Lyosha caught any of us fidgeting, he'd have harsh words and harsher actions for later. As subtly as I could, I let my eyes and mind wander over the motifs on the walls. They told the story of the duchies—the duchy Above, and the duchy Below. Our duchy, which sat on a frozen lake, and the land that thrived beneath the ice. More than anything, I wanted to see what truly lay Below. But I would never get the chance. Only Father was allowed to enter that realm.

I focused next on a hunting scene with a former grand

duke and a cornered bear. I recalled bones, starting with the bear's nose. *Nasal, premaxilla, maxilla. When ground, stabilizer for liquids that tend to curdle. Incisors, canines. Amulets for strength with no demonstrable benefit.*

I was nearing the ilium when the patter of applause interrupted me. The speech was over. I joined in, lifting my chin so that I could look properly impressed. Father offered Mother his arm, and she took it with barely a sneer. They stepped down from the dais together. The brideshow had formally begun.

Prime Minister Eirhan came forward and bowed perfunctorily before murmuring something in Father's ear. Father nodded coldly to the Kylmian ministers, who clustered off to the side. It was no secret that Father and Lyosha fought over the ministers; they fought over everything. Lyosha couldn't mount a successful coup without the majority of the ministers on his side, but Mother's support lent him strength; a coup had been rumored for years. My maid, Aino, had been predicting it once a night for weeks. After all, it was the traditional way for Kylmian children to inherit the dukedom. Poor Aino had taken to double-locking my door each night, and she spent hours fretting right inside it. As though *I'd* be the first one slaughtered in a coup.

It doesn't matter anyway. The coup wouldn't take place in the next five days, and after that, I'd be down south at the university, where the world was civilized and people didn't kill their relatives as a matter of course.

As the brideshow candidates filed down from the balcony, the first of the guests began to greet my father. King Sigis of Drysiak approached, and I slunk behind Velosha. Sigis was an observer, not a delegate, but in my opinion, he was more of a royal pain than anything else. He'd oiled his golden beard to catch the lamplight, and aside from a scarlet-and-diamond pin that signified his own colors, he wore our family blue. He'd fostered with us for five years, learning to swagger like Father and manufacture "accidents" leading to broken legs and broken skulls among more than one sibling. Father favored Sigis over any natural-born child of his own, and he had taught him the worst of his tricks. Maybe it was the cruelty they had in common. The Gods knew arrogance was something we all shared.

Sigis embraced Father, and Father clapped him hard on the back. "Welcome, as always."

"As always, I am honored to be welcome," Sigis said. I didn't snort at that. I didn't want to attract attention. But Sigis's politeness was always an act. He always made me think of a bear—except he lacked the bear's manners. "I was surprised by the size of the magic display."

"It's only the preliminary night," Father said. "I've saved a more impressive show for when the rest of the delegates arrive."

Sigis's eyes glinted strangely. "I look forward to it."

As he moved away, Father leaned over to speak in Mother's ear. "I could have gotten him to stand up in the brideshow."

"Sigis doesn't like boys," she replied out of the side of her mouth.

Lucky boys, I thought.

Father rolled his shoulders. "I could have done it."

"Maybe you should have given him a daughter when you had the chance." Mother sneered. Father shot her a murderous look in response. How those two stayed in the same room long enough to make thirteen children, I'll never guess.

My dress itched in a number of awkward places, and the noise that bounced off the ice walls threatened to give me a headache. But I had to stay until each of the brideshow guests had been greeted and we'd been dismissed from our formal duties. I curtsied to the first candidate, a blushing, stuttering boy. He muttered a name too soft for me to hear, though I ought to have known it from the crest on his shoulder, a wheel flanked by rearing horses. Father and Mother treated him courteously; Lyosha dismissed him with a curled lip. I didn't know much about the candidates, but I did know this: My parents and my brother each had a favorite, and it wasn't the same person.

"Show respect," said Father as the boy retreated. His voice was soft—dangerous.

Lyosha's lip curled. "Why? Omsara is a paupers' kingdom. We don't need them."

"The point of the brideshow is to strengthen friendships, not create rifts," Father said. "I asked you to think about that when you started considering your choices."

The next candidate came up, a girl who was graceful and tall, brown-skinned and wide-eyed, and dressed in a white-and-green shift dress. It looked loose and free compared with the tight bodices we wore under our coats. She dipped a curtsy to each of us, smiling. I stifled a sigh as I curtsied back and pressed her hand. This was going to take *hours*. I could be spending the time packing, or studying, or making my university portfolio. Maybe I could persuade Aino to claim I was ill. Anything would be better than pretending I cared about a brother who thought I'd be more convenient dead and about the poor person who was about to marry him.

I spotted Farhod, my alchemy tutor. Like me, he tried to eschew major functions; unlike me, he usually had more success. I rolled my eyes for his benefit. He shook his head reproachfully. His dark, wide eyes were uniquely suited to disapproval.

"I like her," Lyosha said as the snowdrop girl retreated. "She can be considered."

"Not so obviously, my love," Mother warned him. "Everyone needs to start off on equal footing."

"They're not equal," Lyosha replied. "And I don't see the point in wasting my time."

"Then perhaps I should select a different heir," Father replied. "Being grand duke is a balance, not a life of doing whatever suits you, and when."

Lyosha stiffened, as though he'd been hit by a blast of cold wind. Rage gathered around him like lightning waiting to ground on something. "The future of the duchy is mine. My choice. I don't have to run it as inefficiently as you have."

The next candidate faltered. Father motioned them forward with a gracious sweep of his hand, but I couldn't blame them for moving with reluctance. They introduced themselves in a hurry and retreated as soon as they could.

"Come, now." Mother touched Lyosha's shoulder, on Father's side for the first time in years. "There are many considerations to be met. We can't afford to offend anyone before we know what they're offering for the marriage."

Lyosha sulked. "You just don't like her because she's not *your* choice."

"We talked about this," Father said.

Lyosha spoke in a voice not quite low enough, not quite practiced enough to reach only our ears. "*You* talked about this. You didn't bother to ask."

"This is a political endeavor—" Father began.

Lyosha's voice rose. "I have my politics. I make my choices." A small circle of space began to grow around us. "And if I can't make my own choice, I'll make no choice."

"You are jeopardizing years of statecraft," Father growled.

"The duchy doesn't need outdated relics deciding statecraft," Lyosha choked out. "And neither do I." His words slid through the air like a red sword. The brideshow candidates stared. The tan, dark-haired girl in the emerald-and-gold riding suit no longer smiled. Lyosha's anger crackled, so palpable I could almost see it. "This isn't your brideshow."

11

"This isn't your duchy," Father replied. He sounded almost contemplative. "And the more you try to take it, the more I think it never should be."

The whole hall was silent for a breath, waiting for Lyosha's lightning to finally ground.

"The brideshow's off," Lyosha called, his voice bouncing off the hard ice walls.

Noise rippled across the hall. Father grabbed for Lyosha's arm, but Lyosha had spun on his heel and was already striding through the candidates, who scattered and regrouped like a herd of animals.

Father clapped his hands. In response, the guards around the hall slammed their halberds against the ground with a *crack*. In the silence that followed, he said in an impossibly calm voice, "The brideshow will resume tomorrow. Please enjoy yourselves."

By the time he was finished, most of the foreign delegates had begun to shout.

"Excellent," Velosha murmured beside me, and I shuddered. If Lyosha lost the title of heir-elect, she'd look to win it through a process of elimination—specifically, by eliminating her sibling rivals. Half the court ministers disappeared; the rest decided to settle the matter by arguing at the top of their lungs.

A hand gripped my elbow and yanked me sideways. Aino. She was supposed to stand at the edge of the hall as a lesser lady, but she'd squeezed her way over to me. "Come on," she said, pulling me toward a side door. She elbowed past the minister of the people, and I tripped over the minister of trade's robe. He stumbled past me, steadying himself by putting a hand on top of my head for balance. Had it been a normal night, I would have confronted him for his rudeness.

Aino dragged me past anxious servants to the corridor, barely letting me get my feet under me. The flickering lamps set into the walls caught the red in her auburn hair, and her knuckles were white around my arm. We hurried past officials and servants who rushed the other way, alarmed, no doubt, by the noise. "Slow down," I protested, tripping over the heavy hem of my coat. Aino didn't answer. "Aino!" She wrenched me around a corner, nearly dislocating my shoulder. The iron grips on the bottoms of my shoes dug into the ice.

She didn't slow down until we reached the royal wing and passed beyond the guards there. We scurried down corridors carved with the scenes of my family—grand dukes battling with enemies, treating with the duchy Below, choosing brides from their own brideshows. Winter roses twined above us, their ice petals stretching into a two-thirds bloom.

Aino dug out a key and unlocked my door with trembling fingers. Then she shoved me inside.

The fire was out. The ice walls of my rooms glowed blue-white in moonlight that streamed through thin windowpanes. Aino dumped firewood into the metal basin that served as the fireplace, then started the fire with dry moss and a flint.

The fire basin sat on a thick stone shelf to protect the ice floor beneath, and white and blue tiles lined its chimney. A bearskin rug lay in front of the fire, and I sat in the oak chair there, shifting a blanket to one side. I slid my feet out of my wooden shoes and dug my socks into the rug. A tightness began to uncoil in me. No siblings to murder me, no Father or Mother to examine me, balancing my usefulness and irrelevance against my potential as a threat. I pulled diamond-studded pins from hair that had Mother's paleness but not its curl.

My rooms always meant safety to me, but not to Aino. She locked the door, slid the bolt, and heaved a chair from next to the door until it blocked the handle. Then she went to lock the door to the servants' corridor.

"What are you doing?" I asked.

"Making sure no one separates your head from your neck in whatever happens tonight." Aino's braid had come undone, and she pinned it back up with thin-lipped determination. "This is a coup, and Lyosha and your father are in the middle of it. You don't have to be. How packed are you?"

"Fairly packed." My trunk sat in a corner of the room, stuffed with all the things I thought I'd need at the university—clothes, books, sketches of the biology of Above, a few plates with detail on flora from Below sent up as a sample and gift to Farhod. I was still working on copying his dissection report, a recent—and generous—gift from the duchy Below to expand our academic knowledge.

14

"Good. We'll set out tonight, and we won't come back until one of them is grand duke and one of them is dead."

No one could boss me around like Aino could. She was more of a mother to me than Mother. She was shorter and slimmer than our family, with wide blue eyes that always looked alarmed and a nose made for poking into my business. She knew the intrigues of Lyosha and my parents before I did, and she made sure I was always well dressed for events of the court, well versed in what to say, and well protected from the worst of my family's wrath. She tasted my coffee every morning and ran her fingers along the seams of my new clothes to check for razors my siblings might have slipped in. Worrying for my safety lined her mouth and forehead and streaked her hair with gray before its time. In recent weeks, she'd looked more and more worn out as she updated me on which minister backed which family member and how many siblings were trying to get involved in the imminent coup.

I didn't pay much attention. I cared less for Lyosha's political ambitions than I did for a vial of wolf urine. At least I could learn something interesting from wolf urine. And as long as my chief interests were the flora and fauna of Above and Below, I doubted any ministers or ambitious family members cared about me. All the same: "I can't leave yet." Even if I had no interest in the duchy, I had a duty. Our family *was* Kylma Above, and we had responsibilities to uphold. Father had stipulated that I could go south when the brideshow was over, not before. If I violated his order, he might find some way to prevent me from going at all.

I went over to my desk, skipping across the floor in my wool socks. "What are you doing?" Aino asked.

"I might as well get some work done." I pulled a stack of papers from the middle drawer of the desk. I was copying and annotating Farhod's technical drawings of a dissected citizen Below, and I had to finish the project before I went south. They'd be part of my university portfolio and application. Farhod had warned me that gaining admittance was hard, even for the daughter of a grand duke—but detailed dissection notes of a creature never seen before was sure to catch the attention of scholars and professors.

"You ought to rest." Aino checked the door, then paced back to the fire, dispersing the logs with a poker. "We shouldn't have lit this. What if someone realizes you're here?"

I rolled my eyes as I lit the little candle under my frozen inkwell. Aino was back to her favorite hobby: fretting. "No one can see me, and no one's going to care. Fetch my robe, won't you?"

She stomped off, muttering about ungrateful brats and coups and heads. I was restless, too, and opened the window next my desk, leaning out to let the cold air sting my cheeks.

The palace was quieter than usual. Maybe we really were on the cusp of a coup. Or maybe the brideshow was canceled, and nobody wanted to celebrate. From here, I could just see the bridal tower, and I wondered if the candidates had retreated to it. The girl in the riding suit didn't seem like the type to retreat from anything.

A lone figure hurried across a decorative wall, and four stories beneath me lay the thick ice sheet that separated Above and Below. I wanted to crack that ice so badly that it split my heart to think about it. Beneath that ice swam undulating bodies with serpentine legs, vague shapes I could nearly recognize when I walked on the lake's frozen surface. The duchy Below was our closest ally and our dearest friend. It was the only political matter I had any interest in. It was the greatest thing Father had denied me—and denied me, and denied me.

Aino draped my robe around my shoulders. "Shut the window," she said, reaching past me to do it herself.

I pulled my head inside. "No one's going to shoot me from the palace walls."

"Honestly, Ekata. If there is one night my worrying might save your life, it's tonight." She cinched the robe around my waist. "You've never been the sweet, obedient type. Humor me."

"I'll keep the doors and windows locked." I forced myself not to roll my eyes again. "But don't call for a sled. And let me work for a few hours before bed. There's nothing unsafe about sitting at my desk."

"You can work for half an hour, then I'm dousing the fire. And if anyone knocks, say nothing. You're not here."

I shook my head and tucked my chin to hide a smile. "All right."

I didn't hide it well enough. "Don't treat this like a joke, my lady," Aino snapped. She only used *my lady* when she was really cross. "I'm concerned about your life, and all you can think of is livers and cross sections." She curled her lip at the sheet on my desk, on which Minister Farhod had painstakingly drawn a number of internal organs in a hand so fine they still seemed to glisten.

I licked the nib of my pen. "Aino, relax," I said. "The kitchen boy's more politically involved than I am. Whatever occurs tonight, it's hardly going to concern us."

As it happened, I was wrong.

DAY ONE

CHAPTER TWO

My dreams were cold and lightless. Frost bloomed at the edges of my mind, turning into petals as delicate as spun sugar. The dark squeezed my lungs, my ribs. A presence loomed above me, but when I twisted to see it, my movements were unhurried, pressing through air as thick as honey. I knew, suddenly, that something was going to happen, something I didn't want—but I couldn't stop it. Far beneath me came a tapping, the crystalline sound of a pick on ice.

A hand gripped my shoulder. I opened my mouth to scream. The dark pushed into my lungs, filling me, drowning me—

I wrenched my eyes open. I lay in my bed, covered in the down quilt Aino had given me for my last birthday. I'd kicked the bearskin overlay to the floor sometime in the night. The fire burned low in its grate, but orange flickered around the edges of a charred log.

Aino leaned over me, her fingers digging into my skin. I

tried to swallow my leaping heart and pushed myself up. My nightgown was damp, my skin slick. My eyes felt raw and scraped, and when I reached up, I touched wet cheeks. The faint smell of sweat and roses lingered in the air. I grimaced, but at the sight of Aino's face, I forgot my own disgusting state. Her eyes were wide, and her face even paler than when she'd hurried me out of the Great Hall earlier tonight.

"It's just a bad dream," I told her.

"No. Something's happening." She let go, leaving me anchorless. For a moment, terror seized me, as if the dark could leap out of my nightmare and swallow me again.

I slid to the edge of the bed and stuck my feet into my slippers. "What do you mean?" As my dream receded, my mind started putting together the puzzle pieces, slotting them in place like muscles that made up the working limb in a technical drawing: shouts from the corridor. Panicked tones. Slamming doors and rushing feet. The royal wing was normally silent in the middle of the night. Servants slipped like ghosts from place to place, wary of waking their masters. No one charged through it as if the whole palace were melting.

I grabbed my robe and followed Aino into my antechamber. Moonlight tangled in the corners, catching in the whorls and crevices of the winter roses. The shouting drew closer, then receded, like a wave. I strained to make out voices I recognized. Though they pricked at the corners of my mind, I could match none to a name. I hated going to court, and even when my parents made me attend official functions, I could always stand at the back, wondering about ursine skulls and the toe-fins of Below.

"Check every room!" someone shouted from the end of the hall. Doors banged as they were flung open up and down the corridor. Soon enough, they'd get to me.

Aino's blue eyes filled with fear. She grabbed my wrist. "Come," she whispered, tugging me toward the door on the other side of the antechamber, the one that led to the service corridor.

"Where?" I asked.

"We have to leave."

I swallowed. If we left the palace now, where would we go?

"Any luck?" said a voice from right outside my door. This time, I *did* recognize the voice. Farhod, minister of alchemy. Provider of biology books and technical drawings. Overseer of wolf-urine experiments.

Someone hammered on the door. Aino and I jumped. My heart slammed against my ribs. *Calm*, I begged it silently. It wouldn't obey.

"My lady?" Farhod shouted. A moment later, the silver bell at the top of my door rang.

Aino shook her head and backed toward the servants' door at the rear of the antechamber, pulling on my arm.

"Lady Ekata!" The door rattled. I twisted out of Aino's grip. It was only Farhod, and he'd helped me all my life. He was going to get me into the university. If we were in danger, maybe he was, too. I couldn't abandon him.

"I'm here," I called back. Aino glared at me. "It's Farhod," I whispered.

"When revolutions happen, you don't truly know anyone," Aino warned me.

There were only two people I knew I could trust in Kylma Above, and Farhod was one of them. But for Aino's sake, I settled for opening the door just a crack, dislodging a stray winter rose leaf that had grown over the door in the night. "What's going on?" The blue-white walls of the corridor of the royal wing, carved with the eagle-and-rose insignia of our family, crowded with shapes and shadows that renewed my fear. Though I saw plenty of ministers' robes, no guards accompanied them.

I doubted any minister who wanted to kill me would stoop to doing so personally.

Farhod's dark eyes filled with a strange relief, almost as though he wanted to cry. He looked at me as though he hadn't expected to see me alive. "May I come in?"

"No," Aino groaned from behind me.

"Yes." I stepped aside. Farhod hurried through the gap in the door. As I moved to close it, a hand caught the edge, and Prime Minister Eirhan slipped in behind Farhod.

His oiled black hair hung loose around his shoulders, rather than in its customary horsetail. Deep bags under his eyes suggested that he hadn't slept since the brideshow—though beneath his embroidered blue coat I caught a flash of dressing gown, and his feet were bare. Only a minister in a great hurry would wander our ice palace in bare feet. I couldn't blame him for stepping straight onto the bearskin rug in front of the dying fire. All the same, I would have preferred he'd chosen a different fire in a different wing entirely. Even worse, Urso, a tundra mouse of a man and the minister of trade, ducked through the door without looking at me. I shoved it closed before anyone else could slip through.

"What are you doing here?" I demanded. Farhod I could understand. He was someone I cared about and who cared about me. But the others—Eirhan hadn't deigned to look at me since I'd shown up to Lyosha's heir ceremony three months ago in a dress covered in Experiment Gone Wrong. I barely remembered Minister Urso's name, and he had no reason to remember mine. Now he stood in my antechamber, pulling his gray-brown hair into a knot at the base of his neck with thick, trembling fingers, and I could see sweat stains on the inside collar of his robe.

People were machines, I reminded myself. They were complicated puzzles, but any puzzle could be solved. "Has someone sent for me?" Maybe Lyosha had finally killed Father. The alternative, of course, was that I had to be *taken care of.*

Farhod's brown skin was impossibly pale, even accounting for the moonlight that turned the palace and all within it to blue and bone. His hand clenched around the straps of his large leather examination bag. I'd hauled that bag for him countless times, walking the mountains that surrounded Kylma Above as we looked for signs of bears and wolves and reindeer. All the same, I leaned back when he opened it.

When he straightened, he held nothing more sinister than a bone depressor. "Might I beg the favor of confirming my— Your Grace's health?"

"What?" *Your Grace* was the term used to refer to Father and Mother. Maybe Lyosha, if he'd managed that coup.

Farhod came forward and pressed a thumb to my wrist to check my pulse. It spiked as the bell rang again.

"Don't," Aino said, but Prime Minister Eirhan had already left the rug. He flung the door wide, and more figures came in. Aino hurried over to the fireplace under the pretext of stoking it. I knew better. She gripped the fire poker like a sword. I prayed she wouldn't have to use it.

"Go away," I told them, but it was too late. The crowd swelled, ogling me as Farhod pushed my tongue down and checked the back of my throat. I gripped his shoulder as he examined my ear. "Make them go away." I hated how my voice trembled. If this was how I died, I didn't want everyone to see how afraid I was.

"Please put more wood on the fire. Her Grace has a long night ahead of her," Eirhan said.

"Why are you calling me that?" Eirhan knew the proper titles for every single person in this palace. He probably had some archaic, official names for insignificant ducal daughters. He would never call me *Her Grace* by accident.

But the alternative was equally impossible.

Farhod tapped the back of my left calf. "Will Your Grace lift your foot?"

"Stop calling me that." Panic threatened to wash up from my belly and out of me. I should have done as Aino said. I shouldn't have opened the door. We should have fled out the back stairs, taken a sled and some dogs, and driven until the duchy was far behind us. I bit the inside of my cheek until I tasted blood.

Farhod looked up at me. His eyes were impossible to read in the shadows of their sockets. "I won't be long," he said quietly. "But I must finish."

I swallowed and lifted my foot.

Farhod checked my reflexes, my temperature, and the color of my phlegm. He bent me toward the fire and peered into my eyes. He examined my fingernails. The longer he worked, the quieter my room became. As if the people who'd forced their way in were trying to melt into the shadows and become one with the ice.

At last, Farhod squeezed my hand and turned to Prime Minister Eirhan. "It is my medical opinion that Her Grace is in the peak of health."

The room let out a sigh. I, for my part, wanted to scream. Instead, I did the one thing I knew would get their attention: I acted like my mother. I drew myself up, tilting my chin, channeling her ice and silk, her venom and wrath. *"What. Is. Going. On."*

It worked. Around me, ministers and servants straightened out of habit. They didn't see that I was clenching my fists to keep my hands from shaking, that my hair was damp with sweat, and that my fur-lined robe covered a nightgown.

They saw the daughter of a man who could break ministers with a word, of a woman whose ire could melt the ice beneath their feet. And perhaps it was only that moment of power, but none of them looked so grand to me. Most of them wore nightclothes and slippers, with a coat to stave off the palace's eternal cold. Others, like Eirhan, looked as though they might fall asleep on their feet. Yet they'd dropped whatever they were doing and hurried to my room. To see me.

Prime Minister Eirhan sank to his knees, bending his head, and placed his right hand on the floor. His motion sent ripples around the room and out the door as everyone followed suit. Even Farhod knelt. Even Aino, though she looked as bewildered as I felt, and she still held the poker like she was ready to kill.

No one in the room, aside from Farhod and Aino, had ever shown more than the barest courtesy to me. But no one contradicted Eirhan, who spoke clearly and confidently into the silence. "Long live Her Grace, the Grand Duke of Kylma Above, Guardian of the City and Its Boundaries, Blessed of Kylma Below, Ruler Supreme, Beloved of the Gods."

"Long live Her Grace," the impromptu court chanted.

Impossible, impossible. I was a middle child of thirteen. Even the littlest, Svaro, would be happier as grand duke than I. Not to mention Father, Mother, everyone else who ought to stand in the line of succession ahead of me. "Where are my parents? Has my father died? Lyosha should be grand duke." Unless he'd bungled his coup so spectacularly that he'd killed himself in the process.

Eirhan fixed Farhod with a shrewd eye, and Farhod cleared his throat before saying, "The rest of your family is..." He shook his head, bewildered.

"*What?* What happened?" I demanded.

The congregation was silent again. Then Farhod admitted, "We don't know."

We don't know. I had seven living sisters and four living brothers. Two parents in the peak of physical health. Brothers who still played with toy soldiers. "Even Svaro?"

Farhod swallowed. "Yes, Your Grace."

Eirhan spoke from the floor where he knelt. "Your Grace, in this time of uncertainty, we must do what we can to preserve the safety of the duchy and the government. Will you accept your role?"

I couldn't do that. I had to go study medicine and write treatises on the volatility of magic. I couldn't do that if I was stuck in Kylma Above.

But... we *were* Kylma Above. If something really had happened to the rest of my family, the right and responsibility of rule fell to me. I had no choice. I had a duty.

I focused on the pain of my nails as they dug into my palms. Father always said we were born to rule. Even though I'd never wanted to, even though I'd planned to leave, I was born to this. I had to bear responsibility, and I had to find out what had happened.

Maybe Aino had the answers. But she looked as lost as I felt.

"I accept," I said.

"You are the throne, and the throne is yours," Eirhan said.

"*Long live Her Grace*," the court intoned.

Aino hurried me into my best dress, a heavy velvet contraption the color of deep water under a layer of ice. Winter roses had been embroidered in white and silver silk, and pearls clustered between their leaves. Eirhan had the coronation regalia fetched and handed me the scepter that only the heir-elect and the grand duke were supposed to bear. The cold iron burned against my fingers.

The procession to the Great Hall felt like a dream. As we left my rooms, I ran scenarios through my head. My family had been murdered. (All but me? Unlikely.) My family had murdered one another (more likely than I wished). A plague had struck, and the others were ill (possible, but I didn't have enough information). The rest of my family were the victims of some kind of sorcery (but why had I been spared?). I gripped Aino's hand. Aino held me like a lifeline, too, and that frightened me even more.

We halted in front of the Great Hall. Its closed double doors were engraved with the family crest: a winter rose in full bloom. A line of ministers blocked our way.

One minister stepped forward. I recognized him as Reko, minister of the people. He was a thin, sallow-skinned man, who wore rough robes of turned-out sheepskin, peasant garb that even Lyosha hadn't lowered himself to wearing. He looked like a disgruntled fox trying to hide among the herbivores. His frown deepened as he saw the crowd that surrounded me. "What do you think you're doing?"

Eirhan mirrored his movements, coming to stand in front of me. "We need someone to lead us."

"We have someone to lead us," Reko replied. "We have the grand duke." That counted out a few of my theories. But why was I so necessary if my father or brother was still alive?

"The grand duke and the heir-elect can hardly be expected to lead in their current state." Eirhan's proclamation sent a ripple of murmurs through the growing crowd behind us. "We need a representative of strength, and we need it now. If it is Her Grace, so be it."

I pulled back my shoulders and shifted my grasp on the scepter. I was an Avenko, and ruling was in my blood. My family held the balance between Above and Below, and that made me the most necessary person here.

"You advocate treason," Reko challenged Eirhan. The delegation behind him bristled. I tried to attach titles to faces. I recognized Bailli, minister of the treasury. I thought of him as the walrus because of his bald head and the twin scars that slashed from the corners of his mouth down to his chin. He held the rest of my coronation regalia—the orb, the ducal ring, my father's crown.

"Admit it, Reko," Eirhan said softly. "You don't care about her. You've been trying to dismantle the autocracy for years. If there's no duke sitting on the throne, he can't reject another proposal for a parliament, can he?"

Reko's face turned ruddy. "How dare you—"

Mousy Minister Urso scurried between them. Over the years, he'd tried to be the peacemaker between Father and Mother, appealing to decency, dignity, and whatever else he could dredge up as motivation. I'd always considered him a fool for butting in on family arguments. Now I was glad that someone had dragged him out of bed. "Please, Reko," he said. "I was of the same mind as you at first."

"That mind seems to have wandered off," Reko replied.

Eirhan hissed his disapproval, but Urso continued, hunching his shoulders. "The first night of the brideshow was a disaster. The delegates will continue to arrive throughout the week, and now we have no heir-elect to present to our allies. How many will remain our allies if they see we have no leader?"

I tried to cut in. "I'm not really—"

"They can treat with the ministers. They have no need to see our grand duke," Reko said.

"I don't need—" I said.

"The whole point of the brideshow is to be visible," Eirhan said over me.

All my life, these men had ignored me. It had never bothered me until now. Grand dukes didn't let their subordinates push and belittle them. Lifting the scepter, I used it to shove bodies out of the way until I stood at the front, facing Reko. "Stand aside," I said in the best grand duke voice I could muster.

Reko bared his teeth, and ice skittered up my back. But I wasn't about to show my fear. Fear was the enemy of my family. Fear was a demonstration of weakness. "The proper address is 'Your Grace.'" I punctuated this with a swift poke of the scepter. Reko grunted as it hit him in the midriff. I shoved past him and pushed on the rose-relief doors.

Eirhan rallied behind this new development. "Ministers, Her Grace will have our attendance." He swept in behind me. The others followed.

A sudden clang made me turn. A soldier stood in front of Aino, holding his halberd at a not-so-friendly angle. "Ministers only," he said.

Heat swept through me. Using the scepter as a knife, I sliced through the crowd. Ministers fell away from me like meat peeling from bone. "Aino goes anywhere," I told the guard, and he leaned away from the rage in my voice. "You will refuse her nothing."

He stepped back, and she hurried through the door. Our hands clasped.

The Great Hall was still decorated for the brideshow. Our family crest hung on a two-story banner behind my father's throne, and around the hall, smaller banners were hung for each brideshow delegate. Winter roses wound up the slim ice pillars that held the balconies aloft. This time, I ignored the scenes that lined the walls, and I tried to push recipes and serums and amulets out of my mind. I moved toward the throne, flanked by Eirhan and Aino. But as I walked, the events of the night solidified into weight that dragged at the hem of my dress.

I'm an Avenko, I tried to tell myself. *I was born to this.*

Besides, I only had to be duke until I found out what was going on.

I sat. Aino squeezed my hand, then retreated. The ministers fanned out around me, both those who had marched in my procession and those who stood against me. Minister Reko, glowering, held one hand to where I'd hit his stomach with the scepter.

The doors opened again to reveal my most unwelcome guest yet: King Sigis, foster brother and all-around undesirable. I frowned at Eirhan. What had happened to "ministers only"? But Eirhan bowed low as Sigis came up to us.

"I hear there is cause for condolences." Sigis had a rich, smooth voice that others no doubt found soothing and attractive. He paired it with his most charming face and a royal red coat. Each silver button on the coat was in the shape of a wolf's head. He wore two medals pinned to his chest and one around his neck, as if we'd forget how important he was if he didn't constantly remind us. He drew back as he saw me, surprise flickering over his features. "Ekaterina. Are you truly your father's successor?"

It occurred to me that I should answer him, but Sigis had already begun speaking to Yannush, the foreign minister. Yannush's wiry brown beard, clipped to a crisp point, bobbed as he replied. I heard the phrases "grand duke," "heir-elect," and "rest of the family." Yannush sounded as though he had a firmer grasp on the situation than I did.

I beckoned for Farhod. I wanted to bring Aino forward as well, but when I glanced at her, she shook her head. A servant did not stand next to a grand duke. "Give me the full story," I said.

We ought to have spoken in private. I was too aware of the way my ministry pressed in. And Sigis, as a foreign king, shouldn't have been involved at all. But Eirhan cleared his throat before I could suggest it, and the hall fell silent. "It began after two, Your Grace," he said. "Her Grace your mother was found in a state of—" He licked his lips and looked back at Farhod. The entire hall seemed to lean forward.

Farhod swallowed and bowed to me again. I almost laughed, though that might have had something to do with the onset of panic. Farhod had yelled at me, lectured me, patted me on the shoulder when I'd done well, taken away my experiments when he thought I was going to blow up the palace. Now he had to treat me like a duke. "Her Grace was found in a motionless state and could not be roused."

I parsed the words out in my mind. "Is my mother dead?"

Whispers flurried through the hall. Sigis's blue eyes grew thoughtful, and Farhod raised his voice. "A maid checked on her after hearing strange sounds. Her Grace was asleep and could not be woken, and Doctor Munna was called for. When guards were sent to notify His Grace, they found him in the same condition."

"And my sisters and brothers are like that, too?"

Farhod hesitated. "The entire royal family," he said. "Except you. No one else. I have never seen an illness like it."

Murmuring rose around the hall. Sigis leaned back,

cocking his head; Reko and his delegation surged forward. Eirhan motioned to the guards stationed around the room. A dozen flanked the throne, halberds at the ready. The tips could punch through boiled leather, and my father had decreed that the ax blades be sharp enough to remove a man's head with a single blow.

"This is as good as a confession," Reko barked. "It's obvious that she or one of her allies orchestrated the entire event. How else would a middle daughter have a shot at the grand duchy?"

I almost laughed at the idea of allies, but Farhod was the one who replied. "You're assuming she aspires to the post. Perhaps because that is what you would do in her place?"

Reko's face splotched with red. "In the name of the *real* grand duke, arrest her!"

"*That* is an act of treason!" Eirhan snarled.

Their axes were less than a foot from my neck. If they turned those axes on me, I could watch my life spill out, melting the floor for a few seconds before my brain stopped forever. "Wait," I croaked. "You said it may be an illness. Have they had it for some time? How quickly does it set in?"

"I'm not sure, Your Grace," Farhod said, putting a slight emphasis on my new title. "Munna and I suspect a matter of hours."

"Is it fatal? Is it contagious?"

"I do not know," he said.

Reko's face went from scarlet to ashen. And in that moment, I knew what would make me look better than him.

"The palace must be quarantined until Farhod and the physician figure out whether this can spread. The first priority is protecting the duchy."

Eirhan, for once, looked as though he sympathized with Reko. "What about us—I mean, what about Your Grace?"

"I have some knowledge of chemistry and biology," I said. Farhod's lips twitched at my false modesty, while Aino rolled her eyes. I made a mental note—*declare it treasonous to roll your eyes at the grand duke.* "I'll assist with the cure. Maybe you'd like to help as well. Otherwise, you can conduct your duties from inside the palace."

"Surely Your Grace understands that it's dangerous to confine all the heads of state in a plague house," said Bailli in a gravelly voice.

I glared at him. "Do you think it's good to endanger the rest of the city just because you hope you haven't caught it yet?"

Bailli's cheeks reddened, and his eyes flashed with something darker than anger. I'd made my second enemy as grand duke. My reign was off to a bad start.

"It's not only a matter of us, Your Grace," said Minister Yannush, pointing to the delegates' banners that hung from the walls behind him.

"It would be...unwise in the extreme to hold our foreign visitors against their will," Eirhan added.

"I disagree." This came not from any of my ministers, but from Sigis. He smoothed his beard and smiled. Although his native tongue, Drysian, was the business language of the North, he addressed the court in Kylmian. He always liked to show off.

He strode past the guards before they could decide whether he was allowed to do so. His crotch was face height as I sat on the throne, and I tried to lean away without making it obvious that I was leaning away. He smelled of musk, as if he'd been purposefully wrestling a belligerent sheep before coming to see me. "It's simply a matter of the way you say it. I personally find that with the right leverage, you can get anyone to agree to almost anything."

"That sounds like a threat," I muttered.

"It's not a threat, Ekata." Sigis propped his arm on the back of Father's throne. "An experienced politician could get the delegates to agree to the quarantine. That's all."

Yannush whispered something in Urso's ear. "Perhaps an...interim regent could provide some stability?" Urso said. He sounded anything but sure.

I gripped the arms of Father's throne. "No." If Lyosha thought he could be grand duke, then I could be grand duke, at least for a few hours.

Eirhan stepped in front of me, like a shield. "The Avenko family has been on this throne since the foundation of the duchy. They hold the balance between Above and Below. We cannot select another to sit in their place."

Reko crossed his arms. "For once, we agree. Let the throne stay empty."

38

"Impossible," Eirhan said.

Reko's lip curled. "Why? What will *she* bring that we lack? Experience? Ability?"

"Is that how you speak to your grand duke's face?" I spat, channeling my mother's venom. Reko's mouth twisted in contempt, and my anger rose to match his disdain. Maybe I didn't have the experience or ability of my father, but I *did* have the iron will.

I deliberately turned away from my ministers, ignored Sigis, and focused on the guards who surrounded me. The nearest was shaking, and beneath his helmet, he looked hardly older than me. "What's your name?"

He practically rattled in his ceremonial regalia. "Viljo, my—Your Grace."

Viljo. I focused on his face. Before tonight, I hadn't cared to remember many names. But that would have to change. Father remembered everyone, and so would I. "Viljo, take some men and make sure every palace exit is guarded. No one goes in or out, not unless Farhod or the doctor confirms it. And place guards outside the bridal wing. No one can leave until it's safe."

I lifted my chin. I didn't need to look at anyone else. I didn't need anyone else's approval. Nevertheless, my traitor eyes moved to Sigis. He looked thoughtful. He looked... pleased?

I wasn't so sure I was doing the right thing.

Viljo led five guards out. As the ministers shuffled, Eirhan spoke up again. "I move to have Her Grace declared provisional grand duke." His retinue of allies mustered a hearty enough cheer for me.

Sigis clapped but said nothing. I recognized his calculating look, and I did not like it.

"And what does 'provisional' mean?" Reko sneered. "Will she take provisional coronation trials? Make provisional decisions?"

"There will be no coronation trials. Decisions will be made as they always have. There's no need to catastrophize, Reko," Eirhan said.

Reko's eyes seemed to cut me. "And who's to say *she'll* consider it provisional?"

"You will," I said. "I'm sure Father will be grateful to any loyal ministers who ensure his line is safe while he is . . . resting. And to those who help him once he has fully recovered."

The mutters that circulated the hall seemed more approving than disapproving. Sigis's mouth twitched.

Eirhan snatched the rest of the coronation regalia from Minister Bailli, leaving him to bluster at his empty hands. Eirhan shoved the ducal ring on my finger and dropped the orb in my lap. With a little more precision, he placed the crown, a thin diadem of electrum dotted with pale blue pearls, upon my head. It had last been fitted for Father and balanced precariously. "I declare you—provisionally—the Grand Duke of Kylma Above."

CHAPTER THREE

All was silent for a moment. Three or four people clapped, a lonely sound in the Great Hall, and the noise died out quickly. I cleared my throat. "Thank you."

Eirhan turned to the people below the dais. "Please return to your rooms. Anyone who wishes an audience with Her Grace may leave their name with the captain of the guard and will be summoned if their audience is granted. In the meantime, you will be afforded every comfort."

Reko started forward with a face full of murder. The guards closed ranks in front of me and began to herd everyone toward the door. Someone shouted. Voices bounced off the walls, magnifying the sound. Heightening the closed-in, claustrophobic feeling.

Crack. Crack. The ends of the halberds came down on the floor as clear as bells. I jumped. The crown slipped down over one ear. *Crack.* Guards moved forward, pushing the crowd toward the back wall. *Crack.*

It was leave or get crushed. Ministers began to slip out through the open doors, and though we got plenty of angry looks, no one tried to break through the line. Eirhan's commands were working.

Because Eirhan commands the guards. A chill rooted in my spine, and my fingers tightened around my iron scepter. Eirhan commanded the guards, not me. I was protected only as long as he desired it.

I tried to wipe my face clean of expression, the way I'd seen so many officials do, and straightened the crown on my head. As Eirhan and his guards finished clearing the room, I took stock of who was left. Farhod and Aino had stuck with Eirhan during the guards' sweep and had avoided eviction. Now Farhod conferred with Eirhan.

Sigis was still here, too—the guards couldn't push around a king the same way they could push around the rest of my court. "Well, well, little Ekata. Don't you look…queenly." He slid onto the glass throne reserved for my mother and folded his arms behind his head. Rings gleamed on every finger in red and gold and blue.

I tried not to wrinkle my nose. When Sigis lived with us, I did my best to ensure he couldn't remember my name. My sudden increase in power might protect me from his casual cruelties, but as I'd grown, so had he. Instead of arranging "accidents" or telling tales that would increase Father's ire, he could renege on agreements or incite other delegates to hostility.

"What will you do with all the foreign delegates? Around half have yet to arrive, if I count correctly," he said.

Why do you care? I opened my mouth to say something clever. "You're sitting in my mother's chair." *Great job, Ekata.*

"Your mother's chair, or the grand consort's chair?" He winked at me as he got up. Then he bowed, eyeing the scepter and the orb still clutched in my hands. "If there's one thing the Avenko family has always been able to provide, it is an entertaining evening. Thank you for this one. Do feel free to call on me. I might be able to impart some wisdom for your unexpected ascension, *Your Grace*."

Spending time with my foster brother was the last thing that appealed to me. And why did he say *Your Grace* so silkily, as though he were trying to kiss the words? "Eirhan will arrange it." *Note: Tell Eirhan to avoid arranging anything with Sigis. At all costs.*

Sigis winked again, then turned and strode through the doors of the Great Hall as if he owned them. I tried to rub the crawling feeling off the back of my neck.

Farhod bowed as Eirhan dismissed him, then came up to the dais. Aino joined us and put a hand on my shoulder. "What will you do?" she asked.

About what? The foreign delegates? Sigis? Being grand

duke or potentially losing my entire, terrible family? "I don't know."

Aino smiled a tired, sad smile. "You can't say that anymore, my dear. You're in charge now."

I squeezed the scepter until I could feel a pulse in my fingertips. I took a deep breath, then another, envisioning the slow inflation of my lungs, recalling the spongy press of tissue under a scalpel. I felt my panic recede. Maybe I didn't want to be in charge, but I could be. I focused on Aino's question. "We close off the palace and monitor for any cases of plague outside the walls. Delegates can't be exposed." Any more than they already were, anyway. "And we keep the brideshow guarded at all times. If everything goes wrong, the delegates must get their candidates back safely."

"The confinement of the brideshow representatives could be seen as an abduction," Farhod warned me.

"What do *you* suggest I do?" I snapped. Farhod was more of a chemist than a politician. Of course, a few hours ago, I would have said the same of myself.

His mouth quirked up. "Choose one and send the rest home?"

"Don't you have work to do?"

His smile grew. "Would Her Grace like to excuse me or accompany me?"

I slid off the throne, catching the crown before it could fall off. "When did you become so political?"

"My lady," he said, slipping back to my old title, "I have

served kings, lords, dukes, and every manner of rich man. I would be a fool, indeed, if I didn't learn something from them all."

At least he was on my side. "Maybe if we can find the cure by lunch, we won't have any diplomatic incidents."

We did not find the cure by lunch.

Eirhan settled me in the duke's chamber to the side of the Great Hall. As the sun edged over the eastern horizon, Aino poison-tested cup after cup of strong coffee, and Eirhan tried to wrap my head around my new situation.

"The most important thing for you to do as grand duke right now is to convince our visitors that Kylma Above is under control. We have everything we need—and everything they need, too."

He handed me a single sheet. I unfolded it. And unfolded it. And unfolded it once more. My eyes crossed at the list of names and titles. "I'm supposed to memorize all these?"

Eirhan coughed behind his closed fist. "You're supposed to recognize the delegates as you see them."

"How? I've never seen these people before."

"You have, Your Grace." Eirhan turned his gaze to the ceiling, as if asking the goddess Sjiotha for strength.

I glared at the page. The words swam before me, and I picked a name at random. "When did I last see Bardur Erlyfsson?" From his name, I'd guess he was one of the jarls of the knotty, rain-soaked islands to the southwest. Father had

45

given money and goods to fund wars with them over sea passages that were vital to trade.

"When he came for the peace talks two years ago," Eirhan replied. "I would advise you to watch Erlyfsson carefully, Your Grace. Your father fought him, embargoed him, and opposed him for five years, and neither left the last peace talks with a satisfied heart. Erlyfsson's daughter is part of the brideshow, and his army has been camped along the Kurus border all summer. He could use the brideshow as an excuse to break the peace."

"All right, how about Friedrich von Ilmsbad?"

"Married your cousin."

"Which one?" In my defense, cousins weren't exactly a rare currency.

Eirhan rolled his eyes. I really *did* have to make that illegal. "Marya, your father's niece. His outrageous bride price sponsored repairs to the outer wall around Kylma Above."

"All right. I get the point. I'll start learning the names."

Eirhan and Aino shared a look I didn't care for. "Learning the names won't be sufficient," Eirhan said. "You have to learn the people. You must know who has brought his mistress and who requires an altar in his room. Everyone will look to forward their influence with Kylma. Be prepared to talk of treaties. Be prepared to talk of your family. Be prepared to talk of yourself. And be prepared for every delegate to use the information against you."

"So . . . how do I talk to them without giving them ammunition?" This wasn't possible. Even my father couldn't know everyone in the world.

"We will be here for you," Eirhan said. "All you have to do is think before you speak."

I had no doubt that things would be much worse than that. I resisted the urge to toss the paper into the fire. "Shouldn't I be learning about our current treaties, trade deals, that sort of thing?"

Eirhan had a peculiar expression, as though something I'd said had given him indigestion. "Your Grace would be far wiser to start with the simple things."

I narrowed my eyes. "Just because I was never interested doesn't mean I'm a fool."

"Of course not, Your Grace." Eirhan's carefully bland expression didn't reassure me.

The door opened. "Minister Farhod wishes an audience," the guard said.

"It's not a good time—" Eirhan said.

I spoke over him. "Of course." My heart did a little flip. Had we fixed things already? Was my father going to walk in here to see me playing grand duke?

Farhod entered alone. He already had the classic look of a long day in the laboratory—sweaty, in a loosened cravat and rolled-up sleeves. "I know you're busy, but I need to show you something."

I set my list to the side with a groan of relief. "What is it?"

Farhod's hand went to his wrist, before he remembered his sleeves weren't there. "I don't...entirely know."

I looked at Eirhan, who frowned but said, "Go if you wish."

Aino and I followed Farhod toward the laboratory, and Viljo fell into place behind us. "Has the doctor been working with you?" I asked Farhod.

"I'm afraid so," Farhod grumbled. He'd butted heads with my father's doctor, Munna, on more than one occasion. I'd never been able to stand the doctor, either, so I'd trained under Farhod and hoped that I could make up any gaps in my knowledge later.

Farhod's laboratory was a tower room built as an annex to the palace so that if it blew up, nothing else would go down with it. I'd trod the path so many times I could take it in my sleep. For a moment, I almost tricked myself into believing we were back in the routine of the curious lady and the besieged tutor. "I was thinking," I said, trotting a little to keep up with his long stride. "Maybe I can work with you more on this."

"You have a lot of duties. I don't wish to add to them," Farhod said, fishing for his key as we approached the laboratory door.

"But if I can help you with the cure, I can include it in my university portfolio," I said. "They'd have to accept me with an accomplishment like that."

I waited for the smile that Farhod always gave me when I thought of something clever. Or the tilting of his head from side to side as he considered. But Farhod hesitated over his keys. A tiny crease appeared between his eyebrows. Finally, he said, "Is that really what Your Grace is taking away from all this?"

"Why not?" I asked, but he'd already pushed open the door to the laboratory. I followed him in.

The laboratory was a small, clean space with a worktable and a few stools. The walls were lined with shelves that held ingredients and experiments, neatly labeled and kept in glass jars. The worktable held vials, one for each member of my family. Farhod uncorked the one marked *Lyosha* and held it out to me. I sniffed at the contents. They smelled...sweet? Clean? "Sweat?"

"It came off the body like sweat, but it tastes more like water."

I knew that a good scientist and doctor wouldn't shy away from bodily fluids, but the thought of tasting something excreted from Lyosha made my stomach twist. "Something interfered with his systems?"

"And look at this." Farhod went over to a shelf and pulled out a glass jar. Within it sat a white powder—pulverized winter roses. He took a long-handled wooden spoon and dipped it in. "Do you remember what winter roses do?" He dropped the spoonful of powder into the vial. The fluid began to change color. Farhod swirled it around, and the color deepened, becoming the clear blue of water beneath ice.

"They react with magic," I said.

My family hadn't fallen ill. They'd been cursed.

And I'd been spared.

My mind spun. Magic was a highly regulated resource, which meant no dose left the royal treasury undocumented. So if I tracked down the magic, perhaps I could find the culprit. And if I asked the wrong people, or made the investigation too public, or told someone who couldn't keep their mouth shut...

"Okay." I tried to push the foggy web of court politics out of my mind. "What do we know? It's magical. Which means it's probably deliberate. Could it still be contagious?"

Farhod shrugged. "Magic is too unstable to predict an outcome. It could be that whatever happened to your family wasn't the original intent at all."

"But there was some kind of tampering," I said.

"I'm not sure how else they could have fallen ill. They must have touched or consumed it." Maybe Lyosha had done it. Maybe he'd intended to poison everyone, but somehow things had gotten mixed up and I'd ended up without the curse.

"But we can treat this like poison, can't we?"

Farhod shook his head. "There are still too many things we don't understand. We don't *know* it isn't contagious. We don't know if our patients will live long enough to facilitate thorough experimentation."

Something icy gripped my stomach. "What do you mean?"

Farhod hesitated. "I don't know whether the goal was

to put them in their current state or something worse." He spoke carefully, neutrally. Almost matter-of-fact.

A chill skittered over my skin that had nothing to do with the laboratory's ice walls and low-burning fire. Farhod was only stating facts, and I knew that. All the same, it almost felt as though he didn't care. *You don't care about them, either,* whispered a nasty voice in the back of my mind. *You only started caring when it interfered with your plans to leave.* "And you're sure it was no accident."

"I don't understand how it could be," Farhod replied. "I've been working my way through panaceas, but the best way to find answers would be to find the culprit."

Which meant politics. I wrinkled my nose.

I put on my gloves, and we got to work. Ground-up bear bladder, bezoar, mercury—nothing seemed to react. How would I find a cure for a magical ailment?

And if only the grand duke controlled magic, did that mean I had access now that I was the duke? Could I possibly use it on the illness itself?

But when I brought it up, Farhod said, "You know better than to bring unknown elements into the search for a cure." He was busy with a little pot over a burner. A sharp, sweet smell, like apple blossoms, emanated from it.

I didn't like not knowing things. My exhausted mind drifted down, down to the hole in the ice, to where fishmen waited Below. They knew about magic. Maybe they'd help.

A knock sounded at the door, and the physician looked in.

Munna had always jealously guarded my father's health, and they seemed to take it as a personal affront that he'd fallen ill. They also took that affront out on me. Their eyes were red-rimmed, their sallow face drawn, and while they'd taken the time to put on a fresh coat, they didn't bother to hide their contempt as they bowed. "Your Grace," they said, and the words dripped like poison. No doubt they were part of the faction that thought I'd planned this myself.

"What is it?" I said, too tired to keep my own tone civil. If Munna wanted to hate me, let them hate me. Their loyalty to my father would never make me fully trust them.

"I'm here to confer with the minister. Though I have been…instructed to inform Your Grace that Prime Minister Eirhan has requested your presence in the duke's chamber."

My vision swam. A faint ringing had persisted in my ears for the last ten minutes, and my legs ached as if I'd been up in the mountains scavenging for winter herbs. I pushed myself to my feet. "Did he say what he wanted?"

"I didn't ask," Munna replied.

"Take off your apron," Farhod reminded me as I started for the door.

I unknotted the string with fumbling fingers. "Send a message immediately if you find anything. I don't care what you interrupt."

As I approached the duke's chamber, I spotted Yannush and Urso exiting. They bowed to me but hurried away before

I could ask what they'd been doing. "What—" I said as I went in.

Eirhan had already started talking. "—sent a letter. She'll be arriving by the end of the day, so we'll have to have your quarantine plan in place by then. What did Farhod want?"

Don't tell him. Mistrust prickled my skin. I didn't owe him answers; he owed them to me. "What did Yannush and Urso want?" I countered.

"What's important is what *you* want—support. Yannush and Urso have simple needs, which means it was easy to secure their help against Reko."

Bribery. "No wonder you let me go so easily."

"Your Grace?" I was no expert in all things Eirhan, but his voice sounded as if he'd chipped it off the palace walls.

I didn't care. I was the grand duke, not him. "Was that your plan? To make deals behind my back while I was trying to save the duchy?" My heart stuttered. "Did they offer *you* something?"

We were silent for a moment. Eirhan's voice was far too quiet when he answered me. "They offered support. For you."

For me, or for him? I couldn't know. Eirhan had ensured I wasn't there to hear what they said. I willed my heart to slow down. "I thought you told the court they could apply to meet with me. Do I not have to be at a meeting in order for it to be a meeting with me?"

Eirhan's face broke into an expression of incredulous disdain. It was the sort of expression Father would have executed a man for giving him. But it stole my voice, and the fire from

53

my belly, and left me ashamed and weak. "Over two hundred people are clamoring to see you. Do you really think His Grace your father took every petty request, settled every tiny argument, heard the inconsequential grievances of every single person who wanted to speak with him? You don't run a country by yourself. You trust others to help you."

"Don't lecture me," I snapped. "Ruling is in my blood."

"Is it?" Eirhan picked up a stack of papers and selected a single sheet from among them. "Your tutors reported abominable skills in political affairs, a complete lack of interest in getting along with everyone from new acquaintances to your closest siblings, and an inability to play an instrument, sing, recite poetry, or be otherwise charming in public." He regarded me with cold eyes. "Politics requires a finesse you don't have."

My skin was on fire. Part of me wanted to rage at him, part of me wanted to cry. Part of me wanted to run. All of me prickled with humiliation.

He wasn't wrong. I'd never sought to be a politician, a performer, or even nice. And now I needed to be all those things.

I wondered what would happen if I ordered Viljo to kill Eirhan on the spot. Probably nothing.

Eirhan tucked a greasy lock of hair behind his ear. "You can learn all these things if you pay close attention and let me help you. It's not your fault you've been thrown into a delicate situation with no training." He rubbed at one eye, the first sign of discomfort I'd seen since he stormed into my rooms. "Yannush and Urso are powerful men, and Reko's been pushing for a parliament for years. This disaster could turn them to his side—or we can secure their loyalty and ensure your stability. If, somehow, your father never wakes, you will need to be a more attractive choice than Reko's revolution. You will need to be competent and strong, and you will need a competent and strong ruling machine. If we play to your strengths *and* to mine, we can ensure that you remain grand duke as long as you are needed—and that when you step down, there is some place for you among the living."

He had a point. Once Father and Lyosha woke up, they were more likely to see me as a rival for the throne than a member of the family. All the same, Eirhan was conveniently installing himself as the most important, most competent man in the duchy. As the man I couldn't afford to cross. But he might be the man I needed.

"All right." It felt more like a grumble than a graceful concession. "But you can't make decisions without asking me first."

"I never would, Your Grace. Perhaps we can begin our politics lessons by discussing the implications of what Yannush and Urso were hoping to get out of supporting you? Yannush is the foreign minister; Urso, the minister of trade. They work closely together to determine the demand for our goods and to determine the number of foreign traders who can enter Kylma Above. What they most want now is to relax policies your father put in place, which made it more difficult for foreign merchants to enter the city and buy magic."

I held back the urge to yawn. "Fine," I said, but out of the corner of my eye I saw Aino stiffen. "I mean—did Father know? What was his position on this?" I didn't want him waking up to discover I'd ruined everything in his absence.

"Your father believed that a man-made shortage of refined magic would keep it at a high value. He also required foreign traders to buy a certain amount of goods from Above if they wanted the right to buy goods from Below. And naturally, he favored our own merchants over outsiders."

I tried to wrap my head around the deluge of words. "So if we relax the policies on trade, as Yannush and Urso want, Father will be angry?"

"This is only the start of the discussion, Your Grace. We've promised nothing yet, but we'll keep Yannush and Urso on your hook. Any parliament they backed would have to be established before new trade agreements could be ratified, and that could take much longer and be much less fruitful. And if your father wakes within the week, they'll hardly want to pretend they treated you like a duke."

I had one advantage over Eirhan: He didn't realize we weren't dealing with illness. "So what does that mean?" I said, trying to keep my expression neutral. This was somewhat ruined by the fact that my eyelids stuck together every time I blinked, and my stomach flipped sourly.

"It means you need to read up on trade and be prepared to

discuss options at a cabinet meeting. Now, Minister Itilya and Minister Rafyet—I'm sorry, Your Grace, am I boring you?"

Yes. I didn't say it. I was busy looking at the smooth black bowl on the corner of the table, polished as a mirror, and the water that swirled inside it as though stirred by an invisible hand.

I wasn't supposed to know what it was. It was a messenger bowl, and I'd been using them for years.

Messenger bowls sat in all the state rooms, filled with a water that never froze. My earring had fallen into one at a party, and I spent the evening hiding from my mother in the family library, afraid she'd accuse Aino of stealing it. Hours later, the water in the messenger bowl burbled, and I found my earring suspended in the water. As though someone had known I'd lost it and had known where to return it to me. It was only proper to write a thank-you as a lady of our house, and thus the correspondence had begun. I'd learned about the city Below, carved in black stone, warmed by hot water that jetted up from fissures in the lake floor. I learned about the battles citizens Below fought with beasts that lingered outside the city, using iron spears from Above. Notes came twice weekly and were always short, written on a waxy green paper with ink that never smudged. And no matter how I begged, nothing was sent besides letters. I had never even seen the hand that wrote them.

"That was quick," Eirhan murmured. "The duchy Below has realized there's a new duke Above."

The water turned faster and faster. Something glinted at

the bottom of the bowl, a flash of reflection. But as I watched, the flash came again and again. And then it wasn't a flash at all, but a piece of debris caught up in the water. I reached in, gasping at the water's cold bite, and pulled out a folded slip of green paper that was waxy to the touch. I angled away from Eirhan as I opened it. I'd assumed it would be from the same anonymous hand that had always written to me. But the handwriting in dark blue ink was unfamiliar and nearly illegible.

> *We send our heartfelt condolences to*
> *Grand Duke Ekaterina Avenko regarding*
> *the health of her family. Please accept*
> *this invitation to receive further regards,*
> *in person, at the hour of half past one.*
> *Delegates will be waiting to escort*
> *you Below.*

Below. My heart squeezed strangely, painfully. Images of fishmen with spears, of glimmering magic, filled my mind. My skin grew cold, then hot, then cold again. "Below?"

Eirhan leaned over my shoulder to read the note. His brow furrowed. "It's traditional for new grand dukes to be received by Below. And it's one thing I think you'll be well suited for."

"You think I'd be good at something?" I asked flatly.

Eirhan's smile seemed more polite than amused. "Your

Grace will need to be aware that the grand duke Below is as masterful a politician as we are Above. He became angry when your father reduced the trade of magic, and we haven't exchanged goods in some time. He will talk to you prettily and attempt to charm you into reversing your father's policies. Promise him nothing."

We were under embargo, yet Eirhan thought I could manage the situation. My mind stalled. "I . . . can really go?"

"Unless you'd like to meet the minister of agriculture with me?" Eirhan's smile seemed almost kind. "I will have a gift arranged. You have twenty minutes to get ready. And . . ." He licked his lips. "I implore Your Grace not to be taken in by all the new things you see. Our relationship with Below is—"

"Political. I understand." I grabbed Aino's hand.

Below. A whole world that no one Above got to see. A world of flora and fauna that I would be the first to study. A place that held the secret to magic. A place that might know how my family had been cursed and how I could fix them.

Below. Let Eirhan abuse his power while I was gone. I had to go Below.

CHAPTER FOUR

The entrance to Below was a stone-lined room with a bench and steam room in the corner. In the center of the room, a circular hole had been cut in the three-foot ice sheet. Black water lapped at its edge, ripples hiding whatever lay beneath.

"Your escort awaits you," said Olloi, minister of Below. He looked as if he'd spent so much time observing fish he'd tried to become one. His long coat obscured his figure, and he seemed to sweep rather than walk around the room, so silent I almost bent down to see if he had fins or feet. He stared at me without blinking. I half expected his mouth to pucker.

"What's the protocol?" I asked as Aino braided my hair and loosened my gown. I couldn't embarrass myself beneath the ice. I had to make a good impression so that they'd invite me back. So that I could see all there was to see, study all there was to study.

Olloi stared at me a moment too long. Then he spoke, slowly, as though drawing the words out from a difficult place. "The duke Below is your elder, and he takes precedence. You are there by the grace of the citizens Below, so don't be rude. Follow your escort, and do not stray to look at some interesting flower. Do not argue with anyone from Below."

The water before us bubbled. A dark, slick head emerged, covered in long scales that slid over its scalp like a mane. The face was more woman than fish: long, with sharp cheekbones that cut down toward her nose. Her large, dark eyes fixed upon me. They were mostly pupil, with a thin, gray iris. When she smiled, her teeth made little points and did not meet. I leaned forward to see if she had an extra set tucked in her gums. Aino hissed in a breath behind me, but the representative merely lifted a webbed hand and beckoned.

My own breath caught. Below.

Olloi handed me a bundle of electrum ingots—a gift for the duke. I belted them to my waist, sat on the ice, and slid one foot into the water. I'd been in the moat before, but you never truly got used to the shock of the cold.

Aino's hands lingered on my shoulders. I sent her what I hoped was a reassuring look, then levered myself off the ice shelf and dropped beneath the water's surface.

For a moment, panic rose with the shock of cold, carrying some memory that lurked right beyond my grasp. Then my escort ran a dark green finger down my forehead and over my nose and lips. The pressure on my lungs disappeared, and the intensity of the water lessened. My limbs became looser and my heart slowed to its normal beat.

Above me, a solid white sheet—the ground floor of the palace—stretched out as far as I could see. Tiny fish nibbled at the algae that clung stubbornly to its underside, and farther away, larger shadows swam in the water. The surface of the ice was uneven, and I wondered if it was the weight of our lives that had caused it to buckle. I wondered what else grew on the bottom of the ice, and what else scavenged for its food up here.

The fishwoman brought her legs forward and curled in on herself, touching her forehead to her knees. Their version of a bow, I supposed. It was rude to stare, but I followed her form as she uncurled, past the point where her trunk bifurcated and to her feet. Instead of toes, her skin fell away in long ribbons of fin that glinted silvery pink against the dark green of her body in the pale light under the ice. Her fingers were likewise long, longer than any human's could be, and they ended with blunted tips like mine. She extended them toward me. "We may speak now. Welcome, Your Grace. My name is Meire, and it is a pleasure to meet you at long last."

Her smile did not seem so full of teeth this time. Something in her earnest, solemn eyes begged me to recognize her. *At long last.* "Did you . . . are you the one who wrote me letters?" I said.

She dipped her bow again. "I begged my duke for the

chance to be your guide. I look forward to showing you all the things you have wondered about."

And there were so *many* things. But what caught me first was the musical quality of her voice, lilting and distorted by the water. I'd expected her to...well, burble. "How can I hear you?"

Something sparkled on the edges of her fingers. Magic. "Would you permit me to take you Below?" She took my hand.

My legs kicked weakly. I couldn't help staring at Meire's legs, long and lean and powerful. Her toe-fins splayed wide to push the water. I felt like a doll being dragged by the arm. Maybe I could make something, some kind of flat web for my foot, something to make me swim more like her. The smoothness of Meire's skin surprised me, too—the scales on her palm were so small and interlocked I could hardly tell where one ended and another began. The scales grew in size as they crept up her forearm, turning darker as they spread over her breasts and reached her sternum, until they were the deep green of algae.

Above us, the ice sheet creaked. It diffused the sunlight, giving the lake a soft glow—but ten or fifteen feet down, the glow disappeared in the murky blue-black. "Where is this city you always wrote to me about?" I asked.

"It is down, of course," Meire said, and down we went.

The water grew warmer and darker as we swam. Soon I could barely see Meire's fingers wrapped around mine. Little eddies brushed across my skin, and I thought of the things that created currents like that. I craned my head, but it was useless. I was lost in a lake of ink, with Meire as my only lifeline.

My finger brushed against something smooth and slick— something that flicked around my wrist and tugged. I gasped. Water filled my mouth, all salt and seaweed. Even though I didn't have to breathe, I felt it in my lungs and coughed.

Something flashed, a little stroke of light that illumined my wrist. The strand released its hold.

"My apologies," came Meire's voice from the black beside me. "Can your kind not see in the dark?"

"Not this dark."

"Permit me to help." Meire found my loose hand and brushed her fingers over my knuckles. Something cold broke over my skin and I felt a strange jolt in my belly. A moment later, it began to glow in wide stripes where her fingers had connected.

I held my hand up, squinting in the sudden brightness. Behind it, dark shapes pulled away, long tendrils whipping like shadows as they retreated. "What is this?"

"I only gave you a little magic," Meire said. I gasped again, and Meire's head tilted as she watched me cough.

"You *gave* me magic?" I sputtered.

"Should I not have?" Meire didn't frown, not as a human might, but her eyes widened in what might have been concern. "Is it bad for you?"

"It's—" I stared at the marks on my skin. Magic had been forbidden to us. Its combination of expense and volatility made it a poor choice of toy for fratricidal children. Why let us try to cram it down one another's throats when Father could make pretty spells and sell it for a fortune instead? "I've never been *given* magic like it's nothing."

"We have more than enough to give." Meire tugged on my arm and led me farther down.

More than enough. The thought of it was unfathomable. I'd never really considered what the citizens Below did with the magic they kept, but if they had so much they could waste it on turning my hand into a lamp...I'd have to ask Eirhan why Father had restricted magical imports so considerably.

The light emanated from my hand with a strength that surprised me. "Did you know it would do this?"

"Of course," Meire said. "It does whatever I wish."

Questions rustled against the edges of my mind like the long fingers of the creatures around us. Why could anyone Below shape magic while only Father could Above? Was it an anatomical difference? Had we spent so much time relying on magic as a system of wealth, as a fancy toy, that we'd lost its actual purpose?

I wanted to ask all my questions at once. Instead, we swam, and the things of the deep moved out of our way. I never saw more than a tail fin or a tentacle; even though I twisted and whipped my hand through the water, the creatures were always faster, shying away from the light.

A pale green haze appeared in the gloom. As we drew near, the haze began to distinguish itself. Hundreds—no, thousands—of little spheres jostled one another as they moved with the current. In their light, I began to see new shadows in front of us that were less afraid of the light—long eels and teardrop-shaped fish with jutting teeth. A tendril drifted in front of my face, and Meire swatted it away. I twisted back to look at it but saw only darkness behind me. "What are they?"

"You might call them sentries," she said. "They ensure we are protected from any unwanted visitors."

"Can I—" I stopped just shy of saying *take one*.

Meire looked at me as though she knew what I wanted. But she nudged the spheres aside and pulled me through. And we were inside the city Below.

Meire's descriptions of the city Below hardly did it justice. Slabs of black rock, shaped into curves by the current of the water, reflected the light. Spires twisted, buildings swelled and cut back like waves, and in open windows more spheres glowed. Coral bloomed along the crests of buildings. Schools of silver fish no larger than my fingernail nibbled at the algae growing over their surfaces. A shark half as large as me lurked in an alley between two smaller dwellings.

The lake floor was paved with more algae, and long, translucent bones jutted from the dark fronds. Vertebrae lay scattered among them like flowers, and ceratotrichia waved like hands, beckoning. More lights had been fixed to sconces in the sides of buildings. "What are they made of?" I asked, reaching for one before I remembered that a good grand duke kept her hands to herself.

"They are a type of fungus," Meire replied. She smiled, and it was so strange—those pointed teeth were capable of rending flesh with a simple twist of the head, yet I did not fear her.

As we swam, I began to see the denizens Below fluttering between buildings, following us. I could spot an undulating shape, a flash of fin, but no more. When I stopped to get a better look, Meire pulled me onward.

She let me go when we came to a wide boulevard. Mushroom lamps had been placed at regular intervals to create a clear line of sight, past buildings that grew grander and grander the farther away they were. A current tugged on my wool shift.

This was the processional road. Meire had written of the market and the goods she bought here and the palace at its end. Today the road stretched empty before us, with the palace lurking like a shadow. To either side waited figures, half hidden behind the odd fungal lamps. Silver and blue and coral sparkled on wrists and throats. Wide, dark eyes regarded me as I passed. Mouths opened to reveal teeth like knives. I saw noses like dolphin snouts, and blank spaces with flat gills. Some bodies had scales that looked more like skin, and some overlapped like Meire's, in a manner reminiscent of hair. They all had bifurcated trunks, as far as I could see, and I was trying not to look too conspicuous in my curiosity. They were naked and had mammalian sex and nursing organs. Did they lay eggs? Did they have one child at a time, as we did?

The figures said nothing as we passed. The only sounds I heard were the shifting of waters, the song of some mournful creature, and from far above, the creak of the ice.

My toes skimmed the tops of the algae. The tips became luminous, bright, and they seemed to stretch toward me. Intrigued, I reached for them—

Meire pulled me up. "Apologies. I should not have let you drift so far."

"It's beautiful," I said, turning to look at the bioluminescent patch we left behind.

"It is carnivorous."

My knees tucked up of their own accord. "Oh."

The citizens Below thinned out, and soon we passed behind a low wall and out of their sight. We drifted past floating gardens, masses of seaweed and coral with blooms in purple and pink. The light there changed color, becoming softer and paler. Ahead lay the long, low palace of the duke Below.

The palace's stones had been fitted with such skill that I couldn't see their seams. Meire took me up to the gates, double doors of electrum wound about with seaweed and seaflowers. The guards at the front of it held halberds I recognized too well. The iron shafts were pitted with rust, and sharpened fish bones had been tied to the iron tips with seaweed. Below must have traded with us for them, and not recently.

The guards' fins flicked, and they bowed to me. Then the wide, arched doors of the palace opened, and we were led inside.

The Grand Duke of Kylma Below had ascended to his throne when I was a child. I'd begged and screamed when Father refused to let me accompany him Below to pay our respects. Back then, I'd assumed he was spiteful and cruel. Those appellations weren't untrue, but I'd later learned that it wasn't his fault. The dukes of Below had strict invitations for those of us who stumbled around on the ice Above. Only the grand duke was allowed to visit, perhaps because only a grand duke could use magic. Even when Farhod had been permitted to dissect a citizen of Below, he hadn't been able to collect the body; it had appeared at the entrance to Below with a waterproof note regarding ceremonies for their dead.

I never, ever thought I would go Below as a ruler in my own right.

The palace Below had surprising similarities to my own. We both had tapestries lining the walls, though seaweed poked through the back of theirs, and when I touched my finger to one, I could feel the wax coating over the thread. Another thing we must have traded with Below. The tapestries depicted a romanticized life of Above—processions of strange people in stiff dresses, scenic fights between hunters and bears, prowling wolves, stark mountains.

"We are here," Meire said, and the guards bowed to me again. A new set of doors opened, and we entered a vast hall.

There were no mushroom lamps in the hall; bioluminescent flowers wound about sconces set into the walls. Light bobbed in rotting iron lanterns. Seaweed brushed my feet, and some tiny thing nibbled on my toe. Around the hall stood ministers—well, I assumed they were ministers. They held electrum staffs, and some of them had brushed the scales on their heads with bright colors, just as some of us at court wore makeup.

The duke Below didn't have a throne. He and his companion reposed within delicate silver cages attached to the ceiling. Winter roses looped around them, a pale offering in comparison with the bioluminescent blooms. The duke had an electrum staff not unlike my scepter, which had been set into a wire basket on the side of the cage. A little side table held a few notes fixed to a spike, and a bowl pale as ice, with something odd that shimmered beneath the water. Air, I realized—air Above. This was their messenger bowl for us.

The duke swam away from the cage, and the ministers around us bowed their foreign bows. I tried to imitate them, bringing my knees up to touch my forehead and scraping my skin against the wool of my shift. The skin of my arms and legs was corpse-like in the strange light of Below, and my fingers had begun to prune.

"Welcome," he said, and I took that as my cue to straighten.

The duke had a deeper voice than my guide. "And met with sorrow, Ekaterina Avenko."

"Thank you," I said, fumbling for the electrum ingots at my belt. A minister with darting eyes and an eel snout flitted forward to take them, quick and nervous as a minnow.

"We were disturbed to hear of your father's troubles," the duke Below said. The ministers flicked their fins, as though an electric current had passed through the water, and stared at me with their wide fish eyes. As though they expected me to throw my arms wide and laugh that I wasn't sorry at all.

"I was, too," I admitted. My heart flipped, and I rallied my courage. "My father isn't ill, precisely. He was cursed. With magic."

The room went still. The ministers lining the walls cocked their heads. I thought I heard a faint hissing, and when the duke Below swam forward, I nearly ducked. But Avenkos didn't duck. "I don't—um. Not that I think it's you." *Keep it together.* Grand dukes didn't say *um.* "But if anyone knows how a curse is made, or broken, it would be you."

Silence fell over the room for a moment, leaving my foolish words to hang in the water. If the duke Below was insulted, he could send me home without answers—and worse, without letting me investigate more of Below.

"We do not meddle in the affairs of Above, and we do not refine magic for it. Any curse that took place must have been developed by one of your own subjects, and that subject will have the cure," he said. His voice was pleasant, but I heard the undercurrent of iron in it. I'd insulted him.

I didn't know how to reply. Fortunately, the duke continued in a softer voice. "I do wish an elegant solution to your problems. And I wish you to know you are welcome with us, Ekaterina Avenko. Your father spoke of you often. We admired your curiosity together."

That came as a surprise. I'd always assumed that Father had forgotten about me as much as he could. He had so many children to think about, and most of them wanted to try their hand at being grand duke. Being Princess Experiment hadn't endeared me to him.

The duke Below tilted his head. He expected me to say something, so I did. "I am curious—especially about Below." I touched a bioluminescent bloom, and my awkward, pruney fingers came away dusted with light. "This might be the greatest place I ever travel in my life."

I heard a rustling from around the hall—the ministers, drumming their scaled fingers against their staffs. The duke Below smiled. His teeth were thinner than Meire's but wickedly sharp. I resisted the urge to peer into his mouth. "They approve," he said. "They like you."

My heart swelled. It was the nicest thing anyone had said to me since this mess began.

"We are grateful to you for visiting us at what must be a fraught time," the grand consort said. Her voice was soft, not harsh and biting like Mother's. Nor exasperated, as Aino's so often was.

"I'm honored to be received," I replied. "Even though I hope my station is only temporary."

The duke's fins fluttered. "Hard to know what the future brings us. But our families have always been friends, and I extend this offer of friendship to you, Ekaterina."

I tried not to gape. Yesterday I wouldn't have dared dream of going Below. Now the grand duke was proposing friendship. I bowed again and tried to keep Eirhan's warning at the front of my mind. The duke Below wanted me to solve his problems, too. "I hope that I may one day repay your kindness and hospitality."

The duke laughed at that, a warm and indulgent sound that puffed out water around his gills. "Not your father's daughter, I think. He would never have offered so openly."

I pressed my lips together. What should I say to that? Should I try to take back my own words?

The duke Below continued as though he hadn't noticed my hesitation. "We must first arrange the coronation trials. It is not precisely condoned to share plans with a contestant..." His smile gleamed again, pointed as thorns.

"I won't be having coronation trials," I said.

Around the hall, heads cocked again. Had I said something wrong?

"Are you not the Grand Duke of Kylma Above?" the grand duke Below asked.

"My father is," I replied.

The duke's fins fluttered again, and his ministers imitated him. I tried to decipher their emotion. Nervousness? Unhappiness? "Ekaterina Avenko, you must have the coronation trials. An Avenko must hold the throne," the duke Below said.

I tried to explain. "I am holding the throne. It's only temporary—"

"You know of the bargain our families made three hundred years ago," the duke said.

I nodded. Three hundred years ago, my ancestors had been the first to speak with the citizens Below. The Avenkos had been the first to refine magic, the first to make Kylma something more than a frozen wasteland everyone avoided. And they'd been the first to discover that magic was temporary, but its effects were permanent. So they'd cast magic over our frozen city. They'd arranged for our walls and our palace and our markets to thrive without cracking the ice sheet. And as long as an Avenko kept the throne, we held the secret as well.

"This agreement is delicate in times of succession. If you lost your position..."

"To whom?" To Eirhan? To one of my other ministers? When he didn't reply, I tried a different tactic. "Maybe you can just give me the secret. I won't tell anyone." Not even Farhod, who would probably bargain away years of his life to know. "I can cast the magic I need, and—"

And try to ignore that I knew something spectacular? Try to never use magic again? That was probably the most obvious lie I would ever tell.

The duke held up a hand for silence. For a moment, I wondered if I'd offended him. But then he gestured, and a servant came forward bearing the ice bowl. The duke dipped his long fingers in, drawing out a note of creamy paper with ink that quickly feathered.

His dark pupils widened. "Your father left you in a state indeed."

I swallowed. "What do you mean?"

All stilled around us. Heads bent as the court Below turned one ear up, listening.

"It seems there is an army on the ice," the duke Below said.

Meire led me back through the city. I had no chance to admire the architecture, the merchants who flitted past with baskets of wares hanging from their shoulders, the hunters who returned from the lake hauling fish that rivaled me in size. I wanted to see it all. I wanted to see the lowliest hovel. I wanted to see the place of their god. I wanted to see them fight and build and try to sell me something. I wanted to stay until my eyes grew round and luminous, until my pale skin sloughed off, leaving scales behind. I wanted to see if magic obeyed me now.

But Meire's powerful legs pumped, and all too soon she

was brushing the green lamps aside, taking us back into the dark of the middle of the lake. This time she didn't draw magic on my hand, and it didn't glow. "I apologize that your visit has been cut short," she said. "The guards will be called to our stations at the moat. We will be ready to assist you."

"I'll be watching for you," I said. And I didn't say the private, foolish hope that I would be back soon to learn the rest of what I did not know.

The water grew lighter as we approached the ice. The white expanse should have called to me—it was my home, after all—but dread weighed me down and dragged me back. I knew nothing about politics. In all likelihood, my ministers would rather kill me than teach me. And now I had an army to contend with.

You are the throne, and the throne is yours. The thought hardly reassured me.

Meire stopped at the jagged edge of the ice. "I wish you well." She bowed again, fluid and flawless. I resisted the urge to bow back. "And much prosperity between our peoples. We will help in the coming days, where we can."

She pressed her webbed fingers to my mouth.

My lungs burned. I clapped a hand over my nose to keep from inhaling. Dots started to pop in my vision. With a final bob of her head, Meire flipped around and swam away.

CHAPTER FIVE

Aino and Minister Olloi helped me out of the water and hurried me toward the warmth of the steam room. My arms and legs trembled, and I weakly snatched for the towel Olloi proffered. As I squeezed out my braid and wiggled into a fresh shift, I told Aino about the army. She did up my dress with quick fingers, and we set off toward the study at a rapid pace.

Eirhan looked up as I flew in. His demeanor was as calm as ever, and for a moment, I wondered if the duke Below had been wrong about the army. "I suppose he wanted to discuss the trade agreements and the coronation trials?" Eirhan asked.

I had to stop myself from rolling my eyes. Of course he would ask about that first. "We got a little distracted. What's on the ice?"

Eirhan smiled without humor. "It's Sigis."

"What?" Sigis ought to be sleeping after inserting himself

into last night's excitement. "The palace is under quarantine. He can't leave."

"He hasn't left." Eirhan's smile twisted sourly. "His army has simply come here."

"So he's invading?" It made no sense to stay in our palace and leave his army out in the cold. We could take Sigis hostage.

"I expect he'll use it as a bargaining tool," Eirhan said.

"Bargaining for what? He only came for the brideshow." Even as I said it, I realized how wrong I was. I stared at Eirhan, waiting for the same realization to cross his face, but his expression remained impassive. I went on. "Sigis was dressed in new clothing when he came to the coronation ceremony." He'd been wearing his rings and medals. He'd looked like a king. "He planned this, didn't he? He planned for my family to fall ill so he could sweep in and annex us."

"You cannot claim the head of a sovereign nation has deliberately targeted your family. You'll bring us to war."

"He's got an army at our door. What am I supposed to do?" *Show no fear.* "The walls of Kylma Above have never been breached. The army of Below is ready to help us."

"A siege is *not* our first and best option," Eirhan bit out.

"What is?" I snapped. If Eirhan wanted to rule the country for me, the least he could do was provide answers.

"We need to see what Sigis wants, exactly," Eirhan said.

The duchy, no doubt. If Eirhan didn't realize that, maybe he wasn't such a formidable political enemy after all.

Eirhan, Viljo, Aino, and I went out in four layers of fur, with our hoods pulled up and our mittens wrapped snugly into our sleeves. My braid froze stiff as we hit the cold air, and I thought I heard Eirhan mutter a curse. A high wind whistled in the gaps between the peaks to the west, and the air smelled wet, clean of smoke, promising storms. By nightfall, it would be the kind of wind that drove a man to his knees and kept him there till he died.

The palace's outer walls gave us a view of the houses of the city, half-timber structures lined with rubble fill and ice. Their roofs puffed woodsmoke and slanted to keep the snow from piling too high and heavy. Far beyond, the city walls rose, cutting across the lake and veering up into the mountains. Our border faded somewhere in the peaks beyond, but no one had ever invaded from that direction. Our enemies always came from the plains on the other side of the lake. Just as they did now.

A long, dark smudge wound toward the moat. Thousands upon thousands of men trudged toward us, lining up when they reached the moat's edge. I had never been so glad for the waters, wide and dark, and the ice walls that protected us. They came with horses, they came with tents, they came with cannons and turtles and war machines—

"Can we consider this an act of aggression yet?" I said.

"Why don't you ask him?" Eirhan turned, and behind his

furred bulk I saw another shape, standing at the end of the walk, whose bright red coat seemed garish against the blue-white of the city. Sigis.

I swallowed and moved forward. Eirhan put a warning hand on my arm. "Your Grace cannot make an enemy of this man."

"I know," I said.

Drysiak had been a rotten empire when I was younger, riddled with rebellions and fraudulent bureaucrats, hamstrung by weak leadership. Father had predicted its fall in ten years and had accordingly refused when Sigis offered to marry one of the daughters of Kylma Above. Then Sigis took his father's Drysian throne through bloodshed, and now he went to war with a new kingdom every year—and he won.

Sigis had never been small, but with several layers of clothing and several years of growth, he was truly a bear today. His broad shoulders stretched proud and branched into arms like tree trunks. His face screamed *strong*, from his straight nose to the thick blond beard on his chin. His hard eyes fixed on me as I approached, and his smile didn't reach them. "Finest army in the North," he said.

"And what is it doing here?" I asked, focusing on the leaping wolf stitched across his chest. "Is it a wedding present?"

He raised an eyebrow. "Why, are you getting married?"

I blushed. "So you didn't bring it for Lyosha's brideshow?"

"Ekata." His voice was too warm, too familiar. "Don't be absurd. My army was on campaign not far away, so I sent a message. Your ministers are about to revolt, and I thought you'd appreciate some help. I have experience keeping bureaucrats in line."

On campaign nearby, my freezing behind. This was far too convenient to be a matter of coincidence. But did that mean Sigis knew my family would fall ill, as I'd guessed? Or had he come to Kylma to arrange the illness?

"So your army will fire cannonballs at the city walls until Reko agrees not to open a parliament?"

"Don't worry about the cannons," Sigis said, taking my arm. My muscles tensed. "I only use them on my enemies." He moved closer to the wall, and my feet dug into the ice instinctively. The edge of the wall wasn't a place I liked to go, not since Velosha had pushed Pauno off for decapitating her favorite doll. Sigis didn't seem to notice. "But what would you say to a little joining of power? Your ministers will bow to the one who has the most, after all. If we're together, no one will oppose you." He nudged me with his hip, making me stumble, and caught me by our linked arms. When I glared up at him, he winked.

"Careful," he purred.

Was he flirting with me?

Oh no.

He was flirting with me.

I wrenched my arm free and craned my head, looking for Eirhan.

"I'm a powerful friend, Ekata." Sigis moved to cut me off from my guard, my maid, and my prime minister. "My support means a lot, and I'm willing to put it behind you."

"In return for what?" I asked through a dry mouth.

"Nothing you won't have to do anyway," he said, looping his arm through mine once again and turning me back toward the palace. "And we already know each other so well, don't we?"

Sigis paraded me through my own halls, with Eirhan, Aino, and Viljo trailing behind like useless ducklings. The halls were filled with noise like the constant lapping of lake water against the sides of the moat. Yet everyone from minister to servant fell silent when they saw me. And they stared. Sigis all but pinned me to his side, loudly greeting everyone he recognized as we passed. He wanted us to be seen together.

"Annika," he boomed at my minister of agriculture. Minister Annika bowed, flushing. Even when they stood straight, they only came up to my nose, and as they greeted Sigis, they studiously refused to meet my eyes. "I have an answer for your agricultural problems."

The flush spread to their ears. They tucked a brown curl back into their braid, still ignoring me. "I look forward to hearing it, Your Majesty," they replied in a light, high voice.

He kissed their hand. *Don't make a disgusted noise.* Then he steered me away.

Sigis stopped us outside the Rose Room and ordered Aino to get us a pot of coffee. Her nostrils flared in indignation. But Eirhan put a hand on her arm, and she left without complaining.

The Rose Room had been decorated by someone who evidently thought we had to remind our guests what country they were visiting. The rose of our family was evident everywhere: in the upholstery of the couch and chairs, carved into the table, painted on the tiles of the fireplace. Winter roses covered the walls, studded with cold thorns and perfect blooms. They congregated in the corners and twined over the fireplace, where they never melted, no matter how high a fire burned. They were our crest; they were our family. Cold and brittle and untouchable.

They were half open now, the center buds pushing out with some kind of urgency, turning translucent around the edges of each petal. Less open than they'd been this morning, though.

It's just superstition, I told myself. *There's nothing to the stories.*

Sigis took me to the couch, letting his fingers run from my elbow down my forearm, until he held my palm in his unrelenting grip. He pressed his mouth to my glove, and I felt the pressure on my skin beneath. I resisted the urge to tug my hand away and rub off the shine of his spit.

"You look tired, poor Ekata," Sigis said. I found myself being gently and inexorably pushed down until my knees buckled and I fell onto the silk. "Ruling isn't easy, and I know it's a burden you never wanted."

I tried to think how Father would handle the situation, but he'd never be faced with a flirting Sigis in the first place. The thought of Sigis trying to win my father's hand through suggestive flattery nearly made me giggle hysterically.

Sigis still held my hand. I took a deep breath to regain control. "I'm only provisional grand duke," I said. "It hasn't even been a day."

"I've seen coups take place in less time."

I was starting to see why the duke Below wanted me to solidify my place.

I finally freed my hand from Sigis's grasp. He compensated by scooting closer, touching his knee to mine. I fought the urge to leap up. *He's doing this on purpose.* Why was Eirhan ignoring us? I folded my hands in front of me so that Sigis couldn't see them shake. My thumb found the burning space he'd kissed and rubbed over it. Sigis leaned forward. My heart spiked. I'd met wolves in the mountains with Farhod, so why couldn't I keep my head around this lumbering creature?

Sigis smiled at me again, crossing his arms to show off his biceps. The wolf on his coat rippled. "There was one thing your father never wanted, and that was to diminish the power of the Avenko line. How can you be so certain that your ministers won't create a parliament under your nose? How do you know it wouldn't disrupt the balance between Above and Below?"

"Reko's not going to do that," I said with more conviction than I felt.

"Not if you deal with him decisively. Power, Ekata. You need it. I have it."

"And?" I wanted to sound nonchalant. My voice squeaked.

"We can work together." Sigis picked up my wrist and worked his thumb between my folded hands. "You know I always thought a wife from the North would be . . . fitting."

I pushed my teeth together until pain lanced through my jaw. "I believe you told my father any daughter would do."

He laughed, eyes flicking down to where our hands met. "You always had a good memory, my Ekata."

My skin flushed with anger. I was *his* nothing. "And what does my prime minister think of the idea?" I grated at Eirhan.

If I expected Eirhan to be flustered, I was disappointed. He replied without looking up. "An honor such as this is offered to few. Your Grace need not seek my permission."

Wriggling tapeworm, I thought furiously.

"However," Eirhan continued, and a small storm of hope unfolded in my chest. "Choosing a spouse has been a traditional start to the coronation trials, and we have not yet decided to embark on them. You have sworn to be provisional grand duke, and you might imagine how instigating the coronation trials might be seen by others. Especially without any siblings around to compete."

"Exactly," I said, letting my eyes close in relief. As the door opened and Aino entered with a tray of coffee, I pushed myself off the couch. Sigis held on to my hand like a lifeline. "I'm afraid it's not the right time."

"And if someone else initiates the coronation trials? What then?" Sigis said.

My heart did a quick double-beat, and my fingers twitched involuntarily in Sigis's hand. "No one outside the ducal family has instigated the coronation trials for decades," Eirhan replied for me.

Sigis's smile broadened. His fingers tightened on mine

until I was pretty sure I couldn't feel them anymore. "Perhaps two could embark on the trials together."

My fraying temper got the better of me. "Maybe if you move your army, we can talk about it." I regretted the words as soon as they left my mouth. I was giving Sigis the upper hand.

"Certainly. My men have heard so much about your fine city, and they're eager to lodge within it."

"I—we don't have space," I stammered. "You can arrange food trade with Minister Urso, but your men will have to stay outside."

"You can't leave my men out in the cold." Sigis tilted his head, and his hand pulled at mine, keeping me on a leash like a dog. "You can't leave *me* out in the cold."

Don't make a gagging sound. Don't *make a gagging sound.* I forced my lips to stretch. "I'm afraid we can't accommodate a visiting army. We were expecting a brideshow, not an invasion."

Sigis chuckled, shaking his head. Gods, I hated him. "You always had a way with words, my Ekata."

If I had such a way with words, why couldn't I get him to do what I wanted? He bowed over my hand and pressed another forceful kiss into it, then left.

Any daughter will do. I'd never thought I'd be on the receiving end of Sigis's charm. Unease pricked at my skin like an icy thorn. Did Sigis want the duchy enough to betray my father, curse my family, and single me out as the weakest wolf in the pack? Someone had organized the curse and sent the court spinning toward ruin. It could be Reko, hell-bent on a parliament—but wasn't it terribly convenient that Sigis showed up with his army, right when we were most vulnerable?

"Your Grace is having an eventful day," Eirhan observed.

"Did he really threaten to start the coronation trials?" I groaned, taking the steaming cup Aino offered me.

Eirhan steepled his fingers, and he looked far too thoughtful for my liking. "You would be unstoppable if you faced them together," he mused.

No. "You've been telling everyone we wouldn't run them."

"Sigis's ambition is both a curse and a blessing. If he contends with you in the coronation trials, we stand to lose everything. If he joins with you, no minister will dare oppose you. And...when your father wakes"—I was pretty sure he'd stifled *if*—"he will take back the throne and you'll be protected by your new status as queen of Drysiak."

Eirhan had a point. But I'd still be married to Sigis.

Eirhan drew a stack of paper out of his robe. They were stamped with a seal the color of Sigis's coat. "Your father would also be pleased at your political acumen. He corresponded with Sigis for years on the subject of a bride. More than anything, Sigis wants access to trade. Whether he achieves it through diplomacy, through force, or through the coronation trials seems to be a matter of which is easiest."

"And he thinks marrying me will be easy?"

Aino snickered into her coffee cup, and Eirhan tried to hide his laugh behind a cough. "Your Grace is a veritable font of humor," he said, "but you should consider the offer.

You are in a position of weakness, and Sigis is strength. You are eligible, and you must marry. If you select him, you'll never argue with ministers like Reko again. Not with an army like that camped on the banks."

"And in return, I have to surrender the duchy." The duchy Above had been independent for hundreds of years. I couldn't be the duke who gave it all away. And what would happen to it then? Would we break the tenuous bond between Above and Below, destroy the magic that kept our city on top of the lake? Would that crack the ice sheet and send us plummeting into the depths?

"I believe that Sigis is reasonable and that an agreement can be reached that maintains the independence of Kylma without sacrificing its reigning monarch. Satisfactory trade agreements would give Sigis the edge he really wants."

I could cement power and save the duchy by tethering myself to Sigis. Which meant I couldn't do it at all.

Father had always liked Sigis best. They shared a love of power that kept them talking politics late into the night, and Father never had to fear him, because Sigis would eventually go home. I watched Sigis learn over those few years—I watched him learn that he was safe from my family's murder sickness, and I watched him learn that we were not safe from him. I'd watched Sigis carefully enough to know that he took anything that might be useful to him.

And when it was no longer useful, he broke it.

"The rest of the delegates have begun to arrive. Those

who don't have spies within the walls will hear soon enough that the brideshow has met with . . . insurmountable difficulty. You'll need to show them that you're strong, decisive, able. That they have no wish to antagonize or attack you. With Sigis's support, that will be much easier. Not to mention the spectacle of the coronation trials will give them something to talk about, now that the brideshow is canceled."

"I can't." I couldn't let him use me. I wouldn't let him trample the entire North. I cast about the Rose Room, as if the answer hid inside the flowers. They curled and burst in bunches, a constant reminder. *Superstition.* I reached for Aino's hand.

Eirhan regarded us with that strange, inscrutable expression. "What will you do instead?"

I didn't know.

"If Sigis is going to accept you, we'll need strong contracts in place." Eirhan shuffled through the pile of letters.

"Of course we will," I muttered.

"I'm going to draft—"

"*No.*"

"—and ensure that any contract is favorable to us," Eirhan finished. "Bringing it up will imply that you are seriously considering him, without making any commitments. Perhaps a hint that you will acquiesce when the trials are over, if he throws his support behind you now."

"And he won't see through the ruse?"

"Sigis knows that your position is delicate. Starting the

trials will have consequences no matter what. But if Sigis thinks he has a shot at you, he'll make sure you stay safe."

I squeezed Aino's hand to stop mine from shaking. Yes, he'd keep me safe. And then, when my ministers were cowed and my position was secure, *then* I'd have no choice. I could marry Sigis or have the whole thing come crashing down. I could sell myself or go to war.

And if my family woke—*when* my family woke—my father would be happy to get rid of me.

"You want me to marry him," I said quietly.

"Your Grace will never have as powerful a suitor," Eirhan said. "And you have to get married sometime. There are worse options."

That's where you're wrong. Sigis was cruel because he could be. He didn't have the political acumen of someone like Eirhan, but he didn't need it, either. When he could break an arm between his hands, what need did he have for words?

I needed a way out. "Let me think about it," I said.

"Let me draft preliminary agreements," Eirhan countered. We each waited for the other to blink.

I let him think that I blinked first. "*Only* preliminary."

Eirhan nodded, and as he dipped his chin, I thought I saw the curve of a smile. It was gone when he looked back up. "Only preliminary, Your Grace."

Aino and I stormed back to the royal wing, past whispering ministers and servants who kept their heads down as they dusted off tapestries and put fresh wood in the grates and checked for notes in messenger bowls. When we got to my rooms, I slammed the door in poor Viljo's face. Aino took my hand, trying to soothe me as I fumed silently.

"We can still run," she said.

"Where?" I asked bitterly.

It was a rhetorical question, but Aino set her mouth. "South. Why not? We leave the palace first, head for one of the villas in the mountains. From there we pick a route, and we take it." She raised her eyebrows. *South* meant the university, of course.

I felt a little stab of longing. I'd been so close.... "I can't abandon the duchy."

Her fingers tightened on my arm. "You're the grand duke. You can do what you like."

Except choose my own husband and future.

"What if this is your last chance?" Aino asked.

"It won't be," I said, ignoring the jolt of nerves that came with the thought. I *would* find the cure. I *would* win—against Sigis, against everyone. And I'd take my victory to the university.

She relented, dropping her gaze. "Fine, but just—be careful. You're a target now. Everyone is your enemy."

"You're not," I pointed out. Aino gave me her classic *That's not what I meant* look. "Farhod's not. And if Eirhan were, why would he bother making me grand duke in the first place? He could have killed us when he stormed my rooms." I meant it as a joke, but it was easier to imagine than

I'd have liked. How close we'd come to dying, how maybe I only lived on his whim. Because he needed someone to keep Kylma Above afloat.

Aino's eyes brimmed with worry. She spoke softly, slowly, pressing my fingers with hers. "This is my first lesson in politics: If a minister thinks he can use you, he will try. If he doesn't, he will try to kill you."

She'd always been so worried about me. I made her fret at least twice a week, and now she looked as though she wanted to cry.

"I'm sorry," I blurted out.

She frowned. "For what?"

"For making fun of you last night. For ignoring you. You were concerned, and I didn't think it was relevant—"

"My dear." She sighed, releasing my hands so that she could pat my cheek. "Don't dwell on that. You have so much to worry about now."

I sat down at my desk, but I couldn't concentrate. The idea of Sigis slipping a ring on my finger, taking my mother's throne—no, my father's, for I knew he'd never be content as the grand consort when he could somehow connive to be duke—filled me with a buzzing anxiousness. Eirhan said it was only a preliminary treaty, but if I didn't preempt him somehow, he'd have my brideshow announced and closed before I realized it was happening.

Maybe it was better to go south.

The duke Below needed an Avenko to keep the magical

pact between our realms. But he had my father and the rest of my family to do that, sleeping though they were. Kylma wasn't lost yet. And Farhod was the cleverest person I knew; if this curse had a cure, he'd find it.

"Aino?" I went into the bedroom.

Aino stood at my wardrobe, fiddling with my jewelry drawer. Silver and gold flashed in her hands. She tried to shove the door shut as I approached, but it was too stuffed. She threw up her hands as I nudged her aside.

Diamonds, pearls, sapphires, and amethysts clustered haphazardly within the drawer. I frowned at the mess. "This is all Mother's jewelry."

"Well, she's not using it," Aino grumbled.

"*Aino*," I gasped.

She crossed her arms in a pose of motherly severity. "If we need to flee without warning, those jewels might buy the bread that saves your life." When I only gaped at her, her scowl deepened. "You're the grand duke, you can take what you want."

I rallied myself. "When she discovers that you—"

"*If* she wakes up, she'll never notice they're gone."

They *were* incredible pieces. If we left with them now, I could buy my own palace in the South and never think about Kylma again. Some of the stones were rough, while others were so polished they sent firelight bouncing off the walls. I saw chains with links the size of my little finger, and chains so thin they must have been spun like silk. I picked up an electrum ring with a sapphire the size of my thumbnail.

It was cut in a faceted oval, with leaves and roses worked around it. It was the ugliest, most impressive ring I'd seen Mother wear. *Bridal quality*, I thought, and shuddered.

Then I stopped.

I didn't have to run. There was one other thing I could do to keep Sigis from marrying me.

I slid the ring onto my finger.

"What are you doing?" Aino said from behind me.

I turned and put a hand on her shoulder. "Can you distract Sigis and Eirhan for me? Keep them from wondering what I'm up to."

Her brow knitted. "What *are* you up to?"

"Please." I leaned forward to kiss her on the cheek. Then I made for the door. It was an old trick, and one I felt bad for playing, but if I told her my plan, she'd try to talk me out of it.

The doors of the bridal wing were flanked by two guards. I half expected them to make me stop while they asked permission from Eirhan to let me in. But they stood smartly to the side, and I passed without a word.

Fear swelled in my throat. I could do this. The candidates were only people, like me. People had ten pints of blood, could run maybe sixteen miles per hour and lift about seventy-five pounds. And they were here on the sufferance of the grand duke.

I pushed on the ice doors and went in.

The antechamber was a mess of clothes and luggage. I

tripped over someone's lap harp and nearly slipped on a silk overcoat when I tried to right myself. For fifteen people who had been so refined in public, the princes and princesses looked like they were having a private competition to see who could be messiest. The antechamber itself was empty of people, but I could hear whispering behind a door. As I bumbled my way through the room, the whispering grew more pronounced.

At last, a door swung open, and one of the brideshow candidates stuck his head out. "Finally," he said. Then he called over his shoulder, "Servant's here."

"*Excuse* me?" My protest was lost as candidates all but tumbled into the antechamber.

Before Father and Lyosha, they'd been cloaked in manners as fine as their clothes and jewels. Now they formed a wall of outrage. More doors opened as people came out, brandishing books or instruments or pieces of imported fruit.

"This is unbelievable," said one with pale skin and hair the color of walnut. They wore purple, with a white buck dancing on their shoulder. I ought to recognize the sigil. "Some of us have been up for hours while you imprisoned us and stationed guards outside our quarters," Dancing Buck said.

"If my father were here, he'd declare war on this miserable little country," said a candidate who bore a lily sigil.

"Lucky me," I said.

Dancing Buck folded their arms over their purple tunic. "Don't take that tone with me. *Your* masters have trapped us in here without a word of explanation. What's going on? Are we hostages?"

Complaints began to tumble out, as if irritation were a group exercise they'd practiced for the brideshow. Their faces ranged from bored to angry—except for one girl, the girl who'd smiled at me last night. Her muscle-toned arms were bare under a green wool vest, and her dark hair had little light streaks in it, as if it had caught pieces of the foreign sun and spun them into gold. I frowned at her crest, a serpent wound in a knot. She didn't speak—she just drummed her fingers on her belt, where two ax loops sat empty.

She smiled at me again, and my stomach flipped. She had fresh kohl around her eyes, pink on her cheeks, and red on her lips. She looked like she was enjoying herself.

She looked like she was *laughing* at me.

I clapped hard for attention. The candidates fell silent, though more than one curled their lips, daring me to do something so insolent again. "Let me introduce myself," I said when only one or two grumbling candidates were left. "My name is Ekaterina Avenko, daughter of Kamen Avenko of Kylma Above."

The sneers vanished. A few candidates looked a little embarrassed. No one tried to simper or look happy, and I was strangely glad of that. I'd rather have the honest loathing.

"I am...unhappy to say that I am now the grand duke."

More silence greeted this pronouncement. A few of them exchanged looks; a few of them squeezed hands. "What does that mean, exactly?" said the girl Lyosha had liked last night, the one I'd mentally compared to a snowdrop.

I took a deep breath. "It means that I'm in charge of the brideshow now. And I..." The knot in my stomach grew. I didn't need ministers around to know this was a terrible idea. What was I getting myself into?

Whatever it was, marrying Sigis would be worse.

"What happened to Lyosha?" Snowdrop said.

"If he's dead or something, can we leave?" asked Lily Sigil. *Inconsiderate offal heap.*

I fumbled for words. Most of the candidates looked some variation of curious. A few were incensed. But one girl—*that* girl. Her brown eyes were fixed on me, and the curve of her mouth—like the whole thing was a joke—

I'll give you something to joke about, I thought, and stepped up to her.

I was supposed to say something. We'd been taught the brideshow ceremony as part of our lessons, but I'd been daydreaming about the properties of wild garlic and buckthorn bark.

Then again, how would any of them know I was doing it wrong? I pushed my shoulders back and adopted my Father voice. "As grand duke, I invoke the right to choose my bride."

"*Excuse* me?" said Dancing Buck.

The sapphire ring stuck to my glove until I yanked. "I offer you this as a token of my—" *Love* seemed ridiculous. "Affections. And interest. And...and an alliance between our families and nations." I seized the girl's hand before she

97

could pull away from me. "Please do me the honor of exiting the bridal wing as my"—*no time for second thoughts, NO TIME for second thoughts*—"wife."

Her mouth dropped open in a wide O of surprise. But somehow, the smile was still there.

Did she have a choice? Had she acquiesced as soon as she'd come to the palace as a contestant?

I slid the ring onto her finger, and she didn't resist. That was good enough for me.

The sounds of outrage spread. "You can't do that," one girl burst out. "The brideshow hasn't even started yet."

"It started two days ago," I murmured. Or was it yesterday?

"Our delegations haven't arrived," protested Snowdrop.

"That makes no difference," I said. One of my ancestors had picked a candidate weeks before the brideshow had even started. "I'll see about moving you out of the bridal wing and into your delegations' rooms."

I took my new bride's arm. Her shock had given way to a grin so wide it looked as if it were going to split her face.

She *still* looked like she was laughing at me.

"Are you serious?" someone shouted.

"Uh . . ." I reached for the door handle. "Thank you for coming."

I pulled my new wife out and shut the door before someone could think to throw something at us. My ring glinted on her finger, and she didn't look displeased. It helped to dispel the feeling that I was no better than Sigis.

I hooked my arm tightly through hers and began to walk. I expected her to say something, but the only sounds were of footsteps on ice. My servants and ministers stopped to stare. The news would be all over the palace by dinner.

Good.

I chanced a look in her direction once more. She looked as though this was the best joke she'd ever been part of. Her arm pressed against mine, and she didn't seem to mind.

At the door of the Rose Room, I straightened my coat and checked her ring. "I, um, don't know your name," I admitted. Heat flushed my cheeks.

Was it possible for her grin to grow? "Inkar," she said in a low voice that, if anything, made me blush harder.

"Great. I mean, I'm Ekata. Which you already knew." Were people's mouths normally this dry when they got married?

I opened the door myself and led her in. The couch was bare and showing off its hideous pattern. Aino sat behind it. Sigis was at the table with Eirhan, frowning at a sheet of paper. A pounding started up in my chest.

Sigis and Eirhan stood. When they spotted Inkar's arm linked through mine, they forgot to bow. The fat sapphire on her finger caught the light of the fire.

I hadn't thought this through.

"Minister, my bride."

CHAPTER SIX

Inkar's newly ringed hand tightened over my wrist. Her other hand drifted toward her belt to drum on an empty ax loop. "I am pleased to make your acquaintance," she said in precise, carefully enunciated Drysian. She sounded like someone who'd perfected the language through book-learning but hadn't yet learned the art of conversing with contractions.

Eirhan tried to rally himself. "I—ah."

"Is this some sort of joke?" Sigis said. Fury was written in every line of his body, from his hand, whitening around his clay wineglass, to his face, flushed and wrathful. The last time I'd seen him so angry had been on a hunt, when Velosha's favorite hound had brought down a polar bear he'd been stalking for hours. He'd severed the hound's head in one blow, and it looked as though he wanted to do the same to Inkar now.

He turned to Eirhan and said in an icy voice, "You said Her Grace didn't want to start the coronation trials."

To my relief, Eirhan spoke for me. "Her Grace has the right to—"

"*Her Grace* is a child." Sigis's hand squeezed the wineglass. The clay shattered. *Like* you're *the epitome of maturity at twenty-one.* "And it's your job to keep her from doing things like this."

I felt Inkar's muscles stiffen. Anger clashed with my sickening fear. Grand dukes looked after their own. "You can't speak like that to him," I said.

Sigis jerked toward me. *"Or what?"*

I stepped back before I could stop myself. His eyes shone with something worse than hate: the fury of a powerful man hearing *no.*

Show no fear. I took a breath, focusing on where Inkar's fingers dug into my arm.

Eirhan cracked the fragile silence. "The coronation trials have technically begun, but the first trial is only officially complete when the grand consort accepts her duke's increased responsibility—and it would be unwise to do so until the trial marriage is over," he added hastily. I narrowed my eyes. For the next eight days, my marriage to Inkar could be called off by either one of us. Eirhan was clearly hoping that Sigis would hold off on challenging me in the coronation trials until after the trial marriage failed.

Eirhan's gaze settled back on me, sharp and unforgiving.

"I would appreciate the chance to speak with Her Grace alone."

Sigis couldn't resist having the last word. He leaned in until I could smell the lingering sweat on his coat, his sour-bitter breath from drinking wine and coffee. "Don't forget whose army is sitting at your door, little Ekata."

He stormed out, slamming the door behind him. We all jumped. I resisted the urge to giggle in hysterical relief.

Inkar's smile disappeared. Solemnity sat well on her, making her dark eyes look wide and deep and intelligent. "Do you make all your guests so happy?"

"Her Grace the consort rivals Her Grace the duke for humor, I see," Eirhan remarked dourly. "Ekaterina, what could have possessed you?"

"The prospect of waking up next to Sigis every morning for the rest of my short life," I replied. I felt like hiding behind my new wife.

Inkar laughed in a series of soft exhales. Eirhan didn't smile. "Your Grace has just infuriated the most powerful man in the North," he said through gritted teeth.

That was the problem, wasn't it? The most powerful man in the North had decided he and I should be married, and so many scrambled to do his bidding that they hadn't stopped to think about whether *I'd* wanted to be married to him at all.

"Aino, will you see the grand consort to a suite? Her Grace has much settling in to do." Eirhan bowed to Inkar, low and graceful.

I almost pulled Inkar closer. She and Aino felt like armor that Eirhan was trying to peel away from me. I could say something grand, like, *Anything you say to me, you can say to her.* But I hadn't even known her name five minutes ago. It wasn't exactly the romance of legends. "Aino, please make sure she has everything she needs." I disentangled myself. "I'll escort you to dinner."

"*Someone* will escort you to dinner," Eirhan corrected me.

Aino gave me a strange, bewildered shake of the head before curtsying to Inkar. "Please come with me, Your Grace."

Inkar turned her smile on me one last time as Aino led her out. Her mouth was red and full and inviting. I opened my mouth to stammer out a goodbye, then shut it.

I heard Inkar laugh softly as the door closed.

Eirhan folded his hands and let the silence draw out. Finally, he said, "Does Your Grace have any idea whom she has chosen as a wife?"

Only a man made of arrogance would speak to a grand duke that way. I fought to keep my voice neutral. "I was under the impression that any candidate in the brideshow was an eligible match."

"In theory," Eirhan snapped. "But this is not *theory*. This is politics. Inkar is the daughter of Bardur Erlyfsson and the mistress of the Emerald Order."

Bardur Erlyfsson, one of my father's great enemies. The raider who'd attacked our shipping routes, and the last big threat to Kylma before Sigis. I remembered, now, that Eirhan had said his daughter was part of the brideshow. "You should have mentioned her by name."

"Inkar's attendance is an experiment—a test of trust after the peace. She's his twenty-fifth daughter, so if she dies here, there will be no lasting effect on his kingdom. But he'll still be able to legitimize war." He rubbed at his face. "Do you understand the dangerous pieces you've brought into this game?"

All I could think was, *twenty-fifth daughter?* "Were Erlyfs-son and my father competing to have the most children?"

Eirhan growled his frustration. "This isn't the time for jokes. We've spent all day claiming you won't compete in the coronation trials. We hinged an offer of marriage around it."

"*You* hinged the offer," I corrected him, folding my arms. "I said no, and you ignored me."

"Your Grace can't say no to every little thing she dislikes. Ruling means compromise."

"*Not* about him."

We stood for a moment, facing each other, readying our verbal arsenals. Eirhan and I both struggled for power. And while I didn't have enough to completely defy him, I couldn't give in. Grand dukes were unquestionable, even to their prime ministers.

"The trial marriage lasts for eight days, right? I'll just call it off. Then we are where we were before, without corona-tion trials." And I didn't have to marry Sigis.

Eirhan rubbed at his temples. "No one's going to believe that you're not trying to steal power. We'll frame this to the council as you against him: you trying to preserve the throne through necessity, him trying to steal it. And *don't* call off the trial marriage. If you proclaim yourself dissatisfied with Inkar, you need a damn good reason. Erlyfsson could call it grounds for war if he thinks you've slighted his daughter."

"Maybe I can annoy her so much she'll try to kill me," I said.

I meant it as a joke, but Eirhan nodded decisively. "That's exactly what you need to do. Convince Inkar that being grand consort is worse than going home. If she declares herself dissatisfied, you bear the shame alone, and her father will no doubt feel exceedingly smug. He will likely give you a consolation present, and that will be that."

"So be irritating." I could do that. No one could stand me besides Farhod and Aino anyway.

"And don't let her get used to the idea of being grand consort," Eirhan advised me. "Once people get a taste for power, it's hard to persuade them to let go of it. Now, maybe we should discuss the coronation trials further, since you were so eager to begin them."

According to Eirhan, most of my court would expect the coronation trials despite my declaration (*Eirhan's declaration*, I thought darkly) not to have them. The four trials were usually held among the children of the grand duke, but as my siblings were indisposed, a stand-in would be found. Normally, stand-ins were ministers who lost deliberately. But I knew who would volunteer.

The trials were about winning favor, and I would have to start by winning the favor of my wife. Most grand dukes persuaded their spouses with expensive gifts and wooing and compromises until the trial marriage was over. Of course, I was supposed to get my wife to say no, which made it rather difficult to win. All the same, Sigis didn't even have a wife, so I was one up there. Until he plucked a candidate from a delegation or tricked me into marrying him somehow.

The second trial revolved around the favor of the church. I attended church on Wintertide mass, and only under duress, but surely the archimandrite would favor me over Sigis. The third trial earned the endorsement of Below, and the final contest was of the people—and by people, Eirhan meant my council. If they declared that the people had accepted me, I won.

"Why would the ministers ever choose Sigis?" I asked. "An Avenko has to hold the throne."

"Sigis is an Avenko," Eirhan said.

"What?"

"So he will claim. His great-great-grandmother was Ishrana Avenko. She sent a son to Drysiak for marriage, and, well, here we are." He shook his head. "Really, Ekata. You ought to have known that."

My blood grew hot. I'd been grand duke for one day, and I was already sick of Eirhan chastising me for what I didn't know. I tried to keep my voice calm, as Father would. "Surely his blood's too weak for him to be a true Avenko." For him to hold the balance.

"That is something the duke Below and the archimandrite will determine," Eirhan replied. "Just—win the people's trial. If you end up tied for trials, that will be the deciding factor. Now"—he turned back to his pile of papers—"we have an hour before dinner, so you may go. Might I suggest a bath?"

"Maybe you're smelling yourself," I muttered, resisting the urge to raise my arm and check under it.

I'd hoped Eirhan wouldn't hear, but his fed-up expression said otherwise. "I'll sit next to you at dinner to assist you with some of the more advanced political discourse. Your *wife* will sit at your left hand. Aino will pour your wine. Sigis, of course, will take the space of next importance, on the other side of Inkar."

"That sounds like a terrible idea," I said.

"To place him elsewhere would be a snub to his status," Eirhan replied. "Please believe that I've thought this through, Your Grace."

I barely kept myself from saying something uncivil. I had to choose my battles, and Eirhan would be much warier of me now.

"Before you go"—Eirhan removed a pouch from his belt—"I requisitioned something from the treasury on your behalf." From the pouch he pulled a glass jar so small it fit into his palm. It was filled two-thirds of the way with a pink-tinged liquid that shimmered like stardust in a sunrise. "Your father always makes a display for the delegates. He usually takes raw magic and refines it on the spot, but we'll give you some of his prepared stock."

Magic. For the second time today, someone was *giving* me magic. I took it, trying not to seem too eager. "How?"

"Kamen demonstrates the three types of magic," Eirhan said. I knew them well—constructive, destructive, and transformative. "I gave you a transformative refinement. Focus on something simple, like putting color in the floor, and remember that you have to touch whatever you transform. Think about it while you get ready; the clearer you are in planning, the better it will go. And remember—magic is temporary, but the effects can be permanent. So don't get creative and break the palace. But making people think you have the grand duke's secrets will make them think you're the grand duke, long before the trial of the people."

"Right." I tried to take the little jar.

Eirhan's fingers tightened around it. "And don't tell anyone. Let it be a surprise."

Aino opened the door. "Your bath has been ordered."

I tucked the jar into my pocket. Magic. I knew how it worked in theory, but Father had never let us practice. My palms itched to try it.

Aino hadn't seen the exchange and was still busy fretting over my newlywed situation. "Honestly, Ekata. Married?"

"It had to happen sometime." And as long as I avoided

Sigis, I could put up with whomever I got instead. At least she was pretty, and the right gender.

"After careful thought. After meetings. After you know you're going to marry someone you like."

"That's not how political marriages work." No one in my family married for love. We didn't even know what love looked like.

"You only think that because your parents—" Aino stopped and tucked a strand of auburn hair behind her ear. "You should marry for friendship and support. Not because you were told to, and not because that girl gives you an advantage. Especially since you're a political gain for *her*."

I should have been glad that Aino disliked Inkar already. We could conspire together to get rid of her. But my mind lingered on Inkar's dark hair and red smile, on the thought that I needed more friends and not more problems.

As I bathed in my rooms, I recited the names of the bride-show delegates. Aino had to help me only twice. Then I donned a blue dress, unadorned except for a fur lining. As she put up my hair, I said, "Shouldn't my dress be a little... fancier, for a wedding celebration?"

"Don't worry, dear. No one's going to look at your dress. They're going to look at *these*."

She draped me in every diamond and sapphire she'd looted from Mother's wardrobe. Bracelets around my wrist, earrings at my ears, a glittering belt. "You're going to look like a duke," she promised me as she hung a hexagonal pendant the size of my palm around my neck. When I turned, little flurries of light danced around the ice walls.

Aino handed me a pair of white doeskin gloves, and I slid them on. I grabbed the jar of refined magic, and we went out to meet my bride.

Inkar waited for me right outside the royal wing, speaking softly to the two guards that flanked her. She wore a dark green vest and trousers with a white tunic beneath. Half her brown hair had been braided against the side of her head; the other half hung free. She seemed so warm set against the cold walls of the palace. Warm and dangerous. As if she would burn me if I touched her.

I wanted to take off my gloves and find out.

Aino took my arm and pulled me back. A moment later, I realized why. Two axes, edged with gold, hung from Inkar's belt. Gold threaded through the steel in a snaking pattern.

Inkar brushed the tops of the axes. "Do not worry. They are ceremonial only. No good for taking off heads." Her red smile was anything but reassuring.

"How did she get those in here?" Aino muttered in Kylmian.

I shrugged. I doubted Inkar would use her golden axes on me. "What does mistress of the Emerald Order mean, anyway?" I could start the process of killing our relationship with poor etiquette and descend from there.

Inkar looped her arm through mine. "It means I control a thousand men on horseback."

"Who doesn't?" I muttered. Apparently, every suitor of mine had their own army. "Are you ready?"

"I am very ready," she replied, and we began to walk. Viljo and my secondary guard fell behind us, and Aino followed them. I could feel Aino's eyes on our arms. But when I moved to pull free, Inkar tightened her grip. I coughed and pretended I was trying to shift my coat.

My stomach grew heavier with each step. I was about to walk into a dinner where all eyes would be on me. Everything I did would be dissected the way I dissected tundra mice in the laboratory. I could recite bones and tendons and magical remedies all I liked, but here that would do me no good.

Inkar didn't seem put off by my silence. She gazed at the walls, taking in the relief carvings and the tapestries that told the history of the duchy Above. "These are amazing."

"What?" I pulled my thoughts back from their anxious fixation on the dinner to come. "The winter roses?"

She reached up to touch one. I grabbed her wrist and was rewarded with a surprised—and perhaps affronted?—look. "They'll freeze your fingers, even through gloves," I warned her. "They're not like the ice of the rest of the palace."

"Is that why they do not melt near the fire?" she said. "Are they magic?"

"The legend goes that some duke Below gave them to some duke Above, and now they're an invasive species." They grew into all the corners, twisted around pillars, and ran over the windowsills. "There's a superstition that they bloom when the family is in danger."

"They are blooming now." Her glove traced the outline of a three-quarter bloom. "For your father, perhaps?"

"They're always blooming. Of course people see something in them." I pulled on her arm to get her to walk again.

I could feel her observing me. "Perhaps you are always in danger."

She had a point. Being a member of my family had often resulted in untimely death. All the same, I wished I hadn't said anything. "I don't follow superstition." I followed facts and rules, and even magic had those. Even if they were as light as *temporary madness, permanent outcome.*

Inkar followed their trail along the corridor. "I am part of the family now. Will they bloom when I am in danger?"

"Ah." Guilt flashed through me, leaving me hot. "Maybe we'll find out after the trial marriage." *After you hate me and reject me and hopefully never want to see me again.*

If I even survived that long. If I could even make it to the end of dinner—or to the start of it. Now that we'd exited the royal wing, we started to pass people who stared at me, at Inkar, at our linked arms. I could practically hear the gears turning in their minds. Nausea rolled through me, and I stopped to swallow my fear.

Aino's hand landed on my back, soothing through layers of wool. Then it moved up, and she pretended to adjust my hair, whispering, "You must continue. They're looking for signs that you're weaker than him."

Him. Sigis, Eirhan, or my father? What did it matter? "I don't think I can eat."

"Come." Inkar began to walk again, pulling me along behind her. "The creatures around you are nothing but toads. You do not have to fear them."

"If they are toads, what does that make you?"

It should have been the perfect insult for Eirhan's anti-Inkar campaign. But Inkar smiled as though I'd been genuinely funny.

"I am a serpent," she said, touching a hand to her breast, where the golden serpent coiled. "I eat toads for breakfast."

"I'll tell the cook," I said, and she laughed again. My stomach unclenched a tiny bit. Inkar would sit by my side at dinner, and she didn't seem easily offended. Eirhan would sit on my other side and keep me from committing the worst political and social sins. I would survive this.

The translucent ice doors of the audience chamber showed a blur of color as delegates moved about within. Sigis was in there somewhere, as were each of my ministers. "Everyone in that room hates me, don't they?" I asked Aino.

The angry lines in her face softened. "You are the grand duke," she said. "They will respect you as their host. Don't be too grateful to anyone who is kind. They are not kind out of pity or love." She reached for my shoulder. Then her eyes flitted to Inkar, and she stepped back. Aino nodded to the guards. "I'll be right behind you."

The guards bowed low to me and opened the doors. We entered the flood.

A hush spread like ice crystallizing over an open hole in the lake. Heads swiveled our way, eyes settled on Inkar and me, on the way we stood together. Then, in a flurry of movement, the servants at the side of the room knelt. They bowed their heads and placed one fist against the ice floor, as Eirhan had done the night before. As they moved, so did the crowd. The delegates and brideshow candidates knelt in a wave; kings and emperors bowed at the waist, hands over their hearts.

I let my gaze linger on my kneeling ministers. Eirhan studied the ground like a good subject. Reko glared defiantly. Yannush's beard quivered as he whispered to Annika, and Annika's round face was serious. Bailli rumbled at Olloi. Itilya looked calculating.

And Sigis, hand on his heart, kept his eyes on Inkar. The storm cloud on his face told me he was going to be a problem.

The crowd knelt for a heartbeat, then a heartbeat more. I slipped my hand into my pocket and out of its glove and fumbled for the jar. How had Father managed to begin his displays so elegantly? At last, I popped the cork and felt something cold and smooth flow out onto my hand. The lights guttered, and someone at the back of the hall gasped. It was working.

They wouldn't be impressed for long if I couldn't make

the magic do anything more. I spotted the tapestries that hung from the walls, filled with my favorite subjects. *Concentrate*, Eirhan's voice whispered. If there was one thing I could concentrate on—

I went to the wall and touched a magic-soaked hand to the tapestry. Something stirred in my belly, as though the magic drew out a bit of me as it worked. *Hyathae.* The seathorn bush on the edge of the tapestry began to grow, spreading branches until it nudged a wolf. The wolf tilted its head up to howl. An owl winged in front of the moon, feathers shimmering.

The magic spread to the next tapestry like wildfire, and a bear lunged, scraping cloth claws into the air. Two foxes started a game of chase, leaping from tapestry to tapestry, and a stag lowered his head to charge a hunter's horse. The horse reared and sent one of my long-dead relatives flying. Snow and shadows shifted as animals rushed over them; trees grew beyond the edges of the tapestry to spread silk branches into the air.

When the tapestries stilled and light flared in the room, the applause that followed seemed earnest. But the tapestries hung in tatters, with bits of silk torn loose from one spot and tangled in another—a permanent effect of my temporary display.

I motioned for the crowd to rise. Before we could begin milling about, a loud tapping silenced the hall again.

The tapping came from an iron staff striking the floor. The bearer of the staff was an old woman who leaned on it aggressively as she approached. Her robe was white and silver, spun from silk, and electrum chains wound about her neck, dotted with sapphires as pale as the ice of the city streets. The top of her staff glittered with pearls, and rings adorned her white gloves, two to each finger.

Her eyes were as fierce as a hawk's and as cold as the snow, and they focused on me. Whatever she thought, I couldn't decipher, for her face was as cragged as the mountains around us, her skin weathered by snow and salt and wind.

She was the archimandrite, and she was, in theory, my equal.

While she looked as though her voice ought to come wheezing out of her, she spoke clearly, with a strength that made every spine straighten. "The tribute to your father is appreciated," she said, and I doubted I imagined her icy tone. "However, magic does not make a grand duke. The coronation trials do." She raised her voice so that no one in the hall could mistake her. "As is my duty as archimandrite, I officially declare that the coronation trials have begun."

The delegates began to murmur. I forced myself not to look at Eirhan. We'd known this was coming. All the same, sweat prickled my palms.

"Every grand duke must prove her mettle and willingness to serve. The coronation trials are the chance to prove her ability beyond all other contestants and give us the ruler we need. The coronation trials will conclude when the grand duke has won the will of her wife, the will of the gods, the will of Below, and the will of her own people. Who stands against her?"

I was oddly glad that none of my siblings were here. They'd try to win through elimination, after all. Father had killed all his siblings before his trial, so he'd gotten a minister to stand in—none other than Minister Reko.

But I wasn't so lucky. With the clicking of iron-clawed shoes on ice, Sigis came forward. And even though I'd known he would, my stomach twisted until I was sure it sat upside down. He smiled a smile of cold hate. *Don't throw up.*

"I will stand," he said.

Delegates turned to one another. Their muttering took on angry undertones. Sigis was already too powerful a force in the North. If he won the coronation trials, his gains might make him unstoppable. My ministers regarded this shifting landscape, but no one interfered—not even Reko, who looked as though he wanted to proclaim revolution the moment the trials were declared. They had to support my bid for the trials. I was the throne, and the throne was mine.

"By what right do you stand?" the archimandrite said.

"By the right of ancestry. My great-great-grandmother was grand duke of Kylma Above."

The muttering grew. The archimandrite spoke over it. "Can you prove your bloodline?"

"I can," Sigis called back.

Eirhan motioned to the guards. Their halberds came down with a *crack*. Silence rippled over the crowd.

The archimandrite waited a moment longer, then said, "You will submit it to me tomorrow. And tomorrow you both shall be judged by the gods."

Her iron staff tapped three times on the ground, and she walked back to the edge of the room. The court surged to its feet, and the muttering began anew. They clustered together—normal, I knew, but more sinister now that I also knew they were all talking about me.

"Well, that's a start to my reign," I said.

Inkar looked at me. "What did she mean, you must win the will of your wife?"

Eirhan appeared before I had to spin a reply. He'd found the time to wash his hair and put on a royal-blue coat that bulked up his weasely arms. "Your Grace," he said with a blank expression that might as well have said he dealt with coronation trials all the time. He nodded to Inkar. "Your Grace. Have you everything you need?"

Inkar inclined her head. "I dislike my rooms," she said.

It was the first she'd said to me about it. I shrugged. Eirhan's expression did not waver. "I'll send a maid directly. May I present the minister of the hunt?"

Minister Itilya approached. She reminded me more of a tree than a person—taller than anyone else on my father's council. Her thin face and ice-white hair made her seem less human than the rest of us. She eschewed fashionably long coats for garb that left her legs free in leather trousers and scuffed brown boots, and she wore a black tunic with a sapphire-and-diamond pin in the shape of a rose. I'd met Iti-lya a handful of times, mainly when she'd negotiated for the delivery of certain animals to Farhod's laboratory for study.

"Minister," I said, and she bowed.

Eirhan coughed. I shrugged at him before remembering that grand dukes didn't do that. Eirhan jerked his chin in clear irritation. "Minister, may I present, on behalf of Her Grace, Her Grace the Grand Consort of Kylma Above, Inkar Bardursdatre."

I blushed. I should have known to introduce her.

"My felicitations, Your Graces," Itilya said, "and my highest hopes for the success of the coronation trials." She didn't sound as though she meant it. Then again, she was often calm to the point of being inscrutable.

"What lives up here in the North that you can hunt?" Inkar asked.

Itilya leaned forward a little. Was it a trick of the light or was she actually twice the size of Inkar? "Many things. I am a vital part of providing sustenance to the city. Does hunting interest you?"

Inkar's hand went to the axes at her belt. "More men than anything. But I would be intrigued to see how you do it."

"I would be honored to show Your Grace the kennels," Itilya said. At a nod from Eirhan, she bowed again and excused herself.

Inkar frowned. "Kennels? Does she mean stables?"

"No, kennels. For dogs," I explained.

The frown deepened. "I did not express an interest in dogs."

"Did you think we hunt from horseback? Horses can't survive this place." I pointed to the ice walls, the arching ice ceiling carved in deep relief, and tried not to laugh at the look of panic that cracked Inkar's confident mask.

"No horses?" she said in a voice that bordered on outrage.

"I'm afraid not." *Let's see how the girl with the army on horseback likes this.*

Eirhan introduced Althari, Prince of Palaskia, next. She wore blue and orange and so much fur that she resembled a rabbit. Was she a second or third prince? Trying to remember felt like grabbing for snow as it fell.

"It was a true shock to hear about your father," she said.

"For you and me both," I replied, and she gave a short bow.

I was supposed to say something. Something clever? Eirhan would be furious if I tried to be clever. Grand dukes were imposing and correct. But all I could think of was the blue and orange of her suit, like polar poppies that stuck stubbornly out of the snow, like the orange of the seathorn berries that we turned into jam and ate on seaweed bread to combat scurvy.

"Are you all right, Your Grace?" Althari asked.

"I'm thinking about scurvy," I said.

Eirhan sighed, no doubt resisting the urge to drop his head in his hands. Inkar cocked her head. Althari looked between us, nonplussed.

They'd call me the mad duke if I kept doing things like

that. Worse, they'd let Sigis win the coronation trials. But Inkar came to my rescue. "I believe we have met once before. You were a guest of my father's many years ago."

"Yes." Althari's smile took on the special warmth of memory. "Your father sets such a spectacular table, I almost forgot I was a hostage."

"My father is a gracious host," Inkar said. "I hope to have learned that lesson from him."

"Then you will be a formidable consort indeed," Althari said. "You have my sincerest wishes for the success of the trials." Her eyes narrowed as she glanced at Sigis. Then she took her leave.

I leaned toward Inkar. "How long ago did you two meet?"

Inkar considered. "Eight years? Nine?"

"And you remember her?"

"It was my duty to remember faces," Inkar said. "And remembering faces served me well in the Emerald Order."

"Oh." Even the wife I'd picked on a whim could do my job better than I could.

The Baron of Luciato was introduced next, and his name flashed through my mind like one of the silver fish Below. He wore purple and black and had the tanned-leather look that came from years of campaigns. Inkar greeted him with surprising familiarity. "Every horse in the Emerald Order is a Lucian horse," she said. "I would never consider any other."

The baron's smile lit like a candle. "And your father is famous among our traders."

"Their intelligence is incredible. And they are the most loyal creatures I have ever met. Please tell me you have come to teach the people of Kylma how to ride."

"You must admit, the environment is…not suited for them," Luciato said, eyeing me conspiratorially.

Inkar laughed. "This environment is suited to no one."

"That's not true," I said.

Luciato sputtered. "We—we didn't mean, ah—"

"We have reindeer, bears, wolves, snow hares, and polar foxes, and two distinct types of ground birds in addition to flying fauna. And that doesn't take into account *any* of the flora—" I stopped myself. This wasn't the way a grand duke controlled the conversation.

Inkar hastened to fill the silence. "My wife enjoys biology."

Luciato jumped on the subject. "Perhaps you'd like a specimen to study, then. An arrangement could be made for a pair of Lucian foals for you."

"I thought you said they'd be miserable here," I pointed out.

Luciato's mouth worked. Inkar laughed at me. "He did not say miserable." She put a hand on the baron's shoulder. "Tomorrow, you and I shall visit the stable…the *kennel* master, and we shall discuss this most generous gift."

The baron bowed to us both, though his bow to Inkar was deeper and more graceful. Then he wished us luck with the trials and retreated into the crowd.

Eirhan glared at me. I didn't have to look at him to know it. I tried to fight my own irritation—irritation for Luciato, for Inkar, for Althari, for everyone who could play this game of politics with ease.

Inkar, for her part, glowed. "Two Lucian horses is a generous gift. I could teach you to ride."

"What makes you think I want to learn?" I said sourly.

She laughed. "Do not fear. It is terrifying at first, but I will help you. And you will find it less and less terrifying, until, suddenly, it is the best thing in your life."

"I doubt that," I said flatly, and a shuttered look came over her, the sort of look I recognized with a pang. Apparently, I *had* learned one conversational skill from my father: the ability to alienate my wife.

No weakness. No fear. I was supposed to make Inkar regret our marriage. As the next delegate came up, I straightened my shoulders and greeted him as though I hadn't said anything to Inkar at all. Inkar followed suit and had him smiling in ten seconds.

"Your Grace." Eirhan took me by the shoulder and steered me a short distance away from Inkar. "You have to keep her from doing that."

"Doing what?"

"Charming delegates. That's your job, not hers. They're already inclined to like you more than Sigis, since no one actually wants to see him win the trials. You need to seize that. You'll still need their support when you get rid of her."

He made it sound simple. But as I turned back to her, I was reminded only of how much I didn't know. I was so unsuited for this. Nausea began to form a hard ball in my stomach.

Inkar greeted everyone with a smile and could say something about each of them—even the cousins of Kylma Above. Worse, she seemed so *genuine*. Father had been smooth; Mother, regal. Lyosha had been brash and posturing. My siblings had ranged between cold and clipped to overly saccharine. But Inkar looked like she was happy to be there. Happy to be with me. The fixed, polite smiles of everyone who greeted us became expressions—of interest, of amusement, of something *real*. Even the other brideshow candidates seemed happy for Inkar, despite their dislike of me, and they wished us luck with sincerity. Only Sigis didn't approach; he prowled the edges of the room, sparing us a few angry glowers whenever he could. He didn't give delegates more than an acknowledgment, and he spoke to many ministers at length. I'd have to discuss that with Eirhan later. For now, dinner awaited.

We entered the banquet hall together. Inkar's eyes wandered up the walls to the vaulted ceiling, carved with my family motifs. "Everything," she said in a soft voice. "Everything is ice."

"I'd have thought you'd be used to that by now," I said. Inkar shook her head wordlessly. "Well, the food's not ice. Not yet, anyway."

I was seated in the grandest chair, my father's chair. I felt small and strange slipping into it. If Father.saw me in his chair...the first time he'd caught my oldest sister, Eshra, playing on it, he'd struck her with a birch rod hard enough to break skin. She'd carried the scar on her cheek proudly, right up to the day Lyosha had pushed her into the moat and held her down with a weighted fishing net.

I'm grand duke, I thought. The chair was my right and responsibility, if only until we found the cure.

Inkar took the place next to me normally reserved for Mother. Eirhan sat on my other side. And next to Inkar, Sigis sat with a poisonous smile. "Sorry to surprise you with the trials, dear Ekata," he said, looking past Inkar as though she weren't even there. He spoke in Kylmian, and Inkar's puzzled frown confirmed that she didn't understand. It didn't surprise me; Kylma was the smallest sovereign nation I knew of, and no one else had reason to speak our tongue. Drysian was the court language; Kylmian was the language we spoke behind closed doors.

I wondered how much of a diplomatic incident would be caused if I told him to take a long dip in a tanner's vat. Instead, I forced myself to say in Drysian, "You didn't surprise me at all." *Thanks to Eirhan.* "I hope you enjoy your meal."

"I look forward to it greatly. The culinary exploits here have always been...unique." Sigis eyed Inkar as though she were a rotten smell under his nose. "Have you ever had fish?"

Her tone was politely incredulous. "I come from an island," she said.

He laughed. It was a *she's endearingly stupid* laugh, and by the look of things, Inkar recognized it, too. "I meant fish from Kylma. The fermented shark paste is my favorite."

"Is he joking?" Inkar whispered to me.

"I'm afraid not." I'd always been amused by visitors trying our delicacies for the first time. Part of me looked forward to Inkar's reaction. Part of me hoped she'd enjoy every bite and wipe Sigis's smug look off his face.

"You'll hate it," Sigis said with relish. "The jarls have such dull palates."

Inkar straightened. I gestured for Aino. Maybe wine would keep Sigis occupied. As a servant filled Sigis's and Inkar's cups with bright, golden wine, Aino brought me cloudflower juice and a warning look. I'd be useless enough sober.

"Shall we toast your father, Ekata?" Sigis said. "The great man he was and the legacy he left?"

"He's not dead," I said. What would Sigis do if Father woke up in the middle of the coronation trials? What would *I* do? How would Father deal with the ministers who'd crowned me, with Aino who'd stolen Mother's jewelry, with Inkar, the daughter of a former enemy?

Sigis looked at me as though I'd said something absurd.

Inkar investigated her cup. "From what do you make this wine? And why a wooden wine cup? Are you too poor to pay for silver?"

"We'd all love for you to freeze your lips off on a silver glass," Sigis said before I could answer. "As for the wine, it's made of apples. A special kind, all white. Do you remember playing in the orchards at the foot of the mountains, Ekata? We went not long after I first joined you."

I remembered. I remembered Sigis throwing an unripe apple so hard at my brother Kevro's head that he'd been concussed. An accident, Sigis claimed.

Inkar turned to him. "In my country, when I ask a question of one person, I do not expect it to be answered by another."

Sigis smirked. "There's so much more to the world than your little country, my dear."

More servants began to bear down on us with plates. "Dinner," I said without trying to mask my relief.

Dinner was served in the twelve longest courses of my life. We began with a broth of fish, which Inkar said tasted of the bottom of the sea. Sigis, on the other hand, stopped one of the servants and insisted she pay his compliments to the chef for remembering how well Sigis had loved it. From there we moved on to the dreaded shark paste, served on flat seaweed bread. Inkar prodded at the wobbling mass. "This is...celebratory food?"

I couldn't tell whether she doubted the celebratory or the food aspect more. I opened my mouth to tell her that our full marriage feast would be finer, but then I remembered we weren't supposed to *have* a full marriage feast. "It's a famous delicacy."

"Then you eat it, my wife." She slid her plate toward me and reached for my cup. I was halfway through her bread before I noticed Eirhan glaring at me again. Father and Mother would never have shared the contents of their plates. I probably should have insisted she eat it. Instead, I focused on my food so I wouldn't have to look at Eirhan's face anymore.

After oyster and smoked-fish courses, we moved to the meat: fresh, raw caribou; roasted hare; deer with apple jelly; aspic; and goat sausage cured with spices from the South. Inkar enjoyed most of it, though she made a strange face at the aspic and pushed most of it around on her plate.

As we ate, Eirhan tried his best to engage Sigis. "Her Grace and I very much hope you will enjoy the evening of festivities."

"I don't doubt I will," said Sigis in a voice that indicated the exact opposite. "Though I do hope she's made some plans for my men. They get so restless when they've been on campaign. They have only one thing on their minds, and it's nearly impossible to keep them under control."

He's only baiting me. Sigis wouldn't dare have his men attack the city. I smiled and kept my mouth shut.

Inkar, though, hadn't been told to court Sigis. "Are your men so undisciplined? My father would never let me lead the Emerald Order if he thought I could not control them."

"Drysian soldiers are not your average men. They live for the fight and the spoils. They are like ravenous wolves." He nodded at me. "Her Grace knows a thing or two about wolves."

"Mostly how to keep them away from me," I said without thinking. Sigis's mouth curled in contempt.

Remember Eirhan's advice. I smiled again.

Sigis switched tactics. "I'm sure everyone's dying to know—do you intend to honor the Avythera agreement?"

The what? The glint in his eyes told me that he knew I didn't know. As I fumbled for an answer, Eirhan stepped in. "Her Grace intends to study it in greater depth before officially moving forward. Her father spent years on the agreement, and I'm sure we all agree it would be unwise to push the matter so immediately."

"And I know you're concerned that your father might awaken," Sigis added.

Eirhan, Sigis, and Inkar looked at me. I forced my smile wider.

"It is, of course, our dearest wish," Eirhan said. "Regrettably, one requirement of being a grand duke or a prime minister is a certain attention to practicality."

"Not to mention ambition." Sigis shot a look around the table. "One that I feel many of your ministers lack."

That had to be a threat. But whom was he talking about specifically? I leaned forward to scrutinize the ministers who were listening from up and down the table. Who had a red face? Who wouldn't look up from their plate?

"Your Grace is leaning into her aspic," Eirhan observed.

As I dabbed at my chest with a napkin and a servant removed the offending plate, Sigis said, "Amending the

Avythera agreement would allow you to rebuild the eastern guard towers."

"Rebuild? Why would we need to rebuild? Is there imminent threat of war?" Inkar asked. I did not miss her use of *we*.

"I sincerely hope not," Sigis replied. His gaze met hers. Her smile dropped a fraction and became more like a sneer.

"Her Grace is overwhelmed with duties," Eirhan cut in. "She hasn't had time to look over her father's unfinished business, much less agreements that have been all but cemented."

"Yet she managed to get married...for now." Sigis pitched his voice low enough that the other ministers, straining to make polite conversation through our awkward haze, couldn't hear him. But he wanted me to hear. I was certain of that.

Eirhan, to his credit, changed the subject: gossip on the war between Khourzad and Alhatia, an analysis of the continental crop yield for the season and what that meant for trade, Sigis's winter plans. Sigis's poor temper oozed through every reply. He cut his meat with forceful movements that grated on the porcelain plates. He set his cup down so hard it cracked. His laughs were dark and angry, his orders unforgiving.

And Eirhan wanted me to pretend I was considering this man.

The banquet was followed by a reception, during which it seemed I had to dance with or greet every single person in the room. I found myself dancing with Sigis twice, though dancing was hardly the right way to describe it. Mostly he pushed me from place to place, occasionally lifting me to twirl me around. He spoke loud and long of his fondness for Kylma, of the ways he would modernize it, of the great trading benefits that the Avythera agreement would bring us—especially if we changed the agreement entirely to suit him. When he finally let me go, it was to face a sea of delegates that I couldn't remember anymore. Fatigue threatened to drag me under, and no amount of cloudflower juice could keep me awake.

At long last, Aino rescued me. "Coffee?" I mumbled hopefully.

"Bed," Aino said firmly. Eirhan opened his mouth to object, but she held up a hand. "Her Grace had an early morning and has a trial to win tomorrow."

"You're my favorite." I sighed as she hustled me out of the reception hall.

"Don't say that quite yet. You haven't heard what's in store for you tomorrow." Aino let me lean on her as I limped up the ice stairs toward the royal wing, followed by Viljo and the other guard.

"I do know what's in store for me," I said without much hope. "Sleep. I'm going to sleep for days."

"You're not," Aino said. "I'll bring you breakfast at five. As you eat, Eirhan will recount the rest of the night's happenings, summarize correspondence, and make appointments. At eight, you'll meet with your cabinet, at nine with the clerics, and from ten until lunch you'll meet ministers in order of their current support for you."

"And then at lunch I can sleep for days," I suggested.

"Sigis has requested that you lunch with him. No, there's nothing you can do about it."

"This schedule stinks of Eirhan," I complained.

Aino didn't even blush. She would have made a great politician. "I had to step in after your outburst with the foreign girl, and that meant making concessions. Eirhan was ready to defect after your little stunt and overthrow you for some kind of a parliament."

"Where is the 'foreign girl'?" I asked. Aino had whisked me from the crowd so efficiently that I hadn't had the chance to think up a good way to offend Inkar. Maybe leaving without her would do.

Aino shrugged. "She's not my problem."

We entered the royal wing. It was quieter than I'd ever heard it, a combination of the late hour and the near-death state of my family. The silence was strangely peaceful. After the hubbub of the rest of the day, I could pretend that the whole world had stopped, that I had it to myself for a little while.

Well, to myself and Aino. And Viljo and the other guard.

Aino unlocked the door to my rooms and ushered me in. "Help me with my coat," I begged as she shut the door. "I'm wasting precious seconds."

She tugged me out of my coat and began to loosen the

elaborate dresswork that kept me standing. I was tired down to my bones. It hurt to move, it hurt to stand still—it hurt. "Maybe Farhod will have the curse figured out tomorrow," I said, sending a short, mental prayer to whatever god might be listening.

"There's not much use in thinking like that," Aino warned me.

"I know. Get me my nightgown, won't you?"

As Aino went into my bedchamber, I staggered over to the chair before the fire and collapsed into it, kicking off my shoes. The cold air prickled the bare skin of my calves, but I didn't care enough to fetch the blanket that lay over my desk chair. My eyes slid closed.

The door unlatched. I tilted my head back as far as it could go and spoke. "If you've come to assassinate me, now's actually a really great time."

"I would rather wait," Inkar said.

My eyes flew open. She leaned over me, close enough that I could see the unevenness of the kohl around her eyes. I jerked up and narrowly avoided colliding foreheads. "What are you doing here?" My heart pattered. I wasn't used to other people in my rooms. Not since Nari had grown old enough to coat the inside of my sleeves with glass.

Inkar's not dangerous. But I looked at the curve of her mouth, and I knew I was wrong.

"I am the grand consort now." Inkar came around the chair so that I could see her properly. "Are these not my chambers as well?"

I brought my knees up to my chest, tugging my shift over them. "There are special rooms for the consort." Mother's rooms.

"I will not stay in the rooms provided for me. They are too cold."

Aino appeared at the door to my bedchamber. She held my nightgown up like a shield.

"We'll have a servant build you a fire," I said.

"They are not grand consort rooms." Inkar folded her arms. Her biceps and triceps twitched. "People will look at me, and they will say, that is the girl who is not allowed to be grand consort. She is stuck in a side room while Sigis takes the largest suite. While Sigis competes in the coronation trials and flirts with the grand duke."

The door to my rooms opened again. Three servants entered, carrying a chest and a few miscellaneous items. "What's this?" I asked.

"My belongings. I travel light." Inkar nodded to the servants as they set her things down, then pulled a pair of clippers from her belt and clipped three pieces of an armband from her arm. She dropped the metal into their hands, and the servants bowed low, then retreated without saying a word.

"What—you—" Outrage blossomed in my chest. "You can't stroll in here like it's your rooms. You can't bribe my servants!"

Inkar waved a hand. "I am not bribing them. I am thanking them for their service." Her mouth twitched in a bemused smile. "My wife, in my country, married people spend their nights together."

"Yes, yes," I said impatiently. "Biological imperatives and so on. But we..." I stopped, and a blush crept over me. *Biological imperatives* were the last thing I needed to think about right now.

"If I am so horrible, you can cancel the trial," Inkar pointed out.

"No," I said, too quickly, and a sly smile spread across her lips. My face was so hot it was cooking all intelligence out of my brain. "I...don't want to jump into, um, things. All at once."

Inkar's expression softened a little. "I do not wish to sleep with you—I mean, that is all I wish."

We were silent as I contemplated the best way to hide under my chair without looking like a complete fool.

Behind Inkar, Aino briefly covered her face with the nightgown. "Your Grace, may we speak in private?"

"I will leave you a moment." Inkar picked up her chest as if it weighed nothing and squeezed past Aino into the bedroom.

Aino's nostrils flared, but she stepped into my antechamber and shut the door. Switching to Kylmian, she said, "We should move you to different lodgings."

"No." I'd slept in this suite every night for sixteen years. My notes were here. Farhod's dissection illustrations. My portfolio for the university.

"If she stays, you might not be safe," Aino said.

"If I move, she'll follow me. She's not here because she likes my rooms best."

"We can stop her."

"Aino, we can't make her too angry—" I began.

"*We're* making *her* angry?" Aino's jaw was tight, and red stained her cheeks. "She flaunts that sapphire as though it will get her anything she wants. And you've always known that there are consequences to letting the wrong people into your rooms." Like my family.

The problem was, there were also consequences to keeping Inkar out. "She's all that separates me from Sigis. And if she convinces her father that she's been used and snubbed, he could call it grounds for war. We can't just throw her out. We need to move carefully."

"You *need* to show her that she doesn't have power over the palace," Aino argued.

"She wants to stay the night, and there's not much we can do to refuse her," I said.

Aino flapped the nightgown. "Why not say no?"

"I'm tired. I don't want to engage in politics; I want to sleep. Besides, I'm supposed to irritate her, which means spending time with her. Maybe I'll snore. Or bore her to death talking about biology over breakfast. What could go wrong?"

Aino's lips thinned, but she threw my nightgown at me anyway, hitting me in the face. "Have you considered that she might be worse for you than you are for her?"

I pulled my shift off over my head and slid the nightgown on. "If she kills me, then I don't have to get up before sunrise. I'll take it."

"That's not funny, Ekata. She's not a member of your court, but that doesn't make her trustworthy," Aino said.

That I knew. "I'll call if I need anything."

Aino shook her head but leaned in to kiss me on the cheek. "Anything at all."

I staggered to my bedroom door. Inkar sat cross-legged on my bed, wearing a plain nightgown that I recognized from my wardrobe. She'd unbraided her hair, and it fell, thick and dark, to the tops of her bare knees. The light streaks wound like ribbons through it. She held a thin sheaf of papers in her hand and played absentmindedly with a corner as she looked up. That blasted smile was back on her face.

I went to the other side of the bed and slid in, making sure to keep at least two people's worth of space between us. "What are you reading?"

"It is poetry about the North. I thought it might prepare me for coming here."

I wiggled under the quilt. "And did it?"

Inkar exhaled her soft laugh. "Not even a little."

She set the papers on the table next to the bed—the table I usually used—and lay back. Her hair fanned out around her. The candle flickered low in its sconce.

I cursed Inkar silently. Despite how tired I was, my blood buzzed. Strangers in my room had always meant peril.

I focused on the curve of her nose and tried to calm my breathing and gather my arguments. "Look," I tried. "It was very nice to marry you. And then meet you. But...why are you here?"

The guttering light illuminated a slice of Inkar's cheek, and moonlight poured a softer hue over the rest of her, catching in her eyes and on her shoulder. She tilted her head in puzzlement. "I married you."

"Actually, *I* married *you*. Aren't you...bothered that you came for my brother and ended up with me?"

Her smile grew surer. "I do not like to complain about an improvement in fortunes."

It was hot. Maybe we were running low on ice. It was hot, and I couldn't look her in the face. I flipped onto my back and said solicitously to the ceiling, "Don't you want your own space? Time to think?"

"I want to see what I have gotten myself into," Inkar replied.

I bet you don't. "It's a lot of shark paste."

She laughed again, a full, bursting laugh. It was the kind of laugh I heard only from Aino, and it sounded like a song meant for my ears alone. "It's not funny," I protested half-heartedly.

"I know you have had a hard day—"

That turned the song sour. "Don't patronize me," I snapped.

Inkar's laugh faded. We lay in the awkward silence Eirhan

wanted me to cultivate. I had to admit it wasn't particularly satisfying.

"I only wish to talk," Inkar said at last.

"Talk if you want." I closed my eyes. "I'm going to sleep."

It was the perfect rude statement. But Inkar only shifted, rustling the furs. "I cannot believe you live here."

I didn't answer.

"A palace made of ice. People under the water. Cold roses that grow before our eyes." Her voice was...wondering? I'd spent all evening listening to half-baked compliments and veiled complaints. But Inkar seemed interested in this place for itself.

"The citizens Below aren't really people," I said, opening my eyes.

"It is incredible. We hear the stories from my father's company, but I always thought they were...a metaphor. I never understood how someone could live here."

"I can't understand it myself sometimes." What with my father and my brother trying to murder each other for the throne of the tiniest independent nation on the continent, things could get a bit crowded. But no one else had the city Below.

"I think it is wonderful," she said.

I snorted. But when I looked at her, her eyes were big and serious. She had little black freckles in them.

How could I dissuade her from wanting to be grand consort? "You know the ice never melts, right? And I won't buy you horses."

"The ice never melts at all?" Inkar said.

"We'd sink if it did."

"What happens in the summer?"

Now I had her. "We don't have summer. We have days when we can go out, and days when we can't. Now go to sleep. If I wake up for breakfast, you wake up for breakfast."

"I do not think I can sleep," Inkar said.

"Well, read or look at the stars or something." I'd disembowel her if she riffled through my notes.

"I want to know about you," Inkar said.

Did she? Did she want to hear about my dissection drawings, the studies of bear and wolf and deer skeletons from the mountains?

I *wanted* her to be interested. But I knew what Aino would say. She was using me. Just as I was using her. It was best not to get too close.

So I took a breath and thought about the answers I wanted to give and the answers I wanted to keep for myself. "I'm my father's fourth child. I'm sixteen; I speak Kylmian and Drysian and Farduk; I like to read—"

Inkar smiled gently. "I know all these things. I read about you when I found out I was to come to Kylma. These things are boring."

"Well, they're me," I said, stung.

"No. They are part of you. But what kind of a bride would I be if I did not know them already?"

"A bride my brother was supposed to marry?" I suggested.

"I want to know who you are, not how many languages you speak."

This was my cue to talk about bones until she threw herself out the window from boredom. I swallowed. "You first."

Did Inkar hesitate? "All right," she said, quickly enough that I couldn't be sure. "I hate my sisters and brothers."

"All twenty-four of them?"

"You see? You know my boring facts," she said.

Thank you, Eirhan. "You couldn't get along with any of them?"

"We spent my childhood competing for my father's affection," Inkar said.

"How'd you do?"

"I am expendable enough to be sent as a hostage and important enough to start a war over if you kill me," Inkar pointed out.

"So you're saying things could be worse," I said.

She laughed as though I was charming and clever and funny. People didn't laugh at me that way. Something warm curled in my belly. "Your turn."

"Well, I don't get on with my siblings, either," I said.

"Vying for affection?"

That and trying not to get murdered in the line of succession. "Books make better friends."

"What kinds of books?"

"Biology, mostly. The city Below."

Inkar turned to lie on her back, tilting her head so she

could see through the clear window. "It is fascinating," she said.

"It's important." The city Below and the city Above needed each other.

We lay silent for a few moments. My eyes drifted closed. I had to sleep, especially if a vengeful Aino was going to throw me out of bed in less than five hours.

"I want to know everything about it," Inkar said. "I want you to tell me."

That needed to be the *last* thing I wanted to do. Yet it wasn't.

DAY TWO

CHAPTER SEVEN

K ill me," I groaned as Aino pulled the furs away.

"Breakfast," she said. Her tone was like a bucket of water. "It is ready in your antechamber." Inkar sat up, pulling on the blankets and sending a cold wave over my skin. Aino's glare settled on her. "Please don't let us disturb you further, my lady."

Inkar wiped her eyes and stared blearily at Aino. Aino's mouth became a thin gash in her face, and I slid out of bed before actual sparks shot from her eyes.

Aino pulled me into my robe, tugging the sash so tight I thought I heard a rib crack. Then she steered me by the shoulder into my antechamber. "So thoughtful of you to put on a nightgown," she grated out as she shut the door behind us.

"I never took off my nightgown," I said.

Someone in the corner coughed. Farhod stood by my desk, next to a covered plate. Eirhan waited next to him, radiating rage. His eyes gleamed in the dawn with something a little too close to hate.

"That bed could fit four people. We didn't even touch." I was babbling. "She wouldn't go away. I was tired—"

"Your breakfast is getting cold, Your Grace," Eirhan said as Aino turned up the lamps and started the fire.

Breakfast was bread, porridge, and cold smoked fish. As I took a bite, Eirhan shoved a slip of paper under my nose. "Your order of the day," he said. "Sign at the bottom."

I tried to focus my bleary eyes on the first item. Breakfast. How cute. Next—

"Your father met with the council each morning to discuss the affairs of the duchy. This morning...you'll have a lot to talk about. Expect a discussion of Sigis, the coronation trials, and parliament." Then I would have private meetings with my ministers. "You'll need to convince them that their priorities are your priorities. That's your first step."

"What if their priorities *aren't* my priorities?"

Eirhan's eyes lifted heavenward ever so slightly. "This is politics, Your Grace. Pretend. Soothe the ministers and they won't revolt in the next twenty-four hours. Then we can focus on the twenty-four after that."

It seemed shortsighted. "So I make my ministers happy," I said, even though they'd probably be happiest if I abdicated. "Then—" I frowned at the next item.

"You make Sigis happy," Eirhan said.

I snorted a laugh. "Not possible."

"You were his sister for two years. Yet you do not know how to appease him?" Eirhan said.

"He doesn't get appeased," I argued. "He demands more." Being around him was like slipping under the ice of the moat, a shock that ran my blood hot and cold at once, a pressure that sat on my chest and refused to leave. I could think of only one thing when Sigis was around, and that was getting away from him as quickly as possible. Doing what Sigis wanted was worth avoiding the unpleasantness he could unleash, and he knew it.

"Sigis was furious at your little trick, and now that he stands in the coronation trials, he won't back down. But as long as your father *might* be revived, it will be better for Sigis to be your consort than our duke. Everyone sees his actions as a power grab, but if you convince him he can get what he wants without defeating you in the trials, he'll let you win."

He'd let me win the right to marry him. Joy.

After lunch, we had the second trial, the one to win the approval of the gods. "The archimandrite will probably ask you for money. Give her what she wants."

"That's it?" It seemed ridiculous. I thought I'd have to commune with the gods, not bribe them.

"She may push for more. She's a clever woman and has maintained power despite your father's dislike of her. I am not allowed to accompany you to the trial, but I urge you to do what you can to secure her support. Without her, you won't be grand duke for long."

"She can't back Sigis over me." Sigis was a foreigner.

"You need to treat Sigis as a serious competitor until he's disqualified," Eirhan warned.

My bride poked her head out of my room. "Is that breakfast?" She wore Aino's quilt wrapped around her shoulders. She looked rumpled and sleepy and like she ought to be bundled back to bed. My heartbeat stuttered. My wife could be charming without even brushing her hair.

The air turned stiff. Inkar didn't seem to notice. She trotted forward on her toes, hissing as her feet made contact with the ice floor. She came right up to the rug under my desk and leaned over me to survey the remains of my breakfast. "Have you an egg?" she asked hopefully.

"Fish eggs?" I offered. Her face fell. *Horses and food.* Two ways to annoy Inkar, at least.

Aino hurried me into a serviceable black dress with one of Mother's circlets hooked into my hair. Then Eirhan escorted me to the council chamber, where a fire burned high in the grate.

"Have a seat, Your Grace. In the duke's chair," he specified as I tried to take the chair nearest the door. I moved, feeling my cheeks flush.

I'd never been in the council chamber. The table, carved from dark wood, was smaller than I'd expected. The legs held the faces of strange grotesques, amalgams of animals I'd only ever seen in monographs. Eirhan lit the little candle beneath the inkwell in front of me as my council began to arrive.

The council consisted of top ministers only, whose decisions were integral to running the country. Father had carefully stacked the ministry so that they would all be busy arguing with one another, and have little inclination to unite against him. While the current makeup of the council was to Father's advantage, I had no delusions about what they thought of me. I might unite them through sheer hatred of my incompetency.

The first person to open the door was Reko. Soon after him came Annika, minister of agriculture; then Bailli, minister of the treasury; then Itilya, minister of the hunt; then Rafyet, the grizzled minister of fishing; and Yannush, foreign minister. The last to enter was Urso, minister of trade, who paused at the door to murmur something to his secretary. She nodded and slipped out.

I stopped myself from glancing at Eirhan. A grand duke was in control. A grand duke didn't look to others for approval. I swallowed. "Okay." Eight faces turned toward me. "We're not expecting anyone else, are we?"

Reko's sneer became more pronounced.

"No, Your Grace," Eirhan said.

"Right." How should I salvage this situation? I'd never been in a council meeting before. I didn't know which ministers attended them. "I suppose we should talk about my family."

I'd meant to brief them on Farhod's progress. But Reko,

who'd obviously been looking forward to this, jumped in. "I agree. It's past time to talk about the Avenko line."

Bailli groaned, rubbing his bald head. "Not this again." He looked as exhausted as I felt.

"This again." Reko put his hands flat on the table. "It's obvious that we're one bad heir away from ruination." His eyes locked on me, and I straightened my spine in response to his hateful glare. *What have I ever done to you?* "We need a system to provide a fail-safe. We need a steady government that won't fall apart when our grand duke and his son both fall... ill." His lip curled. "We need to establish a parliament."

"Enough with parliament, Reko," Annika said. "Kylma Above has one ruler, not many. Both Kamen and Lyosha felt that way."

"Our country is too small to be ruled by common government," Bailli added. "Other countries have a surplus of politicians and more needs to be met. For us, parliament isn't as logical."

"It is true that we have had an unusual succession," Eirhan said. "But an Avenko holds the bond between Above and Below. An Avenko must remain in power."

"This is more proof than ever that we need protective measures," Reko argued. "Ekatarina's accession has left us with just one Avenko. What happens if *she's* murdered? What happens if Sigis wins the trials? Establishing a parliament would reduce royal power and decrease their runaway ambition."

"I'm not trying to take over the country," I said.

Reko's laugh was like a fox barking. "Are you saying you initiated the coronation trials by accident?"

Grand dukes didn't do things accidentally. "I made the best decision I could at the time."

Reko raised his hands, looking smug, as though I'd proved his point. "We can have a sixteen-year-old doing her best, or we can have an entire parliament of grown people doing their best. Which would be better for the country?"

"Please, some civility," Urso pleaded.

Itilya tapped her long fingers on the table and tilted her head to give Reko a warning look. He leaned back in his chair, folding his arms. Deep circles rimmed Reko's eyes, and his beard needed combing. None of us was getting enough rest. "Representative rule would give us a government the people want," Itilya said.

"And what will happen to my family?" I asked. "The throne is our right." *Our curse.* "We maintain the link between Above and Below. We *have* to be here."

"That does not mean you need to maintain a strong political position, Your Grace," Itilya said.

So she thought I should stand by and let someone else decide how my life—my country—would be run? "We were born for it. We've been trained for it. Would you support an unschooled farmer who wanted to be minister of agriculture?"

Itilya's face registered no change, but her fingers curled

into loose fists. "Not all of us were raised with wealthy tutors and political intentions, yet we manage."

Itilya had been promoted from a hunting position to Lyosha's bodyguard, then to minister of the hunt. She had been a commoner once. "It's one thing for a person to be rewarded for acts of service. It's different to open up the ministry to everyone Above," I said.

"I agree with Her Grace," Annika said. Their blue eyes darted nervously to me. "A parliament will only slow everything down. We can't wait weeks to get treaties ratified, emergencies declared—what will we do if someone marches to war against us? Wait for parliament to construct a war council?" They folded their hands. "Our grand dukes may sometimes act in error, but they act."

Bailli nodded. "Look at Khourzad. Their parliament has been in a state of flux for eighteen months. When Alhatia attacked, they couldn't decide whether to counterattack, beg for aid, or surrender. Kamen never would have allowed even the discussion of a parliament in this room."

"And it would be an insult to open a parliament behind his back. When he wakes up, he'll expect things to be the way he left them," I said.

"And what if that's not possible, Your Grace?" Yannush leaned forward, fixing his bulging eyes on me. "If Sigis cannot win the coronation trials, he may resort to using his army. How will you maintain power?"

"Her Grace won't be ratifying a parliament at this time.

It's not a matter for discussion, it's a matter of fact." Eirhan shuffled his papers. "I suggest we move on."

We bickered about the coronation trials for the rest of the meeting. Reko was silent, watching me, and even when I met his gaze, he didn't look away. Hatred shone from him. I'd never spoken to Reko before my coronation; did he truly loathe me just because I'd refused him a parliament?

I waited until the cabinet meeting was over to ask Eirhan about the parliament debate. "It's a complicated subject, Your Grace," he said.

"I once performed eye surgery on a dog. I think I can grasp it." His eyebrows rose at my tone, but I didn't apologize. Everyone seemed to think me a special kind of stupid.

"When your father was younger, he supported the concept of a parliament, but over time he's become...less enthused. A parliament could reduce the collective knowledge of the ministry, and it will certainly reduce the power. Kylma has no university of its own, so politicians would either be ignorant or influenced by foreign thinking—and your father distrusts much foreign thinking."

"And Reko...wants more of that?"

"Reko wants the influence of the people. He was a commoner, you know," Eirhan replied. "He did your father a service, and another, and another, and Kamen thought it was only appropriate that a man of the people should be minister of the people. Your father valued his bluntness, but they agreed on almost nothing."

"But Reko's not the only one who wants a parliament," I said.

"He's the one who wants it most. Itilya and Rafyet are commoners, too. Itilya saved Lyosha's life and was promoted in response. She is entirely Lyosha's servant, so her interest in a parliament will surface to the extent that Lyosha supports it. Rafyet is a good fisherman and a valuable member of government, but he doesn't have much influence. Your father put him on the council mostly as a measure of support. Yannush once believed in the autocracy, but he's begun to waver since your father's foreign opinions became more hostile."

Eirhan took a breath. For a moment, I thought he'd continue, but he took a sip of coffee, made a face at the cup, and put it back down.

"Why are they so concerned with parliamentary representation?" I said. "Is there unrest? Are the people planning a revolt?"

"Not at this time," Eirhan said, and I heard what he didn't say. "Your father's been trying to solidify trade agreements in a way that supports our traders, which has resulted in a reduced exchange of goods. Some feel that his increased focus on independent subsistence leaves us vulnerable in the event of a disaster. Others think the world will buy magic from us no matter what." He grimaced. "And that Below will soon relent to the new terms."

I fought the urge to rub my temples. I understood maybe half of what he said, which was his intention, no doubt. "So if we don't trade with anyone, who buys our magic?"

"I never said we don't trade with *anyone*," Eirhan said, and a trace of irritation bled through. "We simply trade less. Magic is worth more. The stores in our treasury have created a useful buffer. But the buffer will quickly run out if you can't replace the magic as it is sold, and some feel that even grand dukes can make mistakes—mistakes that a parliament can counteract."

I wasn't sure how to feel about that. I was questioned enough as grand duke. If we did have a parliament, it would ignore me and do whatever it wanted. *Like marry me off to Sigis.*

"An alternative government is hardly what your father wanted," Eirhan said. "And if you think he'll awaken, the worst thing you can do is push to reduce his power. You've already put us in enough of a state with the coronation trials." How quickly he forgot who'd suggested them in the first place. But he ignored my pointed scowl. "You're scheduled to meet with Annika first. Their lands abroad provide most of our agricultural imports. Lean on that in talks with them."

Annika was responsible for the rye flour we used for our fine loaves; the oats we turned into porridge; the tough, dark cabbage we stewed; and the vegetables that arrived pickled in vinegar. We foraged some things from the mountains, had our own apple orchard, and used the bounties of the lake— but Annika had holdings and land agreements in Drysiak and Rabar, so they could manage to feed a city. I didn't know what to trade them for support, either. Some of what I thought must have shown on my face, for Eirhan said, "I will be here, Your Grace, and I'll assist you on talking points."

"More coffee first," I said, and Aino went to the door to speak to a servant. "Eirhan?"

"Your Grace?"

"What do you think? About a parliament?"

He thought for a moment. Then his lips pulled back into a bland smile, and he said, "I am dedicated to the duke Above, whatever your decisions may be."

At that, he swept to the door and let Annika in.

The meetings were a whirlwind of terms and facts that I couldn't keep track of. Eirhan did most of my talking for me. I bit back resentment, focusing on what he said and the way he said it. I needed him now—but only for now.

Annika was excessively polite but wouldn't meet my eyes. Itilya was unreadable and asked after Lyosha. She was better than Reko, who hadn't asked to meet at all and was probably simultaneously plotting my murder and the establishment of a parliament. Urso wouldn't stop patting my shoulder, and Yannush was all business, speaking more to Eirhan than to me and referencing conversations I'd never been privy to. No one else demanded a parliament outright, which I took as an encouraging start. But by the time Eirhan declared lunch, my brain hurt in a way it had never hurt after a day's work in the laboratory.

As Yannush left, a servant slipped in and handed Eirhan

a note. He scanned it, then huffed. "We're lifting the quarantine."

"Excuse me?"

"Doctor Munna no longer believes there's any danger of contagion. Opening the gates now will minimize bad feeling among the delegates."

"Isn't this a decision for the grand duke to make?" I said.

Eirhan's nostrils flared. "Do you wish to make a different decision? To make them scramble for accommodations in the city or beg for hospitality from Sigis's army?"

He was right, and we both knew it. "Of course not. Lift the quarantine," I said.

"Thank you, Your Grace." He took my arm. "I'll attend to that while you lunch with Sigis."

I set my feet so firmly in the ice that the iron grips on my shoes chipped the surface. Eirhan rubbed at his temple, then checked the hallway outside for eavesdroppers. "I know Your Grace wishes to be anywhere else," he muttered. "But Sigis is your biggest threat, and only you can change that."

"He'd backtrack if I worked with Farhod and cured this... problem," I replied.

"Don't be ridiculous. You haven't the time. Remember, Sigis is only a man. There are things he wants, and all you have to do is make him think he'll get them."

"All I have to do," I repeated under my breath. But I allowed Eirhan to lead me out.

Sigis stood in the Rose Room in a resplendent black cloak.

He'd trimmed his beard and put sapphires in his ears. The gems had been a gift from Father when Sigis left our court, and Sigis had no doubt chosen them with care for this occasion. "Hello, Ekata," he said.

I hesitated. "Hello, brother," I finally said. Maybe that would deter him from trying to marry me.

"Have a cup of wine with me." His voice was all silk and softness. "To commemorate your father, the idol of rulership."

"I..." *Don't know how to respond to that.* I'd never seen Father as an idol, but what would he have done? Grand dukes showed no hesitation. "He's not dead yet."

"I've been led to believe it's only a matter of time." He hardly sounded distraught at the news. Poorly concealed glee might have been more accurate.

"Our physician and our minister of alchemy think there's hope for recovery."

"Then I hope, as well." Sigis sat and lifted his cup. We drank.

Something glinted in his hand, shifting colors in the firelight. He rolled it between his fingers, and I realized what it was—a single pearl of magic. Where'd he gotten that? "Strange, isn't it?" He held it up to the light. "Without this, you'd have nothing. You'd be nothing."

"We'll never be nothing." That was what Sigis didn't understand. It was why he didn't deserve to be grand duke.

"Did your father teach you the secret of making it obey him?" Sigis looked at the pearl of magic as though he wanted to kiss it. Maybe he could marry the magic and leave me alone. Then he shot me a derisive glance, judging and dismissing me in the same moment. I shivered, resisting the urge to scrub his lingering look off the front of my chest. By the time I regained my composure, Sigis wore a cocky smile.

"No. You took from the treasury for that display last night, didn't you?" He chuckled, holding the pearl up. "And here I thought I had something to worry about."

I spoke before I thought better of it. "Being grand duke is about more than making pretty demonstrations."

Sigis burst out laughing. "Pretty demonstrations? You think your father's laughable displays are all we get from magic?" He held the pearl an inch from my nose, and his voice turned soft again. But this time, it wasn't the softness of a man trying to woo me. It was a softness concealing a world of ugly threats. "Do you know what I could do with this? I could make an army of men with unbreakable armor and blades that froze the skin wherever they struck. I could raise walls around any city until it surrendered. I could make you a ring with a diamond the same color as your eyes."

"Gray?" Did he really think that was romantic?

"Your father had petty rules about magic—how much he sold, how we could use it. He could have ruled the world if he'd wanted to."

I wondered if Sigis knew that magic had a temporary life span. I wondered if he realized not everyone wanted the things he did. "Magic belongs to the *real* Avenko line," I said.

Something dark flashed over his face—rage that I'd contradicted him. That I'd told him, for the second time, that he couldn't have something he wanted. He caught my wrist and squeezed until my bones ground together. I clenched my teeth. I wouldn't give him the satisfaction of hearing me whimper. "Prove it," he murmured, dropping the unrefined pearl in my palm.

It couldn't be that simple. The power wasn't conferred upon me just because I was grand duke. Logic said so.

But magic was not logical.

I clenched my fist. Light burst from between my fingers as the pearl popped and the fire died. A glimmering fish leaped over our arms. Pain seared me where Sigis's fingers held tight to my wrist. He yelped, and we flew apart with such force that I slammed into the back of my chair. It tipped dangerously. Sigis's knees rammed the edge of the table, sending our wineglasses toppling.

The fire in the grate flared back to life. Sigis smiled, though it seemed forced as he rubbed his knees. "Not exactly a display worthy of an audience."

Wine stained the oak table and spattered the floor with a ruby rain. The silk at my wrist had melted in the pattern of his fingers, and the skin beneath was red and tender. I watched as Aino righted our cups and cleaned up the wine until lunch was served.

The lunch was more Drysian than Kylmian, and I wondered if that meant the cook was on Sigis's side. I glared at my cheese dumplings and cabbage browned in butter. Aino took a little piece of everything, nodding as she determined it safe to eat. I drank enough wine to wet my tongue and tried not to make a face at the sour burn of it.

Sigis toasted again. "To your father, to his legacy, and to the coronation trials." He took a long drink.

I swallowed carefully. My heart refused to slow its patter. My dress and coat pulled at me in all the wrong places, but shifting would make me look uncomfortable, and I couldn't show him that. Grand dukes didn't show discomfort. They acted as though other people were beneath them. And really, Sigis didn't even rate in the "people" category, no offense to the animal kingdom. I started to classify him.

Hunting tactics: keeps prey off-guard, always nervous and fearful.

"I presume you've executed his servants, of course." Sigis shook his head at my blank look. "You have too soft a touch, Ekata. It was the servants' task to protect their sovereign, and in that they failed quite miserably. In Drysiak, we would never tolerate such laziness."

Weaknesses: incredible arrogance and nationalism. "Of course not." I took a bite of pigeon, another Drysian delicacy.

"And your man of the people. You must have done something with him." I frowned, and Sigis rolled his eyes, clarifying. "Reko. Execute him as well. Swiftly and quietly, if you can. Kamen had a soft spot for him, but you don't have to."

I swallowed my pigeon. "Why do you care? Win the coronation trials and you can do whatever you want."

Aino cleared her throat behind me. Sigis's mouth turned up in what more foolish people would have called a smile. "Perhaps I will. And what happens then?"

"Then you can talk to Father when he wakes up," I said.

Sigis set down his knife and fork. "There's one trial I can't do without you, Ekata." He reached for my hand. I shot back. His stare was unwavering, blue eyes clear and shining and dangerous. "I need the will of my wife to become grand duke. No other woman will do."

I could still hear him snarling, *Her Grace is a child.* "I'm afraid I'm already married."

"A trial marriage." Sigis lifted my cup, brought it to his lips. Wine trailed from the corner of his mouth, red as a kiss. "To a horse rider. You can go back to her tiny, peasant islands and be nothing, or you can stay with me and be a queen. Travel the world, learn as you like. Or come back and fix all the things that are wrong with Kylma. But do it with me." He stopped, and his eyes ran over me again. "You'd look so stunning in our royal scarlet..."

"Does that compliment actually work on girls?"

Behind me, Aino let out an explosive cough. Sigis turned red under his beard. "Don't get so cocky," he snarled. "It's not like everyone's lining up to get a taste of your winning personality."

So much the better. I was already trying to get rid of a wife and a suitor; how much more could I be expected to take?

The rest of the meal was awkward. Any small talk I came up with sounded trite in my mind. I couldn't fathom marrying him. Our relationship would be like my parents'. Was preserving a duchy worth that?

"It's time, Your Grace," Aino said at last, and I almost slumped in relief before remembering I wasn't allowed to.

"Second trial." Sigis's polite pleasantness was back. "Best of luck, my Ekata. You won't catch me unsuspecting this time." His smile was all teeth and charm. "I have always been so fond of the archimandrite. She stood against your stubborn father for years. I hope you don't make the same mistake."

"All of Kylma stands together at this time," I said stiffly as I rose.

Sigis made a derisive noise. "You realize no one's on your side because they like you. Don't make the mistake of thinking you have friends."

CHAPTER EIGHT

We retreated to my rooms, where Aino prepared me for the trial and parade among the people. Layer after layer was piled on: cotton, wool, fur, petticoats, bodices, and long underwear. "You'll wear your father's ceremonial cloak, of course," she said.

"Why?" I'd look like a doll wrapped in a full-size blanket.

Aino's mouth twisted. "It's part of the symbolism of the royal house. Your father always looked the part, even for the people."

"Do they hate him?" I said.

She began to braid my hair. "That is a difficult question to answer. Your father has done things...that make it difficult to love him."

I supposed I could understand that. Why should I expect the entire duchy to love my father when I bore no love for him myself? "Aino?"

"Hmm?" She tied off the braid and wound it in a crown around my head, pinning it with diamond-studded hairpins.

"What should I do? To make people like me?"

The tugging at the back of my head paused. "Make them feel like you care," Aino said. "And be strong. You need to look like someone they can trust to get things done." She opened my wardrobe so that I could see myself in the mirror attached to the inside.

"How is anyone going to know what I look like?" I turned around in my enormous dress. It felt as if I'd gathered twelve full sample baskets from one of Farhod's expeditions in the mountains and strapped them to my hips. "No one can even see me. Why can't I go out in something more practical?" I wore a winter suit of fur and a leather split-skirt when I had expeditions with Farhod.

"You're not practical. You're a duke. And you ask me how people will like you more? You act like a duke."

"Literally anyone could stand in this contraption. We could stuff the dress with straw, and no one would notice the difference." I pulled the hood up and faced the mirror, raising a gloved hand in a mock wave. "If I'm such a powerful duke, why can't I get someone to do this for me?"

Aino heaved a sigh. "If you didn't wish to bear the responsibility, you should have run with me that first night. I did offer, remember?"

"I remember." I wished I'd taken her up on it. We could be cozily sequestered in a mansion far into the hills, surrounded by nothing but wind and ice. Instead, I had hourly meetings with countless people who'd prefer to dissect me on a slab in Farhod's laboratory.

"It's never too late to run," Aino said, handing me my mittens.

I took them, but my mind was far away, in the laboratory at the top of the tower. Aino was right—but I didn't want to run away. I wanted to run *toward*, toward finding a cure for this illness, toward saving myself and others. I could solve this—but first, I had to be my father for a little while.

The kennels were a long, low building attached to the side of the palace, warm and musty and smelling of sweat and wet fur and pine. Six dogs waited outside their stalls, hooked up to a pine sled and looking piteously bored as the kennel master finished with their harnesses. Inkar lingered near the kennel door, her bright smile somewhat fixed.

"I told you we used dogs," I said.

"I know," she said, and I noticed an uneasy tinge to her voice. "I simply—hoped you were joking. Do you truly not use horses?"

"You'd have to be very stupid to think horses would function well in this environment," I said.

She didn't flinch. "Stupid like the man who brought his army on horseback?"

"Exactly like that." I couldn't help laughing. What we

said would probably get back to Sigis. But Inkar smiled at the easy joke.

Our sled dogs were long-limbed, with white-and-tan fur and brown eyes. The kennel master hooked them up two at a time. One yawned, showing off wicked teeth. Inkar drew back.

"It's okay," I said, stifling the urge to take her hand. I bent down and scratched the dog behind the ear instead. "Your horse is in the guest kennel, if you want to ride it behind the sled."

Inkar smiled, and her smile, though brittle, was unyielding. "I do not run from things I fear. And I wish to stand with you."

The kennel master approached us and bowed. "The dogs are trained to a slow pace, Your Grace," he said. "Another sled will follow behind in case you have any trouble."

"We won't." I'd driven a sled on family hunts, when I couldn't get out of them, and on expeditions with Farhod whenever I could go. I wasn't an expert, but I'd manage. Inkar muttered something. "I beg your pardon?"

"I am merely reciting a prayer. I do not wish for my first diplomatic incident to be falling on my ass," she said.

"It would be rather anticlimactic for you," I said.

I hadn't meant it as a compliment, but Inkar's smile cracked a little, revealing something more genuine underneath. "I agree. If I do not take off heads, I will be ashamed of my first public embarrassment as grand consort."

"You could always aim a swing or two *while* you're falling on your ass," I suggested.

Eirhan oiled up beside me, wearing a dour expression. "I hope you are preparing to be suitably mournful during the procession."

I tried not to look as though I'd been caught flirting. *I'm not flirting*, I reminded myself. *I don't know how to flirt.*

"Am I—supposed to say anything, or do anything?" I asked.

"Listen to the archimandrite. Do what she wants. Don't bother trying to charm anyone else. No one will hear you anyway." As Eirhan turned away, I heard him mutter, "And what a blessing that will be."

The kennel master brought the hounds out, and we followed, taking our places on the long wooden sled. I had to pull Inkar off the claw brake and rearrange her behind the handlebar. She clung to it, gasping as the sled began to move.

"It's all right," I said. I took a deep, cold breath, hoping the dogs knew their jobs better than I knew mine. If that didn't say something about the state of Kylma Above, I didn't know what did.

The gate opened, and we faced the crowd.

The dogs began to wag their tails and loped out onto the road. I lifted my face to the sky, gray as a pearl, punctuated by the deep-blue ice spires of the Grand Theatre. Snow dusted my shoulders. The crowd looked like a herd of fantastic winter creatures in their coats of white, brown, and black, their leather and fur. A few foreigners stood out in brightly dyed wool. I spotted slices of arms, hoods, faces. I was on display for the entire world to see, but I saw the world in only the briefest glimpses.

The boulevard was lined with soldiers, and the lamps to either side were lit. The crowd pressed up against the soldiers but did not shout. They reminded me of the curious citizens Below, and I imagined their bending the ice sheet, cracking the ground with their weight, sending us Below in our dragging garments. My scientific mind knew the ice sheet would hold, but my unscientific hands clenched around the bar of the sled.

I pushed my chest out and forced my head up. Father wouldn't show fear, and neither would I. Aino said I had to be likable and strong. Father had gotten by on strength alone, and strength was what I needed now. Strength to inspire faith.

Inkar leaned toward me. "How is it so cold?"

Southerners. If I wanted her to leave me, I could give her the rooms with the coldest privy. But I fished for the edge of Father's cloak. "Here," I said, holding it out to her. She stared at me, eyes widening. They were a lighter brown than they'd looked in the gloom of my rooms last night, with a little bit of green in them. "The whole family fits in here."

She inched over, little by little, hands still gripping the bar. I draped the cape around her far shoulder. I could feel hundreds of eyes following my movements, and I could only hope they took our interaction as a good sign. Maybe they'd think I wasn't caving in too easily to Sigis.

Our grandest buildings lined the boulevard to either side—the stock exchange, with its great dome; the dowager's mansion, with a sharp tower at each corner; the Grand Theatre, with its clear fluted columns; and the covered market. Like our palace, they were carved in ice, though the Grand Theatre had an interior lined with wood and thin stone tiles. Behind them lay the rest of the city: the houses, the shops, the little theaters and coffeehouses, and beyond them the less desirable places, like the tanners' quarter and the fishermen's quarter and other parts of the city where I'd never ventured.

I looked from building to building along the boulevard. Silver and electrum threaded through the edges of their roofs, making them gleam even on this gloomy day. And the most opulent building of all—the Snowmount—stood at the end.

The dogs slowed at the steps of the Snowmount. Legends ran that the Snowmount had once been a cave in the ice. Sjiotha, the goddess of winter, had protected the first settlers of Kylma Above by shielding them from the wind and snow. But when spring came, her jealous brother, Morvoi, had broken the ice and dragged citizens to Below to become his worshippers beneath the lake. When the Avenkos had learned the secrets of magic, they turned the cave into a temple, and every duke found a way to make it more impressive. It had five domes and a monastery, and the roof was shingled with electrum, copper, and gold.

The archimandrite waited at the top of the stairs to the temple. She'd exchanged her white-and-silver robe for a black one. The cloak that covered it was stitched with pearls. Her staff tapped out seconds on the ice.

I dismounted from the sled, inadvertently pulling Inkar with me. The archimandrite stood straight as a pillar while we disentangled ourselves. The cloak dragged on the ground as I walked up the steps to the entrance of the Snowmount, as though Morvoi was trying to pull me under. *If there's any time to do it, it's now*, I prayed.

Inkar followed me to the steps and imitated the bow I gave to the archimandrite. The archimandrite did not bow back.

"Welcome," she said in a voice that told me I most certainly was not.

She held out a gloved hand, and I hesitated over her rings. I opted to kiss the largest one, and she didn't complain. She beckoned, and we followed her through the pale doors, into the Snowmount.

The wide hall was all curves and soft angles, like the black structures Below. Ice buttresses fluted from columns carved with roses and wolves and bears and strung through with electrum thread. A shrine to Morvoi was ornamented with ice fish, nonmagical pearls, and a messenger bowl. Inkar's eyes widened as she took in the carved relief on the walls depicting Sjiotha, a wild-haired, wind-tousled goddess riding a sleigh pulled by bears.

At the altar of Sjiotha burned the eternal torch, the light of which was said to have been given to us by the goddess and had never been extinguished. I pushed back my hood and leaned toward the flame.

"Come," the archimandrite said in a voice of iron. I stiffened at her tone. As we started to follow her, she held up a hand. "The candidate only," she told Inkar. "You may stay and contemplate the matter of your conversion."

Inkar raised her eyebrows. "My what?"

The archimandrite turned and walked away without answering. I tried to shoot Inkar a look that was pleading and reassuring and confident all at once, then hurried after the archimandrite.

We left the main hall of the church through a side door, coming out into a small, open space where winter poppies did their best to bloom through the snow. From there we entered another hall and passed into Sjiotha's monastery, where the buildings were low and the walls bare.

As we walked, the archimandrite spoke. "The coronation trials are a chance to renew faith and cooperation with the church. My blessing is required to pass the trials, and I will give it to only one of you. Three grand dukes I have blessed. You would be the fourth."

"Only until my father—"

"I have always despised your family's method of succession," the archimandrite interrupted. "Your grandfather sacrificed his father to Morvoi." That was a fancy way of saying that Grandfather pushed his predecessor into the moat. "Your father poisoned your uncle, and I have not forgotten it. But I have never known a candidate to kill so many at once. Your brother Svaro was only eight. Did you really have to kill him?"

"He's not dead. I haven't killed anyone," I protested.

"What difference does it make? They cannot rise. They cannot work; they cannot rule. You think this is better than murder?"

"*Yes*," I snapped. Because I was going to wake them up.

Give her what she wants, Eirhan had urged me. I took a deep breath. *Nasal. Premaxilla.*

The archimandrite led me into a room without a fire grate. "Sjiotha has been known to speak in this room," she said. "We will commune together."

She tapped her staff on the floor. A door opened, and two acolytes came in, bearing wooden cups. I tried not to sigh. The sour wine served by the archimandrite at mass was worse than Sigis's Drysian offerings.

An acolyte held my glass in one hand and a round mollusk shell in the other. In its dark and shining center, two fat pearls glistened.

My heart skipped a beat. Magic. Did the archimandrite hold the secret to its refinement?

The archimandrite picked up a pearl and dropped it into

her cup. I hesitated, then imitated her. I tried not to breathe in the wine's bitter scent as I drank. I felt a solid mass slide between my lips, burst against my teeth. My tongue tingled, but I couldn't know whether that was the effect of the wine or the magic.

I exhaled softly. I closed my eyes and bent my mind toward creation and control, thinking of the winter flowers we'd passed on our way in. I thought of light, the way Meire had painted my skin with it. I thought of the tapestry animals, dancing with life. And finally I felt the same pull as the night before, the tug of magic drawing something out of me.

I opened my eyes. No glowing fingertips, no flowers. Nothing but a bit of loose thread that looked as though it had unraveled from the bottom of my dress. Half my mouth felt numb. Before me, the archimandrite stood with her arms out, palms up, eyes closed. Something thick and black oozed from her mouth, dripping off her chin and coalescing on the floor in a sludge. She began to sway. Was that what a message from the goddess ought to look like?

I checked myself for sludginess, or murmuring voices, or anything. All I heard was the wind whistling through gaps in the ice. All I saw was the archimandrite. Maybe I was hallucinating. Maybe that explained the way the archimandrite seemed to sway. Maybe it explained the way the threads on the ground turned to ice and began to grow, pressing in on my dress, swirling into shapes reminiscent of thorns.

By the time the archimandrite opened her eyes and wiped

the sludge from her chin, the ice had come up to my shoulders, and I was no longer convinced it was a hallucination. "Sjiotha has spoken," she said in a raw voice.

She has? I shook out my arms and shoulders. The ice around me broke with a delicate tinkle. "What did she say?"

"You could win her favor, but she needs a declaration of devotion to her cause. A new bell tower, with new bells."

Give her what she wants. "Fine," I said, hoping Minister Bailli wouldn't start with some *When your father was grand duke* speech.

"She requires twenty pounds of raw magic as well."

"Okay." That was going to cause an uproar on the council.

"And I want to sit on your council. And reinstate the warriors of Sjiotha."

I laughed. My great-grandfather had disbanded the warriors of Sjiotha when they'd tried to overthrow him. They'd nearly outnumbered the men in our standing army—hardly a feat, to be fair—and the religious tithe they'd collected from the craftsmen of Kylma had been good for no one but the archimandrite. "No on the warriors. I'll think about putting you on the council."

The archimandrite didn't join me in my mirth. "This is not a negotiation, Your Grace. Either you do it, or..."

But grand dukes didn't bow to others. "You don't get to threaten me. I'm not going to buy the duchy; I'm going to earn it."

"What makes you think those two things are different?"

175

The archimandrite moved away from the black mess on the floor, tapping her staff as she walked. Each little *clink* bounced off the walls. "Three grand dukes I have crowned. Don't presume you know better than me."

Except those three dukes had been up against minor officials and dummy contestants in the coronation trials. The archimandrite knew I was desperate. She knew she could push for more. And maybe she thought my inexperience would mean I wouldn't consider the consequences.

"You're my equal, but not my better," I said, choosing my words carefully. "We can make arrangements, or you can see how respectful a Drysian king will be of our Kylmian goddess."

"Did you truly murder your family so you could end your reign feuding with the church?" the archimandrite spat.

"Call me a murderer *one more time*," I growled through gritted teeth.

The archimandrite waved her hand. "Grand dukes come and go. We keep the Snowmount eternal. With you or with another."

I made fists of my shaking hands. *Give her what she wants.* Eirhan would be so angry with me. "We can make a provisional agreement. I'll speak with the council and see what kind of tithe—"

"You agree now, or you fail the trial," the archimandrite said. "And all of Kylma will know it."

We didn't speak on the way back to the shrine of Sjiotha.

Inkar paced in front of the eternal flame. She came to stand beside me, and though I felt her eyes on me, I couldn't bring myself to meet her gaze.

"Best of luck," the archimandrite said in a voice of snow and stone.

The air bit at us as we left the Snowmount. People craned their necks to see around us. Murmurs ran through the crowd, then dropped to an uncomfortable silence when they realized the archimandrite wouldn't emerge. The world was reduced to the creak of the ice and the groan of the wind.

Sigis stood by his horse, having eschewed a trip via sled. When we heard, at long last, the tap of the archimandrite's staff behind us, he handed his reins to an attendant and strode up the stairs without looking at us. He sank to his knees, taking the archimandrite's hand and bowing his head to the proper ring finger. "It has been too long since I've profaned the altar of Sjiotha with my prayers."

"Some atonement is surely in order." The archimandrite spoke to him as she would speak to a favorite son. She urged him to his feet, and they went inside.

I drew my cloak around Inkar and pulled it tight, as though I could keep the fire that had ignited in me from bursting out. My limbs shook. The whole world was that one point, the door through which two traitors had gone. "Please do not pull me over," said Inkar. I let go of the cloak a hair, and she nodded. "Perhaps we should go back? I am cold, and I do not think we can do any more good here."

"Yes." Father would pretend as though everything that had happened was planned. Well, either that or tear down the Snowmount, and I didn't think I could get away with that. Not with the whole city watching me. I let Inkar guide me down the steps and onto the dogsled.

The dogs brought us around, and we began to trot back up the boulevard toward the walls of the palace. "Perhaps it is for the best," Inkar said. "I have never wanted to adopt a religion merely to impress someone else."

Religion, food, and horses. The annoy-Inkar list grew.

The crowd on the road to either side was silent, and I did not find that to be a comfort. Why didn't anyone cheer for me?

Have you ever given them a reason to? Maybe I should hand Sigis the throne. But that image, of Sigis sitting snug and smug in my father's chair, lit a fire in me. I couldn't let him win. I couldn't be the one who caved in to his invasion after centuries of independence. And I certainly wouldn't do it without a war. That chair was our gift, our right, our responsibility. And grand dukes didn't shy from responsibility.

But my chances in the coronation trials didn't look good. If I couldn't change the archimandrite's mind, I'd have to win the next two trials.

Or I'd have to stop the coronation trials in their tracks.

I knew my family had been cursed via magic. I knew where we stored it, too. Every single shipment, whether it consisted of a pearl or a barrel, had to be approved to leave the royal treasury.

When we arrived at the kennels, my knees were stiff and my hands had frozen around the bar of the sled. My bad temper wrapped around me like a shroud.

Eirhan appeared before I'd even gotten off the sled. "*Give her what she wants*, I said. What did you fail to grasp about that?"

"Nothing." I pulled the ribbon of my cloak and let it fall around Inkar.

"Then how have you failed to win the simplest of the coronation trials?" he snapped.

Grand dukes didn't bear the brunt of their subordinates' attitudes. "Shut up," I told him, and was satisfied to see his mouth fall open a fraction. "Get my guard."

Viljo hopped off his sled. "I am here, Your Grace."

"No," I said, turning the impatience in my voice to iron. "Get the *entire* guard." Grand dukes made grand gestures, after all.

Minister Bailli found me as I was trying to get Viljo to kick down the door of the treasury. He stopped in the middle of the hall, and Minister Urso and his secretary walked right into Bailli's back. "What *are* you doing?" Bailli wiped his head. "Your Grace," he added, as though it would soften his insubordinate tone.

"Give me your key," I said.

"I...what?" His hand went to his belt, touching the large iron ring of keys.

"*Your key*," I snarled.

"I . . . what need does Your Grace have of entering the treasury?" Bailli blustered. The iron grips on his shoes chipped the ice as he shifted from foot to foot.

"I'm the grand duke, and I want to," I said.

For a moment, I thought Bailli would refuse me, but I didn't care. I had a dozen guards who would arrest him on the spot. A moment later, he moved forward, coat swaying, shoulders hunched, and head down. He pushed past me and inserted his key into the lock.

The crowd behind us doubled. I saw Eirhan against the wall, brows drawn together in worry. Reko leaned next to him, arms folded, smiling like a fox that had come upon a goose with a broken leg. "A dictator's first move is always to seize the means of power," he remarked.

The door swung open. Viljo and another guard shoved past Bailli.

The treasury's front office was lined with oak shelves weighed down by book after book of accounts. A desk sat in the corner, drawers open and half-filled with papers and books. I picked up a ledger and began to flip through it.

Bailli's jowls quivered with rage. The guards stood awkwardly, awaiting some order. "Take it all," I said. I turned to Bailli. "We'll be running an audit on your accounts."

Bailli's chest puffed out. "How dare you? No Avenko has audited me, not in thirty years."

"Every account from the past year," I said. If the curse

had been intentional, it would have been made from refined magic my father had prepared for export. And the newer it was, the stronger.

I closed the ledger. "We need access to the treasury itself."

His black eyes flashed. "That's too far." He crossed his arms. "I still consider your father to be the grand duke. I follow him, not you. And only on his order will I open the treasury."

Bailli was a foot taller than me, but I could tell he feared me from the way his throat bobbed, from the way his chest stopped moving. "Resist if you like. I don't need you to open the treasury. Maybe I don't need you to be treasurer at all."

I unclipped the keys from his belt myself. It felt strangely intimate, for all the air between us buzzed with fear and growing anger. Two days ago, I barely knew Bailli's name, and now I was fumbling at his waist. Heat burned in my cheeks, and I didn't look at him as I made my way toward the door leading to the treasury's vaults.

The door was of iron and wood. Five locks separated me from the goods inside, and the guards gathered behind me as I went through key after key.

At last, one of the keys turned and opened on a long, dark hall. As a guard went down the wall, lighting sconces, he revealed a neat, bare room stacked with cloth, barrels of grain and beer and preserved meat, furs and leathers—all of which belonged to the grand duke.

And, of course, the magic. The magic sat at the far end,

in small barrels of the darkest wood. "Which of these were treated and refined by my father?" I asked.

"You can't possibly want to open them," Bailli said.

"Of course not." That came from Eirhan. He gathered the guards with a twist of his hand. "Collect the magic, both raw and refined. We'll keep it in my personal safe."

The guards picked up the barrels and filed out, and with that my power was gutted. "I need access to any magic my father might have treated," I said.

"Why?" Eirhan tucked a stray lock of greasy hair behind his ear.

Now wasn't the time to talk about how the whole family had been cursed. But when I didn't respond, Eirhan's mouth twitched. "Anything Your Grace needs can be discussed at a more...private time?"

I didn't sigh. Eirhan might have thought he'd won the round, but I'd find some way around his guard. To please the spectators, I said, "Take the books to my rooms. If Minister Bailli tries to interfere, arrest him."

Bailli's face was so red I thought it would burst. His eyes glittered with rage. I passed him without saying another word, and he did not speak to me.

At long last, someone was taking me seriously.

CHAPTER NINE

Eirhan imposed himself upon me as Aino helped me change for dinner. "Bailli has always been a staunch monarchist. You may have done the only thing that could push him toward supporting a parliament," he said as I dressed behind a screen.

"We needed the information in the treasury." I stepped into a cream-colored dress with gold embroidery and fur edging. "Grand dukes don't ask."

"Nor do they throw temper tantrums," Eirhan said.

I snorted at that. Father's rage was powerful, but it was still a tantrum. And Lyosha had been worse.

"What are you looking for, exactly?"

Like I'd tell you. He'd already seized the evidence; if he knew what I was searching for, he could destroy it. Could Eirhan be in on a plot against my family?

When I didn't answer, he sighed. "If you can't come up

with a reasonable explanation for confiscating every drop of magic in the treasury, you'll face outrage."

"I'll be fine." I grunted as Aino pulled the back of my dress closed to button it. I'd present my evidence when I was good and ready.

"Sigis and Reko will use the incident to strengthen their positions," Eirhan added.

I sighed. "Why did Father never get rid of Reko?" How did he end up as my problem?

"Your father and Reko had a friendship that...transcended politics." Eirhan sounded as though the very idea was offensive. "Kamen thought more like Reko when he first took the throne. But people change, and Kamen and Reko changed in different directions."

"Would Reko consider forcing an issue like parliament?" By, say, cursing my entire family?

"He has the political motive, but he isn't whom I'd suspect first. The problem is, your tantrum in the treasury put Reko and Bailli on the same side for the first time in over a decade."

"So Bailli will turn into a populist?" I closed my eyes so that Aino could apply kohl.

"Doubtful. But perhaps he'll consider alternative options for a grand duke. Ones that have spent the day charming the archimandrite, for example."

Right. The ever-present problem of Sigis.

"This is why you need to follow my lead. You don't know what you don't know."

"I don't," I agreed with a sigh. *And I don't know* anything *about* you.

"Now, for the matter of dinner," Eirhan said.

"I suppose I'm sitting with Sigis again?"

"You are. And please try to keep your wife under control tonight."

"I can't force her to behave," I protested. Nor did I want her to.

"If she oversteps her bounds, we might have an excuse to dismiss her, so I suppose things could be worse. As for your other needs, keep away from the archimandrite. She's furious. And try to keep her away from Sigis, too. Rafyet's been pushing for a fishing agreement, so it's best not to speak with him until you have all the details. Reko will use whatever ammunition he can against you, and he'll no doubt try to goad you into saying something stupid." Eirhan paused. I could imagine him thinking *It wouldn't be that hard.* "Bailli will probably avoid you as much as you need to avoid him. I have no idea what Itilya thinks, so whatever you do, don't offend her. Actually, don't talk to her, either."

"Is there anyone I *am* allowed to talk to?" I said, coming out from behind the screen.

"I'm sure the delegates will be clamoring." Eirhan clasped his hands. "As long as you avoid sensitive topics and remember everyone's name, you should manage. Oh, and keep Inkar from charming them."

"I have an idea," I said. "Why don't you send my dinner

to the laboratory, and I can work on finding the cure with Farhod?" Or I could visit Below. An unfinished note to Meire was stuffed in a drawer of my desk. I'd been trying for an hour to ask her the secrets of magic, and I still couldn't formulate my request correctly.

"Please try to take this seriously," Eirhan said in a long-suffering voice.

"I am," I protested. Eirhan didn't want me to speak with anyone. And he wanted me to control my wife. And he wanted me to make Sigis happy. He wanted me to do everything short of swim the moat naked. "No one wants me around. The least I could do is try to bring back someone they *do* want."

Eirhan hesitated. "Your father...is not necessarily *wanted*," he said carefully. "But he could maintain control. If you can do the same, you'll survive."

I didn't want to survive. I wanted to thrive. I wanted to do so far away. *Find the cure, and you will*, I promised myself, and pretended not to see the strain around Aino's face as she pushed the screen aside and began to sort through my gold and diamonds.

"I have brought in doctors from the city," Eirhan continued as Aino slid jewelry through the holes in my earlobes and draped it around my neck. "They'll be of great help to Minister Farhod, I'm sure."

Doctors. Under Eirhan's pay, no doubt, who would report findings to him.

The door to my antechamber opened. "I am ready to try

more terrible fish foods," Inkar called from the other side. I buried my smile before Eirhan or Aino could scold me for it.

Eirhan rose. "Are you ready?"

"Nearly." Aino pulled my braid back. "One last time, Ekata. Von der Pahlen," she said.

"From Birustra. Wearing red and silver. Tall, pale, and old."

She tugged gently on my braid in approval. "Arlendt."

"Natterdalen. Wearing blue and yellow. Pale hair, enormous nose, and old."

"Good," Eirhan said. "Ngamo?"

"Osethi. Very tall. Bards probably sing about his mustache. Old." I turned my head up to stick my tongue out at Aino. She pushed me straight again, but not before I caught her smile.

"Triadus?" Aino prompted.

"Um..." I wrinkled my nose as she finished lacing up my back. "This is a trick one, isn't it?"

"No. He's a cousin," she said.

"The one who paid for the ring wall."

"No."

"The one who married the second Prince of Anbertane and is living in exile in Trollundheim?" I guessed.

She sighed. "He's your grandfather's nephew, and he's representing Bruxon."

"Is it really my fault for not remembering my dozens of family members?" I said. "They're all the same. They come from all the neighboring kingdoms, they all disapprove of me, and they're all old. Why are they all old?"

"Because all the young ones came to be brideshow candidates," she replied. "Do try to think of something nice to say to each of them." She sounded as though it were a prayer more than a directive.

"Can I tell them how distinguished they look?" I asked.

"None of them will take that as a compliment. Don't." She slid the last pin into my hair and pointed me toward the mirror.

I looked grand and cold and regal. My gray eyes lacked color, and white powder had been swept over my cheeks to erase what little pink I had in them. I adjusted the diamond tiara that sat on my blonde hair. More diamonds spread across my chest like a constellation of stars, held in place by a web of thin gold. I drew myself up tall, and something of the movement reminded me of my mother. I forced myself straighter. It would be better for people to see her, not me.

Aino's smile seemed bittersweet. "You look beautiful," she said, and I wondered if she was reminded of Mother, too.

I squeezed her hand and led the way to the antechamber. Inkar stood by the fire, admiring the winter roses. She shook her head and adjusted her sapphire ring. "They are still amazing, even though I cannot touch them," she said. She wore a sumptuous green-and-silver overcoat that someone had found to make her vest and trousers a little more celebratory. Her hair had been pinned up as well. The small ruby studs in her ears made her brown eyes richer—or perhaps that was the reflection of the fire. I could smell the sharp tang of sweat on her, and it wasn't the worst thing I'd smelled today.

"I hope Your Grace has had a pleasant afternoon?" Eirhan said to her.

"You do not know what I was doing?" Inkar asked him. "I thought the servants following me were yours."

Eirhan coughed. Was that a hint of a blush I saw on his cheeks? "They were there for your protection and comfort, not to satisfy my own curiosity."

"I did have a pleasant afternoon," Inkar said. "You have a dedicated and enthusiastic guard. I also spoke to your minister of fishing. He does not believe he has anything less disgusting to serve us for dinner."

"Your Grace will simply have something to look forward to for the next fifty years," Eirhan suggested.

The reception before dinner was worse than the first. As we approached the hall, we could hear the murmur of voices, a torrent that dropped to nothing the moment the doors were opened. From Reko's expression, I knew what they'd been talking about.

The people knelt. None of them would look at me. I tightened my grip on Inkar's arm and bid them rise, and the second night's festivities began.

Delegates swirled around me like a current. I spent most of my time trying to remember Eirhan's list of *don'ts* and despairing at my inability to keep Inkar in check.

She seemed to have a magical touch. She told the Prince of Genobia that his national dish was the worst thing she'd ever tasted, and she made him laugh. She mocked the horsemanship of the Natterdales to Arlendt's face, and in return she got a compliment. She challenged another delegate to a shooting contest—a rematch, by the sound of things—and scheduled it for the morning. Inkar shone.

Resentment warred admiration within me. Half of me wanted to take notes and beg her to teach me later. The other half simmered with bitterness—at her effortlessness, at my hopelessness. My father had never let anyone outshine him. And if Inkar brought all the charm to our union, what would happen when she broke off the marriage? There would be just one more aspect of ruling I couldn't handle.

As a determined-looking Rafyet approached, I detached myself from Inkar, who was too busy arguing the merits of Stenobian steel with a count to even register my departure. Remembering Eirhan's warning to avoid Rafyet, I gestured to Viljo, who stomped over with his usual tactlessness. "I need you to pretend to be telling me something important."

"What? I mean, I beg Your Grace's pardon?"

"Minister, will you give us a moment?" I said, and Rafyet bowed and fell back. I strode across the floor with Viljo trailing behind. The ruse worked: People cleared my path, bowing as I passed. Maybe this was how my father had managed to look so polished all the time. Even though I wasn't sure where I was going or what I'd do when I got there, striding with purpose fooled everyone.

I went up an ice staircase at the end of the audience hall that led to a mezzanine, dark and quiet. I pushed through a pair of doors onto an empty balcony. Snow had drifted up against the side of the palace, and I kicked through soft powder as I approached the balcony's edge.

I wanted to hit something, perhaps myself. I would be more useful doing anything than struggling to keep up with gossip on policy I didn't understand. Maybe that was why Eirhan had insisted I attend. So he could show everyone how terrible I was.

I fought to calm myself. *Nasal, premaxilla, maxilla.* Reciting the bones was a familiar rhythm—I was clever, I was an Avenko, I could do this. Checking that Viljo still stood by the balcony door, I put my hands inside my sleeves and leaned out over the edge. Cold stung the tip of my nose and the tops of my cheeks. Beneath me, snow flurried in the halo of light surrounding the lamps that dotted the palace wall. The noises of the city were muffled. I felt so gloriously alone.

Being alone had always been best. Alone meant I didn't have to contend with any siblings for the approval of my parents. It meant no Velosha to slit open the seam of my coat and let the cold air in, no laughing Svaro to command the dogs to kill me. No Lyosha to hiss all the ways he would make it look like an accident. No Aaronika to drop foxglove into my coffee. No Fenedyo to lock me out in the middle of the night and force me to sleep in the kennels. And no oppressive presence of Father or Mother, presenting me with a bitter future.

I huffed a cloud into the cold air. I'd spent the last three years planning my escape from this place, from my brothers and sisters and the people who'd spawned them. But now, if

I wanted to escape Father, I'd have to save him. And to save him, I'd have to become him. Become someone too fearsome for ministers to cross.

"Your Grace?" Viljo shivered. "The dinner won't start without you."

"We can go back. But slowly." I still needed to think all this through. Needed to understand the role I was supposed to play in this grand puppet show, needed to see who else was trying to pull the strings. But I couldn't unravel the solution by thinking logically. These weren't the kinds of puzzles I liked.

I went back through the balcony door but paused inside the mezzanine. A servants' door was to my left, carved seamlessly into the ice. I used to slip through those doors when I wanted to escape the attentions of my family. I would pretend that I'd found another world in the servants' corridors, one where no one existed but me, where I could run through parallel halls and be the master of my own empty kingdom. Then I'd grown too old, and Aino taught me that I couldn't act like a servant anymore. That's when I'd begun hiding with Farhod instead.

"Your Grace?" Viljo said tentatively.

"Yes. A minute." I moved toward the door. Aino and Eirhan would tell me off if they found me sneaking around, shirking my duties and leaving Inkar to wreak charming havoc in my absence.

Of course, that was the allure of it.

"Stay here," I ordered Viljo, and without waiting to see if he objected, I went in and shut the door behind me.

The corridor was cooler than the mezzanine. Only every other sconce had been lit, and there were no tapestries to keep in the heat. This was not a space for comfort. It was a plain, unadorned hallway, without even winter roses to grace it.

The silence of it was almost perfect. I heard the echo, far off, of servants hurrying up and down the stairs, from the kitchens to the banquet hall, but here there was no one. I needed only a few moments. Then I could go back and fail at being grand duke. I walked, letting my hand trail along the smooth ice wall.

A rumble of voices made me pause. No one was supposed to be on this level—not to mention that it was impossible to reach these rooms through the mezzanine. Unless they'd used the servants' entrance, as I had.

Reko. I lightened my steps. He would know to slip through the servants' corridors if he wanted a clandestine meeting. He would have access to the law library, which was through a door right ahead. But as I crept toward the door, the voices resolved, and it was not Reko I heard.

It was Sigis.

"Wait? Waiting has led me nowhere. I waited for the curse to take, then while I was waiting for *Her Grace* to give me the time of day, she married someone else."

"I had no idea that was going to happen." The second voice was high, breathy, panicked. "Who marries a marauding pony-rider? She's out of her mind."

"She's too much trouble," Sigis said. "Put her under and wake up a different one."

"We can't do that. We have to move delicately." The second voice dropped, and for a few moments, I heard the soft hiss of someone whispering. Before I had time to think better of it, I slipped out of my shoes and crept forward on my wool socks. The servants' door to the library was cracked, and I could see a thin slice of bookcase beyond. "You can still win the coronation trials. But we can't be too bold too early, or we'll all lose our heads." The unknown voice paused, then said, "And you'll lose your chance," with what sounded like an attempt at rallied courage.

"Kings are made of chances, my dear," Sigis's voice turned soft, and I couldn't help wincing in sympathy with my traitor. "Remember, you came to me. With one word, I'll have you hanging from a cage outside the palace wall, and I won't lose a single trade agreement."

The air around me was as thick as lake water. My throat closed up.

"Your Grace?"

I gasped, and the sound was as loud as thunder to me. I clapped a hand over my mouth. "What was that?" Sigis snapped. My heart pulsed so loudly I could hear it. Footsteps clicked on the floor. I hefted my skirt off the floor and slid backward, grabbing my shoes on the way.

"Your Grace—" Viljo said again.

"*Shh.*" I shoved him until we both stumbled back into the mezzanine. One of the iron teeth snapped off my shoe. I felt a surge of anger. I was grand duke. I didn't run from things. Sigis didn't get to have more power than me in my own realm. I could have confronted him. I could have caught his coconspirator.

"Is everything...?" Viljo trailed off.

"It's fine." I shoved my shoes back on with trembling hands and let Viljo escort me downstairs.

It wasn't fine. My most powerful enemy had conspired to curse my family. And I wasn't nearly as safe as I'd assumed.

The moment I stepped off the stairs and back into the hall, figures crowded me. Delegates wanted to wish me good nuptials, to inquire as to my health, to proffer meaningless condolences about my father. They reminded me of a flock of wolfrooks waiting for me to die so they could feed on my corpse.

As I struggled forward, nodding and thanking and pretending I knew whoever was speaking to me, I caught Eirhan's eye. Only the steely glint of it in his otherwise composed face told me how angry he was. He looked as though he wanted to say something cutting. The heat of his glare made my back prickle. I gritted my teeth and focused on finding Inkar.

It wasn't hard. She seemed to be the only person enjoying herself—she and whomever she was talking to. But she broke off her conversation with Osethi as soon as she saw me, and her mocking smile was almost secretive, as if we shared a joke. I felt my blush coming and pressed my thumb into a diamond-studded ring to distract myself.

"Is everything well?" Inkar slid her arm through mine as though it had always belonged there.

Not remotely. "Fine."

We went in to dinner and sat for our first course. Before I could explain to a dubious Inkar what was in it, Sigis stood up. "I'd like to say a few words," he said, and the noise of the hall subsided. His deep voice rumbled, clear and confident. He sounded exactly the way a grand duke should sound, exactly the way I didn't sound. He caught my eye and winked.

Don't throw up.

"I'd like to congratulate my dear foster sister and her wife," he said. "The first twenty-four hours of a marriage are always the most tumultuous, so I've heard."

Laughter rippled through the room. When Sigis made a joke, people laughed, no matter how uninspiring the humor.

I didn't realize my hand was shaking until Inkar found it and squeezed. I squeezed back. Eirhan might want me to get rid of her, but having her next to me right now was infinitely preferable to facing Sigis alone.

"I first came to Kylma five years ago. If any of you had told me I'd be competing for that chair…" He shook his head. "And with my cleverest foster sister, too." He raised a glass in my direction.

Don't throw up.

"As shocking as it was to hear about Kamen Avenko, it is in times of tragedy, I believe, that we discover who we really are. Ekata, I look forward to discovering who *you* really are over the course of the coronation trials."

The archimandrite stood as though she'd practiced this moment with him. She probably had. "The gods have made their will known. The God Below has acknowledged King Sigis as a member of the royal line, and the Goddess Above accepts the submission and faithful declaration of His Majesty, King Sigis Casimaj of Drysiak."

Odious owl pellet, I thought furiously at her.

Applause and unease sounded in equal measure. Sigis and I were tied at one trial each.

"Two trials remain," the archimandrite called over the noise, and the hush spread accordingly. "The trial Below will take place in four days. The final trial, to determine the will of the people, will occur the day after. Prepare your strength and cunning."

She sat. Sigis lifted his glass to me. "To the trials," he said. The entire hall drank.

Eirhan's spoon hit the back of my hand. "Your turn," he muttered.

"To do what?" I whispered.

"Say something. Remind them who has the better claim."

Couldn't he have warned me, or given me more magic, or something? I pushed back my father's chair, and the scrape of oak on ice made the delegates turn their eyes toward me. I still held Inkar's hand, but I shook too much to risk letting it go. I pressed my thighs into the table to steady myself.

"Thank you for coming," I said. The words came out slow and raspy. "I...hope more than anything that the true winner of the coronation trials will be my father. He valued each and every one of you." Everyone knew that for a big fat lie, but no one shouted their disagreement. "I hope he'll be well soon. And in any case..." I lifted my own glass. "To new beginnings."

I sat down before I realized I'd forgotten to drink. As the rest of the hall set their glasses down and the first course came, Sigis leaned over. "You've always had a gift for words," he said in Kylmian. "When I lived here, you used to have entire lists devoted to insults and responses to insults." He laughed into his wine cup. "Do you still have it?"

What do you think, you walking refuse bucket? "I make other lists these days," I said in Drysian.

Inkar looked between us. "What are you talking about?"

"Nothing." Sigis smiled tightly at her.

"Old lives," I said. Old wounds. New problems. "Sigis was my foster brother for some time."

"A hostage exchange." Inkar nodded. "I, too, was invaluable enough to serve as a hostage."

"Value is measured by our actions," Sigis replied. "That's why I'm king of the largest country in the North, and you are..." He frowned thoughtfully. "What is it you are, again?"

Inkar's smile was bright anger, steel and snow. "I am the Grand Consort of Kylma Above."

"For now," Sigis replied, unperturbed.

Inkar chose to ignore Sigis. She took a cautious sip of her soup, and her eyes widened. "I like it."

It was warm and creamy, dotted with chunks of salmon and onions. "It is the finest food we have to offer."

"I thought I have been getting your finest since I came here," Inkar said. "No matter. I will enjoy what I can."

"It is hard to enjoy the comforts of civilization when you are not used to them." Sigis took a sip of wine, eyeing Inkar over the top of his cup.

"It is equally hard to find civilization in the North," Inkar replied.

Eirhan cut in. "Your Highness, we've heard interesting reports from Solarkyet. Has their border caused you any trouble?"

"Hardly." Sigis rolled his eyes as he put his cup down. "The Ennthu region has declared itself independent again. The satrap has been hanged, and they've tried a campaign along the border. But they're undisciplined and ignorant in the ways of war." His eyes flicked to Inkar again. "When people begin to rely too much on horses, it becomes easy for them to forget the benefits of alternative strategies. They have no concept of how to besiege a fortress. They don't know how to sit still." His eyes found me next. "I find it to be true in all aspects of their lives, in fact."

"Ridiculous," Inkar said serenely. Her knuckles had whitened around her spoon. "Those who live by the horse are not devoid of education. My father has successfully besieged dozens of cities."

"I do seem to recall a little story about the monastery at Thrios," Sigis replied. "How many months did you sit outside while the monks drank their wine and played with their relics? Six, wasn't it?"

The look Inkar gave him was, for once, devoid of even the pretense of humor. "Five."

"And then, of course, you ran home to Papa, and he slaughtered every monk in that monastery for you."

"That is untrue. Most of the monks became hostages."

"Nothing to say about your military exploits?" Sigis raised a brow.

"I was fourteen. I was not head of the Emerald Order then."

"Is this the wife you want?" Sigis asked me. "One who's incapable of taking responsibility?"

Inkar's jaw worked. "Here," I said, pouring cloudflower juice with honey in her cup. I floundered for something to say. "Um. What good are monks as hostages, anyway?"

"The rich religious orders will pay sometimes. Otherwise, they make good tutors. I learned Drysian from monks," Inkar said. Then she lowered her voice. "Though I often regret it."

"At least he doesn't speak your native language," I muttered back. "I'll never get away from him." Inkar laughed, and Sigis shot us a dark look.

"You seem to have a problem with horses," she added as our smoked caribou arrived. "Do you need a lesson in how to ride?"

"On the contrary. I don't consider them the only tactic in my arsenal, that's all." He tore a piece of caribou off his knife with his teeth. "For example, I can shoot *and* use a sword. Maybe *I* could give *you* a lesson."

Inkar's hand went to her side, then came up again. "Do you think I wear axes only for show?"

Sigis put his knife down and steepled his fingers. "That sounds like a wager. I'm interested."

Inkar smiled dangerously. "The Baron of Rabar will meet me for shooting tomorrow morning. Join us, and we will exercise a little."

"Done."

Eirhan put a hand on my forearm. "Your Grace could do *something* to prevent her wife and the King of Drysiak from killing each other tomorrow."

"Why don't you step in?" I muttered back. "Sigis might actually listen to you." Even saying it stung. If I had to be duke, I didn't want to be known as the impotent and incompetent one.

Course after course passed, with Inkar opining on the food and Sigis slinging barbs at both of us. I'd hoped he'd get drunk and render himself incoherent, but he was too smart for that. He switched from wine to cloudflower juice, and the only thing that seemed to happen was that he switched his attention from Inkar to me. "I'm surprised you've been able to provide fresh meat. Hunting treaties were on hold, were they not? By order of your father? But I suppose that's a matter for your minister of the hunt."

Sigis knew Reko had reported discontent among the people. He knew that Annika had complained of low grain stores and that Yannush had pushed to increase the military budget. He knew everything, and I so clearly knew nothing. The only respite I got was when the meal was finally over and people began to move about. Even then I had one eye on Sigis, tracking him as he talked to my ministers. He charmed Annika, who let him kiss their hand. Bailli's eyes flicked toward me during their conversation, and Itilya wore the same inscrutable coldness she'd always shown. Sigis was angling to win the will of the people out from under me.

I followed the movements of my ministers around the hall. Yannush and Urso provided me with a welcome cup of coffee, then retreated to the sides of the room, talking only to each other and their secretaries. Annika and Itilya had a brief argument. Had one of them been Sigis's companion in the law library?

I was so busy following them I failed to notice my own prime minister until he was right next to my chair. "Your Grace," Eirhan said, and I jumped.

"What can I do for you?" I asked sourly. I'd forgotten to look after Inkar again, and she'd sneaked off to a knot of cheerful delegates.

"I will have some men escort you to bed. Your Grace must be up in five hours, and we have a long itinerary tomorrow."

I noted the two men who stood next to him, all leather and steel. He wanted to keep me under a tighter watch. "Any chance I could make amendments to the itinerary?"

Eirhan's smile looked pained. "Your Grace is quite amusing."

"I thought so." I pushed to my feet and took Aino's hand.

Eirhan's guards flanked us, and my grip on her tightened involuntarily. Inkar joined us as we approached the doors of the hall.

The trip to the royal wing was silent. I didn't want to risk saying anything that the guards could take back to their master. When we arrived, the guards detached, nodded to Viljo and my other personal guard, and took up their posts on either side of the double doors. If I tried to leave through that entrance, they'd stop me or tell Eirhan.

"We have adapted one of the rooms of the wing for you, Your Grace," Aino told Inkar as soon as we were on the other side of the door.

Inkar blinked. "I am not going into another room."

Aino's voice turned sharp. "You aren't staying with Ekata."

"That choice is not for a servant to make," Inkar said. She turned to me. "Am I to go home to my father and tell him that you used me as a pawn? That you have endangered our relationship with Kylma?"

"That's not what I'm doing." The lie sounded weak.

"Prove it," Inkar said, and this time that challenging smile, the one she turned on Sigis and Eirhan, was for me.

I knew what Father would do. He'd always called Mother's bluff. But Inkar could cause me far too much trouble, and she was more useful as my ally than as my enemy. I was tired of everyone fighting around me. And I had to get up in five hours. "You're my wife. You choose where you sleep."

We walked to my door together, and Inkar remained in my antechamber as Aino and I retreated within. Aino undressed me in silence and brushed out my hair as I wiped my face clean with a warm cloth. "Just because she's nice to you doesn't put her on your side," Aino said at last.

"I know." But a dozen people could depose or kill me. Inkar wanted to keep me around.

Inkar came in and slid under the covers with a contented groan. Aino doused all the candles but one and banked the fire. "If you need anything," she said, her eyes flickering to Inkar.

"I'll call for you." I leaned in and pressed my cheek to hers. "I promise I'll be fine."

My bones hurt; my body ached. My eyes felt as though I'd dipped them in the water Below and popped them back into their sockets. But Inkar's presence was a thread unraveling my attention. Her hair splayed over the pillow like a corona, and her dark eyelashes were like a smudge of ink against her cheeks. She looked soft, as though she'd taken off a piece of invisible armor. As though she needed *me* to protect *her*.

No. Inkar didn't need me, and I certainly didn't need to have mushy thoughts about her. I went into my antechamber and sat at my desk, lighting the candle under the inkwell and picking up Farhod's technical drawing of a fishman's heart. With a sluggish hand, I began copying the labels. My eyes fought me every step of the way, and my hands began to shake with cold.

After ten minutes or so, I heard the covers pull back. A moment later, Inkar appeared in the doorway. "Are you truly so afraid of me?" she asked, and I could tell the invisible armor was back.

I cupped one hand around the ink candle for a tiny bit of warmth. "I'm not afraid of you. I..."

"You merely married me to avoid marrying him."

I nearly dropped my pen, catching it by the nib and smearing ink over my palm. I muttered a curse as I set it down. "That's not true," I said in a voice that convinced no one.

Inkar cocked her head. "Then why did you do it?"

The seconds stretched. Eirhan was going to eviscerate me. Inkar blinked. My cheeks began to heat, and I scrambled for something to say. "I like hearing people complain about fish?"

Inkar laughed. There was something in that laugh—it wasn't pompous, like Bailli's, or nervous, like Urso's, or arrogant and demanding, like Sigis's. It was nice that someone thought I was funny. "Do not fear him. I would fight him for my wife's honor." She dropped her eyes to the floor and laced her fingers together. "Provided you truly wish to be my wife. Provided you meant your offer, and I don't have to write to my father."

I stifled a groan. It was too calculated a statement to be innocent, and her sly smile only confirmed it. "Of course I meant my offer," I said, and I didn't really care whether I sounded sincere or not. "May I escort you to bed?" I couldn't deny I was exhausted. Besides, I'd survived one night with her. I could do so again.

We lay down. I edged away from Inkar until my shoulder hung off the side of the bed.

"You do not have to be so awkward with me."

That was a fine thing to say after she'd all but coerced me to keep up this ruse. "Maybe I'm an awkward person."

Inkar was studying me, but not in the way Sigis did. I got the feeling she was trying to understand something in me, not strip me down until she found the right way to use me.

My heart began to skip again. But this time it wasn't accompanied by the fear of a stranger in my rooms.

"You are not awkward with Aino," she said.

"Aino is different," I replied.

"You care about her."

"Obviously."

Inkar turned onto her back. Finally, she said, her voice tentative, "Perhaps it would be of benefit to show some of that compassion. In public."

I snorted softly. "My father never showed compassion. Compassion makes greedy people reach for more. It makes hard people think you're soft." He would always rather be seen as hard than weak.

Inkar was silent for a moment. Then she said, "You do not like your father."

"Not at all," I said.

"Then why do you wish to imitate him?"

Defensiveness flared up in me. Father had ruled the duchy well. "I—he's my father. He was successfully in charge of an entire country. He must have been doing something right."

And he'd infuriated someone so much they'd decided to destroy us.

DAY THREE

CHAPTER TEN

I woke from dark, heavy dreams full of ice and roses. The night outside had cleared up; the moon had set, and the sky was a deep blue, with stars dotting it like snowflakes.

"What time is it?" I whispered.

I expected Aino to answer, but a stranger loomed over me. I jerked away, adrenaline rising. One of my sisters had sneaked in; one of them was going to kill me—but then she shifted, and I saw the dark waterfall of her hair, and I remembered all that had happened.

"I am sorry," Inkar said, and for a moment, I thought she was sorry for marrying me. "I agreed to the shooting contest this morning. I did not mean to wake you."

"Well, you did." I tugged on the blanket. My eyes felt as if I'd opened them in salt water, and my skin was slick with sweat.

I heard the soft thuds of her slippered feet as she went over to her trunk. "You may come with me, if you like."

"I'd rather go back to sleep." My pounding heart might make that difficult.

Aino opened the door a crack. "I thought I heard you," she said in her steel-cold, for-Inkar voice. "Good. A grand duke's schedule starts before dawn."

"No, thank you," I muttered.

"Eirhan's already here," she continued, as if I hadn't said anything at all. "He has your order for the day."

Of course he did. Precisely defined by him, determined by him. He had my schedule fixed from the moment I rose to after I should collapse in my bed. And I had no say in it whatsoever.

I turned to Inkar. "I'd love to watch you shoot." And Inkar's grin, conspiratorial and triumphant, gave me the flash of warmth I needed to ignore Aino's pursed lips.

The training yard was a patch of ice on our western side, maybe thirty-by-thirty feet, packed over with snow and circled by a low wall. A guardhouse, more decorative than anything else, held weaponry and targets that the weapons master hauled out and propped against the wall. Kylma Above's standing army was a joke compared with the monstrosity that lined the lake's edge, but our soldiers took pride in their work. And Below gave us the advantage we needed in times of siege.

As I sat on a bench with my coffee, Inkar handed her overcoat to Viljo and went over to the weapons master, rubbing her arms. She'd braided her hair into a long, silken rope that highlighted the length of her neck. She shook the weapons master's hand.

The Baron of Rabar arrived in a magnificent yellow cloak embroidered with red and blue poppies. He approached and knelt before me, smoothly enough that I almost missed the surprise on his face. "Your Grace honors us with her presence."

"I want to see what my wife can do," I said. I didn't mention the pleasure I got from defying Eirhan. It didn't seem like ducal behavior. "And how is your wife this morning?"

The baron's face clouded momentarily. "She is well, I assure you," he said. "She wished to travel, but she's resting after the birth of our son." He got to his feet, crunching snowpack.

I'd seen the baron with a pretty woman in velvet. "I . . ."

"You must take Her Grace's greetings home with you," Eirhan said, coming up behind us. "Please, don't let us interrupt your match."

The baron went to join Inkar. Inkar clasped his hand and said something that made him chuckle. As they took their bows from the weapons master, Eirhan said quietly, "The young lady the baron brought with him from Rabar is not his wife."

"I gathered that," I said.

"You have insulted him by inferring that he *ought* to have brought his wife."

"I'll be extra complimentary at dinner," I offered.

He sat on the bench next to me. "I told you to remember who brought their mistresses."

"You tell me a lot of things, Eirhan."

"Perhaps you understand why, Your Grace."

I didn't answer. For a while we watched Inkar and the baron as they nocked arrows and let them fly. The baron's struck right on the line between the center and the closest ring. Inkar's was almost dead in the middle.

"Minister Urso is meeting the delegate of Avythera," Eirhan said as Inkar and the baron shook hands and trooped to the targets to retrieve their arrows. "He'll join us shortly."

Avythera wasn't the largest country in the North, and it wasn't our neighbor, but it did have important trade routes. And Sigis wanted it. He'd prattled at me for ages about it the night before last. It said something about us both that I couldn't remember the details.

"Why not bring out the rest of the council?" I said. "We can have our meeting right here."

"Don't tempt me," Eirhan said. "Anything to get Your Grace to sit still."

Urso trotted up to us, pulling his scarf down and bowing low. "Your Grace. I'm sorry I'm late." He cast about for a suitable place to sit, but when he saw the only option was on the bench next to Eirhan, he elected to stand, clasping his hands together and bouncing on the balls of his feet. "The delegate from Avythera was...eager to speak on the matter of our agreement. And passionate."

"And what did he have to say?" Maybe that would clue me in as to what the agreement was actually about.

"He was, ah, interested in striking up an independent relationship with Your Grace." Urso gulped. "As opposed to with her father."

Urso looked at me. Eirhan looked at me. I tried to look clever. Eirhan took a deep breath. "The Avythera agreement was a free-trade agreement between Kylma Above, Drysiak, Avythera, and Solarkyet. Your father withdrew from the agreement when Solarkyet revolted, and imposed a restriction on the number of foreign goods Kylmian traders can purchase. He wishes them to spend their money at home." Eirhan smiled pointedly at Urso. "And I suppose the delegate wishes us to spend it abroad."

Urso shifted from foot to foot as he tried to find some way to sweeten his words. "Very much so," he finally said.

I ran over what he said twice more in my head. "Why not trade abroad? Won't it be better for our standing?" I asked.

Urso's head bobbed. "Your Grace is correct, naturally. But your father had his reasons. And Sigis has made us a counteroffer to make exclusive trading agreements with Drysiak instead."

I looked at Eirhan. "Any special requirements to that counteroffer?"

"I'm sure Sigis would adjust his offer if your relationship was...of a closer nature than trade partners," Eirhan said. He turned back to Urso, who was trying to cover his confusion by inclining his head. "Is Avythera aware of Sigis's counter?"

"They have threatened to declare war if the agreement is not ratified," Urso said, drawing his shoulders in as though he expected me to shout at him.

War in my first week sounded about right for the way things were going. But Eirhan laughed. "What a ridiculous notion."

"Which agreement do you think is best? Sigis's, theirs, or ours?" I asked Urso.

Eirhan cut in before he could answer. "Your father destroyed whatever good faith we had with them. Consider Sigis's offer carefully—and don't make him angrier." He flapped a hand at Urso in clear dismissal. "Have a copy of the agreement sent to Her Grace."

Urso hesitated. I opened my mouth to tell him he could stay. But I took too long, and he bowed deeply and hurried off.

Some grand duke I was turning out to be. I sighed, watching my breath puff out. "I wanted his opinion, not yours," I grumbled.

He snorted. "Why? The only opinion he'd offer is the one he thinks would make you happiest."

That was probably truer than I'd like. "Fine. Now what?"

"The day's order, naturally." He produced it and handed it over. "We can discuss it as you relax and...enjoy yourself?"

214

Truth be told, my fingers and toes were feeling the bite of the cold, but inside meant more conversations I didn't understand, conversations that Eirhan could use to manipulate me and to push me toward Sigis.

First: breakfast. I rolled my eyes. Next, a meeting with the delegate of Avythera, which I'd missed. I had a council meeting soon, then some ceremony to thank the rejected delegates of the brideshow. More meetings, more arguments, more everything. I scanned the list a couple of times before handing it back. "I was hoping to spend time with Farhod."

Eirhan pursed his lips. "There's simply no time to spend. You have to put your scientific interests on hold, for now." *And possibly forever*, he didn't say, but I heard it all the same.

"I need to figure out how this illness works," I said. "Do you want my family to die?"

Eirhan drew back in astonishment. "What a thing to say, Your Grace. But I wonder at the idea that you, and you alone, can save them. *Minister Farhod* needs to find out how the illness works. Your time is better spent elsewhere."

"I suppose Farhod could save them, too," I muttered, blushing.

"Your Grace's loyalty to your family is admirable," Eirhan said. "But I have called for every doctor in Kylma Above to attend at the royal palace, and they have been trained and educated in ways you have not. They can see to your family while you prepare for the possibility that you will be on the throne for the rest of your life. If your family never wakes, what then? How will you ensure that the city Above remains safe? When will you start taking this seriously?"

I *did* take this seriously. Seriously enough to dive into the work of finding a cure myself. I was taking this seriously enough not to trust Eirhan. But he had a point. I needed to act like a duke. I had to be ready to seize power.

Inkar and the baron shot three rounds in all. She won two; he won one. "Have you thought about how you'll get her to renege after the trial period?" Eirhan said.

"Maybe I could...talk to her." I decided not to tell him that she'd already worked out my awkward position. Inkar laughed at something the baron said, and they shook hands again in mock-solemnity before making their way slowly toward us.

Eirhan pinched the bridge of his nose. "Please do not tell her you want to break the marriage," he said, as though he were explaining politics to a child. "The more leverage she has, the more damage she can do. She could demand that you give her treaties, or land, or any number of things to get you to call off the marriage."

If she had such leverage, why hadn't she used it yet? "Well, she seems to be settling in."

"That is precisely what you were supposed to keep her from doing," Eirhan said. "Make her feel unwelcome. So unwelcome that the position of grand consort isn't enough to tempt her to stay."

"How?"

Eirhan glared at me in exasperation. "You're your father's daughter; act like it."

Why do you wish to imitate him? Inkar's question resonated in my mind, and I couldn't justify an answer. Especially when it came to how my parents treated each other. I didn't know how they'd ended up in their poisonous marriage, but it felt wrong to crack open their relationship and use it to hurt other people. Surely I could get Inkar to break the agreement some other way.

Sigis strode up as Inkar and the baron did, cloak flapping at his ankles. "Your Grace. And...Your Grace." He smiled coldly at Inkar, who returned the favor. Sigis nodded to the baron. "I trust you're upholding the Rabari traditions of good shooting."

"I'm afraid my paltry skills are no match for Her Grace's," the baron replied. Why couldn't I be more like him in politics—smooth and suave and in control?

"I don't believe it. You weren't going easy on her, were you?"

Inkar's eyes flashed. "Would you?" Her bow came up a fraction.

Sigis beckoned the weapons master. "Of course not. But I'm a man well aware of my faults. I'm not one to put courtesy above competition."

I choked back a snort at that.

Inkar went to the target. Sigis tested a bow, shook his head, but took up a place beside her.

"If they attempt to kill each other in earnest, you will be held responsible," Eirhan muttered out of the side of his mouth.

"Understood. Viljo?" I said. "Keep Her Grace and King Sigis from murdering each other."

"I'm serious," Eirhan said as the shooting began again. "Sigis should never have won the will of the archimandrite. If you don't want him to win the trial Below, you'll need to give Below a reason to support you instead."

"The duke Below *begged* me to start the coronation trials."

"If I may give Your Grace some political advice: Never assume that your allies will have to take your side. They might have options that you never considered. And even if the trial Below is an easy victory, the trial for the people may not be. Every time Sigis speaks to one of your ministers, he threatens you." Eirhan rubbed his face. "Marrying him might be more than the convenient solution. If he defeats you in all the trials, it might be the only way to preserve your life."

I wondered if his insistence that I marry Sigis was about more than preserving my life. What sort of deals had they made with each other? Eirhan couldn't have been the voice I'd heard in the law library. But he could have manipulated the person I'd heard.

Sigis and Inkar shot. Sigis's aim was dead in the center of the target; Inkar's was off by a hair. Sigis all but strutted to examine his arrow.

"I'm going Below today," I decided.

Eirhan coughed. "Your Grace, that's simply impossible. Arrangements must be made—"

"I thought it was your role to *advise*." I didn't look at him, but I could feel the anger radiating from Eirhan like heat.

"His Grace the Duke of Kylma Below invited you once. That doesn't make Below an extension of your land, which you may visit whenever you like. The duke Below must be aware and willing to receive you."

"It's important."

"Why?" he demanded. He sounded angry, but when I didn't answer, the air between us became thicker, prickling not with anger but with unease. "Your Grace, what's so important about going Below now?"

At the end of the yard, Inkar held herself stiffly as she shook Sigis's hand. I watched Sigis and Inkar troop back and draw again.

"Does it have something to do with the illness?"

"Never mind," I said, and squared my shoulders.

Inkar lost the second round, and the third. Her smile became more and more brittle, threatening to snap every time Sigis said something like, "Well, I do have experience with war," or, "I learned that trick at the battle of Bledna."

She didn't throw her bow to the ground, though it looked as though she wanted to. Her gloved hand clenched around it, and instead, she strode over to me. She took my hand carefully, gently, and pressed her lips to it. "Is our guest not accomplished?" Her merry tone was strained.

"I used to watch him shoot all the time," I said, attempting to shrug it off.

Sigis raised an eyebrow. "I didn't realize you paid me so much mind back then, Your Grace."

Ew. Disgusting. Don't throw up. "Weapons practice was mandatory, and you were always best at it."

"I came here to shoot against the baron," Inkar said. Her low voice was soft, on the verge of threatening. "I came here to use my axes on you."

"If you're looking for another lesson, I'm happy to oblige." Sigis drew his sword and moved away from her, swinging it in a figure eight pattern.

Inkar drew her axes, laughing as Viljo stepped smartly between her and me.

"Viljo, you may stand down," I said.

"No, Your Grace."

Eirhan nodded in approval. "Don't even try, Your Grace. I told Viljo that protecting you sometimes included ignoring you."

I glared at Eirhan and settled back on the bench. The golden detail on Inkar's axes caught the light. She lunged forward, hooking one ax over Sigis's sword and pulling it down as she swung the other. He danced back, pulling his sword free and counterattacking in a smooth, strong movement that made Inkar duck and slide backward.

She parried his next attack, deflecting the blade, and jabbed at him. He sidestepped, and her ax chipped into the ice. Sigis swung down, hard. Inkar rolled to the side, and his sword bounced off her handle. She lunged to her feet, slipping on the snow, one ax down. She breathed hard, shifting her grip.

My heart pulsed hard enough to make my deep fur collar vibrate. I sucked in a freezing breath. Sigis couldn't kill her. He wouldn't be so stupid.

The savage triumph in his eyes did not comfort me.

"Need a break?" Sigis asked.

"Of course not," she puffed. "Why would I make it easier for you?"

She attacked again, ducked a counterattack, and ripped her ax out of the ice. Her body rippled like silk, fluid and graceful and breathtaking. I'd never have stood a chance against her. But I could see that Sigis was even better.

Sigis parried easily, sliding his blade under her arm to rip her vest. He bared his teeth. His face lit with joy. His blade flashed in the sunlight, too fast to follow. It would be so easy to manufacture an accident. Suddenly, I remembered the time he shot Velosha in the shoulder. It had been impossible for her to prove that Sigis was the culprit, but I'd seen him pull the bowstring.

Sigis laughed and spun away as Inkar lunged, slamming the flat of his sword against her ribs. Inkar gasped and fell to her knees.

I launched to my feet. "Viljo!"

The dutiful Viljo trooped between Sigis and Inkar. Sigis backed off, still laughing. "You can't let me win so easily, Your Grace."

I extended my hand to Inkar, but she got to her feet on her own. Her eyes burned. "I am not finished."

"We're all finished," I said in my best Mother voice. Maybe the tone would mask the fear. Inkar might act invincible, but she had ten pints of blood, just like everyone else. And I wouldn't let Sigis spill even one drop. "I have meetings, and I don't give you permission to murder each other while I'm gone."

Sigis's bloodlust smile turned on me. "I take offense at that. I had no intention of causing *her lady* harm." I was sure he'd forgotten to call Inkar *consort* on purpose. He sheathed his sword and let his lip curl contemptuously. "I thought she'd be a more formidable opponent."

I offered Inkar my arm. Her fingers tightened around my wrist as we began to walk. I shook with fury, and so did she, but we steadied each other. Neither of us could laugh him off, but neither of us would bow to him.

"I'll see Your Grace at lunch," Sigis called after me.

"I think," Inkar said softly, in a voice full of pain. "I think I quite despise him."

CHAPTER ELEVEN

B ack in my rooms, Inkar sat by the fire, and I picked up
a bowl of porridge that had gone cold. Farhod had left
a note on the curse's progress—neither better nor worse.
My family had been moved into my father's suite, which
was the only place they would all fit, and arguing doctors
crowded around them, draining their lungs and trying cures
for pneumonia.

We weren't getting anywhere with solutions Above. I
hesitated over a note, but when Eirhan poked his head in
to summon me to my council meeting, I dropped a hasty
and probably impolite request into the messenger bowl in
the family library. Then I spooned up the last of my porridge, took a cup of coffee from Aino, and followed Eirhan
to the council chamber.

I didn't realize the depth of trouble I was in until we

entered. Reko's eyes glittered with malice as they followed me from the door to my seat at the head of the table. Urso sweated next to him, and Yannush kept his bulging eyes on the table. Annika sat in whispered conference with Itilya. Only Rafyet presented a friendly face. *One of you*, I thought. One of them had to be the whispered voice in the law library.

We discussed minor issues between delegates for a drowsy, wasted half hour. Then we moved on to Farhod's report. "No change," Eirhan said. "Their illness seems to be stable. And no new reports of infection." I wondered, not for the first time, if he knew it wasn't an illness at all.

"Because it's fake." Reko waved a hand. "Whatever poison you've used, we'll find it."

"Watch your tongue," Eirhan warned him.

"Why? Will Her Grace, the *provisional* grand duke, have me poisoned, too? Or will she merely ransack my offices for no reason?"

I hardened my voice. "I don't see why I shouldn't."

"I'm not surprised. We've all seen how far you'll go to get your way—"

"Enough," Eirhan said. I pushed down my anger. I should be the one to bring Reko to heel. "One way or another, Ekaterina is grand duke. Unless Sigis wins the trials."

Bailli waved a hand. "Surely he can be persuaded to forfeit. What does he want?"

"Besides winning? He wants to marry Ekaterina," Eirhan said.

There was a short, ugly silence. "How do you know this?" Itilya asked.

"It is the way he can best legitimize himself. The citizens of Kylma Above may be grumbling, but they're not in open revolt yet. People will adjust to him better if he marries into the family."

"And the trial marriage?" Annika said.

"We all know the girl can't be grand consort." Eirhan didn't even say Inkar's name, and I flashed hot with anger.

"We can pick a different brideshow delegate. There are many other young ladies to choose from if Her Grace is not partial to anyone else," Rafyet suggested.

"Why not make Sigis consort instead?" Bailli said. "Remove him from the trials, place Ekata in the lead, retain the line. When her family is revived, we don't have to bother with the question of succession. She can go to Drysiak; things resume as normal."

I opened my mouth to tell him *he* could marry Sigis and move to Drysiak if he loved the idea so much. But my ministers, only newly reminded of my existence, had no trouble talking over me.

"Impossible," Itilya said. Her clear blue eyes and raised chin didn't look to me as if she'd be caught sniveling under Sigis in the library.

Yannush's eyes darted around the table, like an eel sizing up the smallest, weakest fish. "Not to mention, what happens if her family is *not* revived?"

Reko nodded and crossed his arms. "I agree. That plan could backfire and leave Sigis in charge of the duchy. Though, of course, if Ekata were removed immediately—"

"And allow Sigis to win the coronation trials by forfeiture?" Eirhan said.

Reko's smile was sharklike. "Parliament."

Annika tugged at the collar of their coat, eyeing me from beneath their lashes. "A parliament would keep things stable."

"It would allow for an equal discussion," Yannush said.

"It would put less pressure on Your Grace," Urso said to me.

"It's not up for debate." My voice echoed loud and harsh in the room. "You're my advisory council. You *advise* me. You don't decide whether we get a parliament or whom I marry."

Reko looked as though he very much wanted to disagree. But Eirhan shuffled his papers, and we moved on to the Avythera problem. Avythera had put us under embargo, which was starting to affect our charcoal and firewood stores. The kingdom of Rabar had provided us with some aid, but unless we found another source of trade—or cracked their negotiations—we'd be up against a wall.

Arguments flurried around me like snow, and names I couldn't keep track of flew back and forth across the table. Reko sneered, while Annika seemed to lose their train of thought whenever they caught me watching them. Yannush swung his head back and forth until he made me dizzy. They could all be betraying me in a thousand different ways. I tried to ground myself in logic. What did they want? What could be their motives? But the reality was, I knew my ministers as well as I knew the guests in my palace: not at all.

The conversation changed faster than I could open my mouth. Ministers weaved old debates into new ones, referencing problems and people they'd been discussing long before I became grand duke.

I focused on my coffee, on the table—oak, sturdy, used in shipbuilding and storage and to make half-timber walls for some of the houses in the city. From there I went to the tapestries. Bears, wolves, marmots, snow hares, pastoral scenes from the mountains surrounding the duchy Above. The corners were embroidered with plants that thrived in the cold and had various medicinal properties. Before I knew it, Eirhan was calling the meeting to a close, and I'd missed more than half. If I'd hoped to win anyone to my side during the cabinet meeting, I was a dismal failure.

I left the room first so that Eirhan couldn't block my exit and make me feel useless, or come up with more ways for me to flirt with Sigis. I was tempted to give Reko the parliament he wanted so I'd never have to sit through a meeting like that again.

As I entered the royal wing, Viljo trotted up. "Your Grace, I have been given the preliminary results of the audit. Everything seems to be in order. Bailli is...scrupulous with his funds and how he tracks them."

I bit my lip instead of letting Viljo bear the brunt of my

frustration. I didn't have time to chase after the wrong culprits. "Maybe he has a second set of books."

"It's possible, Your Grace." Viljo sounded as though he believed the exact opposite.

"Do you have a list of transactions involving magic?" I asked.

"Yes. The last person to requisition magic from the treasury was Minister Farhod, four weeks ago, and that was an order of raw magic."

Out of the question. It wasn't Farhod. "Who else?"

"Your Grace, may I say something?" Viljo asked.

You just did. "Go ahead."

"Minister Olloi reported broken locks on the gate to Below. Two, maybe three, weeks back. He said nothing had been vandalized or stolen, but..."

But no one would break into the entrance to Below for reasons of theft. They'd break the gate to go...Below. "I presume the guard told someone."

"An official report was made, which went to the captain, Your Grace. He would have told Prime Minister Eirhan if he felt the crime constituted a threat."

So. Not only did I need to ask Below for help breaking the curse, but I needed to accuse them of hosting visitors behind my back. Wonderful.

Aino waited in my rooms, fixing one of my shoes so that the iron spike on the side was firmly attached again. "Farhod came by," she said.

"What did he say?"

"He didn't look happy. Said something about a fluid increase in the lungs. Certainly nothing about your family getting better."

I tried to bury my frustration on that, too. It wasn't Farhod's fault that the search for the remedy was going poorly. "Anything else?"

"There's a message on your desk." She frowned at my shoe.

I went over. My heart skipped a beat as I spotted the pale green paper.

> *Your request for an audience has been granted.*
> *Yours in friendship, etc.*

"Get me a change of clothes," I told Aino. "We're going Below."

Olloi met me at the entrance to Below. His unblinking eyes examined my hands, then my belt. "Your Grace risks great offense by going Below without a gift." Olloi unlocked the rusted padlock that secured the iron bar across the door.

"I'll have one sent. Below knows we're living in unusual circumstances." Besides, could they afford to offend *me*? I was the head of a sovereign nation, one that Below relied on for any contact with the world above. "How fast does that lock rust?"

"One or two years, Your Grace. We're due a replacement."

"Hmm." Had Viljo been lying to me about the break-in, or was Olloi lying to me now?

I caught a flash of silver beneath the dark water. My problems Above would have to wait. Aino helped me out of my dress and finished pinning my hair to my head. "Are you sure about this?" she murmured.

"I'm sure." I wondered whether to say something to Olloi, but Meire's crest lifted above the surface of the lake, and I was out of time. Better for me to act once I had more information.

I slid into the water, gasping as my muscles seized. A hand found mine and tugged me down until I was face-to-face with Meire. Meire's fingers brushed over my eyes and lips. The pressure on my lungs lifted, and I let the excess air go in a stream of bubbles.

Meire coiled her lithe green body in a bow. "Hail, Your Grace." We began to swim down together. "We were delighted by your request to meet again so soon," she said.

"I wish it were under better circumstances," I admitted. "But an urgent matter has come up." Or two.

The ice creaked above us, pale, dotted with seaweed and thick as any of the city walls. A long line ran where something's dorsal fin had scratched against it. Soon it disappeared as we swam into the gloom and the darkness enveloped us.

Meire flipped her feet, pulling up short. "Hold out your hand," she said.

I hesitated. "Can...can I try?"

"Magic is notoriously fickle around your kind," she warned me, but a moment later, I felt the soft press of her hand on mine. The pearl was slick and a little bit slimy. I focused, pushing my mind toward light and vision, and squeezed my fist until I felt the pearl burst between my fingers.

I felt that tug, as though the magic drew on some part of me I couldn't name. Then I cried out as a stabbing pain shot up my arm. Light flared from Meire's hand. Long, thick spines, red at the base and fading to white, ran up my arm, ending in wicked points. The skin around them swelled. I touched one gingerly; it was rubbery beneath my finger and I winced as it bent, pulling the skin beneath.

Meire hissed something, and her long fingers pressed against the base of the spines. "Perhaps we should fix this before we visit my duke."

"Sorry." I should've let Meire do her job, instead of wasting time and fixating on a magic I couldn't master. "I just..." Again, I hesitated. But whom else could I tell this to? Meire had been kind to me before she'd had to be. "The grand duke is the only one Above who can do magic."

"Yes," Meire said. She did not look at me but tugged a spine free, leaving a white welt behind. I clenched my fist. It felt like pulling needles.

"I sort of thought"—*hoped*—"that when I became grand duke, I'd inherit the secret." It sounded foolish when I put it that way. The knowledge wouldn't simply appear in my head.

"It is a symbol of trust between us," Meire said. "The greatest secret. I know my duke is eager to give it to you once the coronation trials are over."

"Do you know it?"

Meire went still, one hand holding mine, the other pinching a spine near my wrist. I shouldn't have asked. All the same, if she truly was debating telling me...

She spoke carefully, quietly, focusing on my arm. "When I was learning, my tutors always said that the secret to magic was inside us." Her wide eyes darted to mine, and she blinked.

I squeezed her hand in return. I knew it was more than she should have told me, and warmth filled me that she'd answered at all.

But it wasn't enough. I needed to search until I held the secret of magic in my hands. If I did that, my council would forget Sigis even existed.

No one had prepared for my arrival Below. Figures crowded the processional way, haggling with vendors who wore suspended cages of corroding iron and nets of seaweed. Scales shone in the bioluminescent light, red and green and blue, and black eyes gleamed. Fishwives hung fish, still breathing, from chains at their shoulders. Seaweed reached green-black fingers out, brushing at the finned feet of the crowd. Tiny sharks stole from their wares.

"Is it a market day?" I couldn't help asking.

Meire moved her head, and a cloud of silver fish around

her mane shivered and dissipated. "Every day is a market day. But come. The grand duke knows that you are here."

Together we swam on. As the fishwives saw us, their bodies moved in surprise, curling in deference and undulating as they swam out of the way. Spikes glistened on elbows and arms. I wondered if they were there by magic, as mine had been.

The sea shifted and pulled us toward the palace. I held tightly to Meire's arm, keeping my feet up so I could avoid the reaching fronds and the tiny figures that darted between them.

The guards at the palace gates bowed and moved to the side, and we swam into darkened halls. The shadows seemed to have grown since I'd swum here last—was it only two days ago? Something roiled in a corner, flicking a tentacle out to test the water as we passed.

We stopped at the entrance to the duke's throne room. Meire released my hand. Her black eyes seemed pensive. "What is it?" I said.

"My master…" she began, but she didn't seem to know how to finish. Her shoulders hunched, and she turned toward the guards, bowing. The guards at the inner doors opened up, and I swam into the throne room once again.

It was much darker than it had been the other day. The glow of the bioluminescence illuminated silhouettes more than faces, and I saw only thin slices of body and fin as they swam in from the edges of the room. The half-cages that held the grand duke and the grand consort Below were barely visible in the gloom, and my skin was the pale grayish-blue of bodies shortly before we burned them. I bowed.

"We must apologize for the lack of light," came the grand duke's voice from a shadow in front of me. "We don't have as much need of it as your kind do. But we will bring a lamp, and we will talk of treaties and good friendships together."

I swallowed, rallying my courage. "How can you be so certain that I am the one you should treat with?"

"Whom else would I treat with?" the duke Below replied, and the amusement in his voice was diminished.

I wished I could take a deep breath, or tighten my grip around something heavy and protective, like a sword. "You declared my foster brother eligible to defeat me in your trial."

There was movement, an eddying of water. The winter roses above us refracted the dim light, glinting like razors. "He is of the line," the duke Below said, and, suddenly, the shape of him loomed before me, a shadow in front of shadows. The spines at his elbows were tipped in yellow. A warning to predators? Was it significant that he was the grand duke and that his spurs were a different color? *Focus.*

Father was a large man, but the duke Below had to be nine feet from crown to toes. His shoulders were broad, and his arms powerful with muscle. I could see no sympathy in his eyes. I knew if I tried to flee, I wouldn't stand a chance. I had to use my words—the words I was so terrible with

Above. "We do not meddle in the affairs of Above." His teeth flashed in the gloom. "Unless..." He extended a hand, and a servant set a roll of seaweed paper into it.

The agreement. I should just sign it. But even I wasn't foolish enough to sign a contract I hadn't read. "Send it to my prime minister," I said.

The duke Below's voice was low in my mind, and did I imagine the cold current that wrapped around my limbs? "You do not have much time."

"Nevertheless." There was no reason to feel anxious. No reason to panic. "I came here to investigate magic, not negotiate." Not until I had a stronger grasp of the situation.

His fins swished. "You *are* bold. I respected your father, for all we disagreed. I hope it is not a mistake to extend the same courtesy to you."

"No," I said, feeling the rising panic. "I want to work with you. I only..." I told him of my suspicion that someone had been Below without me.

The duke's eyes gleamed. "I have given your liaison dispensation to escort you wherever you need to go." His smile grew, and I imagined those teeth fastening around me, dragging me down to the seaweed of the royal road, to lie among the picked bones. "Come and go as you need, if you think you can discover defiance of my law, Your Grace."

His words were the height of generosity. His tone was a warning. I bowed and allowed the guard to see me out.

Meire waited for me outside. "I will take you to the treasury," she said. "But would you like to see the fields where we grow it first?"

"Grow what?" I asked.

"The magic."

My heart quickened against my ribs. "Lead the way."

Magic came from a particular type of seaweed, Meire explained as we swam. It produced little white flowers, which, in turn, produced bloodred stamen, which, in turn, produced sap that beaded and congealed into the pearls that Meire kept in a little pouch on her belt.

"And you use it every day?" I said, still astonished.

"We do have it in excess," Meire pointed out.

"Isn't it dangerous to use it so much?" I said.

Meire's head tilted. "Why would it be?"

Because magic was unstable. Because magic was expensive. Because magic was uncontrollable. But only Above.

We swam away from the palace complex and its swooping walls. Eels darted from coral gardens. Citizens swam among them, seemingly unbothered by sharks and seven-foot fish. Rocks jutted from the lake floor, and in the small, cavernous spaces fish nibbled at algae.

Meire stopped at the edge of the city and unhooked a lantern from its post, showing me the space where pearls of magic were inserted so that light would be emitted. "We will be going into the dark. Can you hold the lamp?" I pressed my hand against the fungal sentinels, reveling in the spongy feel of them, then took the lamp by its glass handle, another item they must have traded for with Above. Meire's hand grasped mine again, and she drew a six-foot spear from the sheath at her back. The tip thinned to a barbed point. The wood was soft and rotted in places, the iron point browned and flaked. "What is that for?" I asked.

"It is only a precaution," Meire said. Precaution against what? It looked like I could snap that spear in half. She pushed aside the lights of the city, and we swam out into the dark.

I held the lamp before me, but it illuminated only a small swath of water in front of us. Meire swung her spear slowly through the water, and ink-black shapes moved out of our way. More sentinels, I hoped. "Does anything ever attack you out here?"

"You hunt Above, do you not?" Meire said. "We hunt, too. The fish you catch Above are the slow, stupid ones. For us, it is a rite of passage to go into the deep, to pursue the angriest and largest of creatures."

"What did you fight?" I asked.

Meire hesitated. It occurred to me that perhaps it was too personal a question, that I'd put her on the spot by asking something she didn't want to answer but couldn't refuse a grand duke. "Never mind. I'm sorry."

"Do not be sorry." Meire moved her right arm closer to the lamp, and I saw a spiral of perfect rings winding from her elbow to her wrist. "It was a . . . squid, you might call it."

"A kraken?" I guessed.

A stream of bubbles hissed out of Meire's teeth. Had I made her laugh? "Nothing so large," she said. "I am alive, after all."

"What's the largest thing anyone's ever killed down here?" I asked.

"Ah. That was many hundreds of years ago. It was a shark as large as the city itself. It is said that one tooth was the size of a whole man. He swallowed entire villages, until a hero resolved to be the one to end his terrifying control over us. That was *our* first grand duke."

"Did he defeat it?" I asked.

"He beseeched his brother from Above for iron and fashioned a spear and an enormous bow to launch it. Our mer-wives stood as bait. When the shark attacked, our grand duke killed it with one shot. It is said the shark's blood flowed over the lake floor, creating the carnivorous processional road. The meat served for a feast that united all the people Below."

"And the skeleton?"

"Became the walls of the grand duke's palace." Now it was my turn to laugh. "Consider it," she suggested.

I thought of the gleaming walls, their polished stone. They looked more like volcanic rock than cartilage, as romantic as the legend sounded. Maybe the grand duke would grant me leave to take a small sample of the building material, and Farhod could help me analyze it.

But my first priority was to find out how someone Above had gotten magic and learned how to use it. My second was to figure out a cure for my family. And when I managed that, I'd probably have to leave Kylma before I could learn more about Below—before my father decided I was too much of a threat.

Meire put her hand over mine and lifted the lamp. Something dark fluttered away from the lantern light. "We are here."

The magic fields stretched dark over the lake floor, dotted with pale, round blooms like the moon at its peak. As light fell on them, a few flowers swiveled toward the lantern. I caught the glint of red stamens, and the shining, pearlescent sap at their center.

Farhod had one tiny jar of pearls, allotted by the treasury once a year. Here were thousands of them, nestled in paper-thin petals—the wealth of Kylma and more.

I ran my hand over a velvet-soft bloom. The pearl's skin broke, leaving a trail of glittering white across the dark water. The trail grew fins, a tail, a gaping jaw—and my finger, smeared with sap, became long and pointed, as pale as bone and as ridged as a tooth. I reached for the little fish, and at the touch of magic upon magic, it splintered into shards of ice, to be snatched up by even smaller fish that flashed beneath the flowers. They swarmed my finger, nipping at the remains of the magic, softening the look of my hand until only the shadow of scales remained. Then they darted back to the protection of the seaweed.

"Amazing," I said, bringing my finger close to my face.

"The pearls aren't so fragile Above." My fingers glowed a moment with the final traces of magic, then faded to their dull, pale human forms.

"These are not entirely ready to be harvested. We allow the pearls to mature before sending shipments Above. It hardens their skin and makes them less potent."

"But it means that anything you shipped Above would have been sent within a certain time frame," I guessed. That was a start. "Meire, how does a curse work?"

Her hand tightened fractionally against mine. "It is entirely a matter of will. Of the actor."

"I don't suppose you know how to cure one?"

Was it wishful thinking, or did she hesitate for a moment? "No, Your Grace."

"Hmm." I sighed, releasing a stream of bubbles even though I wasn't technically breathing. The nearest flowers danced in the little current I'd created. The ground beneath them swarmed with life. Everything over the fields seemed to shimmer. "Why grow the magic all the way out here? Why not within the city?"

"The flowers require the dark," Meire replied.

"And what lies beyond this?"

"The deep places." Meire's forearm turned so that I could see the puckered scars again. "Do you really wish to see...?"

I laughed. "It's not necessary. This time."

"You are a curious one," Meire said. "It is a trait we like Below."

"Lucky me."

We turned away from the fields and made our way back toward the archives. "Do you wish me to take the lantern?" Meire asked as we swam.

"Does that mean I can try the spear?" I said.

A trail of laughter escaped from her mouth. "My master would be most displeased if you stabbed something by accident. I regret that I must keep the spear."

"It was worth a try." I felt Meire's hand squeeze briefly around mine.

We swam back into the city. I tried to imagine it as it once was, according to Meire's tale—a barren rock bottom swarming with frightened citizens Below. One fishman, with a seaweed mane and shoulders like an aurochs, winding a winch that would launch a spear the length of my Great Hall. A shark with a great, gaping mouth, with teeth the size of my father, eyes like twin eternities. What had happened to the skin of such a creature? Was the wide arch of the palace truly part of its nose?

Meire took me to a low building on a street with more of the strange orange and green gardens that surrounded the palace walls. We swam through the wide door and into the bare foyer of the treasury. The small room had a vaulted ceiling dotted with blue fungal lamps. Long shadows moved over my arms. When I looked up, I saw only dark rock.

A fishwoman hovered before us, pressing webbed fingers together. Her scales were a deep orange-red, tinged with blue around the outside edges. Delicate fins rippled down her back, over the top of her head, down her chest. Her nose was of the flat, gill type, and her eyes had a thin orange iris. She paused before us, and Meire swam in front of me. She inclined her head, and the fishwife returned the gesture. Then Meire gestured to me.

The fishwife executed a graceful bow, fins fluttering. "Welcome, Your Grace." She turned and motioned to the guards at the end of the foyer. They opened a set of doors behind them. "Please, follow me."

We followed. My grip on Meire's hand became tighter. "Did you tell her who I was?"

"Naturally," Meire said. "I cannot simply swim to the royal treasury and demand access."

"So you can speak to other citizens Below telepathically?" This would be a fascinating tidbit to present to Farhod.

"No." But Meire sounded unsure. "It is more that...we can speak to each other without your being able to hear."

"What's the difference?"

"Your Grace, we will have the book of receipts brought up immediately," the fishwife said.

As she disappeared, I turned to Meire. "Is it possible that someone could sneak Below?"

"I do not know, Your Grace," Meire said. She kept her eyes on the room around us; clerks floated at stations set out on the walls. Iron spikes had been fastened into the walls to keep their waterproof documents from floating all over the room. Between the spikes, tapestries hung, depicting the wealth of Below—softly glowing magic, ingots of iron and electrum, scenes of trade and prosperity between citizens. "I have never known it to happen in my life. We do not *want* visitors. Present company excepted," she said, flashing her teeth at me.

"What about the moat?" I pressed. "Someone could get Below from there."

Meire's eyes widened, her mouth turning into a small O of confusion. "Swim from the moat to the city Below? That would be impossible. And the moat is patrolled. You would be..." She shook her head. "You would accuse our guard of conspiracy and treason."

My stomach jolted unpleasantly. If I wasn't careful, I'd endear myself to Below as poorly as I'd endeared myself to my ministers Above. But I had to find the answers. "What about the messenger bowls? Could someone else have used them? The way we did?"

"They are personally monitored by His Grace's staff," Meire said. "Only your family is allowed correspondence."

As far as she knew.

The treasury records came as a slim book made from pressed algae paper. Meire held the lamp above my head as I flipped through it. Harvested seaweed, fishing permits, coral, and pearls. And then came the magic.

The jars were measured by weight and stored so the pearls at the top didn't crush the ones at the bottom. I read through the ledger with growing frustration. "It's all accounted for."

"Is that not good?" Meire said. "It means that the error must come from your treasury."

"Every scrap of magic in my treasury has been accounted for, too. Any extra magic that was obtained had to come from here." I sighed as her scales rose defensively. "I'm not claiming anything. I just have to find out what happened before—" Before I lost the coronation trials. Before I had to choose between marrying Sigis and death. Before the person who created the curse turned it on me.

I ran my fingers down the ledger column, pausing when I hit a fuzzy patch. I frowned and traced over it again. "Feel this."

Meire caressed the page with her long, four-jointed finger. "I do not understand."

"Hold up the lantern." I angled the book so that the page in question was isolated in the light. The fibers were scraped and cut in a crosshatch pattern. The ink feathered lightly around them. For a moment, I was distracted by the ink. What did they use? How did they keep it from dissolving? "It's been scraped," I said. Like vellum when Farhod needed to amend a report. "Look at this." I flipped to an earlier page. "The addition was off in this column, so the accountant corrected it by scratching out the number and writing the correction in a free space."

"And added a signature." Meire indicated a squiggle of ink. My stomach lurched. "To verify that the change was valid. In case anyone had a question later. Meire, this means that whoever changed this number, here where it's scraped, didn't have permission. They covered it up by changing the ledger. Whoever it was could be our illegal seller."

"His Grace will be displeased," Meire murmured.

But I wasn't. I finally had solid evidence there was a buyer from Above.

Chapter Twelve

Meire took me back to the surface and released my hand to bow. "Thank you for your help," I said. "And thank His Grace for allowing it."

"I am honored to assist you," Meire said. "You are welcome Below any time you might wish. Merely send word."

"Could you send news?" I said. "If you find out who altered the ledger?"

"I will do everything within my power." Her crest flattened slightly, and her feet swished from side to side. Finally, she added, "And if you address a note to me, only I will see it."

Without thinking, I held up my hand. Meire's pressed against it. Her longer fingers and wide palm dwarfed my own, and for a moment, I wondered if magic properly applied could bridge that gap, give me fins for toes and webbed fingers, a new life Below. "Thank you."

Her hand separated from mine, pressed against my nose and mouth. A prickle started in my lungs. She flipped and swam down, down into the dark.

I kicked upward toward the hole in the ice that was the entrance to my duchy and surfaced with a gasp. Aino and Viljo hastened to pull me out of the water, and Aino hurried me behind a screen to change before my shirt could freeze to my body.

"Please tell me you found something useful," she said.

"I did." I took a deep breath, willing the mantle of my father to fall over me. Grand dukes had grand rages. Anything less was a childish tantrum. "Minister Olloi, tell me about the break-in."

"I—excuse me, Your Grace?"

Why was he gaping like that? "The break-in," I repeated, trying to push my forceful tone around my urge to chatter. Grand dukes didn't like to repeat themselves. "The one that occurred before my family fell ill. The one you reported to the guard."

Olloi blinked. "I don't understand what that has to do with—"

"I didn't ask you to understand."

Olloi's mouth worked like a fish's. "It—must have occurred some time in the night. I check the gate to Below every morning and evening, and one morning I came down and the locks were broken."

I looked at Viljo. He shook his head once. "And then

you had them replaced with the rusty locks you just opened for me?"

His face turned red. *Guilty.* I turned from him and went to the door. The padlock still hung from it, and I bent to examine the iron and the wood around it. "How were the locks broken?"

"Ah." Olloi sounded closer and closer to tears. "An ax? A knife?"

I looked back at him. "Why are you asking me?"

"I don't know what it was; I can only guess!"

"Ekata," whispered Aino. Behind her, Viljo frowned.

I watched Olloi carefully. "There's no trauma to the door." No mark, no chip in the wood.

Olloi began to tremble. "I don't understand," he said.

I pushed down my pity and folded my arms. "You lied, didn't you? This door wasn't forced. There are no broken locks. That's because someone unlocked this door with a key. That someone is you. Viljo, arrest the minister of Below, if you please."

Viljo coughed. "I, ah—was ordered by Prime Minister Eirhan not to arrest anyone on Her Grace's behalf."

That little traitor.

A fist closed around my heart. Grand dukes commanded obedience. "Now, Viljo."

"Wait," Olloi said, and panic ran deep in his voice. "It was Annika. They forced me to open the gates and lie."

Viljo hesitated, and I did, too. Encouraged, Olloi began

to babble. "I thought that if I reported it as a break-in, someone would investigate and find out. But no one ever questioned me."

He could be telling the truth. If Olloi had told the captain, and the captain told Eirhan, and Eirhan told him to forget it...I nodded to Viljo, who stood down, then went to the bench and sat, reminding myself that grand dukes were regal even when they had soaking-wet hair.

"I'm loyal to your father." Olloi knelt and bowed his head.

I snorted. "I can't say I believe that, considering."

He flinched. "I am, but my wife—Annika threatened to hurt my wife if I didn't leave the door unlocked and let them go Below."

"So your wife's life is more important than the grand duke's?" I said. That was an unfair question; I would probably have preserved Olloi's wife before my own father.

"I didn't know what Annika would do," he said, and the remorse in his voice was not entirely motivated by fear. "I thought they wanted to sell magic for a personal profit. I thought they wouldn't get far without the help of someone from Below."

His shoulders shook with fear, and I knew it was a selfish fear, entirely centered on preserving his own life and that of his family. But unlike my other ministers, Olloi feared me. I held the power of life and death over him. And that was a power that could be shaped, used, wielded. Warmth filled me.

I counted out careful seconds. "I don't think you're lying," I said at last. Olloi's head whipped up. "If I'm wrong, your death will be public and brutal. If you try to run, it will be the same. Don't leave your rooms." I stood. "And *don't* tell anyone we had this conversation."

Olloi sagged so heavily I thought he'd fall backward. "Thank you, Your Grace. Thank you."

It felt stranger to be on the receiving end of gratitude than of fear. "Don't grovel. Tell me the truth. And tell me if anyone threatens you again."

"What reason would Annika have to betray us?" Aino asked in an undertone as we left the entrance to Below.

"I guess we'll find out. Get me Annika's schedule, won't you? Discreetly," I added. We couldn't have a repeat of the treasury disaster.

Aino nodded. A strange, proud look came over her face. "You were impressive," she said.

"I was like my father, you mean." And it was what I wanted—it was what I needed—but it didn't make me happy.

I itched to write to Meire and update her on my new findings. Instead, I went back to my rooms and dried myself by the fire, waiting for Aino. "Annika has a meeting with Eirhan and Yannush at three," she reported when she came back.

That wasn't for another hour. "A nap?" Aino suggested.

"Farhod." I was long overdue for a visit to my family.

Aino rubbed at her brow and smoothed her frizzy auburn hair. "You should leave him to his work, Ekata."

"It's my work, too," I said. It *should* be my work. It was what I was good at.

My father's rooms were thirty steps down the hall from mine and guarded not by two guards but four, who bowed to me as I passed through. I stopped at the entrance to his antechamber. The stink of his rooms—sour sweat and soiled bedclothes and bitter medicinal remedies all mixed together—nearly sent me back out again. And the heat— it was a wonder the floor hadn't collapsed on the rooms beneath. A cold drop of water from the melting lintel hit the back of my ear and slid under my dress.

Six of my siblings lay in the antechamber on mattresses. The rich furniture—brocade chairs and velvet couches in vibrant purple and gold—had been shoved up against the carved ice walls, wrinkling tapestries of previous grand dukes. The antechamber was as large as my entire suite, and had two fireplaces, both roaring. Two doctors knelt; one checked Nari's pulse while the other slid a long, woven straw up Fenedyo's nose. As I watched, the doctor sucked on the straw, then spat a long line of clear fluid into a bedpan next to him.

Don't be sick. It's what doctors do. It was what I might end up doing someday. The doctor who monitored Nari looked up at me. His frown became recognition, and he bowed his head. "Your Grace. Do you need something?"

Nari had once impaled Velosha with an iron nail, aiming for the stomach but missing any vital organs. Fenedyo made me think of bitter winds, of searing panic. When he'd locked me out of the palace, I'd known exactly what hypothermia would do to me, and it had taken me longer than I wanted to admit to remember the kennels had warmth and safety. I looked upon my siblings with no love. Why was I trying to save them?

I headed to where the smell was worse, sweeter and bitterer and sicker. The rest of my family lay in the bedchamber—Father and Mother on the enormous oak-and-brocade bed, the rest of my siblings on more mattresses and cots. Father's cherrywood desk had been filled with most of Farhod's medicine cabinet. Farhod sat in my father's chair, peering at a solution in a glass dish. Munna tended Kavrosh.

"Any progress?"

Farhod stretched his shoulders. "There's been no change. They're halfway drowned and they can't wake up. Their breathing is labored, and there's a bubbling in their lungs. We drain them sometimes, but it doesn't really do anything."

I touched Father's wrist. It was clammy, and his pulse threaded. My father looked smaller, suddenly, thinner and frailer and paler.

The doctors moved quietly around me, pretending I wasn't there. I went to examine the ingredients strewn across the desk. "What have you tried?"

"I prescribed bloodleaf and sapphire kelp. No improvement."

I ran through my list of breathing agents. "Mint and ulna?"

"Done that."

"Wormwood?"

"Some debate on the efficacy," Farhod said.

"It was fruitless," said Munna. Their gray-brown hair was greasy, and some unnamed fluid stained their coat. "Your Grace, this is hardly the place for you."

"It's not contagious, is it?" I challenged them.

"It would seem not." Munna looked as though they wanted to say something more, but I set my jaw.

"Farhod, magic made the curse." I tried to keep my voice low. I still didn't trust that Munna and the other doctors weren't in Eirhan's pocket. Eirhan might know more than he claimed. "Maybe magic *can* unmake it."

"Magic doesn't do whatever we want, Ekata," Farhod said. "It only obeys your father, and he wouldn't have done this to himself."

Unless someone else had bought the secret from Below. Or discovered the secret on their own.

Winter roses bloomed around the bedposts, dipping toward Father's head. "Farhod, they use magic Below all the time. They have the secret of it."

"The creatures Below might be people, but they're not human," Farhod warned me. He rubbed his temple, and I spotted a swipe of gray I hadn't noticed before. "Don't assume that magic will work for us the same way it does for them."

"What if we can tap into it but don't know how?" I said.

"Ekata, your forefathers have had three hundred years to experiment. Magic is volatile. You're not going to change that, and certainly not in two days."

"Father must have used something to refine it," I said. Desperation ran like fire through my veins. If refinement were something like alchemy...something I was good at...

Munna pushed a stray hair out of their face. "He almost certainly did. But whatever it was, we don't know."

Then Farhod said, "You might as well show her," and they beckoned me to Father's desk. The water in the messenger bowl there rippled, but when I bent over it, I saw nothing.

Munna pulled open a drawer full of neatly labeled jars and wooden boxes. Father's own little medicine cabinet. I spotted charcoal, mustard seed, nux vomica, juniper, and slippery elm. He was ready to combat an arsenal of poisons. "He wouldn't keep his greatest secret in a drawer anyone could open."

Munna reached down and popped the bottom of the drawer up. Of course Father would have a secret compartment. I wondered how Munna knew of it. But when they lifted the false bottom out, I saw only evidence that something *had* been there. Brown circular stains dotted the drawer, ingrained in the wood. "You think whatever was in this drawer was part of the process?"

"I cannot say, Your Grace," Munna replied, and went to check on my father.

Dead ends. Dead ends and nothing to study. I glared at the antidotes and emetics. *It's a puzzle.* But I was missing a crucial piece.

Farhod touched my arm gently, and there was more concern than irritation in his gaze. "Ekata, we've tried every remedy we can think of. We've seen no change. So far the illness hasn't gotten worse, but...if it does, I don't know if we can stop it."

My duke voice came back. "You can't say that." The whole duchy was a mess, and it was unfair that my father had abandoned me to deal with it. Unfair that all I'd worked for, all I'd studied, was, suddenly, nothing more than a hobby, and one that I had to set aside for some greater good I wasn't sure I believed in. "We have to have something. I must have progress for the council. By tonight."

"Or what?" Frustration bled through in Farhod's voice. "You can't force this. We'll help them when we help them— and maybe we won't be able to help them at all."

"*No*," I said, pulling Father's demeanor around me like a cloak. The word came out strong, cold, authoritative. Everything he was. Masking my panic and turning it into my strength. "I'm not going to die on that throne. Not tonight, not tomorrow, not in fifty years. You're going to find me a way out of it."

Farhod took a deep breath. "Ekata," he said gently. "Sometimes things don't happen the way we want—"

"Don't patronize me," I snarled. Farhod recoiled. Rage boiled in me, and I knew it was wrong, but I couldn't stop.

"I'm not stupid. I'm not a child. Don't you want to save them?"

"You know I do." Farhod's even tone was strained.

"Then do something!" I shouted. My voice cracked.

"*I can't!*" Farhod shouted back. "This isn't a test, and it isn't a lesson, and we're not in my laboratory. These aren't even your father's *rooms* anymore! This is a hospital, and I can't put my work on hold to coddle you when you're supposed to be running the country."

Farhod had never yelled at me. Not even when I was being my most recalcitrant. The doctors stopped what they were doing to stare.

My first thought was that Father would have killed him for saying these things. But my defensive arguments melted as I looked at him. He was sallow and thin-lipped. Anger and fear warred on his face.

The anger won. "You know that the best way to cure them is to find the culprit. So what are you doing here?"

I fought to keep my tears in. I had a thousand excuses, but that was all they were. The truth was, I was too scared to do what needed to be done.

But Father had never been scared. "Fine," I said, and the word sounded cold and bitter. "You're right." I dipped my hands in a bowl of water and dried them on the edge of my coat. "Thank you for your candor."

"Ekata, I didn't mean—"

"I know what you meant." I cut him off, fighting to keep my voice even. "I understand. I'll let you work."

Farhod reached for me. "Why don't you sit down?" His tone was carefully kind. I hated it.

"I would, but I don't have time. I've a country to run."

I sounded like my parents, and I hated that, too. This had never been the way Farhod and I acted toward each other. Becoming grand duke had taken more than my family. It had taken my friends, and that hurt more.

I hurried out before the first tears could fall, wiping them on the back of my glove as I opened the door to the hall outside.

I set off toward the civil quarters. It was time for me to be in control. It was time for me to do something. And Annika would be in their meeting, which meant I could do things a bit differently than I had during my disastrous, too-public audit of the treasury. If I found evidence in their rooms, I'd arrest them. If I didn't, I'd arrest Olloi. Grand dukes made grand gestures.

Annika made sense as a suspect. *Someone* had been talking to Sigis in the law library. They owned land in Drysiak, and they'd switched from opposing a parliament to supporting one in the matter of a day. And if the uneasiness grew in me, if I felt as though I was sneaking around, I reminded myself that I was the grand duke and that my word was law.

Annika's rooms were locked, but I motioned to Viljo. He

came forward warily. "Break the lock," I ordered. He stared at me, uncertain, and my temper flared again. "Do you need to hear it twice?"

"Ah, no," he mumbled. "Your Grace."

He took out a knife and fumbled with the lock until I heard a brittle snap. The door to Annika's rooms creaked open.

The apartments were green and gold, with a low couch in the antechamber and a desk carved from a pale wood in a series of intricate knots, more in the style of one of the Western countries than our little snowbound place. Maybe Annika owned land there, too.

I went to the desk first, opening each drawer in succession. Land agreements, taxation records, farming leases, and serf reports. All were dated in the last three months. And all were for land within Sigis's empire. They would make good evidence.

"Your Grace," Viljo said nervously.

"Watch the door." From the desk, I moved on to Annika's bookshelves. If I were to hide truly damning information, I'd do so in the most boring-looking book on my shelf. For me, it would be a biology tome. For Annika...

I pulled *On the Technological Advances in Soil* from the shelf and flicked it open. No luck. I picked up the book next to it, and the book next to that. Each one looked less interesting than the last—but none of them hid anything.

Under the bed. Behind a sconce. In the cushions of

couches and chairs. In the lining of tapestries. As I took a quick inventory of the rooms, my pulse increased. *You're the grand duke. You don't snoop. You investigate.* This palace was my right. Serving my family was Annika's privilege.

"Your Grace," Viljo repeated. Did he have any *other* language in his vocabulary?

"I told you to watch the door," I snapped.

"Why?" said an all-too-familiar and unwelcome voice.

I whirled, dropping the stack of books I held. They bounced off my toes. I tried to look like the kind of person who dropped books on my shoes for fun. "Minister Reko. What are you doing here?"

"I must ask you the same question." Reko's eyes fluttered from the bookcase to me to Viljo. "I wasn't aware you had business with Minister Annika—" His eyes swept the room again. "*Without* Minister Annika."

"And you just happened to come this way?" I challenged him. "Your quarters are on the other side of the palace. Are you following me around?"

He didn't answer. That only solidified my certainty, like ice freezing over the dark lake. He had been waiting for me to leave the royal apartments to see what I'd do next. But he cocked his head and said, "And what *are* you doing here?" as though he had all the right in the world to be in Annika's rooms, and I had none.

His insolence rubbed at an open wound. "I am the grand duke. I can go where I please in my own palace."

"That it is your palace does not make it all your property. Would you demand that the entire duchy open its doors for you to stomp around and throw their books on the floor?" Reko sounded both amused and outraged.

"If that's what will bring my father back, yes."

"Even a grand duke must abide by the law," Reko said.

I called on the cold rage of my father and mother. "I am the law."

The sneer began at his lips. It pulled back, and back, twisting his face, darkening his eyes. "*You* are the law?" he seethed. "How dare you? Your father was the law. You're nothing but a despot. This is a person's private room."

"That's enough," I said, and tried to signal the paralyzed Viljo.

"It is *not* enough," he said, and from the way he pitched his voice, theatrically loud, I knew he was trying to signal people to come. And it was working. I heard footsteps in the hall, saw half a face behind the doorframe. "You have violated a sacred rule. Are you planting evidence? Are you setting them up? Orchestrating their downfall so that you can replace them?"

"I'm trying to find the truth." I wanted the truth. The chance to escape. Freedom. Not the scrutiny of the servants and delegates and lesser ministers who had begun to crowd the hallway, curious.

"Whose truth?" Reko said.

"Truth isn't subjective. It's scientific." And there was a truth to all this.

Reko laughed, bitter as poison. "Of course. Your truth is the only truth. I should have expected."

"Reko, stop." I hated how pleading I sounded. But I hated the spectacle more. I hated that people peered around the corner and didn't avert their gaze when I glared at them. I hated that my plan was truly awful and that I was only now starting to realize it. I hated that if I'd understood even the simplest politics, I probably wouldn't be here.

"No," Reko spat. "Not until you've stopped the coronation trials and abdicated. I won't stand by while you seize power. You're not fit for it."

I know, I wanted to scream in his face. I knew better than anyone.

Reko stepped toward the door, and his voice rang out down the corridor. "I'd rather have no grand duke and let Kylma fall into the lake than have a thief and a murderer for my grand duke."

The murmurs that fissured through the corridor picked up in volume and speed. Syllables punched through the air like the sound of ice cracking. *Murder. Curse. Stealing.*

I was going under.

I grabbed Viljo by the arm. "Arrest him." I dug in my fingers and gave him a look that said plainly, *It's him or you.*

Viljo opened his mouth to dissent—then marched over to

Reko. Reko didn't try to resist as Viljo turned him against the wall and twisted his arms behind his back. At Viljo's nod another guard came forward and took Reko away, their shoes clicking on the ice in a disjointed beat.

The crowd parted as they passed. The look Reko gave me over his shoulder was bitterly triumphant.

Silence followed, as thick as honey. I needed to save face, and I needed to do so before anyone else left. "And arrest Minister Annika, please. On suspicion of treason." Viljo nodded, and another guard was dispatched to find them.

I lifted my head and gathered the cloak of my mother about me. My spine was rigid. Let them talk. Let them think me a despot.

Grand dukes made grand tyrants.

Chapter Thirteen

Father probably would have made some magical demonstration to remind everyone who was in charge. I retreated. Aino followed me, but wisely kept her mouth shut until we were in my rooms. Then she said, "What's the point, Ekata?"

"Don't start again," I replied in a voice too hard. "I'll arrest whomever I need to."

"This isn't like you. What's the point of staying? What are you fighting for that's worth destroying yourself?" She stood by the door, forehead creased, her mouth turned down. Waiting for me to break her heart.

I couldn't bear to look at her. I went into my bedroom, forcing cheer into my voice so that it wouldn't wobble. "Nothing's destroying me. Don't be dramatic."

I heard the telltale sigh of Aino giving up on me. Then she followed me in and helped me change into a high-collared black dress with gold embellishments. As she held a pair of ruby earrings up next to my face, I studied myself in the wardrobe mirror. The bags under my eyes had not grown smaller since the night Eirhan had crowned me. My face seemed thinner, too, though perhaps that was the effect of the long earrings that framed it. The black collar of my dress made my skin ghostly. My gray eyes were dull, my pale hair greasy. The frown I presented was entirely too much like Mother's.

I was in such a mess, and I didn't know how to get out of it.

We turned at the sound of the door swinging open. "It is only me," said Inkar cheerfully as she came in and began to peel off layers. "I will be ready in a minute." She slid her tunic over her head, exposing her stomach and the bottom of her breast band.

I squawked and whirled back to my wardrobe—forgetting the full-size mirror there that reflected not just me but a view of her. I pulled my dressing screen between us before I could be caught staring. My face was warmer than any fire. "Wh-what are you doing?" I sputtered.

"I have been sweating," she said. "I did not think you would want to smell it during dinner."

"You could have warned me." *Why* couldn't I keep my voice steady? "Aino could have helped you get dressed." Aino smacked me lightly on the shoulder.

"I apologize. It is not odd in my country to change in front of other women."

"I'm not *other women*." I was her wife. My mind lingered on the cut of her hip, the curve of her belly. Was her skin as soft as it looked?

Think about something else. "What made you so sweaty, anyway?" I asked into the wardrobe.

"I was practicing with the guard," Inkar replied.

I hadn't expected that answer. I turned in surprise, granting myself a face full of woven screen. "Why?"

"I have been lazy here. Your guard are kind opponents. And they are funny. I like them."

"Now she's cavorting with guards," Aino said in Kylmian. She held up a necklace of pink sapphires.

"No," I said. "Mother always wore that one."

Aino's eyebrows drew together. "I thought that would help to connect you with her. Remind people what you're capable of."

They already know what I'm capable of. Bungling politics and throwing temper tantrums. But was that really anything different from what Mother and Father used to do? They just had more style. I nodded assent, and Aino helped me fix the necklace's clasp.

When I poked my head out from behind the screen, I was relieved to see that Inkar wore a black shirt. She'd exchanged her green vest for a white fur coat, and her axes hung prominently on a thick belt. "I will guard you. What do you think?" Inkar spread her arms.

She looked ready and willing to kill someone for me. She looked good.

Aino pursed her lips. "Should Your Grace not attempt something more...regal? We'd hate to give the impression that you spend your day lounging with the guard." She paused so that Inkar could appreciate the fullness of her sneer. "A grand consort must act a certain way."

"As a grand duke must act a certain way?" Inkar said.

Aino stepped between us, as if to protect me. "Are you insulting her?"

"Of course not." Inkar tapped on her axes meditatively. "I think an unconventional grand duke deserves an unconventional consort."

"Oh, you do deserve each other," Aino muttered in Kylmian.

"Aino," I snapped.

She shot me a resentful look but switched back to Drysian. "And would Her Grace like to make any demands of me before dinner?"

"Of course not," Inkar said. Was that a hint of resentment in her tone, a hint of challenge in her smile?

"How relieving." Aino carefully repinned a stray lock of my hair. "In such a case: Ekata, you're ready." Her voice dropped, and she added under her breath, "Though only the gods know how."

The Great Hall was silent as we entered. *Father never accomplished that*, I thought darkly. I bore the usual awkward obeisance from my subjects and guests and had them rise. Would I ever be good at small talk, at remembering the right faces at the right times, and the right terms for every treaty, agreement, and dispute? *You won't have to*, insisted a small part of me, and I clung to that with more determination than hope.

I scanned the hall for my enemies. Most of my ministry stood as far from me as they could get, at the edges of the hall with the servants. Sigis had cornered Yannush and they seemed to be in the throes of an argument. The only one who approached was Urso, who pressed my hand with bare fingers. They slipped under my cuff to touch my wrist and I stifled a yelp. They were freezing. "Has Minister Farhod made any headway?" he asked in an undertone.

"Why don't you ask him yourself?" I said, pulling my hand away.

"He's...not here..." Urso stepped back. "Good gods," he said in a voice a touch too loud. "You didn't arrest him, too?"

"No." But the damage was done. Heads turned at my vehemence, and Urso slunk back to his secretary and Minister Itilya.

Someone laughed. Sigis, of course. "If there's one thing I could learn from you, it's how to make an entrance." He bowed. "You've got people talking."

It's getting certain people to stop *talking that's the trick.* I couldn't even muster a false smile. How had he gotten behind me so fast?

"I'm taking bets on who's next. Your ministers are all afraid to play." Sigis leaned in, bringing a shoulder between me and Inkar. My hand tightened reflexively around her arm. "My money's on the alchemist. I don't know why you haven't arrested him already."

"Imagine that," I muttered. "Something you don't know."

"I beg your pardon?" he said in that soft, *I'm-going-to-murder-you* voice.

"Have you had a difficult campaign this season?" Inkar asked, forcing him to step back and acknowledge her.

Sigis answered her grudgingly. "Campaigns are never easy, and my opponents fought honorably. But I'm sure news of my victories traveled as far as your little island."

"It may surprise you that I do not follow your every move," Inkar said.

"It shocks him," I said.

Sigis froze for a moment, and I thought I saw a brief flash of hatred, quickly replaced by a bland smile. He touched a diamond rose pin at his neck and gave me a half bow.

I took Inkar's arm and directed her away from Sigis without returning it. All the self-preservation of sixteen years surviving my family screamed at me not to provoke a narcissistic foster brother with his eyes on my throne, but I was tired of playing nice.

Inkar hailed a guard at the door to the banquet hall. He wore a half grin, half grimace, and a spectacular purple bruise just under his left eye. "Declared fit for duty, Your Grace," he said.

Inkar laughed. "I am sorry for that. My arm is still numb where you hit it."

I stared at him blankly. "You hit her?"

For a moment, the guard looked like a man standing between a bear and her cub. But Inkar laughed again. "Do not be angry. That is the point of training. I hit him; he hit me." She put a hand on his arm. "You did well. I will see you tomorrow."

We went into the hall in silence. Inkar seemed hesitant, glancing at me two, three times before she spoke. "I like the guards, and I like to train. I hope you do not punish them for it."

"I'm not angry." I was thinking. What if Inkar was my key to winning the guards over from Eirhan?

Dinner was dull in the worst possible way. Sigis focused not on me, but on my ministers—flirting with Itilya, who looked at me before giving each reply. Haggling trade points with Urso and bringing up the Avythera agreement more than once. His conversation flowed so smoothly, and I was so awkward, that I couldn't come up with the right thing to say before he turned the conversation again. I resigned myself to being silent and moody until dinner was over.

But after dinner was worse. As delegate after delegate

whom I didn't know and didn't care about came up to me, I lost track of whom Sigis talked to and for how long. I craned my neck so much looking for him that I got dizzy and sent the Baron of Rabar off in a huff.

"You seem distracted." I jumped. Of *course* Sigis was right beside me.

I bit back a curse and said the first thing I knew would make him angry. "I'm looking for my wife."

"Your wife." Sigis laughed. "I still find it ridiculous. You need someone you know, Ekata. Someone who knows you." Suddenly, he was right next to my ear, voice soft and crushing as velvet. "It would be easier, you know. No coronation trials. No risking it all. I could take care of the horsewoman for us."

I wanted to scrub the back of my neck until it bled, just to get the feel of his breath off me. I wanted to peel out of my skin and slip away.

I wanted to take one of *the horsewoman*'s axes and see how hard it really was to get those ten pints of blood out.

"Ah." How did I stop thinking about this? "Yannush wants to talk to me."

He caught my elbow as I maneuvered from the throne to the open floor. "Careful, dear. I'll think you're stalling."

Call me dear again, I thought, but it was a hollow threat. Then, conscious of his eyes on me, I made my way to where Yannush conferred with Urso and Urso's secretary.

Urso noticed me first. "Your Grace." He bowed. Yannush's

bulging eyes widened in a way that might have made me laugh if I were in a better mood.

"What did Sigis think was so interesting at dinner?" I asked Yannush.

"He was discussing the export of raw magic," Yannush said, and I had no way to know if it was a total lie. "Everyone wants the secret to stabilization, of course, so that they don't have to rely on your father to provide the more expensive, refined magic."

"How much raw magic do we export?" I asked.

Yannush looked vaguely affronted; apparently, I ought to have known already. "We export far more refined than raw," he said. "Though many who buy raw magic use it here. Foreigners believe that magic is more potent within Kylma's limits than without."

That was interesting. "Is it?"

"I wouldn't know, Your Grace. I don't use magic for frivolity." He shut his mouth. His face took on a closed look, as though he'd said something he shouldn't have.

I knew magic lost power as it aged. But what if there was more to it? What if proximity to Below made it more potent, more stable? It had been grown and harvested Below, after all. What if the people Below could manipulate magic because it was in its natural element?

What if I could find some way to re-create that natural element? Would that be enough to gain control, to refine the magic without knowing my father's exact formula?

"Your…Grace?" Yannush said. He was looking at me oddly, as if I were a fisherman and he were the eel on my line.

"Yannush." I put my hand on his arm. He tensed. "You might be brilliant." And though I wanted to savor the look of shock on his face, I slipped around him and hurried for the servants' door, Viljo close behind, praying that Eirhan's back was still turned.

I faltered outside Father's rooms, though for once, it wasn't Father I feared. I'd been cruel to Farhod, and unfair. He deserved better. Under normal circumstances, I'd have waited a few days, until we could both pretend this had never happened. But if I didn't act immediately, Sigis might win the coronation trials before Father woke up.

Grand dukes don't apologize, I thought. All I had to do was march in and act like myself. All the same, it felt as if a barrier separated me from the door.

The guards to either side of the door eyed me. Behind me, Viljo coughed. "I know," I said irritably. "Open up."

The antechamber was much as I'd left it. My sisters and brothers stank and were soaked through with sweat. The door to Father's bedroom opened, and Farhod poked his head out. "Ekata?"

Something inside me broke loose. If he were still angry with me, he'd have called me something else—*my lady* or

Your Grace. All the same, the air between us was stiff, like being outside on the cusp of a snowstorm.

"Um." I bit the inside of my cheek. *Sorry* rose on my tongue, but I quashed it. If I couldn't think of a regal way to say it, I couldn't say it at all.

Farhod inclined his head, as though gracefully accepting my nonapology. "It's late. Is everything all right?"

"Everything's fine." I took a deep breath. "I want to try something."

Farhod was careful not to look at me. "Something dangerous?" *Something foolish?*

"Maybe. Unless you've made progress." I knew he hadn't. He'd have sent every servant in the palace to find me if he had.

His hand went around and around his cuff. "Sometimes it takes weeks or months to find a cure, you know." I could practically hear Farhod trying out arguments in his head. I knew he hesitated only because of our fight.

"I don't have weeks or months." I had until the end of the coronation trials. And if Sigis won... "I've come up with a hypothesis."

"Oh?" He sounded relieved.

"The environment of Below is conducive to magic. The people can manipulate it however they like. It's not unstable. But you didn't find any organ of magic when you performed the autopsy on the citizen of Below."

Farhod frowned. "Not that I could identify."

"What if the secret to magic is in the environment? In the water?" What else could it be? If I truly focused, I wouldn't fail.

"Have you tested this theory?" Farhod asked.

"Meire—my liaison Below—said the secret to magic was within us." Farhod's frown didn't abate, and I went on. "I can do this." I needed to do this. "I'm grand duke."

"Being grand duke doesn't automatically give you power over magic." Farhod was trying to keep his tone gentle, still afraid to anger me.

It didn't work, but I did manage to squash the flash of frustration. "Has anything else worked so far?" I said.

"No," Farhod admitted. "No emetics, no remedies. At the university, we'd have tried a biopsy, but Kylma has no doctors trained for it."

"Surely cutting my family open isn't better than trying my way," I said.

Farhod didn't look as though he entirely agreed. "Why not try experimenting with the magic on me first?"

"You're not ill, for a start. And I have a time limit. Farhod, I can do it. What other options do we have?" Doctors siphoned fluid out of my family's lungs. If Sigis won the coronation trials, he'd let them all drown.

Farhod sagged. He looked so much older than he had a few days ago. His skin was dry and cracked, and his expressive dark eyes seemed dull. "Maybe...start with a sibling."

I went to Father's table. The black messenger bowl sat

unperturbed, still as the moat on a clear day. This was what I had of Below.

The little jar of magical pearls was fetched from the laboratory. I dipped a cup into the messenger bowl, then popped the latch on the jar of pearls. They nestled, glistening, coated in ever-shifting color. I dropped a pearl into the cup, as the archimandrite had done. Then I crushed it with a pestle and let the magic disperse through the water.

"Are you...?" Farhod didn't say *sure*.

Because I wasn't. I looked around the room. Whom could the family live without? Whom could *I* live with, if I succeeded?

I knelt next to Velosha, who lay on a cot at the foot of Father's bed. Her venom wasn't the worst, and I doubted my ministers liked her more than they liked me. I knelt before her, cupping one hand under her neck to raise her head.

Grand dukes make grand decisions. No one else would do it for me. I leaned forward and let the cup moisten my sister's lips. Her head moved a little, and the liquid flowed down her throat.

I became aware of the small crowd standing behind me. Disapproval rolled off Munna. "What now?" they said.

"We'll have to wait." I put two fingers to her neck, checking her pulse.

"For how long?"

Velosha's pulse hammered against my fingers. Her eyes flicked open. I hissed in a breath. "It's working—"

She began to writhe. I was thrown to the side as Munna pushed me out of the way. They fixed a mask to her face and sucked at the catheter that slid up her nose. Water poured from Velosha's mouth. They pulled her up by the shoulders, reaching one hand around her to slap her back.

My blood was thorns and ice inside me. This was supposed to save me. This was supposed to work.

This was killing her.

"Ekata." Farhod gripped me by the elbow. "Ekata, come. Get out of the way." He pulled me up and tried to steer me toward the desk.

I sagged in his grasp. "Maybe—it's dispelling all the water. Maybe it induced vomiting." Maybe the flow of water would stop, and instead of her burbling breath, it would be her voice I heard.

Then the others began to seize.

Lyosha was the first. A doctor rushed to him, swearing. Then Svaro began, then Mother.

Then Father.

Farhod dropped my arm and shoved past me. He sucked hard on the catheter trailing from Father's nose, spitting the fluid directly onto the floor. Father's eyes fluttered. The room erupted in shouts. My mind faced a wall, as blank and smooth as ice. There had to be a solution to this. There had to be.

You thought you had one, whispered part of my mind. I'd

tried, but I wasn't clever enough. I wasn't capable enough. I couldn't be grand duke, and I couldn't be a scientist, either.

"Lobelia," Farhod shouted between breaths. *"Ekata."*

My mind turned over and over. Lobelia. A pale purple flower, imported dried. Emetic. A poison. Father had ordered that I should never touch it, for fear that I would use it on my siblings.

Farhod slid off the bed. "Hold him," he growled, and shoved me at my father.

Father wasn't so terrifying now, with spit and salt water dripping down his chin, snot hanging from his nose, eyes staring at nothing. His graying beard and hair were matted, his cheeks hollowed and waxy. For a moment, I was amazed I'd tried to save him. Would he thank me when he woke? Give me the chance to travel south? Or would he always hate me for seeing him like this?

His body convulsed. More water slid from his nose and mouth. I fumbled for the catheter.

Farhod crouched beside Velosha, crushing lobelia in a mortar. For a moment, my fog lifted as a fresh wave of fear hit. "Don't," I said. He looked up. "Let me do it. If you accidentally…"

If he accidentally killed her, his own life would be over. Whereas I was practically expected to do my family in.

A glaring doctor handed me a long syringe. I took the mortar from Farhod and filled the syringe. Then I leaned over Velosha and put a few drops down her throat.

She stilled for a few moments. Then her abdomen spasmed as she reacted to the poison. She coughed one dry cough—then it poured back out. Sweet salt water spattered my dress, stained pink and as warm as my sister's feverish body. Magic sparkled, feathering into capillaries that bled into the cloth like little red trees. Velosha's body shook.

She flopped like a fish for over a minute. When she finally stilled, her breathing seemed less labored, but it rasped as though her insides had been scraped raw. Magic still fizzed on the front of my dress. And behind me, I could hear the rest of my family begin to breathe as normal.

I choked on a hysterical laugh. To think of this as normal.

I let Velosha fall back to her cot. "Thank you," I muttered as I stood. "I'll go now."

I pushed past the doctors, through the antechamber, and out into the cold hall, where I leaned against the wall and slid to the floor. I drew up my knees and made a cradle for my head. I didn't care that I was covered in questionable fluids. I didn't care that the soaking hem of my dress was turning stiff and freezing to the ice floor.

I'd been so sure my idea would work. Because I was clever, and because grand dukes had grand solutions. Because I thought Below could solve my problems. Because I thought magic could solve them.

The door opened with a quiet click. Farhod sat next to me, stretching out his legs along the floor. For a long while, we said nothing. Tears rose again, and this time I let them come. How could I have been so stupid? How could I have thought this would help?

Nothing else did, whispered that little voice. But it could shut up. All it did was give me stupid ideas and then tell me how foolish I'd been.

"Ekata, it happens," Farhod said.

"Does it?" I asked flatly.

"Yes. To doctors *and* to grand dukes. You make decisions with the information you have, and sometimes those decisions are wrong. Sometimes you haven't slept enough, and you haven't eaten enough, and things seem clear right up until everything falls apart."

I forced myself to look at him. He did look as though he meant everything he said.

"You need to get some rest," he said. "In the morning, you'll have to convince the council that you were trying to help, not hurt."

I shook my head. If he thought I could manage to sleep . . .

He caught my hand and squeezed it. "Ekata, I know it's bad. These are the kinds of days you'll have as grand duke sometimes. But I'll stand behind you. This will pass."

The problem was, this wouldn't pass. The council would swing favor toward Sigis, and he'd win the coronation trials. Then it wouldn't matter what I'd been trying to do.

Footsteps clicked down the hall. The bottom of Aino's

dress came into view, and Farhod led her away, murmuring. I put my head back on my knees and tried to forget it all.

Gentle arms tugged me upright. Aino kissed me, feather-light, on the cheek. "Poor Ekata," she murmured. "Come sleep."

Aino led me to bed and made me drink a soporific, and Inkar pulled my quilt up to my shoulders. For once, they didn't snipe at each other, but I couldn't care enough to be grateful. I slept unwillingly, and the dark that pulled me down seemed deep and hopeless.

I was suspended, with darkness below me and light somewhere far above. It filtered through to me, white to blue to gray.

I couldn't breathe. My heart pounded, and my lungs spasmed. As I flailed and choked, I spotted my hands— corpse-gray, speckled with shadow from something far above. Frost burst over my skin in sharp crystals, all thorns. It wound about my wrists, binding me. Dragging me down.

I screamed. Water filled my mouth, salty-sweet. The thorns tightened. Frost crept up my arms, blooming into my shoulders. It dug into my skin. I couldn't make a sound. I thrashed; I wouldn't go quietly—

I woke up just as I spat a mouthful of water onto Inkar's face.

She held me by my shoulders, her dark eyes wide in shock. Her hair was wet. "Aino!" she screamed.

I was wet, too—every single part of me. My nightgown was as soaked as if I'd tossed it into the moat. Water dripped from my hair, and the inside of my mouth felt slimy. My legs slicked against each other. Aino burst in and shoved Inkar aside, grabbing me by the shoulders, then leaning me forward and slapping my back hard enough to leave a handprint. I choked on fluid and indignation. Warmth and pain burst inside me. But the next breath I took was free. "What happened?" I gasped.

"I thought you were having a fit," Inkar said. Her carefree smile was gone. Her mouth was dark in the light of the stars, surrounded by the pale moon of her face.

"Are you all right? Are you well? What happened?" Aino said.

"How should I know?" I looked from Aino's serious face to Inkar's petrified one. My face burned. All I remembered was fear, but now that I was awake, things didn't seem nearly so real. "It must have been a bad dream." I wiped at my soaking front, feeling foolish.

Aino looked at me for a long moment. "Yes," she said slowly. "Let's get you into something dry." She rubbed at my still-wet arms. "Inkar, won't you excuse us?"

"No." Inkar slid off the bed to stand on the bearskin rug at the foot of it. She knelt before the fire, and I heard steel on flint.

I needed to calm down. I wanted to forget the frost blooming all over me, the depths dragging me down.

I coughed. Water sluiced over my chin, and I put a hand up to my mouth. Inkar and Aino stared at me. I felt small, suddenly, childish and immature and repulsive. "I'm sorry," I said, bringing my knees up and tugging my sodden night-gown away from my chest. "I must have...I don't know."

Inkar returned to the bed and ran a finger down my bare arm. She brought it up to her nose. "It does not smell like sweat." Her tongue darted out. "It does not taste like sweat." Her hands went to the hem of my nightshirt, squeezing. "It did not look like a nightmare. Not the kind I have seen. It looked like..."

She frowned, but it wasn't the disgusted frown I'd expected. It was a puzzled one. I was a mystery she needed to solve. "When I woke up, I thought you were drowning," she said.

Drowning.

Aino trembled as she pulled the soggy gown over my head. I ran my tongue around the inside of my mouth again, tasting this time. I'd smelled this sweetness once before. And the salt of the water—it wasn't sweat.

It was lake water.

Inkar was right. I *had* been drowning, like the rest of my family. Which meant that whoever cursed them was trying to curse me, too. A flash of memory ignited, the sense of cold and damp, the image of frost in my mind. Three nights ago, I'd had this same nightmare. Only it wasn't a nightmare.

I'd already made so many mistakes in my young reign, but

this might be the biggest. *I* was the mistake. My ascension to the dukedom was a mistake. I should be lying next to my father, slowly drowning.

Aino and Inkar bundled me into a new nightgown and robe and set me before the fire. Aino fetched new bedclothes, and she and Inkar fitted them while I sat and shivered. Aino moved as if her joints had aged ten years in the night. But she worked without complaint, and in silence.

"You may go," Inkar said when they were done.

"Excuse me?" Aino said in a voice like cut glass.

"We are finished. You may sleep." Inkar's voice was brisk and neutral. As though Aino were beneath her anger.

"Someone just tried to kill her. I'm not about to leave."

"I will watch her." Inkar sat cross-legged on the bed. "I have kept watch before. On campaign. You and I will take three-hour shifts to ensure one of us is always wakeful."

Aino glared, thin-lipped. "She has a point," I said, and nearly recoiled when that glare turned on me. "I mean— wouldn't taking shifts be better?" If I could sleep at all. "We all have things to do tomorrow."

"We can't trust her," Aino said in Kylmian.

Poor Aino, always so worried for me. I took her hand. "No matter what she wants, she won't get it if I die. Let her take a watch. You can rest." She needed it. Her eyes still swam with tears, and she looked as if she hadn't slept since I'd become grand duke.

"Don't be a fool for her," Aino warned me softly. Then she stepped back, straightening. "Wake me when it's my turn. And call for me if anything happens," she said in Drysian, in a tone that indicated Inkar would pay if she didn't.

Inkar only nodded. Aino shut the servants' door, but not quietly enough for a graceful exit. "Why does she dislike me so?" Inkar asked.

"You treat her like a servant," I said.

A line appeared between Inkar's brows. "She is a servant. And if she were a servant in my father's court, she would be executed for the way she speaks to her betters."

"You're not better than her," I snapped.

Inkar raised a brow. "I am sorry," she said. "I did not know you would be angry."

"That's because you don't know me. Aino does." I walked over to my side of the bed and flopped without taking off my robe.

Inkar did not lie down. She still sat, upright, cross-legged, regarding me. Her dark eyes blinked, shuttering away thoughts that I could not fathom. And I was strangely sorry for that.

I pulled the covers up to my chin and lay still with my hands folded over my belly. But sleep refused to come. My skin tingled, and my blood rushed. All the coffee in the world didn't help me in the daytime, but now I couldn't even close my eyes. My lungs heaved without my permission. "Forget it," I said finally. I sat up and adjusted my robe. "I can't sleep,

anyway. You might as well rest while I get some work done."
Maybe I could use my experience to make a few notes on
the curse.

"I will not sleep. I have promised your—I have promised
Aino that I will look after you."

"Well, I can't lie here."

Inkar looked out the window at the blue-black night, the
pinprick stars that wove through the sky like a tapestry. "Take
me to see this city I have agreed to live in," she said abruptly.

"What?"

"I would like to take a walk."

"Do you realize how cold it is out there?" I said.

She smiled that sly, sidelong smile. "Are you asking me to
keep you warm?"

"No!" I grew hot. *Yes.* "I only meant—you're going to
have trouble keeping *yourself* warm."

She considered. "We go out. We walk until it is too cold.
We come back in."

"It's already too cold," I muttered. But if Inkar wanted
to see what she'd gotten herself into, this was a good way to
show her. Maybe I could find some way to annoy her without accidentally freezing her to death. "All right. But there's
no way you brought warm enough clothing. You'll have to
borrow some of mine."

I peered out into the hall. My guards stood at either side of
the door. One nodded to me, then frowned in confusion

when he spotted the fur snowball behind me. "It's Inkar," I said. "We're going for a walk."

"Yes, Your Grace," he said. He followed at a sedate pace.

"Saljo, I command you not to laugh at me," Inkar grumbled. I looked around, confused, then I realized that Saljo was the name of the guard. How could Inkar know his name better than I did?

Saljo snorted. "Yes, Your Grace."

"This is awful," Inkar said. She kicked the inside of her skirt. "How am I supposed to protect you in a skirt like this?"

"You're not supposed to protect me," I said. "The guards protect me. They protect you, too."

"I do not need protection," Inkar replied. "Except you buried my axes under an entire sheep."

"Right," I said. I tucked my head, trying to stifle my smile. She was pretty and charming and clever. Was she really allowed to be adorable as well?

Focus on the negative, said Eirhan's voice in my mind.

I'd almost drowned tonight. My mental Eirhan voice could stuff it.

"Are you sure we should not tell Aino where we are going?" Inkar said Aino's name delicately.

"Completely sure. She'll forbid us from going outside and probably mobilize the entire guard to stop us. This way, how will she ever know?"

"She will open your chamber doors to check on you. She will find that both of us are missing. She will panic and mobilize the guard, as you say. She will be furious when she discovers that your life was never in danger."

"And I'll tell her that I'm the grand duke and that I can do what I want." I was proud of myself for saying that with a straight face. Grand duke or no, Aino would treat me like her disobedient daughter. "It's always easier to ask forgiveness than permission."

"You say that knowing it is not you Aino will hate," Inkar reasoned. "She will think the whole thing was my idea."

"It was your idea." I grabbed her mittened hand in mine, and though there were layers between us, the pressure of her hand as she squeezed sent a bolt up through my arm and into my belly. "It's too late to back out now. You're not even slightly cold yet."

The night was blessedly still when we stepped outside. No wind to chill us, no snow to settle on us. The stars were a riot across the sky, and the moon a·thin, sideways smile. Inkar gasped, coughed, and gasped again.

"Bracing, isn't it?" I said smugly.

"I have little hairs on the inside of my nose," Inkar began.

"I didn't really need to know that."

"They are all frozen." Inkar pulled up her scarf to cover the lower half of her face.

"We can turn around, if you like," I offered.

Her eyes were alight. "No chance. Let us walk."

So we did. We walked to the palace gate, and Saljo opened the side door for us.

The streets Above were quiet. Most people were inside, asleep. We passed the inn quarter, where light and noise spilled out onto the street, but soon the lane became silent again, lit only by streetlamps. Our shoes chipped away at the black surface of the lake. Under the thick ice, we saw the outlines of fish darting unperturbed beneath our shadows. Inkar knelt and pressed her mitten to the ice. "This is amazing."

"More than amazing." I knelt, too, but I was searching for bigger shapes, the citizens who swam and fought denizens of the lake and had their own lives and problems and conspiracies.

"Where I come from, the sea is green, and we cannot see to the bottom," Inkar said. "We do not walk on the water. We sail, and we pray that the water does not see fit to take us."

She sounded in awe. She sounded— "Are you afraid of it?"

"You are not?" she retorted.

"Never," I said, and it was true.

I had seen Inkar flushed from a fight and laughing at a joke; I'd seen her angry and happy and curious. Now she just looked—beautiful. Her face was alight with wonder, so palpable I could almost feel it.

She was looking at me. "Are you all right?"

I had no idea what I was. "You wanted to see the city. Let's go."

I took her to the stock exchange, the dowager's mansion, the grand hunting lodge. I showed her spires and columns and domes carved from ice, and though I could not see her mouth, her wide eyes told me all I needed to know. I took her past the merchant palaces and to the market. The tall houses, with birch frames and rubble fillings, were dark at this hour, but I pointed them out to her one by one.

"That is a bank?" she said doubtfully of one building.

"What do banks look like where you come from?" I asked.

"We do not pay with notes. We pay with silver and gold." Inkar touched her arm, where her silver coils sat under four layers of sleeves. "We keep our money with us and clip off pieces of our armbands when we wish to buy. No banks necessary."

"What do you do with all the clippings?" I said.

"We melt them down and make new things. We melt down the coins we bring home, too."

"And use the notes as fuel?"

A line appeared between her brows. "Of course not." But her eyelids crinkled, and I knew she was smiling. "My father will bring a dowry of these bands. If you prefer, he will trade them for notes. They make for nice decoration."

"Um." I kept my eyes on the road, watching the fish dart like my thoughts. Trying to pick the right one carefully. "Why would your father come with your dowry if you never intended to win the brideshow?"

"I wrote to him as soon as you presented me to the court. He has not had time to organize a full dowry, but he will make you many pretty promises." Her eyes dimmed a little, as though she'd told a bitter joke.

289

"But..." I cast about for the right words. What did Eirhan want me to say, and what did I want to say? "It's only a trial marriage."

Inkar cocked her head. "Until eight days have passed."

"Unless one of us breaks it."

It was the wrong thing to say. Inkar's grip on my arm tightened, and her voice took on a stilted quality. "You intend to break it."

"No," I said, feeling a burst of shame. I didn't know what I wanted anymore. "But you didn't come here thinking you would stay forever."

"No." She looked down the road of high-stacked houses, pressed together as if for warmth. "I wanted to see something new." Her boot scraped against the road.

"Your father's using you. He used you to get better terms on the treaty, and now that we're married, he'll use you to get more."

Inkar shrugged. "So?"

"It doesn't bother you?"

"I am the twenty-fifth daughter. It is part of my life. People use me." An emotion I couldn't quite place gleamed in her eyes. "You are using me, and I do not mind."

"No, I'm not," I said automatically.

"Of course you are. Everyone says that if you were not married to me, you would already be married to *him*." She squeezed my arm. "I do not blame you. Sigis likes power too much. He would not be content to stay grand consort, as I am." She raised a brow at me, as if to say I could do worse. "My father despises him."

"Any expanding warlord would," I muttered.

"Excuse me?"

"Nothing." We walked along the fishery stalls, where blood and scales froze to the walls and beams of the tents. "Forgiving your father, I understand. I guess. You didn't choose to be his daughter. But why would you choose to stay married to me?"

Inkar was silent for a long time, gazing at the snowflake stars. Finally, she said, "I have spent my life trying to show others that I can make something of myself. Living to others' standards. But when I came here, I resolved to live only for myself. And you chose that."

"And you'd rather be here than with the Emerald Order?" Not to mention be largely ignored by her father, something I'd tried and failed to accomplish every day before I became grand duke.

Inkar adjusted her scarf. "The order was a challenge. I have conquered it. Some people still say it is not enough, that I am too fragile or that my father helped me." The sly smile was back. "But even my father said this marriage was impossible."

I leaned in, pressing my nose to her cheek. Heat rippled over my skin and pooled in my belly. "Lyosha would never have known what to do with you."

Inkar laughed. "Your brother would never have selected

me. I knew as much when I agreed to come. He dislikes...
horse riders."

My wife had the gift of understatement. Lyosha's entire
platform for ruling had been closed off and nationalistic.
Originally, he hadn't wanted a foreign consort at all. It was
only through Mother's great coaxing that he'd agreed to the
brideshow. "If you knew he'd be so dismissive, why come?
And why..." I searched for the right words. I actually liked
Inkar. I cared what she thought about me. "Why were you
so pleased to marry me?"

Her hood turned toward me. "The first time I saw you,
you looked as bored by your family as I was. Then, when
you came into the bridal wing, you were so helpless..." She
exhaled softly in laughter.

"Helpless?" I nearly choked on my outrage.

"Helpless. Panicked. You were like a doe."

"I was not." I laughed incredulously. The sound bounced
off the silent buildings to either side.

"You were. And I think it is why you chose me. Because
I am the hunter. Good for pursuing does." She squeezed my
hand again. "And fighting off pale bears."

I was surrounded by hunters. Sigis hunted my title. Reko
hunted my power. Someone hunted my life. But Inkar protected me. She wasn't my hunter; she was my herd.

"Do you know why I picked you?" I said. "I picked you
because you laughed at me." And perhaps I shouldn't have

told her, but it made her laugh again, and I found I didn't mind that.

After thirty minutes, every step Inkar took wobbled, and I dragged her back to my rooms. Her cheeks were an angry red and she leaned over to stoke the fire with a groan. "I will never be warm again."

"Of course you will," I said. The best way to get warm would have been to press together in my bed to share body heat. But I wasn't about to suggest that. Instead, I pulled off my clothes, shuddering as I was reduced once more to my nightgown and bare legs, and slid under the covers.

Inkar sat next to me. "I hope you are sufficiently tired."

"I'm sufficiently cold," I admitted, burrowing down.

"In fifteen minutes, I will go find Aino and tell her it is her turn to watch. Perhaps she will not yell at me."

We fell silent, enjoying the warmth, the crackling of the fire, the pale blue of my bedroom walls and ceiling. My bones ached, but the weight of my blankets reassured me. My eyes grew heavier, but I needed to say one thing before sleep took over. "I'm sorry I snapped at you," I murmured. "Aino's special to me." Special didn't really begin to define my relationship with Aino, but I was too tired to think of what did.

"I forgive you," Inkar said. "You did almost die. It makes a woman a little..."

"Irritable?" I suggested.

"I suppose. Vengeful, as well." Her hand snaked under the covers and found mine. "It will not happen again."

Our fingers knotted, a complicated tangle of threads. I thought about pulling on those fingers until her face was right above mine, then pulling again until the gap between us closed completely. I thought about her offer to keep me warm.

I'd never have the courage to take her up on it.

"I begged him to let me come here," Inkar said, almost too quietly for me to hear.

"Hmm?" I pulled my loose thoughts together.

"I was the one who came up with the plan. I wanted to see this place, and my older siblings did not want to come. I convinced my father that my life was worth it."

"That's..." I struggled to find the right word.

"Clever?" Inkar cocked her head. "Romantic?"

"Sad." That her father had thought her disposable in the face of political gain, when she was so much more. Then again, what did my father think of me?

"I do not regret it," she said, and our fingers tightened. Two daughters who had nothing else, holding on to each other.

We were still holding hands when Aino woke me.

DAY FOUR

CHAPTER FOURTEEN

H er breathing was still labored in the night," Inkar said as Aino shook me by the shoulder.

"She's fine, thank you," Aino said, and I could have sworn I saw another layer of ice frost over the windows.

"I simply thought you should know." Inkar stretched and ran a hand through her dark hair, momentarily obscuring her face. Behind her, the winter roses half bloomed against the wall.

Aino muttered under her breath as she put my robe around my shoulders. I waved to Inkar as I was shuffled out.

"And whom is Your Grace planning to arrest today?" Eirhan said as I shut the door to my bedroom behind me.

"Whomever I need to," I said.

"Let's start with the council meeting, shall we? It will be easier to arrest the entire room than loot offices and bedrooms one by one."

"You're hilarious." I picked up a piece of salmon and stuck it on a slice of seaweed bread. "I thought you wanted me to arrest Reko."

"And Annika?"

I couldn't admit that ransacking their rooms might have been a mistake. "They have ties to Sigis. I know they're plotting something with him. But I have to figure out what."

"You can begin with the fact that they signed two land agreements with him as soon as he arrived."

"What?" I gaped at him. "Why didn't you tell me before?"

"It's in the documents you, ahem, rescued from their room." Eirhan brandished an example.

I snatched it from him. "I was getting to that," I said, blushing. I'd already read the contract through, but I hadn't made any sense of it.

"I might recommend getting to it *before* your entire council revolts, and not after," Eirhan said.

If I brought the council a confession, maybe I could justify the hasty actions and the bad look I'd brought upon myself. "I'll tell them everything once I've talked to Annika and Reko."

"*Now* you want to talk," Eirhan muttered. But he didn't challenge me further; he nodded and said, "I'll be meeting Rafyet to discuss his new proposal for fishing agreements. Anyway, do remember to let your guard protect you."

My guard. Of course, they would be Eirhan's eyes and ears. Could I bribe them to stay out of the room? "What else would they do?" I asked darkly, and as Inkar came out for breakfast, I retreated to get dressed.

Annika rose as I entered but did not bow. Their round face was paler than usual in the morning light.

I wore my mother's jewelry like armor. I needed to maintain control. I needed to keep Annika fearful and defensive. I motioned for them to sit in a low chair while I towered over them. "So," I said, narrowing my eyes. "You make agreements with my enemy. You support a parliament to reduce my family's power. And now I discover you've traveled Below."

Annika folded their hands. They'd traded their opulent coat for a suit that drew tight across their shoulders and hips, and they kept their legs pressed together. They looked small—deliberately so, I guessed. But they met my eye and held their chin up. "I can assure you that's not true."

"None of it?"

They licked their lips. "Many claims can be made, Your Grace, but I can explain them. To your satisfaction, I hope."

I held up the paper Eirhan had cleverly noticed. "You signed this after Sigis arrived for the brideshow."

Annika was as still as a hare poised to flee. "I had your father's permission for that."

"Can you prove it?" I said.

They didn't reply. Nor did they look away. Their blue eyes turned pale and angry.

"Why do you want to depose me?"

"I don't, Your Grace."

"You want a parliament."

Their words were measured. "You seized the treasury. You've arrested me. A parliament doesn't mean you can't be duke. It just means you can't be an autocrat anymore."

"You had no problem with my father's being an autocrat," I pointed out.

"Kamen has thirty years of experience in politics." Their eyes dropped to their lap. "But he taught you more about fear than politics. I would have supported a parliament no matter who succeeded him. Perhaps it's time for a change."

"And supporting a parliament would make it easier for Sigis to marry into the family, wouldn't it? The parliament could maintain control. In theory." I doubted Sigis would make things any easier on a governing body than he would on me. "And what about Below?"

Annika raised a pale eyebrow. "I've never been Below."

"Minister Olloi says otherwise."

They snorted. "Minister Olloi hates me. He's wanted to be minister of agriculture since before you were born."

"Why is that? Why does everyone want a post that has no meaning on an ice-covered lake? Is it because you can make special deals with powerful kings?"

Annika lifted one shoulder in response. "Being minister of agriculture gives me a say in trade and imported goods. Olloi's job is to guard a locked door."

That was fair. "Being minister of agriculture means you can make lucrative agreements, too." I examined the papers. "What did Sigis offer you?"

Annika was silent. I let the silence draw out. Their heel tapped on the floor, ice grips *click-clicking* in the silence. "I want to make a deal," they said at last.

The side of my mouth twitched. "Offer me something."

"Olloi arranged for Sigis to access untreated magic from Below. I don't know who collected it, but Sigis has talked to everyone. I can tell you who supports him, who avoids him, and who's undecided."

"So tell me," I said.

Annika wet their lips. "I want promises first. I want to maintain my seat on the council, and Kylma buys my produce before trading with foreigners."

I narrowed my eyes. Annika should be begging for their life, not negotiating an agricultural agreement.

"More grain means a better life for citizens Above. The tax will enrich the treasury. You'll have an ally on your council. There's no drawback for you."

I'd hardly call Annika an ally. "And how do I know you didn't go Below?"

"I cannot prove that I haven't been somewhere, Your Grace," Annika said. "I can only tell you that Olloi has his reasons for framing me."

Be Father. They didn't fear me enough if they thought staying on my council would benefit them. "This is my problem, Annika. If *you're* lying, I'm only handing you more power. Executing you would be cleaner and easier for me."

Their hands clenched into fists. "My holdings would revert to Sigis, not you. You'd lose a valuable asset. I can help you." Now I heard that hint of desperation. "I can give you names."

I folded my arms. "So talk. And if your information is decent, we'll talk about what you get to keep." Their position, their agreements, their head—let them wonder what was on the line.

Their fingers twitched; then they forced them to relax. And they began to talk.

Reko sat at his desk, writing. When I entered, he glanced up, then scrawled his signature at the bottom of the page and set it aside. "How pleased I am that Her Grace has blessed me with her presence."

Reko didn't have to like me, but he did have to respect me. "Surely you would never have spoken that way to my father."

"You are not your father," Reko said.

There was a short, ugly silence.

"I'll get to the point." I took the armchair by the fire. "I've been speaking with Minister Annika. They had some interesting things to say about my council."

Reko picked at a bit of invisible dust on his sleeve. "I'm sure they painted me the very picture of villainy."

"Actually, they said you'd refused all of Sigis's attempts to sway you. They said you were the only one."

Reko raised an eyebrow. "I'm loyal to Kamen. Don't confuse it with being loyal to you."

Anger flared in me again. *Well, he's honest.* Something that no one else on my council seemed to be. "It means we're on the same side."

Reko snorted at that.

"We are. We both want my father back. And I think we can help each other." I folded my hands. "You help me, I look for the cure. My father returns, things go back to normal."

Reko's mouth twisted as though he were amused at my trying to be an adult. "Let's say you're right. Do you really think things will go back to normal?" He shook his head, as though I honestly couldn't be *that* stupid. "This reckoning has been coming since before you were born. We need a representative parliament, whether or not your father recovers."

"I can't—" I stopped myself. Grand dukes could do anything. "Surely if I declare a parliament, that looks as though I consider myself to be grand duke permanently, not merely provisionally. Something you've been against from the beginning."

Reko folded his hands and tapped his forefingers together. "Here's the deal I want. Call for a representative parliament immediately. I've drafted preliminary documents, which you can present to the council. Once you've decreed it—publicly—I'll help you."

"That's not the way this works," I said, feeling my temper

start hot in my belly. "You don't tell me what the deal is. I tell *you*, and you obey."

"If you want my help, Your Grace, you'll have to give me a parliament. And I think you need my help."

"I don't need anything," I snapped. "I don't have to give you anything, either. I was willing to overlook your outburst in the hall, but if you won't cooperate, I'll have to think about what my father would do in these circumstances."

A strange look crossed Reko's face. At first, I couldn't place it, then I realized—it was grief. Pain and anger, too, but more grief than anything else. "Your father was my friend."

"Well, I'm not. And I'm grand duke if I don't find a way to cure him. Think about that before you refuse me again." I got to my feet.

I expected him to say something—to tell me to wait, or to fling some insult after me in defiance. But Reko merely tapped his fingers and watched me, and the longer I waited, the harder it was to speak.

I left his chambers. I ought to storm somewhere dramatically, but his refusal had put me at odds with myself. If I couldn't inspire fear in Reko, I didn't yet have what it took to control my court. I was still vulnerable. I needed to do more.

But I wasn't sure what.

I thought I'd be able to contemplate Reko's insistent treason at my council meeting and ignore my ministers as they had ignored me. But the moment I stepped into the room—five minutes early—I saw them sitting straight-backed and nervous, and I knew I wouldn't like what they had to say.

I took Father's seat next to Eirhan. The room was quiet: shuffling papers and cleared throats and slurps of coffee. I focused on the tapestries and their flora: cloudtree, wolfthorn, galanthus. The fauna: lepus arctos, canis lupus nixus, ursos isabellinus. When Rafyet finally arrived, on time and blinking in confusion, I'd identified about a third of the tapestry.

I waited for Eirhan to call the meeting. But he simply picked up his coffee cup and turned to me. "Okay," I said. "I suppose we should start."

I looked from minister to minister. But not all of them looked to me. Itilya, Bailli, and Urso turned slightly toward Yannush. Yannush set down his own cup and took a breath. "What's the point in starting, Your Grace? We can't discuss the Avythera agreement without the minister of agriculture present. The minister of Below should be arranging your coronation trials, but he's confined to his rooms. The rest of us walk in fear that we'll be next."

"And why is that?" I asked.

I'd meant to sound sardonic, as though they clearly had something to hide. But Yannush leaned in and said carefully, "Because Your Grace arrests everyone who irritates her."

"That's ridiculous. Eirhan's still here, and he's been irritating me for days."

No one smiled, not even the pained smile of We-Have-to-Laugh-at-Her-Grace's-Jokes.

Yannush bared his teeth ever so slightly, then worked his mouth into a neutral expression. "We have to face the facts. Your Grace is overwhelmed. Your interference in your family's health nearly killed them, and your paranoia is destroying this council. We can't make the decisions we need to make."

Anger rose in me like a tide. Paranoid? Someone tried to curse me last night, and I was paranoid for wanting to find out who it was? "You don't make decisions," I reminded him. "You're my advisory council."

"And we advise you to step back," Yannush said.

Step back. And let Sigis win the coronation trials without trying? And let Eirhan be grand duke in my name?

"My father would kill you for saying such a thing," I hissed.

There was silence around the table. My stomach curdled with cold knowledge. None of them cared, because I wasn't my father. My edges weren't hard enough. Grand dukes commanded respect, and I didn't.

The water in the messenger bowl began to swirl. Eirhan reached forward, but I swatted his outstretched hand, standing to take the green-tinged note myself.

You are cordially invited Below, where answers are to be found for your questions.

Eirhan peered over my shoulder. "What does that mean?"

I folded the note. "It means this meeting is over." My heart began to patter. The note couldn't have come at a better time. "If you want to do something useful, you can keep Sigis from winning the coronation trials." Assuming, of course, that the council hadn't arranged his coup in the first place.

The palace Below was hung with color and light, a riot of lamps in more shades than I would have guessed could grow here. I wanted to press my hand against them, but Meire held my wrist tight and swam without speaking to me, her crest flat against her head.

Instead of leading me to the throne room, Meire took me through a low arch and a winding, open corridor until we reached a bare courtyard. A wire cage stretched up and over our heads, keeping us inside and the yard exposed. There was no decoration here; the space was lit only by a few deep-blue lamps. Everything looked stranger in their light; Meire's skin took on an obsidian sheen, and my own looked dead and bloodless.

"What is this place?"

Meire did not look at me. Her eyes were dark, and the gills at her neck flickered like a panicked heartbeat. "It is a tribunal. It is why you are here."

I frowned. "Am I on trial?" And for what? For taking too long to sign some agreement?

"Of course not," the duke Below said from behind me. I turned around and bowed, and he nodded to me, taking me by the hand. His hands were larger than Meire's, multijointed and silver at the tips. One of his hands could have enveloped both of mine. "You may think of this as a gift, if you like."

Behind him swam a shadow, and at his nod, the shadow flipped backward and disappeared under a dark arch. When it returned, it solidified into the shape of a fishman holding a thick seaweed rope who tugged three bound figures after him. With a sinking feeling, I recognized the fishwife who'd given us the accounts. She did not look at me; none of the three did. None of them struggled. They let the official drag them by their bindings through a door in our cage and into the courtyard's desolate center.

"These are the citizens who broke the law and consorted with an unfit citizen from Above," the duke Below said. "We gathered evidence, and I tried them by my own hand. Now I present their execution to you as a gift."

A gift of execution. The concept curdled my stomach. But I looked at his flashing teeth and nodded.

"We have come to tensions in recent times," the duke said. "It is something for which we blame your father, not you. And it has turned some of our citizens desperate. Desperation is no excuse for lawbreaking. We still hope for good relations between Above and Below. On that faith, do you wish to speak with them before their sentence is exacted?"

I wrapped my fingers around the wire mesh that separated us. "Who? And why?"

The citizen on the right flashed their crest, fanning it out in bravery or defiance. "One man can halt the trade that built us? It is not right."

"One man can make us weak and defenseless without

paying a price? It is not right," said the second one. They'd clearly rehearsed.

"Who helped you?" I said again. This time, their jailer jabbed at the fishwife with his spear. The dull, rotting tip scraped against her scales, denting them. I flinched.

She looked at me, and her eyes seemed sorrowful. "We met them at the top of the ice. Not at the moat, where many might be watching. While they kept guard, I traded. Iron and wax and electrum, spears to hunt the deep things. The pale king did not come into the water. But his servant did."

"What did the servant look like?"

Another silence, this one longer. At last, the middle one answered. He had a red-and-orange pattern on his scales, a sunset of color. It broke my heart a little. I'd spent my life wanting to observe these people, their culture, their customs. Not their executions.

"He said he was a powerful man." *Eirhan*. "He said he spoke with all foreign nations." *Yannush*. "He said he cared for the plight of all people." *Reko*.

"What was his name?"

"He sits on your council," the fishwife said. "He is pale of skin, and his hair is dark on his head and on his chin."

Rafyet. But that was laughable. Why would Rafyet brag about knowing foreign nations?

He wouldn't. Yannush had a beard, too. Yannush, my foreign minister. Yannush, who had argued with Sigis last night and tried to depose me this morning.

Something uneasy touched at the back of my mind. "Wait. You can see my council room?"

The duke Below nodded to the jailer, who jabbed the fishwife in a clean, brutal move. This time, the pitted iron dug through her flesh and tore a hole in her shoulder. With two powerful kicks, the jailer swam out through the opening of the cage, dragging his spear behind him. Red billowed from the fishwife. The duke Below latched the cage again.

The fishwife began to twist against her bonds. The gills along the side of her jaw fluttered frantically. Her coconspirators trembled, and muscles bulged in their scaly arms as they pulled against the seaweed rope with no success.

I didn't notice the first shark until the fishwife's head hung by a thread, mouth opening and closing uselessly. Her knife-sharp teeth had done nothing for her in the end. Another little shape darted back and fastened its teeth around her shoulder until something made a popping sound.

Farhod's autopsy report of the citizen Below had contained cross sections and technical drawings. I'd seen intestines on paper, the muscles of the arms and legs. But it was so terribly different to see these parts spilling out into the water. The other two prisoners threw back their heads and began a keen that boiled through the water; the keening turned to screaming as the sharks set upon them, ripping a leg free at its knee, pushing their snouts into the hole of a belly.

And then the screams stopped, and that was somehow worse.

I looked down, watching the hair on my legs rise as the sounds of ripping things faded. The sharks moved silently, cutting through the water and the ropes and the meat, shaking the pieces of their prey.

Meire took my hand. "You are disturbed."

"You aren't?"

"This is the reality of our world." A shadow passed over Meire's face. The scent of blood had drawn larger predators, sharks that made the duke Below look slim and small. *So many things here.* Suddenly, our cage seemed scant protection.

"It is done, and we have seen it." The duke Below offered me his arm, and I released Meire's hand to take it. "We do not take pleasure in it, but this is how we rule. It is how we keep our rule." He gave me a calculating look. "I sympathize with my people, and I feel grief and shame with their families. We fight and control the things of the deep, and we cannot do that without your assistance. People have become desperate now."

He led me to the edge of the palace compound, and we bowed to each other. When Meire tugged on me to go, I resisted. "I have to ask," I said, but words failed me. Despite the whole world being made of water, my mouth was dry.

The duke Below brought his head forward, listening.

"My family. Can they be cured with magic?"

The duke tilted his head. "That is not a question I can answer, Your Grace."

"It is a magical curse," I pointed out.

If I was hoping to make him feel guilty enough to give up the secret of magical dominance, I was disappointed. "A magical cure could be attempted. But citizens Below cannot travel Above, and no citizen Above can use magic as the citizens Below can."

"My father can."

"The grand duke is given special dispensation." The duke Below turned his staff around in his long, thin fingers. "It is only natural that you would wish for it."

"Ah." I was hoping to get around to that part a little more diplomatically.

"I relish the sharing of this knowledge. But you are not grand duke yet." His fins flipped. "You must win the coronation trials."

The way things were going, Sigis would become the arbiter of all magic and use it to obliterate everything.

"We could give you the secret," the duke said. "We could help you win the trials. In exchange."

"You'll cheat." Even Below was up to its neck in our politics. The duke inclined his head, dark eyes unblinking. *Don't ask. Just say no.* "In exchange for what?"

"Reexamine your father's declarations. Widen trade. Make our countries equally prosperous again."

Why not just do it? Make the deal, do the trade. Get the power. "I can't," I said, sounding less like a grand duke than ever. "I—I swore I would give the throne back to my father the way he left it. If I were grand duke, I wouldn't hesitate, but…"

"I see," the duke Below said. "We do, naturally, wish for his recovery." His dark eyes were impossible to read. "And we hope you will tell him how we assisted his daughter." He bowed again. "May I give you some advice?"

"Of course."

The staff spun in his hands. "You think it is barbaric, what I did to our traitors. But this is what it is to rule, Ekaterina Avenko." He sounded a little sad. "Sometimes you must be brutal and unforgiving, even to people you once considered friends."

Inkar waited in my rooms, reading a Kylmian grammar book and rubbing one hand against her temples. "Why do you always wander your palace with wet hair?" she asked. "It is a wonder you have not taken ill and died."

"Cheerful sentiments, as usual," Aino grumbled as she went to my wardrobe. "Which dress, Ekata?"

"The most imposing one," I replied. The one that said *Don't touch me, don't even look at me.* As Aino retrieved it, I studied Inkar. She had controlled a thousand men on horseback; maybe she could help me now.

Inkar mouthed a few words, then ran her hand through her hair in frustration. Then I saw a hint of red in her cheeks. "You are looking at me." The blush was joined by a sly smile. Inkar closed the book and tilted her head.

"I want to ask you a question." I tried to ignore the sick feeling in my belly. "When you led the Emerald Order, did you ever execute anyone? One of your own?"

The smile dropped from her lips. "When I had to."

"Do you regret it?"

She hesitated, then shook her head. "What is necessary is necessary," she said. "And sometimes people need to know that you will take that final step."

Yes. People had to know that I could be brutal. Maybe they'd take me seriously if it was Yannush's blood spilling all over the floor of the Great Hall.

Eirhan knocked on my door as I was getting dressed. "You asked me to assemble the council," he said, frowning as he took in my severe look. I wore a high-necked black velvet dress with a skirt that had room for three people. Silver and sapphires were strung over my arms and chest.

"Have the council convene in the Great Hall."

Eirhan's expression flickered. "The Great Hall is a public space, Your Grace."

"Did Father hire you to point out the obvious?" I asked. "Tell your guard to release Annika, and have the council convene in the Great Hall." *Don't make me tell you again*. I picked up the tiara and slid it onto my head. Strength. Pride. Rage. This was the legacy of my family, and if I had to use it to win, I would. *Grand dukes made grand statements*. I paused at the door. "Inkar? Will you come?"

She said nothing, but she slid out of her chair and took the arm I offered. A grand duke and her consort. Aino arched an eyebrow in disapproval.

Eirhan's lips pursed momentarily before he smoothed them. "What of Reko, Your Grace?" he asked as I exited my rooms.

"Reko can stay in prison," I replied. Until he learned that grand dukes were to be feared, not defied.

Eirhan disappeared down the hall ahead of us. I shoved down my fear until I could barely feel it tickle at the back of my spine, then began to walk. I had to be swift and brutal, as the duke Below had been.

Aino's pace increased slightly, and I felt her hand brush my shoulder before she spoke in Kylmian. "Are you sure you should be mixing Inkar in with politics?"

"She's already mixed in," I said. And it felt better to have her support. A partner, even if she was a temporary one.

We came to the Great Hall. I walked toward the throne with trepidation, but without hesitation. The guard was silent; the only sound I could hear was the swishing of my dress and the scrape of our ironclad shoes against the ice floor. I took a seat and rested my forearms against the armrests, then I lifted my chin and sucked in my cheeks, trying to give myself the hard, angry face of a grand duke. I resisted the urge to touch my crown. *You're the most powerful person in the room*, I told myself. *Everyone here should fear you.* And by the end of this meeting, they would.

My ministers slunk in one by one. Itilya wore her usual

unruffled expression, but her eyes did not reach mine. Urso's face was the color of day-old fish. Rafyet looked bewildered. Whispers spun around the room as Annika entered, and intensified when Sigis came behind. I clenched my fists as he winked at me.

Eirhan hurried to me. He leaned low. "What is your intention?"

"Take your seat," I said. *I don't owe you anything.*

"If you're going to make some grand pronouncement, we need a strategy—"

"No," I said, loudly enough to get the attention of every-one in the room. Silence dropped like a curtain. Eirhan leaned away from the vehemence in my voice. "I have some-thing to say, and everyone's going to hear it." I shifted. The sick feeling in my stomach grew. "My family isn't ill. They've been cursed." This didn't get the gasp I'd imagined. Instead, the silence deepened, as though everyone had stilled every part of themselves to make sure they heard what I said next. "I think Minister Yannush can say something about that."

The silence extended a moment longer, so still that I thought I could hear the winter roses growing on the other side of the room. Then Minister Yannush said, "I cannot," with a confidence that didn't reach his too-large eyes.

"You cursed them with magic you bought personally when you went Below."

That broke things. Whispering flew through the room.

316

Inkar turned to me with questioning eyes. I shook my head slightly.

"That's impossible," Yannush said in a high voice that shone with fear.

"Your cohorts Below admitted it was you," I said.

"And you believed them?" He tried to snort, but his bluster was gone. People began to shift away from him. Sigis wore the shrewd, calculating look I'd seen on him when he'd entered the hall the night of my coronation. *Recalibrating.*

I turned my attention back to Yannush. "Why shouldn't I? Who else would they have identified?"

Yannush swallowed. I watched his eyes, hoping they would dart toward a coconspirator. But they remained steadily, disappointingly on me.

"You have committed treason. The price for that is death." My words echoed in a cold, quiet hall. Why was it that my ministers could never keep so silent in private?

They were waiting for me to say *but.* They were waiting for me to commute his sentence.

"You'll be escorted from your rooms tomorrow morning for the execution. I suggest you put your affairs in order."

Then came the uproar. "You can't!" cried Bailli. Other voices joined his.

"Wait," said Yannush, who stumbled forward. I glared at two of the guards who lined the wall, and they hurried to meet him. "I have allies. There are others!" The guards hesitated, looking back at me. I waved for them to continue. *"I have the cure."*

His voice was almost lost in the crowd. Urso stood, pale as the outer wall, with his hat pressed to his chest. Some had elected to shout abuse after Yannush; others proclaimed the need for mercy, as Bailli had done.

"Get them under control," I told Viljo. His halberd came down on the ice, hard. *Crack.* More guards joined him, from all around the walls, setting up the familiar rhythm. But this time, the rhythm was under my control. Even Eirhan looked nervous.

When the hall was silent again, Viljo thrust his halberd in the air. The guards froze. "Minister Olloi," I said. Olloi gaped at me. "You lied to me. I told you what would happen. Make your peace by the morning."

Olloi swayed on the spot. He didn't resist as a guard led him out. Whispers swept the hall again, but at one *crack* of a halberd on the ice, they died away.

This was power. This was what I'd needed. I'd merely had to sign two men over to death to get it.

I spent the rest of the afternoon speaking with delegates—those who weren't too terrified to keep their appointments. I kept Inkar with me, a move that made Eirhan shake his head.

"I hope you're making her unhappy," he muttered in Kylmian. He paced around the room frenetically, something I'd never seen before from him.

Inkar was fast becoming my best ally. "Everything's going

according to plan," I replied, neglecting to mention that the plan had changed.

"Arlendt has a suggestion for a replacement foreign minister," Inkar said when the Baron of Arlendt had gone.

Eirhan stopped pacing and contrived to look so astonished I thought he'd fall back into his chair. "And how is his opinion relevant, Your Grace?"

Inkar shrugged, took a sip of my coffee, and wrinkled her nose. "I did not say his suggestion was relevant. I said that he had one." She looked at me. "You will have to choose a new minister, will you not?"

Yannush's arrest left a power vacuum, but I had no notion of whom to fill it with. Nor was I invested in making what my father would perceive as a power play when he woke up. "That's not my first priority."

Eirhan's shoes clicked on the ice like clockwork. "You've demonstrated that you're Kamen's daughter at last. Now you need to consolidate—immediately. Pick an aristocratic second child for foreign minister. Then they'll owe you something. Then move on to trade discussions with Urso. Terrify him sufficiently and he'll be too afraid to bring a mediocre deal back for you to sign."

"What trade discussions?" The pit in my stomach was morphing, changing into something too close to panic again.

"Any trade. Particularly trade with Below."

I shook my head. Even as I did, a small part of me marveled at the girl who could order the taking of two lives but couldn't decide basic policy. But I knew what made me so afraid. Father would have expected me to kill his cabinet if they'd even hinted at treason. Making these decisions would make *me* his enemy.

"You can't leave us in a precarious position because you think Kamen *might* wake up," Eirhan said. Was that fear I heard in his voice?

"You can make the agreements if you're so keen," I muttered.

I hadn't intended him to hear or to take me seriously. But Eirhan said, "Your Grace has refused us parliamentary representation. You can't order me to take the power you've denied me."

As if he could convince me he was powerless. "You declared me *provisional* grand duke. My father's condition isn't better, but it's not worse. I can't pretend he's as good as dead after four days, and I won't do anything—*anything*— that I can't guarantee he'd do."

Inkar looked between us. Eirhan stopped his pacing. "A deadlock is a dangerous thing, Your Grace."

"Is that a threat?"

"Don't be ridiculous." He reached back to retie his slipping horsetail with shaking hands. "It's advice. People will start taking drastic measures, and dealing with them may be worse than making the decision in the first place."

I had to wait until after dinner to slip into a servants' corridor. I followed it to a staircase and sneaked up to the second floor, hoping that Viljo and Aino wouldn't get into too much trouble for my absence.

If the guards outside Yannush's door were surprised to see me, they didn't indicate it. "I haven't been here," I told them coldly as they let me in. I considered giving them something; Inkar paid servants in silver from her own arms. But grand dukes didn't make bribes. They received obedience.

Yannush looked awful—half his horsetail had come undone and hung in knotted tangles around his face. His skin was sallow in the firelight, and his eyes were dark pits. His beard looked dull and untidy.

He swayed as he registered me. Then his face twisted bitterly. "What are *you* doing here?"

Maybe it *was* a bad idea I'd come alone. "You said you had a cure."

For a moment, I thought he hadn't heard me. Then he began to pace. "I didn't want to do it, you know," he said, as though he'd been rehearsing.

I could tell him to shut up and give me my answers, but I held back. Maybe he'd reveal his allies. According to Annika, I hardly lacked for candidates.

"My hand was forced. Your father went mad, and we had no alternatives to stop him."

"We?" I said.

"We'll go bankrupt if you don't do something," Yannush said. He ran his hands over his arms, and I saw the scratches in his leather coat where his nails had scraped carelessly. "Not to mention that you've led us to the brink of war."

I almost laughed at that. "You're the one who tried to give Sigis the keys to the country."

"We need his power. We need his strength." Yannush stared me down. "We need his allegiance. Your father risked revolution and worse. Sigis might take some measure of independence, but he'll offer stability. We need this. The Avenko line is selfish. You could have made an industry out of refining magic, but your father hoarded the secret. Sigis will make us a trading center. Sigis will make magic relevant, not just a curiosity for kings. And Sigis, unlike you, knows how to run a country."

"Such a hero," I sneered. "I'm sure you didn't spare a thought for the rewards Sigis would give you. Land, titles, powerful positions in government. Did I miss anything?"

The fervent light in Yannush's eyes guttered. "I've only done what I think must be done. And I didn't do it for Sigis, but for Kylma."

"Liar." I stepped forward, testing my limits. Yannush fell back. *Excellent.* "How willing are you to die for him?"

For a long moment, all I could hear was the moan of the wind outside. Yannush's hateful gaze gave way to something more desperate. Finally, he said, "What other option do I have?" in the hoarse voice of a man who had thrown his lot in with the conspiracy and lost.

What would Father do? Rage at him? Promise a painful

death? Or would he act as Yannush's friend right up to the point at which he killed him? "The illness is magical. Which means if you had something to do with it, you know how to manipulate the magic. You have the secret."

Something flickered in his face. Hope, cunning, fear? "You want me to give it to you."

I tried to keep my face blank. "I want to know how you got it."

"And if I said it was your own father?"

"I'd call you a liar again." I regretted not bringing Viljo along; the only way I could think to threaten Yannush was with a fire poker, and that didn't seem fitting for my station. So I tried to soften my voice instead, to use pretty words instead of dire threats. To start from a different direction. "Tell me about the curse, Yannush. Tell me who worked on it with you, and tell me why you cursed them all." *All except me.*

"We need the Avenko line to survive," he said, grudgingly. "Whatever magic binds Above and Below relies on your line. We hoped we could keep you all...sleeping."

"But you chose not to."

Yannush wouldn't look at me. I felt ice melt into my blood, and I was taken back to that night, standing in the servants' corridor, listening to Sigis hiss at his unknown accomplice in the law library. *We'll wake up a different one.* They'd wanted to replace me with a more pliant Avenko.

But why hadn't the curse worked on me?

Focus. I needed answers, not more questions. "So you kept them all alive, in case you needed them again."

Yannush swallowed and dipped his chin.

"You can wake them up." *I* could wake them up if I could unlock the secret of using magic.

Footsteps sounded in the hall outside, brisk and purposeful and loud in a way that servants were never loud. I bit back a curse. "All right. Give me the cure, and your death will be private and quick, with no shame to your family."

The footsteps stopped at the door. Yannush's eyes flicked toward it. The corner of his mouth turned up. "Counteroffer: I cure your family, I live."

Fists hammered on the door, and I jumped. "Your Grace?" The guard sounded remarkably unfriendly for someone whose job was guarding my life. "Your Grace, you must come out immediately."

"Final offer: You provide the cure, you provide a list of names. And in return, you get a sled and I'll never tell my father where you went."

A key grated in the lock. "Your Grace!"

Our mirrored looks of desperation were almost funny. Both of us were seeing our lives slip away, though not quite in the same way. Yannush grabbed my wrist, nearly grinding my bones together. "Done," he said hoarsely. "Send the alchemist. Prepare the pardon."

The guard broke in.

I was marched back to my rooms under a cloud of discontent. The entire trip from Yannush's apartments was punctuated by admonishments like, "You can't *leave* like that, Your Grace," and, "You've put the entire palace in an uproar." As if I'd stopped putting the palace in an uproar since I became the duke.

Aino and Inkar sat inside—Aino by the fire in the antechamber, Inkar on my bed. Aino shook her head. "I know," I said, putting a hand on her shoulder as I passed. Ever since I'd become the duke, her worry for me had increased tenfold. I ought to try behaving, for her sake if not for my own. But I didn't regret what I'd done.

"Where did you go?" Inkar had a blanket pulled over her knees and the Kylmian grammar book propped upon them. Her hair fell in front of her face, making her look smaller somehow, more vulnerable.

I should have lied to her. The trial marriage would be over in four more days, and she would be gone by then. Instead, I shut the bedroom door and went to my wardrobe. "I was visiting Yannush. He'll help me in exchange for exile."

"I thought you were going to execute him."

"I still might." He'd crossed lines that should never be crossed. "Father would."

"You keep talking about him as though he is everything

that matters." Inkar set the grammar book aside and drew up her knees, propping her chin on them and tucking a sun-streaked lock of hair behind her ear.

"He—it's difficult," I muttered, trying to undo the button between my shoulders. I should have called for Aino, but I'd had enough of her sniping at Inkar and making snide comments in Kylmian.

"I can help you." Inkar slid off the bed, hissing as her bare calves touched the air. A few moments later, her fingers brushed the back of my neck. My skin prickled. She slid the first button free and began to work her way down my back. Each light touch made my breath hitch.

"That's not what I meant," I said, struggling to focus. Father was far from everything that mattered, but he reached *through* everything that mattered. Like an illness that rooted in a specimen and spread through a population. His cruelty had become normal, and if I didn't pretend I had it, I'd be torn apart. "I can either be him or be used by people who want to be him. If those are my only options, I know what I'll choose."

She was silent for a moment as she finished unbuttoning my dress. Then she said, "My father often told me that I had to think about what kind of leader I would be. He said we would discover ourselves in battle. You have not been given many battles to discover yourself. But I do not think you will discover what kind of leader you are if you are always chasing after him."

Her hand appeared around my side, holding the long lace of my corset. I turned to take it and met her eyes. They were too close, too kind. No one in my family had eyes like that. I could see the soft fuzz on her cheek, and firelight tipped her eyelashes with gold. Her mouth was slightly parted, her brow furrowed in concern. How could she be so sincere? Among my family, such sincerity would crack us open, and the wolves would descend. I'd only been safely myself with Aino and Farhod.

I took the lace and her hand, too. "I don't have time to learn to be the right kind of leader." Every misstep brought Sigis closer to winning the coronation trials, no matter what I learned from it.

I felt Inkar's soft exhale on my cheek. Goose bumps prickled down my neck. Her gaze fluttered over my lips. Then she retreated, getting into bed and pulling Aino's quilt around her. "Perhaps your father was not the right kind of leader, either," she said.

I was tired of everyone questioning me. Nothing I did would ever be good enough. Suddenly, nothing my father had ever done was sufficient, either. "He has thirty years of experience, which is more than us," I said, yanking on my corset. Only when I'd finished tugging it loose did I realize that I'd snapped. I glanced at Inkar. She sat cross-legged, picking at something on the quilt. Refusing to look at me.

I put my dress away and got into my nightgown. Neither of us spoke. The longer the silence drew on, the harder it was to break it. I felt a flush of irritation—it wasn't untrue, what

I'd said. But beneath the irritation lay a deeper melancholy. I'd brought Father's persona into my own room, and now there was nowhere I could truly be myself.

Maybe this was how Father and Mother had become each other's enemies. By trading cold, unfeeling comments, backed up with bitter excuses. Cut after little cut, until nothing was left but the hate.

"I'm sorry," I said, sliding into bed on the other side. "I didn't mean to be angry." Grand dukes didn't apologize, but Ekata did.

Inkar finally looked at me, and it was the same flinty gaze she reserved for Sigis. I nearly scrambled back out of bed. Inkar was a serpent, poised and ready. And I was the lowest of toads.

"I am trying to help you. You may speak to me how you like, but I am not your servant, and I will not scrape to you."

This was the sort of argument Eirhan had wanted. But I was finished with Eirhan's plan. I put out a hand, fingers splayed. "I'm sorry," I said again. "I'm listening." Because a grand consort commanded grand respect, and there was one way I would never be like Father: I wouldn't encourage my wife to hate me.

Inkar contemplated me for a long moment. At last, our palms touched, sending an electric shiver up my arm. "Mercy can be a great thing. A mark of understanding and hope. And I have found that keeping your word is something many consider admirable."

"Mercy for a traitor who cursed my family?" I tried to make the words heartfelt.

"You must do what you think is right. I do not know much about your father, but I have spoken with delegates who do. He is a hard man, and not many people love him. Is he how you wish to be?"

Being loved wouldn't make me a good ruler. But neither would being harsh. Good rule had to come from knowledge and experience. And since I didn't have those—maybe sincerity would see me through.

You don't have to sit on the throne for years, I reminded myself, tightening my grip on Inkar's hand. *You only have to sit until tomorrow.* If Yannush kept his word.

"Sleep," Inkar said. "I will watch over you until it is Aino's turn."

I lay down. I didn't want to sleep, but exhaustion was a beast that I couldn't escape. "Don't leave me," I mumbled, pulling the quilt up to my nose.

She laughed softly. "Not today."

And I slept, dreaming of rage, of blood billowing in the water and Yannush weeping for his life. I dreamed I was surrounded by a cage of winter roses, and every time I touched them, another part of me turned to ice. I dreamed murky things until Aino shook me awake, pulling my hand free of Inkar's. "Breakfast?" I mumbled.

"No." Aino's voice trembled. I blinked, and I saw the tears that swam in her eyes. "Your father died in the night."

DAY FIVE

CHAPTER FIFTEEN

That's not possible," I whispered.

"I'm sorry," Aino said, and I thought I saw something in her eyes—guilt? Fear?

Inkar sat up, rubbing her face with one hand. The other still held tightly to me. "What is wrong?"

"He can't be—" I didn't say it. Yannush had promised me a cure. Tremors ran up and down my arms, and nausea settled in my belly. I pulled away from Inkar, who looked from me to Aino.

"What are you doing?" Aino said as I reached for my robe.

"I'm going to see him." I slid into my shoes. I didn't wait for her or Inkar. My insides felt hollow, though my brain was awash with noise. Impossible.

"Who knows?" I asked in a rusty voice.

"A doctor reported it," Aino whispered, tiptoeing after

me as though afraid to disturb the silence of the royal wing. "I don't know who else knows."

I headed toward the corridor, picking up speed. I heard the clank of Viljo following me, the click of the door as Inkar shut it behind her.

The sick feeling in me doubled. What if Yannush had used Farhod to kill Father?

You promised, I thought, and I couldn't think of anything else. He'd promised.

Sounds began to break through the haze in my brain. Rapid commands, the rumbling undercurrent of many people in one place, muttering things. I began to notice people being herded in the opposite direction. Their hair was unkempt, their robes and coats covering nightclothes. Many were running. Some looked back, faces full of fear.

A servant grabbed my arm. "Don't gape; bring more water!"

Viljo ripped his hand off me. The servant practically threw himself to his knees when he saw what he'd done, hard enough that I heard the crack of them as they hit the ice. "I'm sorry, Your Grace, I didn't realize—"

And I didn't care. "What's happening?"

He swallowed and lifted his head, staring intently at my stomach. "Fire. In the foreign minister's room."

I pushed into the thickening crowd, leaving Viljo, Aino, and Inkar to make their own path behind me. Despite the early hour, ministers lingered in the hallway. As I drew closer, I saw the light that flickered from Yannush's open door.

I recognized the broad shoulders and bald head that stood in front of me, and I tapped Minister Bailli on the shoulder. "What?" When he turned and saw me, his face drained of color, and he performed a hasty bow. "Your Grace, I beg your pardon."

"Who's in there?" I said.

Bailli looked as though I'd asked him who was the Grand Duke of Kylma Above. "No one, Your Grace."

I shoved past him and headed into Yannush's rooms. Smoke seared my throat. Yannush's room wasn't technically on fire—his desk was. Papers had been piled on top of it, and tapestries had been torn from the walls and set alight. A puddle had formed beneath them.

Eirhan stood in the middle of the room, holding a hand-kerchief over his nose and mouth. Of course. His guard scoured the place, overturning every stick of furniture that hadn't been set on fire. "Where's Yannush?"

Eirhan removed the handkerchief from his mouth, pre-sumably so that I could experience his full surprise that I could ask such a stupid question. "He's killed himself."

That didn't make sense. I'd granted him immunity. *Maybe he knew I told a lie*, I thought. But how could he? Even I didn't know the truth yet.

"He seems loyal to his coconspirators, even in his death." Eirhan gestured to the burning documents. "We've gone through every unburnt scrap and rescued what we could. But we've found nothing."

"I want to look anyway," I said. It was too convenient that Eirhan arrived before I had.

Inkar appeared in the doorway and made for the inner door of Yannush's bedroom. "I don't recommend it, Your Grace," Eirhan told her. "It's not a nice sight."

Inkar gave him a contemptuous look and pushed on the door. I followed, hesitating as I caught sight of one slippered foot dangling over the bed. Then I hardened my resolve.

Yannush lay on his bed. His sheets and quilt were one dark stain. For a moment, I pushed aside my empty panic and pressed one hand to his forehead. Pallor mortis and algor mortis had begun to set in, but I doubted Yannush had been dead more than half an hour. His skin was slick, almost slimy, and his beard was strung with droplets. I brought my fingers up to my nose and sniffed. I dabbed at the fluid with my tongue.

It was a taste I recognized too well. But had he died from the curse or from the bone-handled knife that stuck out of his chest?

Next to his bed, a wide chest of drawers bore the blackened scars of a recently extinguished fire. I heard footsteps as Eirhan joined us. Inkar's hand slid into mine, and I gripped it as though it was the only thing keeping me standing. "He killed himself?"

"Who else would have done it?" Eirhan said, and his voice was higher than it should have been. "*You* were the last to see him alive, were you not?"

Suspicion pricked at me. "Other than your guard, I assume."

Eirhan waved his hand. "The staff saw no one enter or leave around the time of his death."

But... "Why?" I said. I'd seen the man devoid of all pride, begging for his life in front of my court. He'd been given the chance to save himself. It made no sense. And where was Farhod?

"He was obviously mad, Your Grace. His display in the Great Hall was enough to prove that." Eirhan's greasy face was pale, and his eyes shifted around the room. Searching for something? Avoiding me?

The guards would have told Eirhan I'd been to see Yannush. Eirhan could easily have slipped in to kill Yannush and used them as an alibi.

If Eirhan had murdered Yannush, he'd murdered my father, too. The knowledge was a hot knife in my belly. And he couldn't have done it alone.

Eirhan was frowning at me. "Is Your Grace all right?" He took my elbow. "You don't need to see this. My guard will escort you back to your rooms and cancel the morning order."

"What's the point?" I said, too weary to try to pretend. Too weary to try to cross him.

"You still have to prepare for the trial Below. It's unlikely your father will be better by then, and—what?"

He spoke so naturally. As though my life hadn't changed forever half an hour ago. "You don't know?"

Eirhan's face drained of color, and the sinking feeling in my stomach was back. *Your life just got a lot more complicated,* said the detached part of me. Or maybe Eirhan was a better actor than I'd believed. "Know what, Your Grace?"

The smell hit us like a wall as we entered Father's antechamber. I pressed my hand over my nose and kept moving, though I heard Aino cough in the doorway. The chamber was strewn with my siblings, all lying motionless. "Are they...?" I said through my fingers.

"Alive, Your Grace," said Munna.

I passed them and went into my father's bedchamber. There the smell was worse, and my empty stomach flipped. I focused on the table at the side of the room, overfilled with Farhod's herbs. Wormwood, lobelia, mountain poppy, seathorn root. Herbs to purge, to clear airways, to reduce swelling. If I looked at the herbs, I didn't have to look at my father.

Eirhan walked past me to the bed. Mother's chest rose and fell shallowly. Next to her, Father was terribly still. "What's going on? What *exactly* happened?"

"It began around three," Munna said. "Everything was as it had been, then... his lungs filled faster than we could drain them. It was as though he drowned."

I didn't look at my father's pale hands, at the gray cast to his skin. I didn't look at his soaking clothes, at the fluid that still dripped from his chin, from the side of his ear.

"We tried what we could. But... it was difficult when the alchemist fell, too," Munna said.

"What?" My hand flew away from my mouth, and I nearly dry-heaved as I gasped in the full acrid stench.

"Interesting," Eirhan said.

Interesting? I would kill him. I would obliterate everything that had ever been his.

Not Farhod. Not one of the only people who believed in me.

"No one else has fallen to the curse since it took hold. Why him?" Eirhan said.

"Where is Farhod?" I interrupted. Munna nodded to a corner, darker than the rest. I'd been so fixated on my father I hadn't stopped to count the number of shapes sleeping on the floor.

Farhod's brown skin had grayed. When I touched a finger to his neck, I could barely find a pulse. A catheter dangled from his nose.

"Why was I not immediately informed?" Eirhan demanded of the guard in a low voice.

"We sent out messengers to alert Her Grace and the council—"

"That's not how things work around here. *I* am told first. You don't determine whether to interrupt Her Grace's sleep or what the council needs to know. You tell me when there's a development."

"Her Grace would have wanted to know," Aino said.

"Her Grace is under too much pressure as it is," snapped Eirhan. "Look at her."

I lifted the blanket and tugged it gently under Farhod's

chin. Then I drew in a breath to sob, and my stomach revolted. I leaned over the bedpan next to Farhod and noisily threw up.

Aino and Inkar installed me in the family library and gave me a cup of coffee to warm my hands. Breakfast sat untouched on a silver tray. Snow fell, turning the world to a gray palette. Fitting, really. Gray was the color of mourning.

Messengers had been sent out to cry the news among the people. On the horizon, a bright dot burned—a bonfire set by Sigis's army to celebrate the dead duke or the living king, or to proclaim that they were still there. I imagined Sigis and Eirhan together, wearing identical smirks, watching their plans come to fruition. My blood fizzed.

The winter roses twined in the corners of the room, reaching out with blue-tinted petals. They seemed to crowd me. I pulled my knees up to my chest.

The door clicked, and Eirhan came in. "My condolences, Your Grace."

"Thank you," I replied without much attempt at sincerity.

He took a breath, as though he wanted to say something. Then another. I should have felt victorious for making Eirhan uneasy. But I couldn't bring myself to feel anything. Finally, he spoke in Kylmian. "I realize it's a difficult time, but we need to plan your next move."

I shrugged. I looked at the messenger bowl, silent in its corner. Did Below know? Did the faintly rippling water provide them with something more than a portal for notes and lost earrings and other useless things? "What's the point? I only wanted to stay until Father woke up. And now—" Now he was dead. And one of my only allies might as well be.

"Stop whining." Eirhan's voice was full of venom. I looked up, too surprised to say anything. Eirhan began to pace, tapping his pale fist against the air as if he held a conductor's baton. "The trial Below is tomorrow. Your father's death means that no one will trust Lyosha to wake. If Sigis wins the trial, your ministry won't think twice about making him duke instead of you. And what do you think will happen then? Will Sigis send you off to live in exile? Will he let you study at the university or make you stay in the palace? Right now, you have three choices: win the trials, marry Sigis, or die. And if you lose the trials…"

Grand dukes got grand weddings. Or grand deaths.

"You can't speak to her like that," Aino said coldly.

"When Her Grace starts acting like an adult, I'll start speaking to her like one," Eirhan replied. "You've had five days to impress the court, and what have you done? Insisted *you* should find the cure for the uncurable, failed to broker relations with any of the delegates, and married the worst possible bride."

Inkar followed the exchange with a wrinkled brow. "I do not understand what he says. But I do not like it," she said to me in Drysian.

"I never wanted to be grand duke—" I began.

"Well, you are," Eirhan snarled. "Are you willing to do

341

what it takes to survive? Are you willing to do what it takes to keep the people around you alive?"

The air was as thick as water. Was he threatening Aino? Inkar? Would he kill them to keep me in line? Should I let Eirhan act as grand duke for me if it meant he'd leave them alone?

Eirhan took my silence for compliance. "Good. I'll have someone answer your letters of condolence; they're already piling up. Now: the plan. We'll make Below a counteroffer on their trade agreement. If they like it, they'll help you win."

I tried to clear my mind of its fog, to focus on what Eirhan said, and not on how much I hated him right now. "I have to win by cheating?"

"Don't act so noble. Your throne is on the line, and Sigis will do whatever he can to take it. But if you win the trial Below, you'll look stronger in the eyes of the court. You'll have demonstrated strength and spine. That's when you send Inkar home."

He hadn't looked at her, hadn't given any indication that he was talking about her. But her eyes narrowed. She'd heard her name.

"I..." My stomach lurched, though I wasn't sure whether that was from the guilt or the shock of Farhod and Father. I couldn't look at her. "I guess."

"No guessing. You can't have her ruining what comes next. Because once you win the trial Below, you *will* make Sigis an offer of marriage, and he *will* accept you."

"No." It was a quiet plea, devoid of fire.

"Yes. Because if he refuses you, he demonstrates to the court that all he wants is power, and they'll never choose him for that. But if he marries you, he has to make only small sacrifices."

Like put up with me for the rest of my life. Like be the power behind the throne, instead of the power on the throne.

And what would I sacrifice? My everything.

"What are you talking about?" Inkar asked, looking from me to Eirhan.

He didn't bother to answer her. In his mind, she was nothing. I was nothing. Part of the grand game.

Eirhan raised his eyebrows. "Are we clear, Your Grace?"

"We're clear," I said. And it wasn't exactly a lie.

"Good. Meet with Sigis. We'll get out of this."

We? Did Eirhan truly expect me to think he was still on my side? As he scurried away like the weasel he was, I fought the urge to scream obscenities at his back.

Aino crouched next to my chair, putting a hand on my arm. Her blue eyes were full of pain for me, and puffy from crying. "I know things look bad now, with Farhod and your father," she said. "But you can't give in."

"Why not?" My mind was so cold that I barely felt the first tear slide down my cheek and drip into my coffee. "What's the point? I only stayed because I thought—" My voice cracked. "I thought I could fix things." I'd been so sure that I could solve the puzzle. I'd assumed my father would sweep back into his role, that I could disappear south and my problems would melt in the warm sun. Now Eirhan planned to make a prison of my life.

To him I was a useful creature. Inkar's doe, perhaps, ready to be caged. But does fled at the scent of danger, and so would I.

Aino rubbed my back as I cried. When I finally looked up, she wiped at my cheeks with a handkerchief. I took it and blew my nose.

"Can we still run?" I said.

Aino's mouth fell open. It would have been funny under other circumstances. But she shook herself and said, "Our bags are packed. Come." She took my hand. Inkar followed us, a bemused look on her face.

We didn't speak again until we were in my chambers. "We'll head to the mountains, but we can spend only one night in the safe house, if that. We'll wind around to the east tomorrow. And from there"—Aino looked at me—"south?"

"Maybe I shouldn't go south." I went to my desk and began removing my papers. Hollowness grew in my stomach. South didn't seem right anymore. I was leaving behind an unfinished puzzle and a half-drowned mentor. I was giving up.

Aino took me by the shoulder. Her blue eyes brooked no argument. "Ekata, you don't need the cure for university entry. You don't need to prove to the world how smart you are."

Maybe I needed to prove to myself how smart I was. "We have to take Inkar with us," I said to change the subject.

"Why? She's the daughter of a prominent jarl. She'll be fine."

"She'll have to pay for whatever mess I leave behind, and that's not right." She'd probably leave me the moment she realized I wasn't grand duke anymore, but I didn't care. "Get the jewelry."

Inkar frowned at me as Aino bustled off. "What is happening? Are you all right?"

"We're leaving," I said in Drysian, tapping the edges of papers on my desk until they all aligned.

Her eyebrows drew closer together. "Why?"

"Because my father is dead. Because no one wants me to be grand duke." *Not even me.*

She took my hand in hers. It was cold, cracked at the knuckles from windburn, and a warmth spread through me at the touch. How could it seem so different from when Sigis had seized my hand? "I want you to be grand duke."

Aino snorted softly from the bedroom. I said, "That's—" *Irrelevant. Self-serving. Obvious.* "—kind of you. But when it comes to me and my ministers, you don't have much influence. Sigis does. And Eirhan does. And if they want to wield that power so badly, they can stop trying to wield it through me. It's time to give the people what they want." I smiled humorlessly.

Inkar's hand tightened around mine. "This is not what people want. This is what you want. You cannot run, Ekata."

"Why not? If I cure my family, Lyosha will kill me, and things will go back to the way they were. If I leave, Sigis will take over, and things will go back to the way they were." Or he'd wake up a sister and marry her. Either way, it made no difference to me.

Inkar's dark eyes searched my face, and I couldn't decipher her expression. "That sounds...terrible." Her dark hair fell over her shoulder as she tilted her head. "Everything that happened, happened because of the way things were. You took responsibility for what happens now."

"And look how well I did," I said bitterly.

"Ekata." Inkar looked down at where our hands linked. "You have fled your problems for five days. Fleeing again will not fix them. It will take them longer to find you, but it will be worse when they do. A good leader does not run. A good leader talks to her ministers and—"

"I don't want to be a good leader," I said with a force that made Inkar stiffen. I tugged my hand away from hers and made a fist until it stopped shaking. "I'm sorry if it means you don't get to be consort, but I won't let this be my life."

A fire burned behind her eyes, the same fire she used on Sigis. A chill started in my spine, moving outward as I noticed how her jaw had tightened and her hands had clenched. "Do you think this is about my being grand consort?"

"I just meant—" But I wasn't sure what I meant.

"This is about your responsibility. You took it, even if you did not want to. Now you have to face it. And if you do, I will stand with you. But if you run, I will not go. I do not follow cowards."

"It's too much," I shouted. The responsibility had driven

my family mad. It had made us greedy and complacent. It had turned even the children murderous. My father had hoarded secrets and goods, and no one could stop him. He'd thought to increase the power of an already powerful duchy, and instead, he'd brought us to the brink of destruction. "My family doesn't deserve this power. We shouldn't have it." Power in the wrong hands had ruined us. And where my family was concerned, there were no right hands.

Inkar wouldn't look at me. She turned to my desk and picked up the inkwell, turning it over and letting the frozen brick of ink fall out into her hand. "Maybe that is true," she said. "What are you going to do about it?"

Run. But that wasn't the answer she wanted. And it would solve my problems, but not the problems of the duchy.

We needed the Avenko family to keep the connection between Above and Below. But that didn't mean we should hoard all the power. Father had done that, and where was he now? All the same, I could hardly trust my ministers enough to delegate to them. At least one more was in on the conspiracy to betray me, and the others thought Sigis would make a better ruler than having no ruler at all. The only minister I could count on not to be a complete traitor was Reko, and he—

The laugh started in the back of my mind, growing until I couldn't help but let it out. A giggle turned to hysterics, taking the rage and the sorrow and the fear that had coiled inside me with nowhere to go, and turning them into fuel. "What did you do to her?" Aino said.

"I—I do not know." Inkar sounded concerned. That only made me laugh harder.

I wished I'd been less foolish, less adamant. More clear-headed. But grand dukes could be grand fools.

"I know what I'm going to do about it," I said. Inkar looked as though she regretted everything she'd said in the past five minutes. "But first, I need—"

I hesitated, then knocked on Reko's door before I opened it. Grand dukes showed at least mediocre courtesy.

Aino, furious that I'd refused to run after all, had stayed in my rooms. Inkar stood behind me, dressed in the blue and white of the royal guard. The helmet she'd borrowed was far too large. Inkar said something that made one of the guards snort and then stood at attention as though she were meant to be there.

I went in alone. Reko sat at his desk, staring. Baffled. "To what do I owe the"—his mouth turned down—"pleasure?"

He was probably expecting threats. Or a promise of execution. I took a chair near his fire. "You said you have a preliminary proposal for a parliament."

His dark eyes flickered to the door, as though he suspected the guard to burst in and burn everything down. "What do you want with it?"

"I want to save my family from ourselves." I wondered, briefly, if anyone had told Reko about Father's death. Now wasn't the time to find out. "I will grant you a parliament if you support me in the final coronation trial. And if you agree to be the parliament's first prime minister."

Reko's lips pulled back. "You must be joking."

At first, I thought that he didn't believe me or that he wouldn't support me in the trial. But then he said, "Openly oppose Eirhan? You might as well execute me and save him the trouble."

"What do you mean?"

He sat back. "The man will do anything to maintain control. He'd kill anyone."

Anyone. "Even my family?"

Reko leaned forward. "Anyone," he said, and his eyes fastened on me, saying what he didn't say:

Even you.

If I wanted to outsmart Eirhan, I'd have to make him think he still controlled me. So I went back to my rooms and prepared my best trading arguments and my most queenly garb, and prepared to meet with Sigis.

"Eirhan doesn't think you should come with me," I told Inkar as Aino helped me into my father's massive cloak. Her lips were still pursed, her movements angry.

Inkar waved a hand. "He dislikes my cavorting with your guard, or with you. But he does not command us."

Easy for her to say, with her powerful jarl of a father. But her tone warmed me. She hadn't changed from her guard uniform, though she'd removed the helmet. She was all dazzling white and blue. Her axes hung from a belt tooled with the family roses, and more roses were stamped into her breastplate. "Are you sure you should wear that?"

"Of course. I must protect you from bears, after all." She flashed me a knowing smile. "And the guard has made me an honorary member." The smile turned sly.

I ducked my head so she couldn't see the color rising in my cheeks. Her smiles could be an undermining tactic, an attempt to gain control of my household and make it impossible to break the engagement. But my stomach fluttered stupidly, and I fought the urge to laugh.

"I want to look like someone who protects you. Your ministers mutter when they think I do not notice. They think I only want to rise above my station." She frowned, and for the first time since I'd met her, she looked unsure. "But I do not want to distract from your real purpose. Is it all right?"

"I think it's perfect," I said. Inkar was useful in a fight. And dressed in our Kylmian uniform, she looked both like herself and like one of us.

Sigis had taken up residence with his army again, presumably so that he could give the order to attack at any moment. Viljo frowned when I told him we'd be leaving the city. "I don't approve, Your Grace. We might be on Kylmian territory, but we'll still be disadvantaged if he decides to hold you hostage. Or other things. Why not invite him here?"

Because then Eirhan would be listening. "We have to do it outside. I'm sorry."

Viljo considered this for a moment. "I will put a regiment together and contact the kennel master."

"No regiment. A few men you trust." When Viljo opened his mouth to object, I fixed him with my mother's favorite look.

"It shall be as Your Grace commands...." Viljo shifted uncomfortably. "My old guard's master warned me that dukes make foolish moves, at times. I think this is one of those times."

"You can consider your duty accomplished and your words noted," I replied. But perhaps it was good to have Inkar with me. If Sigis made a move, he'd bring himself into conflict with both our countries.

"Dogs." Inkar sighed as he set off. "Maybe I do not want to go."

Viljo's idea of a few trusted men was two sleds of guards riding before us and two behind. We left the palace gate and made for the edge of the city. The dogs set out at a trotting pace, tongues lolling, enjoying the exercise.

"Hold on, and enjoy the view," I advised Inkar.

"That is impossible," Inkar informed me, gripping the sled so tightly that the leather of her gloves creaked. I scooted closer.

We avoided the main roads, driving instead down side streets and smaller trade avenues, winding to the edge of the city with few people to witness our departure. When we came to the main gate, Viljo stopped and spoke briefly to the guard there. The guard nodded, and the gate opened.

A few feet beyond the gate, the ice ended and the moat stretched. Our guards used tridents to break up ice as it formed on the water's surface. On the moat's other side, a thousand men stood, silent. Watching.

Viljo dismounted his sled and crunched toward me over new snow. "I don't like this, Your Grace. They're ready for an attack."

"We'll be fine. Lower the drawbridge."

I hopped off my sled and helped Inkar down. She gasped as she sank up to her knees in snow. Across the moat, I saw the line of soldiers stand a little straighter. None of them looked directly at me, but they were watching. Waiting.

The bridge came down from the outer wall with a thud.

Viljo started across. A figure with a star on his coat met him at the other end, one hand on his sword. They leaned toward each other for a few moments, then Viljo motioned for us. The other figure turned and called, "Inform His Majesty that the grand duke and her consort have arrived."

Inkar straightened. Our hands found each other.

As we crossed, we looked down at the waters of the moat, blue and still. I wondered if Meire was down there patrolling. The idea of it comforted me. I leaned in to Inkar on the pretext of steadying her. "If things go wrong, come back to the moat," I whispered. "The citizens Below will help you."

Inkar touched her axes. "No one and nothing will make me run from a fight."

Sound buzzed, low and rumbling, from the other side of the camp. As a soldier led us through the clusters of white tents, the rumbling increased to a dull roar. This was the kind of party we didn't have in the banquet halls.

A bonfire burned high and angry, blinding and smoky from an excess of wet wood, overlaying the smell of horses and unwashed men. Sigis sat in front of it, in a chair far too grand to be something he hauled around on campaigns. He didn't wear mourning colors, but rather the uniform of his army: red and black, with a gold sash that showed off his numerous military achievements.

He wore a smile, too, which I dearly wanted to wipe off his face. His men stared at us frankly, amused, sneering at Inkar. Their eyes scraped over me until I felt naked and raw. I pretended my spine was electrum, my skin gold. Grand dukes didn't turn tail and run.

Sigis slid off his throne and walked over to us. "What can I do for you, Your Grace?"

I swallowed. "I want to talk to you," I said, and my voice was only a little higher than normal.

Sigis spread his arms. "Talk, then."

"Alone," I said.

His army shifted and murmured, and Sigis's smile turned clever and arrogant and suggestive. I held my tongue. Saying *not like that* would only embarrass me further.

"I can refuse Her Grace nothing, of course," he called, and the men around him cheered. Someone whistled.

"I think this was a bad idea," Inkar whispered.

"We'll be fine." *He can't kill me now. He can't kill me now.*

"This way, my dear," he said. The party silenced as we walked through it, then rumbled to life again behind us. "What do you think of our wake for your father?"

"I appreciate your kindness," I lied.

He brought us to a tent like all the others, with the exception of a guard out front. "After you."

I nodded to Viljo, who stepped back unhappily. Then I ducked inside with Inkar at my heels.

The interior was smaller than the suite we'd offered Sigis at the palace, but no less grand. Fur lined the inside of the tent. A brass brazier had been placed in a pit on the floor, and a wooden desk and chair sat to one side; a bed, to the other.

"Didn't you want to speak alone?" he said in Drysian, eyeing Inkar. She pushed back her hood, and he smirked. "Have you demoted your so-called wife? The uniform suits her. Maybe the next time we meet, her battle skills will be as good as she says they are."

"I—" Inkar looked at me and fell silent.

"Inkar stays," I said.

Sigis shrugged, then kicked his boots off and sat in front of the brazier. "Very well. To what do I owe the pleasure of your visit? You might have invited me to the palace, for Your Grace's comfort."

I got to the point. "Minister Yannush is dead."

Unease flickered over Sigis's face. A few days ago, I would have missed it. Now it gave me the answer I needed most. "I'm sorry to hear it," Sigis said. "You'll have to remind me who Yannush was, though."

"I don't think I do," I replied. "He offered you the chance to be grand duke, didn't he?"

Another moment of silence. "A number of people think I'd make a better duke than you."

"But Yannush was in touch with you before. He told you Father would be ill. He stood to gain from an alliance with you."

Sigis shrugged. "Most people do, Ekata." He rose, picked up a scroll and a clay carafe from his desk, shook the carafe experimentally, then took them over to the fire, sticking the carafe in the coals. "It's what comes from being the most powerful man on the continent. But there's a big step between courting my favor and committing treason."

"There's a lot I can't do as grand duke, but I can extrapolate from evidence. Yannush spied for you. What did you offer him?" My traitorous voice shook. Inkar slipped her hand through mine.

Sigis laughed at that. "What did *I* offer *him*? He came to me. Kylma struggles with high taxes and low imports. No one's been able to get the things they need, and your father was too obsessed with controlling his magic and fighting his son. Not to mention that annexation would be good for you.

355

Tariffs would be all but demolished, trade would be simpler, and you'd have access to a wider range of nations. Face it, Ekata. Kylma is too small, and the world is too big."

He drew a long, curved knife from his belt. Inkar stiffened, but he unrolled the scroll on his lap. It was a map of the North. He'd painted his conquests in red, radiating from Drysiak outward. He began to trace the tip of his knife over the new boundaries of his kingdom. "You think your frozen wasteland is the height of civilization, when in truth your army is fifty years behind mine in equipment and a hundred in tactics. Your people can barely subsist on the fish and meat they catch. If it weren't for your magical friends Below, you'd be nothing at all. Your father was holding this place hostage. It could be a part of something better, but he was never willing."

"So Yannush just wrote to you, offering an entire duchy."

Sigis looked up, smiling blandly. "More or less."

"And he didn't want anything in return."

"Of course he did." Sigis picked up the clay carafe from the fire and poured amber wine into a wooden cup. "He wanted to be prime minister."

I remembered Reko's words. *The man will do anything to maintain control.* Clearly *anything* meant the murder of other ministers, but did it also mean treason? "And you didn't see a problem with marching here and taking Kylma."

Sigis took a sip. "Not really. It's what I do." He saluted me with his cup. "And I'd be better at it than your father, or your brother. Or, with all due respect, you." Inkar narrowed her eyes at him. He leaned back and yawned. "Is that all you need to know? That Yannush begged me to save Kylma from your autocrat madman of a father? Or is there something else?"

"Did you know I'd survive the curse?" I hadn't meant to ask, but my curiosity had gotten the better of me.

"Honestly, Ekata, it makes little difference," Sigis replied, as if he could sidestep the question and I wouldn't notice.

"So kill me now." Inkar glared at me, wide-eyed. *Why* was I saying these things? "Win the coronation trials."

Sigis only laughed. "Believe it or not, I'm not in the habit of killing royalty. If I do it, it's only a matter of time before the commoners think that anyone can do it. And that's hardly a good message to send." He raised the knife, and Inkar leaned in front of my heart. "Make no mistake—if I must kill you, I will. But I have such fond memories of you, little Ekata. Besides, why kill you when there are other ways to achieve my goal?"

His eyes flicked to Inkar. "Reject the horsewoman, and marry me, instead. You can even keep your title."

"I'd rather die the way Yannush died than marry you," I said. Inkar laughed her soft laugh.

Ugliness passed over Sigis's face. "So be it. When I'm finished with you, we'll see how willing to die you are."

I stood. "You're not really different from when you lived with us."

"Nor are you. Better suited to books than to leadership, I think. And far too easy to get into trouble." Sigis rose and pulled aside the tent flap. His eyes burned through the back of my coat as we walked out.

The cold nearly knocked my breath out of me. Inkar's black-freckled eyes were serious as she pulled my scarf over my mouth and nose. She cupped my chin in her gloved hands. "You are very foolish," she said.

"I know." I waved at Viljo, and he rounded up the guards with a shout.

"You are also very brave." Her brown eyes were warm with pride. "Are you certain you can win the coronation trials?"

"Not remotely."

"But you need to win," Inkar said. "He said he will take the whole city if you do not."

"I heard him," I grumbled. And I knew the ugly truth, too. If he lost, what was to stop him from attacking anyway?

"I am having a thought," Inkar said that night as we prepared for bed.

Aino rolled her eyes in my mirror as she brushed out my hair. I returned her look with a stern one of my own and said, "What is it?"

"Sigis said he did not kill royalty. But what does he do with the kings and counts of the lands he conquers?"

How was I to know? "Exiles them?"

"That would encourage revolution. And I do not think Sigis would take kindly to revolution," Inkar said.

Most leaders didn't. "Maybe Sigis has a special dungeon

where he locks them all up. Or maybe he does kill them."
Maybe he worked out coups with *their* ministers and got the
kings killed that way.

"I wonder if there is a special reason he should not kill
you," Inkar said.

"Aside from my being the leader of a sovereign nation,
you mean."

"Yes. My cousin was the satrap of a small country Sigis
conquered. He was hanged."

"Oh." I fumbled for words. "Sorry to hear it."

But when I looked at Inkar, she waved a hand. She had
changed into her nightgown and was untying the cord around
her braid. "I do not cry for him. He was an unpleasant man."

She had a point. Perhaps Sigis wasn't convinced that he was
enough of an Avenko to maintain our agreement with Below.

Aino put a hand on my shoulder. "You are ready, Your
Grace," she said in Kylmian. "Are you sure you don't want
me to send her away? I don't want you to sleep badly."

"I won't. Inkar's . . . helpful."

Aino raised an eyebrow. I shrugged and focused on trying
not to blush, at which I was a spectacular failure.

"Remember the trial tomorrow," Aino said.

"How could I forget?" I tried to sound confident. Instead,
my voice trembled, and my eyes suddenly blurred. I was tired
of pretending that nothing would go wrong. I'd tried to do
things the way I thought I should, and I'd only gotten myself
into more trouble.

Her tone softened. "We can still do it."

I knew what she meant—we could leave. I shook my head. Aino's hand squeezed around my shoulder, then she left.

"What was that about?" Inkar asked.

"Nothing." I didn't want her to think me a coward. "It's—I don't really know how to say goodbye. Or deal with the possibility that I might—" *Die tomorrow.* I couldn't say it. "I don't know how I can win." I felt the familiar bite of fear in my stomach. "I should have trained with you and the guard. I'm not strong enough."

"Ekata." In her mouth, my name sounded like warm wine, like a chair by the fire. She held out a hand, and I couldn't keep myself from taking it.

She pulled me gently until I sat next to her. I was close enough to count her eyelashes. "You will not defeat Sigis through strength," she said. "You must outthink him."

"Outthink the master strategist?" Yes, I was smart, but Sigis hadn't gained control of the entire North by being unintelligent.

"You know more about Below," she said. "You know what...strangeness...lies down there. You must use that to your advantage. It is not a matter of strength. You know the battleground, and he does not."

"You make it sound easy." I pulled away and climbed under the covers. Inkar slid in next to me.

The fire burned lower, and cold moonlight mixed with the orange-yellow of the flames. Her dark hair soaked it up, and the light streaks at the top took on a burnished sheen. I resisted the urge to run my hand through that hair, to see if it was as silky as it looked. A crescent of light shifted on her cheek as she swallowed. "It is simple. But that does not make it easy."

"If I lose—if I don't come back—" I said.

Inkar's brows drew in. "You will."

"—help Aino. Nobody else will protect her."

"You will come back," Inkar said. Her fingers found mine and slotted between them. Something in my heart squeezed.

"What if I don't?"

Inkar's large eyes swept my face, down to my collarbone and back again. "What kind of power do you think I will have to help anyone if you do not?"

"You'll still be the twenty-fifth daughter of Bardur Erlyfsson. No one will be after your head."

Her ankle hooked around mine, and her other hand came up to my shoulder. Her touch left a burning trail on my skin. For a moment, I forgot what we'd been talking about. I forgot the coronation trials. Her knee pressed against my thigh, and her hair fanned across the space between us. "I am more interested in what happens if you win."

"You'll still be grand consort." That was starting to seem like less and less of a problem.

"That is not what I mean." Her eyes were serious. "If you win, you will be grand duke. What does that mean for you?"

I wanted to make some quip that would turn her mouth,

scrunch her eyes. But her question unfolded in my mind. "Things have to change." I'd thought about it, sitting in Reko's rooms, hammering out preliminary agreements until I wanted to squeeze my brain like a wet rag. But I hadn't really *thought* about it. What it meant for me.

If I won the coronation trials, I would turn around and give that power away. Not so much that it broke our spell with Below, but enough. "I can't be him."

"Your father? Your brother?"

"Both." I met Inkar's gaze. Her dark eyes seemed to drink me in. "I've spent these past days trying to live up to something I never could. Because pretending to be my father was easier than trying to be me and failing so miserably. And—"
The only person I hadn't wanted to fear me was Inkar.

"I wish I hadn't tried to be him from the start," I said instead. "I'm going to die tomorrow, and I didn't even do any good for the duchy."

"You will not die." Inkar said it gently.

"It doesn't matter what advantages I have. Sigis wouldn't have risked challenging me if he weren't sure he would win."

"You will live a long and prosperous life, and everyone in Kylma will love you," Inkar said. I snorted. "I mean it. When you are being yourself, you are..." Her hand moved from my shoulder to my jaw. My breath caught. One finger traced the line of my cheek, and her eyes followed it. The touch was feather-soft, the skin of her fingertips velvet.

"What am I?" I said.

Her mouth curved in that eternal smile. "Interesting."

Her palm cupped my cheek. I could nearly taste my heartbeat. Slowly, as if I were trying to touch a wild hare, I rested my free hand on her hip, adding my weight fingertip by fingertip until I could feel the crest of her pelvis under her nightgown. Muscle and sinew shifted beneath her skin.

"If I die, help Aino," I whispered again. For the life of me, I couldn't say it louder. I didn't have the breath. "Help Aino, and she will help you."

"Aino hates me," she replied in the same whisper. Her nose brushed mine. For a moment, I thought she would lean in, close the gap between our lips. But she seemed to be waiting for something.

"Aino does what I say. And I say you're my consort, and everyone must obey you."

"Everyone?" Her voice was rich and low, on the brink of laughter. Her nose slid against mine and brushed my cheek. Her lips were softer than I'd imagined, pressing first into the corner of my mouth, then against the whole of it. Her hand slid up into my hair. Suddenly, more of her was pressed against me: her knees, her stomach, her chest. I gasped against her mouth and pulled her in. Her kiss became surer. Her hand moved to my neck, brushing from my jaw to my collarbone. She smelled of sweat and cloudflower.

I didn't know what to do.

I started to shake. First, it was my calves and thighs, but when my spine went rigid, Inkar pulled back. Her eyes were dark wells. Part of me wanted to lean in, to see how long it might take me to get to the bottom. But another part of me—

"Are you all right?" Her hand moved up to cup my cheek.

"I'm afraid." I hadn't realized it until I said it. But I was afraid. Afraid of tomorrow. Afraid that I'd kiss Inkar now and hate her later, and afraid that she'd hate me. And I was afraid of myself.

The curve of Inkar's lips turned down. She shifted back, leaving a cold gap of space between us. But her hand stayed on my cheek, and her legs still curled between mine. "I will do nothing if you do not want it. Do not be afraid of me."

I ran my thumb over the hair above her ear. It really was as soft as it looked. I leaned in and kissed her, a feathery touch of mouths before I could turn coward and freeze. "I'm not. I won't."

I thought she might try again. Her hand ran from my cheek to my waist and rested there. But she didn't move in. She said, in the softest voice I'd ever heard from her: "Are you sorry you married me?"

"I've never once been sorry," I replied. And though that wasn't such an achievement for a five-day courtship, she laughed, and that was enough for me.

DAY SIX

Chapter Sixteen

The morning of the trial Below bloomed cold and cloud-less. Aino woke me when the sun was a red fire on a smoky horizon. As I slid out of bed, Inkar stirred. "Go back to sleep," I said, tucking my head so that Aino wouldn't see how I blushed.

"No." She was already sitting up. "I must be ready, too."

"For what?" muttered Aino. She was as pale as I'd seen her the night of my haphazard coronation, and she discarded over a dozen items from my closet until she settled on a coat—velvet the color of the night sky, lined with ermine and dotted with tiny diamonds like stars. "And the white dress to go with it."

"I'm only going to take it all off again," I said.

Aino shot me her classic motherly glare. "You are the grand duke, and you have to look like it." Inkar nodded in agreement.

So on went the dress, with two petticoats and a crinoline underneath. On went the coat, with a tasseled hood and velvet gloves. Aino set my braid and pinned it in a crown about my head, fixing it with studded pins and clasps. As Aino dressed me, Inkar dressed herself in the green of her father and the Emerald Order, with a vest over her black leather tunic and trousers. She pinned up her hair to mirror mine and slid my enormous sapphire ring over her gloved hand for everyone to see. Last came her axes, gleaming like sunlight solidified. I wanted to kiss the freckles on her nose, but the thought of doing it in front of Aino set my ears on fire. I settled for taking her hand.

The kennel master waited with our sled. "They're all out there, Your Grace." Though grand dukes made grand entrances, I still wasn't used to them. Maybe I never would be.

There's still a chance. To wrangle the cure out of the duke Below. To save my family from our ministers and from each other.

All of Kylma had turned out. They lined the road to the gate, their faces peering out of hoods and scarves like little moons as we drove past, solemn and silent. The sun turned everything blindingly bright. The dowager's mansion and the hunting lodge became crystal and gold. The white wall of the city rose up, giving way to sky, as though nothing lay beyond it. And then the gates slid open, and I faced the whole world in miniature.

Every delegate had come out to see the trial, sporting their colors and packed together for warmth. My entire ministry, Reko included, stood at the edge of the moat. All of them had dressed in the family colors and held white roses. I could only hope that meant something good for me. The moat rippled, each little wave tipped in gold, and behind that stood Sigis's army. They gleamed in red and black, brass buttons and helmets catching the sun.

"Are you ready?" Eirhan said.

I nodded. I didn't really trust myself to speak. Inkar held me up on one side, Aino on the other. I contemplated throwing up all over the bottom of Eirhan's coat.

"Sigis will arrive soon," Eirhan said. "I suggest trying to look somewhat regal while you wait."

I was beyond tired of letting Eirhan tell me what to do. *One battle at a time.* First, I had to win the trial Below. Then I could work on firing my prime minister.

Sigis's army let out a roar. A thousand arms pumped in the air. A gap appeared in the lines, and Sigis swaggered through, decked in a fur robe I swore I'd last seen on Father. A beaverskin cap covered his head. Diamonds glittered on both ears and in rings on his gloved fingers. Though his sword remained sheathed, it sat in a prominent place on his hip, and his hand lingered there before he raised it to the swelling of the crowd. His cruel smile played about his lips as he looked around, until, at last, his eyes found their target: me. The smile fixed, broadened, and then his hand sliced through the air. The noise cut to silence.

I curled my lip. *Your army doesn't scare me.* If I thought it vehemently enough, I might even believe it. But it didn't matter how much Sigis showed off now. I had to defeat him, not his thousand men.

The bridge lowered, and Sigis strode across. He walked right up to me, moving in until he knew I was uncomfortable. Inkar put herself between us. He laughed.

"Last chance, Ekata. I have a ring for you," he said over her head.

My insides buzzed. I didn't answer.

Water churned in the moat. A dark blue head, covered in scales, emerged from the wavelets and blinked round eyes at Prime Minister Eirhan.

Urso came forward, rubbing a damp hankerchief under his collar. How could he be sweating? The breeze froze the tears at the corner of my eyes, and Sigis's bold smile was starting to look forced. With a last squeeze of my hands, Aino and Inkar stepped back, leaving me alone. "Your Grace," Urso said, sounding more nervous than ever. "Your Highness."

Sigis and I nodded.

"The trial Below is a test to win the alliance of our dearest partners. Once Below, you will receive instructions for the competition. He—erm, the one who earns the favor of the duke Below wins the trial. Are you prepared?"

"Yes," said Sigis, as though the question itself were ridiculous.

I tried to keep my tone even, calm, befitting a grand duke.

Because that was what I was, and Sigis wouldn't take that away from me. "Yes."

"Then disrobe."

Sigis made a great show of unclasping his cloak and letting it fall to the ground. He pulled his clothes off piece by piece until he stood in a pair of scarlet shorts that made me roll my eyes. It couldn't be often that he had permission to parade his royal butt for his subjects. One of his hands made a loose fist, and I thought I knew what was held inside it. I removed my layers one by one, thankful that Aino had made me wear my crinoline and corset, if only to watch him grow more and more uncomfortable as he waited. By the time I stood in my shift, he was trying not to rub his arms.

More shapes disturbed the surface of the water. Something glittered on the moat's surface, and ice began to spin out in petals and leaves, filling in the water until just one dark hole remained. One way in, one way out.

We moved to the edge of the hole. My toes squeezed together at the cold. "Do you really think you'll be a better grand duke than me?" Sigis asked in a low voice.

Not alone. But I'd vowed to give up my absolute power, something I knew he'd never do.

"I was begged to come save Kylma from you. Why fight for it? Why insist on ruling a country that will never love you?"

Something snapped in me. "Maybe you're right," I said, filling my voice with weariness. "It's not like anyone ever taught me how to rule."

"It's not your fault." Sigis's voice was syrupy-warm. "Your father taught you that hating your siblings was more important than nurturing your own people. You simply don't have the necessary skills, Ekata." He opened his fist. A little ring sat on his palm—far too small for his fingers, but not the wrong size for me. He held it up with a smirk. Behind him, identical expressions of horror crossed Aino's and Inkar's faces. Eirhan looked hopeful, the utter bastard. "Take it," said Sigis gently. "Don't be a grand fool."

I plucked it from his fingers. I couldn't help myself. "Sorry, but grand fools make grand gestures."

I drew back my arm in a wide move that everyone could see. Then I hurled the ring into the moat.

It tumbled into the depths, losing sparkle as it fell. I had the satisfaction of seeing, for a bare instant, a look of utter shock on Sigis's face. Then I dived. The cold hit me, and I couldn't think about anything else.

I began to shake. The moat was so much colder than the water in the palace entrance to Below. I fought not to gasp. It had been too many years since I last dived in. I wasn't used to it anymore.

The water began to feel warmer—or maybe I was losing all feeling. I tried to pump my arms and legs, but they dragged and refused to work. My heart worked slowly, painfully, and my lungs began to burn.

Above me, the roar of Sigis's army was muted by the water

372

as he leaped in, too. His face transformed into horror as the cold hit, and his mouth formed around a curse. Maybe the trial was about who could last the longest underwater.

A shape appeared beneath me, and I recognized Meire's green mane. Hands glittering with magic pressed against my face, and the need for air receded. Next to me, a citizen Below I did not recognize brushed Sigis's mouth and nose.

I opened my mouth to say something, but Meire pressed a long finger to her lips. A kick of her feet took her down, away from me, and I knew not to follow.

Light grew around us. Dozens—no, hundreds—of lamps strung beneath the ice gave it a blue-green glow. Flowers hung next to them, laced through seaweed orbs. Thirty or forty feet below, I spotted a dark net of woven seaweed, meant to keep the rest of Above from Below's business. And as the light grew, so did the warmth. I saw Sigis's mouth turn a slightly less violent shade of blue.

A fishman swam to meet us. He bore an electrum staff that glittered blue and green, and his dark mane was edged with gray. "This is the trial Below. You shall proceed to the Stonemount. There is a pearl, a gift from the duke Below for the crown of the duke Above. Whoever retrieves the pearl receives our blessing to wear the crown."

He looked from Sigis to me, blinking his great eyes. "You will not harm each other. You will not touch or be touched by a citizen Below. You will not leave the light."

Sigis moved first, shoving past him and shooting off through the lamps. I swam after him, though my brain pinged a warning. He couldn't possibly know where the Stonemount was. Could he?

Something flashed beneath me, far enough that I nearly missed it. Meire coiled behind a burst of pink flowers, about twenty feet away. She met my eyes and beckoned. I turned from Sigis's retreating form and set off after her, sticking close to the net.

Meire disappeared as I drew near, showing herself only in brief flashes to let me know I was on the right track. From time to time, I glanced around the hanging garden; Sigis's body became a thin line moving between lamps, then a dot, then disappeared. The tightness in my chest began to unclench. Inkar might be right. I might win this after all. And maybe I wouldn't win through superior intelligence, but who cared? I'd win through making allies, and perhaps that was more important for a grand duke. I set my pace.

Something gripped my ankle, and I let out a short scream. Sigis pulled me back and propelled himself forward until we were shoulder to shoulder. He hadn't tried to get ahead of me at all. He'd let me think I was secure, and now he was going to steal my victory.

He swam with practiced ease. A hot fist squeezed around my heart. Even if I did find the pearl first, he would just take it from me.

Meire had vanished. She couldn't let Sigis see her. As the

net dropped away beneath us, I angled down, feeling the water stir as Sigis followed me. *You must outthink him*, Inkar's voice whispered in the back of my mind. Sigis knew that I'd been Below and would consider that my advantage. And he expected me to lead him to the Stonemount.

I slowed my pace, as though I were tiring. Then I dived straight down.

I heard a bubbling shout of anger as Sigis followed. The water darkened instantly, reducing the ice to a creaking monster somewhere far above. A figure swam up beside me. "Go back," said a voice I did not recognize. I shook my head and kept swimming. The guard didn't touch me. He couldn't touch me.

Sigis's shoulder slammed into mine, sending me spinning through the water. He shot me a look of pure hatred. Two years ago, that look would have pinned me like an insect, made me run off to some servant's corner and hope that someone else would make him angrier before I had to venture out again. Now I bared my teeth, kicked him in the knee, and hurtled into the dark. The guards called after us: *Stop. Come back. It is dangerous.* But I ignored them, and so Sigis ignored them, and we plunged toward the deep dark.

I felt the first brush of something on my wrist and swallowed my spike of fear. But at the second brush, I shot back up. I couldn't see Sigis anymore, but I heard a yelp and guessed that one of the creatures of the deep had fastened itself to him. A tentacle wrapped around my calf, and

I struck out in panic. How ironic if both of us were to die down here.

I kicked again, and the sentinel freed me. Then I swam, hoping I was still headed in the right direction. Gradually my eyes picked up shapes, long and thin, looping through the water around me. My mind attached names to the shapes, questioning.

Focus. At last, I spotted the light, and as I kicked closer, it resolved into lamps. I checked behind me. Fish and fishmen, long things and finned things. But no Sigis.

Two guards appeared beneath me, and two came up to swim beside me to keep me from leaving the lit area. None of them was Meire.

But I didn't need her anymore, I realized. Something floated in the water around me, giving it a strange, oily sheen. As it dusted my fingers, strange eddies appeared in the water. Ice crystals formed like rose petals and fell away from my body. Magic. It illuminated a trail before me.

The trail led to a rocky face that loomed like a mountain. Little flowers, pale as moons, dotted its surface, tilting their bloodred stamens toward the lamps.

They clustered around an opening in the rock. A light flickered from within. I aimed for the light and swam.

As the Snowmount had been carved Above, so had the Stonemount Below. Black-on-black scenes showed Morvoi, the God Below, bringing the first citizens down to be his subjects. Sharks terrorized fishmen, and kraken wrapped their arms around pillars. Little fish and squid as dark as stone swam back and forth above us. The petals that brushed against my body darkened, turning as thin and sharp as volcanic glass. I pressed my legs together, thinking of their knife edges, of the little sharks around us.

The duke Below floated beneath a relief of Sjiotha and Morvoi. He wore his electrum crown, with points like teeth. His dark, dark eyes regarded me. In his hand, he held the pearl.

He beckoned. A guard swam in, bearing a body in his arms. Sigis.

I didn't know whether my former foster brother was unconscious or worse. Welts covered him, wrapping around both legs and his torso, kissing his neck and cheek. The duke Below observed me, as I, in turn, observed my rival. "You match your father for ruthlessness."

It was the sort of statement I'd been chasing after all week. Now it left me cold.

"We are not in the habit of starting wars," the duke Below said. "But you have won your trial." He held out the pearl, sparkling, the size of my little fingernail. It was cool against my fingers, and so light my stomach lurched with the fear of losing it.

"Hail, Your Grace," he said, and curled into a bow to me. Around us, the citizens Below followed him.

"Hail," I replied.

"It pleases me that it is you," the duke said. "We will keep you."

What did he mean by that? *Doesn't matter.* My mouth was dry, for all that water surrounded me. Now was my chance. "And if I'm grand duke, do I not get a grand duke's privilege?"

His eyes hooked into me. "Like your father, you hunger for our magic." It did not sound like a compliment. "What will you do with the secret when you have it?"

"I'll bring my family back."

A low hissing sounded around me. Was it the wrong thing to say? "And after?" the duke asked, never taking his black eyes from my face.

"I don't know," I confessed. I hadn't thought beyond the awakening until yesterday. Maybe a parliament would demand the knowledge, or order the creation, of a guild. Maybe our trade would become less restrictive. But it wasn't a decision for me to make alone.

The duke regarded me a few moments more. Then he said, "You will be a friend to us, Ekata Avenko. As we are a friend to you. So I say, as a friend to a friend, we will give you what you need to stabilize your magic Above. In return, you will not try to wake your family."

Something strange and heavy coiled in my stomach, dragged at my feet. *What?* "Why not?"

The duke cocked his head. "Because we do not want it. We cursed them, after all. We made you the Grand Duke of Kylma Above."

CHAPTER SEVENTEEN

Y ou—you..." Panic wrapped its cold grip around my spine. My feet stilled in the water; my hand loosened around my prize pearl. "You cursed us?"

The duke Below signaled a servant. She bore a messenger bowl, shining, white, strange. The duke withdrew four shimmering pearls from the pouch at his belt and crushed them in his fist. He opened a handful of light that flashed through the water and dipped it through the oily barrier, into the air Above. "We cursed only those who deserved it most. And now that the succession is clear, we can be finished. If you are so reluctant, I do not mind taking on the task—" He began to stir with his fingers.

"No." The word burst out of me, and even I was surprised by the vehemence of it. But I meant it, I realized. "You can't do that."

The duke's mane flattened against his head. "Why not?"

Was it the strange light, or did the orange spurs at his elbows seem brighter?

"You can't kill them. Maybe they don't deserve to live, but that's not your choice." It was for my ministers, for my parliament. Maybe for me, even. But not for him.

"He who has the power makes the choice." The duke's head turned. He regarded Sigis, supine in the arms of his guard. "There is one who understands this. Should we wake one of your sisters and make Sigis grand duke instead?"

"You can't threaten my life. You can't hurt me during the coronation trials."

"We may not *touch* you during the coronation trials," the duke Below corrected. "But we may...adjust things with regard to your family."

"I..." They'd cursed us. It made such horrible sense. But if they had— "Why did you tell me about Yannush?"

"Yannush favored the wrong candidate. He tried to kill you even when we instructed him not to. I told you we are friends, Ekaterina. We did as friends should do."

My stomach twisted bitterly. He'd killed three of his own citizens to make me trust him. "And now you're threatening me."

"I do not wish to. But look at the weapons we hold," the duke said. I didn't think he meant it as a mark of intimidation. Their rotting spears spoke of desperation. "Your father stopped trading iron and wax. Things decay around us, and we cannot replace them. We must defend ourselves from the deep. We are not servants of Above. We are not interesting and exotic things to study. We are our own people, and we have our own needs." He continued to stir the air with his hand. Magic was volatile, magic didn't follow orders, magic couldn't be controlled—except by them. *How?*

"You told me you didn't meddle in the affairs of Above," I said, more to buy time than anything else.

He smiled. "Of course I told you that."

"But if you don't care...why didn't you kill me the first time I came Below?"

"Kill you?" The duke seemed puzzled. "Why would we kill you? You are curious. You are spirited. You are dazzled by us." Easy to manipulate. "And we need someone of the Avenko line." His hand paused. "Tell me it can be you, Ekaterina."

I couldn't move. I couldn't even think.

"We demand respect." His hand made lazy figure eights in the bowl. "If you will not give it to us, then we will stop extending our protection to you. We will find another Avenko—the little one, perhaps. He is young enough to be molded for many uses."

Two figures swam between us. My body flushed with electric fear. "You cannot touch me," I said automatically.

But they didn't need to touch me. One raised his hand, and I felt the magic drawing out of me, the tightening of my lungs, the rising tide of panic.

I flailed, gripping my pearl, grabbing for the little black

petals until their tips bit into my palm. I sliced up out of desperation, hoping that if I distracted him, I might buy my lungs a moment more. But what did it matter? I was so far away from the surface I'd never make it.

The blade of the petal caught his arm as he threw it up to deflect me. It scraped off his scales to bite into a soft, unprotected piece of forearm. Blood ribboned out.

Around the wound, magic began to coalesce. My hand brushed it, and I felt the tug, deep in my belly. The weight on my chest loosened. I no longer needed to breathe. Around my fingers, the water flashed, taking on shape, putting a barrier between me and my enemy.

It was doing what I needed. It was doing what I wanted.

The secret to magic was inside us, Meire had said. I'd assumed she meant in a more general sense. That if I dug deep enough, I'd find it for myself. But that wasn't true at all. The secret was literally *in their blood*.

The guard started toward me, fingers clamped around his arm. The water wall between us shattered. My arm darted out to grab his. I closed my eyes, pulled for the magic all around me, focused my thoughts. My fingers lengthened, growing bluer and extra-jointed. Webbing stretched between them. I shot away from him, through the arch of the Stonemount and toward the surface, swimming too fast and too desperately. Lanterns and fishmen blurred around me. Still I pushed for more speed, more power. Magic was temporary. How long did I have? The water churned behind me as the guards followed. But true to the laws of the trial, they did not touch me.

I swam up in the gloom, past fish that hid behind arrangements of flora. I swam until the glow of the lanterns shone against the dark of the ice sheet, illuminating the jagged hole in the moat. My limbs ached. My fingers took on a pink tinge, growing nails. The magic was wearing off. But the ice was only a few strokes away—

A long body joined mine. Meire's green crest was flat, her pupils wide. She couldn't touch me, but I reached for her. If anyone would help me here, she would.

Between her fingers she held a single, glowing pearl. She kicked past me and pressed it to the bottom of the ice. More citizens Below joined her. Magic broke in glittering clouds around their fingers.

Winter roses burst from the underside of the ice. Blooms erupted, sprouting vines and thorns and new buds that became flowers. They covered the hole, wilting and disappearing seamlessly into a smooth sheet.

I kicked frantically. My legs were on fire. Black spots exploded around the edge of my vision as my lungs convulsed, remembering they needed air. Warmth leeched out of the water around me. I swam for my life, cutting with my pale, small, human hands toward the white sheet above, toward the hole that withered as the darkness in my eyes grew. My fingers reached, splayed, for the last open water.

Frost grew over it like leaves. Icy thorns pricked my fingers, drawing blood. I gasped, and the water rushed in.

This was my end. Drifting to eternal sleep in a place I'd loved without respect. Free of all my problems at last. A drop of blood uncurled in the water. I stared at it, red against blue against white.

Against steel.

A sharp edge sliced into my vision. Far away I heard a dim cracking sound, but I couldn't understand it. I was lost to the vastness of Below.

Gold and silver slashed down. The blade wiggled into the crack of the ice, broke free, then chopped again. And again. Ice grew back, fast, stitching the pieces together—but not fast enough. The blades were a whirl, one after the other, relentless. And at last, they revealed what I'd been seeking.

A leather-clad arm plunged into the water, and a hand tanned by days in the sun wrapped around my wrist and pulled. My brain had enough self-preservation instinct to tell my feet to kick. I fluttered my blue toes.

My head broke the surface, and I coughed and choked, spitting lake water all over Inkar. She braced one knee against the ice and pulled me up.

I gulped air. My body shivered uncontrollably. I fell to my hands and knees, and my skin instantly fused to the ice.

"It will be all right," Inkar whispered as she worked me free, peeling me off the ice minus one layer of skin. I was too cold to feel the pain. She draped one of my arms over her shoulder, then the other. "I have you now."

Black boots creaked against white snow as Inkar staggered to her feet. Even my eyes seemed to glaze over with frost. It didn't matter, I realized, my thoughts as slow as milk in the morning. I would die of hypothermia anyway.

"You can't do this," warned a voice I ought to recognize. "You cannot interfere in the coronation trials."

"Try to stop me, old man," Inkar growled back.

The trip up to the palace was a haze. My mind was mercifully blank for the first time in a long time. When the fog finally lifted, I was in a bathtub in my antechamber, stripped naked, staring at a blazing fire. My fingers and toes burned. I brought up a shaking arm to inspect my fingertips. They were blue, but light blue. Frostnip, but not frostbite. I would recover. The skin of my palms had been tightly wrapped, and the linen was soaked. My knees and the tops of my feet were the same.

Inkar sat in a chair next to the fire. She turned at the sound of splashing water and her body sagged in relief. "Are you with me?"

"Yes. I mean, I think so." My voice sounded like the rasping of ice. I drew my knees up, conscious of my nakedness.

Inkar stared intently at the floor. "I am sorry," she said. "I thought it would be best. I will fetch your robe."

I smiled. *It is not odd in my country to be naked in front of other women*, I almost said. But that would imply things—not bad things, but things I wasn't ready for. Not to mention that I could barely move my arms. I tried to hoist myself out of the tub and hardly rose an inch. "Where's Aino?"

"I do not know," Inkar called back. I heard the creak of my wardrobe door. "She told me what to do and disappeared." Inkar came back in with my robe over one shoulder and a towel over the other, and a small wound kit in her hands. She draped my robe over the chair, near enough to the fire that it might get some warmth. Then she pulled the bearskin rug over to the edge of the tub and gripped my arm, steadying me as I struggled to my feet.

Her hand was so warm. I wanted to wrap myself in that warmth until the trembling stopped.

"Can you stand alone?" she asked.

I nodded. I didn't trust myself to open my mouth.

Inkar draped the towel around me and began to dry. She worked precisely, saying, "arm," or "leg," when I needed to lift, careful never to touch her skin to mine. All the same, her touch left a warm trail wherever it had been, and my tired heart pattered furiously as she moved from limb to limb. Soon she set the towel aside and pulled my robe around me.

"You're very good at this," I said as she tightened it.

"I have been out in the field, remember?" she replied. "I have dealt with hypothermia before."

Her hands rested on my arms. It was hard to concentrate. "But you live somewhere warm," I said.

Inkar laughed. "Only a Kylmian would say that." She led me to the chair, and I sat. "May I change your bandages?"

"Okay."

Inkar knelt, pulling a slim knife from her belt to cut off the wrapping. I hissed at the pressure, but her fingers were light as they ran the edge of my wound. The skin was raw and wept yellow pus. "It looks good, if you can believe it. It will be a little hard to hold a sword for a few days." Inkar met my eyes and flashed a brief smile.

I wanted her to kiss me so badly. Energy fizzed through my body, starting in my stomach and spreading out until my fingers warmed with it. Every brush of her against my skin sent a tingling through me that made me throb.

"This may sting," she murmured, picking up a jar of something thick and pale from the wound kit. She spread the poultice over my palm, and I drew in a breath as her other hand tightened around my wrist. "What is it?"

What did I tell her—that I could feel my heartbeat pulsing in my wounds? That her skin glowed in the firelight, or that her waterfall hair had come half undone from her braid? That the way she wrapped my hand again, so careful, so concentrated, was the most beautiful way I'd ever seen someone look at me?

My floundering mouth came up with, "Do you end up bandaging all your wives?"

Inkar didn't lift her head, but I saw the curve of her jaw as she smiled. "Joking? I think you are feeling better."

She released my right hand and took the left. My fingers caught in her braid, loosening the ribbon. Inkar froze, head tilted down, gazing at my hand. I teased her hair out. The strands separated as easily as water. As I found the base of her skull, she finally looked up at me, still kneeling like a supplicant before her queen. Her lips parted slightly, revealing ivory teeth.

I leaned forward as she leaned up. Our mouths met, awkward in a way that last night's kiss hadn't been, but I didn't fear her now. Her lips burned against me, and I drank up her warmth, letting it spread in waves. I didn't care if she was using me. Everyone would, one way or another. Why shouldn't it be her?

A massive shiver overtook me. Inkar pulled back, and it was like losing the sun. "Are you all right?"

"I'm fine," I said. "Just—cold, still." I leaned forward again to recapture some of that heat. Our foreheads met, our noses touched. She smelled like salt and sweat.

"I should—" Inkar's breath tickled my neck. "Aino will be back soon." She bent over my other hand, and I didn't dissent. I didn't need Aino walking in on us, or her disapproval.

For a few moments, the only sound in the room was the crackling of the fire and the scrape of the putty knife in the jar of poultice. Then Inkar stood and went to my desk. "Aino suggested we bring you out for dinner, if you are not too ill."

I laughed. "Since when were you and Aino coconspirators?"

"Since you went through the ice," Inkar said. She frowned at the various jars on my desk. I liked the way she wrinkled her nose in puzzlement.

The servants' door opened in the antechamber, and Aino appeared, obscured by a large stack of blankets and towels. She dropped them onto the bed, then spotted me through the door. Her eyes filled with tears.

"I'm fine," I said uncomfortably as she hurried over. She bent down to wrap me in a careful hug, an effect somewhat ruined when she started to sob on my shoulder. I patted her awkwardly, trying to hold her without using my hands.

"What happened? First the hole closed. Then Inkar—" She stopped, took a shuddering breath, and tried again, voice softening. "Then Her Grace broke through and pulled you out. Below was pushing Sigis out of the water as we left. He looked..."

"He must be alive. His army would be laying siege to us otherwise." Though I hoped he'd bear some interesting scars.

Aino cleared her throat. "May I...?"

"Here." Inkar handed her a roll of bandages.

Neither of them looked at each other. They seemed... embarrassed? As Inkar slipped into the bedroom to sort through the pile of linens, Aino bent over my raw knees. "Forget what happened with me," I said in Kylmian. "What happened between the two of you?"

"What do you mean?" Aino asked, but she didn't look up.

"You know what I mean. She's not ordering you around. You're not being sarcastic. You're...agreeing on things."

"We've always agreed on things," Aino protested. I snorted. She closed the bandage around my left knee. "You did not see the way she looked when we all thought you were dead. She broke hundreds of years of tradition for you. And she threatened to kill Eirhan."

"At least somebody did," I joked.

Aino smiled, but it was quick, vanishing so completely I wasn't sure it had been there at all. "When she broke through the ice...I thought she'd go in, too. Then I thought she'd give up. But she didn't stop. She didn't even falter. I don't know why she was willing to die for you, but..." Aino slapped more of the poultice on my right knee, making me hiss in pain. "Sorry. I'm not saying that I'll ever think of her as one of my own. But if you have to marry someone, marry her."

If I had to marry someone. The thought opened a strange hollowness in my belly. I didn't want to get married at sixteen. I hadn't really considered getting married at all. Inkar had been a lucky choice, but I'd known her for only six days.

Inkar came back into the antechamber, and I watched as she examined a length of bandage. She was so serious when she thought I wasn't looking. But when she caught my eye, her dark, flirtatious smile came up. My heart jumped. I looked down and fiddled with the corner of my robe.

Aino finished wrapping me up. "There. I think that will hold." She shook her head again. "You should have run."

"No, Aino," I said. I'd wanted to—I still wanted to—but I couldn't say I should have.

A knock came at the door. With a sigh, Aino got up to answer it. "Yes?"

"Compliments from my lord minister," said a woman's voice that I vaguely recognized. I twisted to look, wiping at my cheeks and wincing as I pressed on my wounds. Urso's secretary stood in the hall. "But the final trial has started."

Chapter Eighteen

W hat?" I jerked to my feet.

"No," Aino whispered.

"Urso sent me. The prime minister has allowed King Sigis to begin his speech," the secretary said.

No. No, no, no. He'd obviously decided I'd lost the trial Below—or perhaps I hadn't won it to his liking. "When?"

"He began fifteen minutes ago."

"Get my coat," I told Aino.

"You need to get dressed," she began.

"No time." I limped toward my wardrobe and grabbed the first coat I saw, the dark velvet. Inkar helped me pull it and button it. I placed a hand to my temple as my head spun. Inkar steadied me.

Aino brushed at her tears. "It's going to be fine," I said. She didn't answer.

"Only Her Grace will be allowed in the hall." The secretary tugged at the ends of her gloves. Unease prodded me. Did I know her voice?

Aino frowned. "Kamen's trial was public."

"Minister Eirhan has ordered it," the secretary said in a trembling voice.

Inkar's eyes narrowed. "I am the grand consort. I shall go where I like."

"Inkar," I said. She looked at me reproachfully. "It's okay." I had to complete the coronation trials on my own, and she'd already interfered for me once. And in this last trial, I had an advantage that I didn't think Sigis could match.

"We will escort you, at least," Aino said.

As we left my rooms, Viljo shot me a worried glance, then turned to follow us. The secretary scowled and quickened her pace. "Through here," she said, heading toward the family library. "We'll take the servants' corridor."

She opened the door to the library, and I tottered inside.

One little fire had been stoked next to an armchair in the most open corner. A figure sat in the armchair, so bundled I couldn't recognize them. "Hello, Ekata," said a small voice. "I had a nightmare. And they say that Father died?"

Svaro. *We will find another Avenko.*

The relief dropped out of me like a stone. Aino gasped as the secretary parted our hands with force, her fingers tearing at my bandaged palms. The secretary gave Aino a hard shove, back through the open door, then slammed it and pulled a chair under the handle.

Something twanged. Viljo shouted. Then he crashed into me, and we fell to the ice floor with his shoulder in my clavicle. My spine sang with pain. I pushed on Viljo, gritting my teeth as I tried to ignore my back and my muscles and my palms, and sat up. Blood soaked the front of my robe.

Urso stood at the other end of the room, fumbling with the little crossbow. "I told you to keep everyone else out," he said in a high voice. Eirhan stood next to him. His eyebrows were drawn into a thoughtful frown.

"I'm sorry," Urso's secretary said. "I didn't know how—I couldn't make—"

Her voice. I *did* recognize it—from the law library. I almost laughed. I'd been so intent on discovering whether it was Annika or Itilya with Sigis that night that I hadn't considered that someone who *wasn't* a minister could be conspiring against me. My family's arrogance toward the common people would kill me after all.

"Hardly matters." Urso's hands shook as he put the crossbow down on a little table. "Bind her. We'll do it another way." A dark messenger bowl sat on the table; something fell from his hands into the water.

My mind landed on one fact after another. I pressed on Viljo's wound. "Please, will you call for a doctor?"

"Are—are you serious?" Urso sputtered.

These would be my last moments on the earth, so I might as well do something good with them. I fumbled for the small knife at my belt and cut strips of cloth from the hem of my nightgown. "It's not his fault he was assigned to guard me. Don't kill him for it."

"We can't get out." Even as he spoke, winter roses burst and grew around the room. They crushed over one another, flowing down the wall and blooming in delicate crystal petals before melting into the walls. "That's our security, Your Grace. No one is coming in to save you."

I busied myself tending to Viljo's wound. My hands trembled. I didn't trust myself to pull out the crossbow bolt lodged in his shoulder, so I wrapped cloth around it. Little good it did him. Viljo paled with every passing moment. My paltry bandages grew soaked almost as soon as they touched his body.

"You might have warned Viljo," I told Eirhan. "You might have told him to stay away from me."

"And what makes you think I knew about this?" Eirhan's voice was calm.

"You know everything?" I guessed. "You planned it?"

"My dear, what a thing to say." Eirhan shook out his arms as though the idea clung to him unpleasantly. "After all the time I spent cultivating Lyosha for rule, after the delicate balance I walked between father and son—you think I'd throw all that away to start over? With *you*?"

"Why did you kill Yannush, then?" My eyes prickled. *Focus. Keep applying pressure.*

"The man wanted to be prime minister. It was simply untenable." Eirhan spoke casually, but I was starting to understand him.

He was afraid. He'd spent his life trying to keep his job and his head. He'd never anticipated me, or the trouble I'd bring. He'd been struggling to maintain his place and his power, just as I had.

But just as my situation didn't justify my actions, neither did his. Beneath my hand, Viljo gasped and wheezed. Something burbled in his lungs, and a fresh lance of pain went through my chest. I'd killed him the moment I'd made him my guard.

Urso glared at Eirhan, though the effect was ruined by the shaking in his hands. "Well? Does that mean you've chosen your side, at last?" Urso prompted.

Eirhan watched me silently.

Urso jerked his chin, and his secretary pulled my arms behind me. I struggled uselessly. "Maybe if you cooperate, we'll have all this over with in time to save your guard," she said in my ear, and bound my wrists with a thick cloth.

"I'm sorry." Urso swallowed. His eyes flickered to Svaro. "It was His Grace Below's idea. The Avenko line...it has to be contained. It's nothing personal, you see. But we never had the means to do it until His Grace contacted us to offer more...magical assistance."

So Below had acted first. Though the plan would have come to nothing if Yannush and Urso hadn't been willing. "And where does Sigis fit?"

"We needed someone to help stabilize the country. Someone with experience and power. We didn't think...It doesn't matter." Urso's voice turned pitying. "We thought you would be the best alternative. I am sorry you turned out to be as troublesome as your father."

The funny thing was, he *did* sound sorry. He was good at regret and sympathy. He was always trying to be liked, and even now he wanted me to understand him. All the same, I couldn't conflate regret with having a moral compass. "Forgive me if I don't see."

"You should have married Sigis. You should have done as you were told."

I *should* have been less like my father. That was the bad choice I'd made. And I'd changed my mind too late.

I was done making bad choices.

The walls rattled as someone pounded against the doors. Winter roses twined over them, freezing the handles and the lock and isolating me from the world outside.

"They won't break through," Urso said, and I didn't know if he was talking to me or to himself.

"Why Sigis?" I asked. "Why annexation?"

"I'm sure Yannush explained everything." A fresh tremor shook Urso's hand. "Not that it matters."

"It was money, wasn't it?" I said. "You'll be remembered as a traitor who sold his country for a nice title and a bit of land."

Urso ignored me. "Your Grace," he said to Svaro, who'd been watching the entire exchange from his chair. "Are you ready to take up your mantle?"

Svaro straightened. His wet hair stood on end. "Are you saying I am grand duke?" His voice was curious, even eager.

"If you wish to be," Urso said.

"Does that mean Father is dead?" Svaro asked.

"I regret to say," Urso said.

"Svaro, he'll only use you," I cut in. Urso shot an irritated look over my head to his secretary, and a moment later, a wad of cloth was shoved into my mouth.

Svaro frowned. I could see the question winding across his face. But when he nodded, it was without remorse. What could I expect? My family was my family.

"Very good." Urso turned. "Go," he told Eirhan. "Unless you're going to try some poorly thought-out plan to save her."

Eirhan's mouth twisted in an unamused smile. "My plans are never poor." Then he looked at me for a long moment. "I really did want to help you," he said at last. Fury and fear mixed sickeningly in my stomach. I'd hoped, up to now, that he was playing some long game with Urso, the way he'd played me. "I warned you to think about the consequences of your actions. You have my sympathy."

What good *that* would do me. I curled my lip at him, too, over my gag, but he didn't seem fazed by it. He paused at the servants' door, and for a moment, I thought he'd changed his mind. But the longer he watched me, the more I realized: He was only waiting to see the job through.

Urso poured a dark imported wine from the carafe into the cup. Then he picked up a tiny jar, and I didn't have to see the ever-shifting color to know what was in it. With a little wooden spoon, he lifted a pearl from the jar, so fresh it broke as it caught on the grain. He stirred the wine, closing his eyes, concentrating. And from a little vial that held something darker than wine, he poured a few drops. *I knew it.* My theory was right. Stable magic. Could any blood suffice for this? Could it be synthesized, or was there some extra component to blood from Below that made it possible? Even when I was about to die, I couldn't help wondering.

Urso crushed another pearl in a small bowl with a fresh splash of blood. He dipped his fingers in the mixture and came toward me. "Escort my lady to the Great Hall," he said. Eirhan beckoned, and little Svaro took his hand. In his white ermine robe, he seemed so small, so fragile. He winced as the ice walls shuddered one more time, then disappeared through the servants' entrance without once looking back. Urso's secretary hurried after him.

I made a noise against my gag. Urso pulled it free. "I'm not my father, you know," I said. "There are other solutions to your problems."

Urso's kindly face looked more sorrowful than ever. "Not for me, my lady." And he pressed his fingers, wet with magic, to the side of my throat. As he drew them down, I felt my muscles slacken. My jaw fell open. Urso guided my head back and poured the dark, sour wine into my unresisting mouth.

"I suspect it will be quick," he said. He didn't draw my head back down, and I was left to stare at the blue-white ceiling, listen to his footsteps as they receded, to the deep breath he took as he came to grips with killing his second grand duke, to the click of the servants' door closing like a blade nicking on ice. And then I was alone, with a very still Viljo sprawled across my lap.

Cold brushed like a current against my cheek. The air grew thick, hard to breathe. I tugged at the bonds around my wrists. They'd been tied tight.

Had Urso taken his supplies? I still couldn't move my neck. But maybe—I wriggled against Viljo's body, trying to scoot free. The edges of the ceiling began to turn dark. There was banging on the library doors, far away and fuzzy. My throat contracted as something salty-sweet filled my mouth.

So cold. My shoulders shook, and tremors traveled down my arms, chafing the bindings on my wrists. I levered my knees free of Viljo, then my feet. I tried to push up but slipped in something wet and banged my knee hard on the floor. My head cracked against the ice. I could see the table. If I could make it there, somehow—if I could get my hands out from behind my back—

A door crashed open. I barely heard the shouts. I was lifted away from the floor, and my arms were freed of their bindings. A hand slammed against my back. Water spewed out of me. It beaded on my skin. Winter roses burst on the floor, and I couldn't tell if they were in the room or only in my mind.

My hand found Inkar's wrist and squeezed, holding on with all the strength I had. I was glad I wouldn't die alone. Something cracked with a sound like the ice sheet breaking.

Someone grabbed my hair, yanking me back. I jerked, but Inkar held me steady. "Calm, now," Aino said. "You'll be all right." My free hand found her shoulder and clawed at it.

"Keep her steady." Aino's fingers worked into my mouth, shoving something against the back of my throat. Bitter iron coated my tongue before being washed away. She withdrew her hand and pushed my mouth shut. "Swallow, Ekata." I tried to shake my head. "Yes. Calm. It will be fine." Water all around me. "There you go," she soothed. "You'll be all right. Relax. There you go."

I swallowed, choked, and hiccuped. My mouth sprang open, and I pulled in a lungful of precious air. Then another. The dark began to recede, leaving Aino and Inkar and half a dozen servants and guards staring. My lungs burbled, and I started to cough. "A bowl," Aino snapped, and someone hurried to obey her. She slid a wooden bowl under my chin and nodded to Inkar, who leaned me forward. I vomited a thin stream into the bowl. My sinuses burned.

I was so tired of drowning.

Inkar's and Aino's faces came into focus before me. I expected Aino to ask the question, but she remained silent. It was Inkar who finally said, "Who was it?"

"Urso," I said. "Among others. How did you get in?"

"We hoped the servants' entrance wouldn't be blocked. But we had to take the long way around," Aino said.

"And you didn't see anyone?"

Aino shook her head.

"We should take you to a doctor, Your Grace," a guard said. Saljo, I thought. Inkar's friend. I squeezed her hand again.

"Viljo first," I said.

Two guards knelt by Viljo, while the rest observed the space where the door to the library had once been. Now there was nothing but a tangle of thorns, wild and blue, roses bursting in full bloom between them.

When I was certain that I could breathe without coughing, I stood. Aino put a hand on my shoulder. "Please, Ekata. Sit. We'll take care of things."

The puzzle pieces turned, and the puzzle pieces fit. I couldn't think about the roar that grew in my mind, and I couldn't deal with it, because the reckoning would be bad, and first I needed— "Farhod."

"What?" Inkar said. She brushed her hand across my lips, pressed her forehead to mine. "You are just...better?"

I shook my head. I wasn't *just* better. But I couldn't think about that. "I'm going to Farhod." And if the rest of my family hadn't died in the last five minutes, I was going to shake this curse off once and for all.

I staggered toward Urso's little table. I picked up the shimmering jar. The vial of blood was empty, except for a tiny smear at the bottom. I had no idea whether it would be enough. Aino came forward to support me, and I let her. The anger at the back of my mind reared, but I pushed it back. I couldn't explode. Not yet. My mind had to focus on other things. Like where I'd find more blood.

The laboratory. Where Farhod had so carefully dissected a specimen from Below. Where everything waited in jars.

The laboratory was cold and silent, and I shivered as we entered. Inkar lit a lamp on the wall. "What are we looking for?"

I went to Farhod's anatomy shelf, peering among the labeled jars. Intestine sample, skin sample, a section of vertebrae—any of them *might* work, but I knew of only one guarantee. I picked up a little glass jar. His small, neat handwriting labeled it *blood, dried, specimen male, citizen Below.*

"Don't you think you should stop your brother first?" Aino said as I shut the door to the laboratory.

"No," I said in a voice so cold it clouded the air between us.

Aino paled. She said nothing more as we made our way to Father's chambers. "Wait here," I told her, and beckoned to Inkar, who followed me with a bewildered expression.

The scene beyond was as still as death. My family barely breathed. Munna hurried over to me. "My Lord Svaro—" they said.

"I know." I covered my nose in an attempt to dull the stench. "I'll explain later." For now, I moved to the desk, pushing Farhod's many remedies aside to set down my equipment.

I wondered if I should take anything else. Red poppies, for vitriol and strength, for life in the face of death. Calimony moss, hawthorn, dried bear's blood. In the end, I took a little water from the messenger bowl at Father's desk. I tapped dried blood into the cup, biting my lip. If I ran out of this before I managed the cure...

Munna watched me uneasily. "Your Grace, nothing's changed for the rest of them." Their voice held a note of warning, and I couldn't say I blamed them. The last time I'd tried to interfere, I'd nearly killed everyone.

"That's where you're wrong," I said, and took Urso's jar. Three glistening pearls—that might be enough. They were so fresh they sent a burst of blue into the air as I dropped two into the cup. Sparks wriggled through the water as I stirred the concoction, careful not to touch it—yet.

The cup turned warm in my hand. Color fizzed to the surface of the water. I kept stirring and focused. Colors shattered against one another, new tiny flowers bloomed and died. The ghost of a bear's roar moved through my head, the taste of hawthorn burst on my tongue, all in a moment.

I moved to Velosha first. Some part of me still wondered if this was right. If the world wasn't better without them. Would Father have spared time and effort to keep them alive?

But that was the point, wasn't it? I wasn't Father. I knelt, took a drink from the cup, and shaped the magic in my mind. Then I leaned over Velosha and blew into the catheter. I put a hand on her shoulder and thought about the magic leaving her body—all of it—and I knelt before her until her chest moved, and instead of water, she was breathing air.

The room had gone silent. Everyone had stopped to look at me. "I think she'll vomit," I said, and got to my feet with Inkar's help.

Velosha drew a great, rattling breath. Then she turned to her side and began to heave.

I moved to Lyosha, now that I was certain of my success. Well, more certain. They could relapse, Below could make a countermove, any number of things could happen. But I had to trust what I was doing, then I had to face the rest of the problems I'd created.

I went to Farhod last, lying disregarded in his corner. The doctors had to prioritize the royal family, but seeing him hurt worse than anything else. *For your sake, more than anything, I hope this works*, I thought, and took my last drink.

He lay still for a beat, then a beat longer. How long had it taken the others? Should he recover faster or slower? As I counted heartbeats with no result, I tried not to let my fear overwhelm me. Every patient was different, sometimes things took time—

Farhod convulsed. His eyes opened. I knew he recognized me. He coughed a stream of water over his chin and smiled weakly.

My hands tightened around his shoulders, and I pulled

him into a hug. "I did it," I said, not caring that he coughed lake water and phlegm all over my coat and hair. "I did it."

I woke up my selfish, angry, murderous family.

Inkar touched my arm as we left. "Saljo says they are preparing for another coronation in the Great Hall."

"Sigis or Svaro? My little brother," I clarified when she frowned in confusion.

"The little one, I think. Sigis is...furious."

No doubt. I wondered if Sigis still wanted to marry me, or had encouraged Urso to kill me—or whether the duke Below had demanded my death. It hardly mattered. "I'll have to change," I said, brushing at the ruined front of my coat. "I hope you'll help me." I patted at my pockets, feeling for the lumps that indicated the dried blood and Urso's little jar. All I needed, really, to make my grand entrance.

I hurried into my underclothes and selected the blue dress I'd worn for my coronation. Aino worked without speaking. With every brush of her hand against my arm or back, my stomach turned, over and over, until I thought I'd be sick if I opened my mouth.

But the dark fury had gathered in me ever since she'd saved me, with magic she shouldn't know how to use. "You..." I swallowed and turned my voice as brittle and hard as ice. "You knew the whole time, didn't you?"

Her fingers stilled between my shoulder blades. "Knew what?"

"You knew it was Yannush and Urso and Eirhan. How long?"

Aino paused. Then her fingers worked again, hooking the final buttons. "It wasn't Eirhan." Her voice was quiet, broken. I knew she was crying, but I didn't turn around. "He was trying to protect himself. And I was trying to protect you. I told you to run, remember?"

"Did you plan it?"

Her fingers tightened. "No."

I finally turned to face her. Her face was a mask, but her eyes glistened, tears held back by sheer force of will. As though she didn't want to be ashamed. If anything, it made me angrier. "What did he offer you?" I stepped back, away from her caging arms, still raised to adjust my dress. "Power? Money? Some kind of title? What could Sigis give you that you couldn't ask from me?" My voice trembled. The roaring rage stole my spare breath and I heaved for more.

The first of her tears spilled over. "Ekata, please. It wasn't about him—"

Her hand came to my shoulder. I shoved it away. "*Then what? What was so important to you that you gave me six days of hell? That you jeopardized my life and tried to kill my family?*"

"I told you to run." Aino shook her head; tears scattered from her chin like pearls. "They'd have sorted it out among themselves. But you wouldn't go. And the longer you stayed, the more they thought about killing you, the more we had to do to make sure you stayed alive—"

"*We?*" I reached for her wrist, but she pulled away from me. She feared me, I realized. And it should bother me, but I was too angry to care. "Who's *we*? Yannush? Urso?" Aino didn't reply, but I knew from her stone face I hadn't guessed right. "Below?"

"They wrote to me. From Below. I don't know who. They told me where to find your father's supply of ingredients, and they told me how I could protect you. The night it happened... I didn't take only your mother's jewelry. I took your father's supply of blood, too." She all but fell backward onto my bed, pressing her hands together until they turned white.

Aino, Aino. I wanted to tell her to get out of my sight. I wanted to run away, to Farhod and Inkar, away from her.

But she was still my Aino, more my mother than my own mother. I'd spent six days trying to outrun problem after problem. I had to face this one head-on.

Anger warred with sorrow inside me. Tears filled my eyes. I forced myself to kneel before her and to remember that I didn't want to hate her. "Why didn't you tell me?" I asked softly, taking her hand. "We could have stopped all this before it even began. Instead, you betrayed my family and conspired against my father."

The venom in her voice was a layer of ice over my skin. "What do I care about your father? The rest of your family can drown. All your life I've had to protect you from them. And now that they're gone, no one mourns them. Even your *wife* would rather be with you than the man she came to marry, Ekata." Her voice took on a pleading tone, and her eyes finally met mine. Her grip on me tightened, and I hissed in pain. "I've always tried to protect you, and your family has been the worst threat you've faced. Let's go. They can destroy the duchy without you, and you can do what you always wanted."

"I'm an Avenko," I said, even though I wasn't sure I wanted to be one, even though I had no idea who *Ekata* was without Aino to guide me. And Aino could never stay, not after what she'd done. "No matter how far I go, and no matter how long I stay away, I'm responsible for Kylma, and I can't let it fall apart." Not at the hands of my father, or Sigis, or Eirhan, or any other greedy minister. And my mind, spinning and spinning and spinning, was warning me that my time ran short.

"What's the point?" Aino palmed at her eyes and succeeded only in smearing the kohl around them. "There will be another coup and another. And eventually there won't be anyone left."

I knew she believed what she said. I knew it was a future I couldn't accept.

"You can't leave this room, Aino." I smoothed her hair as though I were the mother now. She hiccuped pitifully, and my tears spilled out in return. "I mean it," I said, voice shaking. "They'll tear you apart if they realize."

"What will you do with me?" Aino asked.

"I don't know." While I wanted to wrap my arms around

her and squeeze as tight as I could, while I wanted to crawl into bed and let her tuck me in and pretend everything was the way it had been a week ago, I knew I couldn't. There were no certainties for us anymore.

"You were shouting," Inkar said as I came into the ante-chamber.

"You never fight with your mother?" I replied, wiping my face.

Inkar smiled at that. "Perhaps I should braid your hair instead of letting her."

She ran her fingers over my scalp. It was a strange combination of soothing and electrifying. We had to hurry; we had to counter Svaro and Urso, and maybe even Sigis. All the same, I couldn't bring myself to rush her.

"I should not have let them lock me out so quickly," Inkar said.

For a moment, I didn't know what she meant. Then I thought of the family library and reached behind me. She took my hand. "It's not your fault," I said.

She sighed through her nose. "Sigis was right. I am soft. Too slow. I saw she was nervous, but I thought..."

"You're not going soft. She tricked all of us."

"It was a foolish trick, and I was a fool to fall for it," Inkar said. Her quick fingers tied her red ribbon at the bottom of my braid. Then they strayed up to my neck, resting in the hollow of my throat, where my heart beat all too quickly. "You need a necklace. Shall I get one for you?"

I swallowed, reveling a little in the pressure of her fingers and relieved that Inkar had offered so I wouldn't have to face Aino again. "The diamonds. The biggest ones you can find."

A grand duke dressed to impress, after all.

We arrived at the doors to the Great Hall with Saljo behind us. "Are you certain Aino will be all right?" Inkar asked in an undertone.

"If she stays put," I replied. If I could keep my grand duke status a little while longer, I could protect her until she went into exile. And I had no doubt that exile would be her kindest punishment.

Two soldiers guarded the doors to the Great Hall. They gaped at me as if I'd come back from the dead. "Aki," Inkar said. One of them bowed. "I am so sorry," she said. "About Viljo."

Aki looked at me, and for a moment, I thought I was still wearing my blood-soaked coat. Her eyes were red-rimmed but dry. "You are very kind, Your Grace."

They still thought of Inkar as the consort. That was a good sign. "Would you like to know who killed him?" I asked.

The guards hesitated, then nodded, and at my order they opened the doors to the Great Hall.

The hall was crowded with delegates and ministers, as it had been the night of my own coronation. Svaro sat dwarfed by my father's oak throne, huddled in his ermine cloak, blue eyes wide. Eirhan stood next to him. Either the coronation regalia had yet to arrive or they'd just finished the ceremony.

"What does a grand duke have to do around here to get a good view?" I asked.

The Baron of Rabar turned, and at the sight of me, he stumbled back so violently I was afraid I'd stopped his heart. His antics caused the Prince of Palaskia to take notice, and she swore loudly enough that several people twisted around to see.

That was all it took. The crowd parted as though answering my inaudible command, leaving me standing, once more, at the head of a clear path to my father's throne.

I began to walk, twisting at the caps on the vial and the jar, tapping out ingredients onto my fingers without drawing attention to my hands in my sleeves. Not that anyone was looking at them. They stared at me, at the whole of me—the grand duke who, for once, commanded a grand presence.

Eirhan's face drained of blood. I would never tire of astonishing that man. Next to him, Urso turned a particular shade of green I'd only seen Below.

"I'll make this brief," I said. "Svaro, get up."

Svaro's face twisted. "Get out. You're not grand duke anymore."

"Oh, I *am*," I replied. I looked around. Sigis wore his rage like a coat, and the hate in his eyes made me shiver. But beneath it I saw shock—and fear. As though he were realizing, for the first time, that he might lose. Annika, Reko, Itilya, and Bailli stared. It was so silent I could hear the soft *plink* of a winter rose petal dropping to the floor.

Sigis recovered his wits fastest. "What sort of strange game is this?" he said. "Did you pretend to die so that you could avoid the last trial?" His eyes flicked to Urso, who was doing his best to impersonate an ice statue.

"Well, I did drown. But my health has greatly improved," I said.

To his credit, Sigis did not roar at Urso's utter incompetence. He merely said, "Then the coronation trials are not finished."

"Yes, they are. I've won."

"Hardly." Sigis's fists clenched. "You've only won two out of three. If I can—"

I brought my hands out. No one noticed the empty vial that I dropped, because every light in the Great Hall went out.

Magic pooled and pulled, growing between my fingers, sparking across my hands as it reacted to my touch, my thoughts. My borrowed blood.

Transformative, constructive, destructive. Links formed, white and cold as ice, stretching in a chain from my hand. They shot out to coil around Urso, around Eirhan, around Sigis.

I took a deep breath, and when I spoke, my voice boomed as though a hundred of me spoke at once: "*I am grand duke.*"

Urso hissed as the chain burned his bare skin. Sigis broke his with a grunt, but I knit it back together with a thought. Fresh magic was almost too willing to obey. I sent another chain flicking toward Svaro. Father's throne cracked beneath him with a sound like thunder.

Then I pulled the magic back. The links burst into a charm of hummingbirds. They fled to hide among the winter roses. "I am grand duke," I repeated more softly. "For the next thirty minutes. Then I will sign papers of abdication, drawn up by Minister Reko"—I nodded to Reko, who seemed too shocked to respond—"in favor of a parliament operating as a joint governing body with my brother Lyosha Avenko."

There was complete silence. Then Svaro leaped up to stand on Father's broken chair. "You can't do that."

"I can do what I want. I'm an autocrat." *For thirty more minutes.*

He drew a knife from his belt and hurled it at my head.

The knife spun wide to bounce hilt-first against the chest of a stunned delegate. All the same, the hall erupted. Inkar leaped in front of me, jerking her ax out of its loop. Everyone began to shout.

I put a hand on Inkar's arm before she could do something reckless. "Have him removed," I shouted over the din. Aki started forward.

"Don't." Eirhan held up a hand imperiously. "Everyone stays where they are until we work this out."

I had the satisfaction of seeing him utterly bowled over for the second time as Aki ignored his orders, pinning Svaro's arms to his sides and lifting him from the chair. She grunted as he kicked at her legs, and another guard stepped in to help. "It's not fair," Svaro screamed as they wrestled him down to the doors, watched by over a hundred aghast faces. "I'm grand duke. *I'm grand duke.*" His tantrum echoed down the corridor long after the doors closed behind him.

Sigis came forward. Inkar turned to face him, too. He moved his shoulders first, as if to remind me how massive he was. "Impressive display, little Ekata. But what does that mean, exactly, with my army at your door? Is it worth the risk, not to let me finish what I started?"

"You'd never get across the moat," I replied easily. "The duke Below will never let you."

Sigis smiled, a dangerous flash of white in the dark. "The duke Below tried to kill you."

I held myself tall—not like Father or Mother, but like myself. Drawing my confidence around me to be my cloak. "Revenge was my father's vice. It seems that mine is compromise." Because Below did deserve amends, for my father's actions and for mine. Grand dukes commanded grand respect, and I'd forgotten that my counterpart Below was as grand as we were.

The guards, taking their cues from Inkar, moved in and stood to either side of me. Not as my oppressors, but as my protection. They moved forward, crossing their halberds so that Sigis had no choice but to fall back. His face twisted. "I hope you're ready for a siege, little Ekata," he spat around their shoulders.

"I'm not," I replied cheerfully. "Luckily, Inkar's father is ready to break one."

His expression was even better than Eirhan's.

I raised my voice to compete with the growing hubbub. "Urso, consider yourself under arrest." The last arrest I'd ever make. "And, Prime Minister—when my brother is well, he'll no doubt want to murder every one of us. It might be useful if he didn't have the absolute power to do so."

I was grand duke for many more hours, as it happened. Even with Reko's extensive plan to guide us, the matter of even a proclamation of a parliament had to be debated and redebated. But no one liked the idea of facing Lyosha after their multiple complicities—not without the option of being exonerated by their peers. Only Bailli complained, and nobody much cared.

When the meeting was done, most of the ministers hurried from the cabinet room as if they expected me to cackle that grand dukes made grand jokes and kill them all on the spot. Only Eirhan stayed behind, scratching at correspondence. At last, he put down his pen, blew out the candle beneath the inkwell, and looked at me. Shadows lingered under his eyes. "Why, Your Grace?"

"Technically, I'm not duke anymore." I waved at the papers that a secretary gathered from the table. I knew what he asked. Why hadn't I arrested him, too? "I realized why you never defected to Sigis. You were afraid he wouldn't gain the confidence of the ministers. So you helped me until you thought I couldn't win. You like to slither, Eirhan. As long as you look after yourself, the rest of us can die as we like, can't we?"

"I don't entirely agree with Your—with my lady's assessment."

"I don't really care." I made a show of examining my fingernails. "The truth is, I've done you a favor. You owe me." I pointed to the parliamentary documents. "You will keep me alive until that goes into effect."

Eirhan didn't blink. "Or?"

"Or Inkar will tell everyone the part you played. They'll find the story in my notes, or diaries, or secret places you won't think to set on fire. Some way, Lyosha will find out. And even if he's the one who kills me, he'll think he has to make an example of you."

Eirhan considered this. "I do hope my lady's university days come with haste," he said at last.

Inkar and I left the cabinet room together. "This has been a day," I muttered.

"Also a night," Inkar said, pointing to a low-burning candle clock.

"At least I don't have to wake up early tomorrow." Or for the rest of my days, I hoped.

Inkar was quiet on our way back to our rooms. I thought

she was being watchful for Svaro or other murderous siblings, but when we were inside, she sat on the bed and spoke hesitantly. "My father will be here in a few days."

"The mysterious Erlyfsson." I flashed her a grin as I reached behind me to unclasp the top of my dress.

Inkar wasn't smiling, for once. "I have decided to reject your offer of marriage."

To my credit, I paused only a moment before tugging the dress off my shoulders. "Okay." I tried to ignore the strange feeling in my belly, as though I'd lost something and wasn't sure whether I wanted to cry or not. I'd known Inkar for a week. I didn't even want to be married. I could hardly fault her for feeling the same way.

Ironic, really. I'd gotten what Eirhan wanted, and now it was irrelevant. And I shouldn't be surprised, I thought as I finished unbuttoning and stepped out of my dress. She'd held her title as long as I'd been grand duke. Now I was back to being no one, and that wasn't what she'd agreed to.

"Ekata," she said gently, and I heard the bed creak as she got up.

"It's fine." My voice was calm. Bright, even. "Really. Thank you for coming to the brideshow." I winced. I sounded resentful and childish, not like a grand duke at all. And while I wasn't technically duke anymore, I didn't want Inkar's last memory of me to be full of petulance and pouting. I hung my dress, then turned to her. *Don't run away from your problems.* "Thank you for standing by me. And saving my life. I couldn't have done this without you, quite literally, and—" I forced myself to think of my parents, locked in an eternal battle of fury, who'd never traded a kind word in my living memory. "I understand."

She smiled, and I hated myself a little for thinking how beautiful she was. "Ekata." She ran a finger down my wrist. Her hands were so small; how could they raise goose bumps up my arm where they hadn't even touched? "I am rejecting the offer because my father...he will try to get what he can. And if I have agreed to be grand consort, he will demand that I remain consort-elect." Her hand drifted down until her fingers rested in my palm. "I do not want to marry Lyosha and stay in Kylma Above. I want to go where I wish."

"Like where?"

Inkar laughed softly and looked up at me through her eyelashes. "I hear south is where the clever people go."

My heartbeat pulsed in our caught hands. I felt dizzy. "So...you're rejecting me so that you can stay with me?"

"Maybe." She dipped her head so that I couldn't read her expression. "Do you need help with your corset?"

We finished dressing for bed and lay down, knees touching, ankles crossed, hands clasped. The shadow of night turned her eyes dark, bottomless, like some creature from Below, and I shivered.

"I do not want promises," she said in a rich, sleepy voice.

"I will not give them, and I will not take them. Maybe next week we will part ways. But this week...would you not prefer to be with me for myself, and not for politics?"

"You'll have to learn to get along with Aino," I warned her.

If Inkar was surprised to hear I'd still be taking Aino south, she didn't show it. "I like to think I can be charming." She wiggled forward to touch her forehead to mine. Her breath kissed my cheek. I had to angle my face only a little for our mouths to touch lightly.

"For some people," I said against her lips. She made a soft sound and pressed in. She tasted like warmth and sun and promises, like the South, like freedom. She tasted like someone who kissed me because she wanted to.

We fell asleep with our foreheads touching, with our breath aligned, while the moon shone full and the winter roses furled into tight buds over my window.

EPILOGUE

The hall below us was packed. The old Grand Theatre on the processional boulevard had been refitted so that the seats were arranged in a semicircle, and the stage held a podium and two tables opposite each other. It was one of the few buildings in Kylma Above that had a wooden interior, and it shone a strange, soft gold in the light of an enormous chandelier.

More than one head craned in our direction. The boxes had been reserved for the royal family and guests, and we were the source of no small speculation. My reign was the second-briefest in Kylmian history, just longer than some ancestor who'd been poisoned his second day—yet I'd made one of the biggest marks. After three hundred years of autocracy, Kylma would have parliamentary representation.

"Are you proud?" Inkar asked. She wore a green wool coat and a serpent pin that glittered like shards of ice. Her hair was half up, half down, the way she wore it when I first saw her at the brideshow six months ago.

"I didn't have much to do with it." After making the decree, I'd left the implementation of a parliament largely up to Reko, who'd refused to be prime minister in the end. I'd endured some screaming from Lyosha, and Eirhan's personal servant tested everything I ate and checked my freshly washed clothing for hidden needles or burrs. But the archimandrite had publicly thrown her support behind me—in return for a seat. That had helped to reduce murder attempts, and now we were down to one a week or less.

"It's still something to be proud of," Farhod said. He had a proper seat as a minister, but he lingered in my box, smiling. The sleeves of his coat were stained with new experimentation. Magical power no longer belonged solely to the grand duke, and Farhod was in charge of discovering the true extent of its properties. I'd examine it, too, in my first year's study at the university.

Aino had gone south to secure rooms for me and live away from the angry reach of Kylma Above. It was going to be strange, seeing her again. Hopefully, a good kind of strange. And strange, too, to see what life was like in places where snow never fell.

The guard at my box bowed, and Lyosha and Mother stepped inside, wearing matching looks of distaste. Lyosha wore the royal colors in a grand suit and elbow-length cape. Mother wore black fur from her ankles to her neck, as she had every day since Father died. For someone who had despised him, she certainly reveled in her widow status.

Inkar moved automatically to stand between them and me. "Are you pleased, little sister?" Lyosha asked in his cold voice.

"Do you even think this experiment will work?" Mother added.

It was still hard for me to speak up around them. I cleared my throat and said, as casually as I could, "Maybe. If you try. But if you make everyone mad and get cursed again, there won't be much I can do from down south."

"Yes, yes." Lyosha rolled his eyes. "Ekata the hero."

"When is it you're set to leave?" Mother asked.

"Day after tomorrow."

She sighed. "So soon. And yet not soon enough." She turned and drifted out.

"I suppose you should write," Lyosha said ungraciously. "Science is a noble enough calling, and we may well need you. Now, if you'll excuse me, I have to go open a parliament that some brash idealist decided was a fantastic idea." He rolled his eyes once more, then followed Mother out.

Inkar shook her head. "They do not understand."

I squeezed her hand. "I don't need them to."

The archimandrite approached the stage, leaning on her iron staff. Slowly she mounted the stairs, and silence fell. When she had crossed to her place in front of the podium, Lyosha emerged. Applause broke out; white roses were waved in the air. His reign was off to a good start. *You're welcome*, I thought.

Inkar pulled me to the chair at the front of the box, and together we sat to watch the show.

ACKNOWLEDGMENTS

Writing this book was an intense experience, and a lot of people stood behind me to help make the experience into an actual book. First and foremost, my family: Mom, Dad, Elizabeth, Elias. Boy, the things you put up with. Thank you for that, and for the encouragement, for cooking for me, for talking me down from the cliffs of writerly despair....

Thank you to my agent, Kurestin Armada, for walking me through proposals, always working with me to hone my craft, and dealing with panicked transatlantic phone calls. And for insisting that this book was good whenever I doubted it.

My editor, Hallie Tibbetts, continues to be fantastic and a person I'd like to work with for eternity. Here's hoping for many more books for your editorial scalpel. For my LBYR team: to Morgan Maple and Valerie Wong for amazing publicity and incredible graphics, to Karina Granda and Billelis for the fantastic look of this book, and to Jen Graham and the managing editorial and production teams.

Thank you to my fellow writers and commiserators, who

can always help put things into perspective (and cheerlead!): the Malmö writers group, the Copenhagen writers group, the #Novel19s and Class2k19, the Armada (best agentsibs ever!). Big thanks to Carina Bissett, mentor and friend—see you in the autumn for your amazing classes, I hope!

Thank you to my sensitivity readers for their poignant comments and fantastic advice concerning Ekata and Inkar's relationship. Any remaining insensitivities are mine alone.

And finally, to all the people who read and loved *We Rule the Night*: Your positivity kept me going, even when I was certain that I could crawl under the bed and no one would miss me.

I enjoy being inspired by history, and the plot of *The Winter Duke* began with the story of Alexander I of Russia's patricide, which was also regicide, and a strangely unlikely coup. I highly recommend reading *The Romanovs* by Simon Sebag Montefiore for a fascinating look at a brutal royal family.